HELL'S ASCENDANT

BENJAMIN MEDRANO

Hell's Ascendant by Benjamin Medrano

© 2019 Benjamin Medrano. All rights reserved.

Contact the author at BenjaminPMedrano@gmail.com

Visit the author's website at benjaminmedrano.com

Sign up for the author's mailing list at http://eepurl.com/cGPT-b

Editing by Picky Cat Proofreading

Cover Art by Nguyen Uy Vu

To my alpha readers, my editors, and my beloved, thank you.

THE STORY SO FAR

Violently betrayed and stripped of her wings, the angel Isalla was cast down into the hells by Haral, a woman she'd believed was a friend. Isalla was saved from death by Kanae, a demoness and healer in the hells, who nursed the injured angel back to health and taught her about the hells, which was a different place than Isalla had imagined. Many demons in the hells lived normal lives, though it was still a dark and dangerous place.

Over time the two women grew close, then their relationship blossomed into a hesitant romance over the course of weeks, at which point Isalla confided in Kanae that she'd been betrayed because she'd found signs of a conspiracy in the heavens, one that seemed to have designs on overthrowing the current ruling council. Concerned about the plans of the conspirators, and the likelihood that a radical faction would destroy the fragile peace between the heavens and hells, Kanae agreed to help Isalla contact her old commander and lover, an angel named Roselynn who Isalla had informed of her investigation.

Unfortunately, Haral had learned that Roselynn was making inquiries of her own after Isalla vanished, and the angel had acted swiftly and ruthlessly, drawing Roselynn into an ambush by demons, who then sent Roselynn into the hells for interrogation. Roselynn woke in the comfortable Spire of Confession, and the unwitting angel was slowly, gently brainwashed by another angel and two succubi into effectively abandoning the heavens and making herself more beautiful. A visit by the demon queen Estalia caused Roselynn, now going by Rose, to fall almost entirely.

Meanwhile, Haral had sent assassins to finish off Isalla, as she had learned that the angel had somehow managed to survive the fall. As Kanae brought word that Roselynn had been captured in a demon raid, one of the assassins attempted to kill Isalla. The attempt failed, but the assassin perished as she tried to flee, leaving the two with unanswered questions. With few other choices available, the two women chose to seek out Roselynn and attempt to rescue her, despite Kanae's deep fear of Queen Estalia.

Their rescue attempt brought them near the Spire of Confession, where they waited to strike once Roselynn was being taken to the capital of Estalia. Their attempt worked nearly flawlessly, despite one of Rose's guards managing to break free of the hypnosis that Kanae had inflicted on them. Kanae teleported the three of them to near her home, and her explanations managed to raise questions in Rose's mind, and also prompted her to guess that Kanae was Queen Estalia's lost daughter. While Kanae didn't confirm her guess, her lack of response told Rose that she was correct.

Kanae distanced herself as Isalla and Rose rekindled their relationship, the demoness avoiding being drawn in, due to worrying that any relationship couldn't last, and believing that soon Estalia would come for her. Unfortunately for Kanae, Estalia had already known that she lived, and immediately set out to meet the three at Kanae's home.

Estalia's arrival threw all Kanae's plans into disarray, as the queen revealed that Kanae's true name was Kitania, and the two managed to somewhat reconcile, though Kanae revealed that Estalia's goal was to end the war by manipulating angels and demons alike into worshiping her. Estalia soon departed for her palace, leaving behind both armor and Ember, the legendary weapon that belonged to Rose, as well as a few guards to keep the angels safe while the plot in the heavens was unraveled.

Before the group of women could come to a final decision on

what to do, and even as Kanae was disposing of the last of her things, Haral's third attempt on Isalla's life arrived, an attempt which was also intended to kill Rose and even Estalia if she was in the way. A group of angels attacked Kanae's home, and the demoness fought a delaying action as the guards left by Estalia and the angels alike prepared themselves for battle. Just as Isalla and Rose came to her aid, the attackers shot Kanae with an arrow that had been intended for Estalia. The arrow teleported her to a fortress in the mortal world, where Kanae was torn apart by a hail of magical arrows.

Enraged by the apparent death of Kanae, Isalla and Rose fought desperately, heavily injuring several of the attackers, but would have lost if Estalia's guards hadn't reached them in time. Their grieving was interrupted by the information that Kanae had been teleported, and the guards took custody of the assassins and transported all the angels to Estalia's palace, where the two angels hoped to learn what had become of Kanae.

In the palace, Estalia informed the two that Kanae doubtlessly lived, for Kanae was truly immortal, capable of regenerating from any known attack. Bolstered by the knowledge that even an archangel couldn't kill Kanae, the two angels vowed to rescue her and drag the conspiracy that had been trying to kill them into the light.

Far away, Kanae woke in a cell, chained to a wall, and with the transmutation that had disguised her for centuries broken, revealing her original body. With an elven guard nearby, she decided that it wasn't worth hiding who she was anymore and introduced herself as Kitania. Kitania soon learned that she was in the palace of the goddess Alserah, an elven goddess known as the Divine Archer, and one who terrified Kitania, at least at first.

Within the walls of the goddess's palace, Kitania was protected from all attempts to magically locate her by Estalia's servants, so Isalla and Rose were forced to wait for new information. The angel Eziel was mentally dominated by Estalia and gave additional information to Isalla and Rose, as well as giving additional hope that Kitania was safe. Estalia chose to retaliate for the attack within her borders and conquered the angelic outpost of Firewatch, taking all the angels within prisoner.

Kitania was soon allowed to move about the elven palace, though she was subject to a good deal of suspicion. This grew worse when an elven princess, Niadra Sellis, invited her to a ball and the two were drugged. When Alserah confronted the two women, Kitania realized that the goddess was infected by a horrible parasite from the hells known as a dream spider and afterward helped Alserah remove it from her head, though Kitania was heavily injured in the process.

In the aftermath, Kitania was given still more freedom, and Alserah chose to abandon her ransom demand for Kitania. As the demoness began breaking down due to her worries about what Isalla and Rose thought of her, Alserah gave permission for Niadra to associate with Kitania and expressed some interest in the demoness herself.

Meanwhile, Alserah's emissary reached Estalia and informed her of Kitania's presence in the Forest of Sighs. After a short time, Estalia dispatched Isalla, Rose, and Vinara, the succubus who'd been teaching Isalla magic, to retrieve Kitania and begin investigating the angelic conspiracy, known as the Society of Golden Dawn. Along with them was Eziel, who Estalia was sending as a servant for Kitania. During their journey there was an attempt to poison them, but it was foiled.

Haral once more acted herself, wishing to learn what Kitania knew and to punish Niadra for growing close to a demon. She ambushed their carriage and kidnapped the two, as well as Niadra's maid, beheaded Kitania with a soul-stealing blade, then had her servants torture Niadra and her maid while Haral left. Kitania resisted the blade's magic and killed the angels left behind, then returned Niadra to the palace.

The reunion between Isalla, Rose, and Kitania was awkward, especially when Vinara revealed that she'd once been one of Kitania's lovers and demanded an apology for Kitania faking her death ages before. Alserah asked for more details on how Isalla had been betrayed, and they began closing in on who Haral was, as well as her plots, but they were a little too late.

Haral and her companions unleashed twenty titanic monsters

on the Forest of Sighs in the middle of the night, consisting of ten hellfire worms and an equal number of storm phoenixes. These creatures were scattered across the country, and any one of them could devastate cities, while Alserah could only be in one place at a time.

Vinara helped track down where Haral was controlling them from, and the group dealt with three of the creatures on their way to intercept the angels, then engaged them in a short, brutal battle. The angels had laid a trap for Alserah, twisting her power to imprison her briefly, and they had an arrow like the one which had nearly killed Kitania. Kitania ripped the arrow away from an angel just in time and managed to severely injure Haral as she took the bracelet controlling the monsters from the angel. Haral managed to escape by using a teleportation charm, but the monsters were quickly killed in the aftermath.

Once things had calmed down, the group returned to the palace, where some discussion of who might get to keep Kitania occurred, and Rose revealed that Isalla had slept with Estalia. However, everyone knew that it was just the calm before the storm, and that far more dangerous times were on the horizon.

And now their story continues.

PROLOGUE

*C*oral stepped into the room, not even pausing as she began speaking. "Lady Anna, I think that Reath needs some personal attention with how her attitude has been of late, and…"

The succubus's voice trailed off as she realized that Anna wasn't in her usual chair, and the room was otherwise empty. Several documents sat on the polished top of the desk, weighed down by a paperweight, while paintings adorned the white marble walls. Even so, Anna going missing was a bit perplexing, and after a moment Coral put her hands on her hips, looking around in annoyance.

"Now where did she get off to? And right when I needed her, too?" Coral asked aloud, then let out a soft sigh of annoyance. Anna didn't vanish often, and when she did it was always for a good reason, so she abandoned the hope of getting help from her superior and chose a different strategy, murmuring. "Maybe I can get some help from Irak…"

She left the room behind, all the while wondering what Anna was doing. The angel had been acting oddly ever since she'd gotten the most recent dispatches from Estalia.

~

THE ROOM SHOULD HAVE BEEN dark, with as dark as the stone it'd been carved from was. It wasn't, but that was due to the glowing crystals which dotted the walls and hung in lanterns. The room was a shallow dome, with polished walls and crystalline lanterns hanging here and there. Only the glowing portal set into one wall allowed entry, and Anna brushed her fingers over the runes carved into the doorway for the moment, admiring them instead of what was in the center of the room. It didn't help, not really, but she treasured the moments of peace that it brought her. When she closed her eyes, though... then she remembered the incredibly short message she'd been sent by Estalia, the words seared into her mind.

Things may be worse than I feared in the heavens. I'm afraid that I may have need of you. Kitania may have need of you. I'm sorry, dear one.

"You shouldn't be sorry, my beloved goddess. We both knew the time would come when I could no longer hide," Anna spoke at last, her quiet words echoing in the musty confines of the chamber. A part of her was grieving for what might happen soon, but at the same time another part of her was awakening after a long slumber. So, she took a deep breath and turned to the center of the room, looking at the items resting there.

A potion rested in an ornate vial-holder on a pillar to one side of the room's center, its contents shedding a radiant blue light. The sight of the potion caused Anna's pulse to quicken, but her gaze rested on it for only a moment. Instead she looked at the armor resting on its rack and the cloudpiercer laying lengthwise on display in front of it.

The armor was for an angel, which was just as it should have been. Unlike almost every suit of plate Anna had seen for a high-ranking angel, this suit wasn't ornate and beautiful. Nor had it been forged of mithral... no, it was made of fine, gleaming steel without ornate patterns or engravings. Only the runes which powered its magic shone, and even those were hidden, as if to heighten the apparent simplicity of the armor, from the boots and greaves to the helm and plates designed to guard her forewings. The armor brought back memories, and few of them were good... but even they paled beside the emotions inspired by the cloudpiercer.

Anna's gaze fell to the cloudpiercer, and she felt herself shudder. She took a step closer, then another, feeling her legs almost quivering beneath her. The cloudpiercer was almost as simple as the armor, with a shaft forged of steel wrapped in black leather, right up until one looked at the blade. The blade burned with power, blazing gold runes seared into the silver-blue metal. Power greater than any other weapon she'd wielded surged through the blade, and Anna let out a soft sigh as she closed her eyes. Memories of the wars she'd fought in rushed through her head, each of them with the cloudpiercer in hand. There were few things she wanted less than to take it up again, and yet... a part of her *lived* for it. She didn't like to think about it, but not all the trembling in her hand was of reluctance.

"For our daughter. For *us*," Anna murmured.

Reaching out, she picked up Infinity's Edge, and the weapon surged with power, almost joyfully welcoming her grasp. Anna couldn't help a smile at the reaction, closing her eyes and basking in the sensation, reveling in how... *right* it felt in her hand.

"Everything has to end, one day," Anna said softly, running a finger over one of the runes, the power within it burning at her finger. "However... that doesn't mean we have to simply accept it."

No one answered, but Anna realized her fingers had ceased trembling, and she smiled.

CHAPTER 1

*K*itania slammed the butt of her cloudpiercer against the ground and grunted as it suddenly extended, launching her upward suddenly, but she wasn't done. It wasn't nearly as smooth as she'd prefer, but she channeled mana into her armor and wings snapped into existence behind her, translucent, black-feathered wings that took her soaring upward in seconds, well outside Isalla's reach.

The blonde angel stared up at Kitania for a moment, then lowered her practice sword as she glowered at the demoness, speaking in palpable annoyance. "Okay, I see what you mean about your acrobatics. Tears of heaven, how do you *do* that?"

"Practice, really, though I couldn't do the flying bit until I had this armor," Kitania replied, grinning as she stabilized, then slowly descended again. She was quite pleased with how her practicing had paid off so far. "I didn't have the extending cloudpiercer, either, so had to pole vault instead. I'm just glad I watched Anna's training so much; otherwise I wouldn't know how to use it while flying. I still need to practice more to get used to it, but it *is* more effective."

"To be fair, I'm pretty sure that Anna must be *far* better with a cloudpiercer than I thought she was," Rose chimed in. The red-haired angel wasn't in practice gear; instead she was wearing a deep blue dress that contrasted nicely with her pale skin and vivid hair, and the rose-shaped hair clasp kept the hair out of Rose's eyes. She'd been watching them, and Kitania thought that she saw a little shock in Rose's eyes. Eventually the angel continued. "I've seen some angels use them before, and they're... well, you have to be careful about your wings with them, and they aren't good when you're trying to keep a tight formation."

"Precisely!" Kitania said, relaxing as she leaned on the cloudpiercer, letting her flight magic lapse. She took a breath, then continued the explanation. "The nature of a cloudpiercer, and the style of combat it's used for, isn't good when you're trying to keep formation. I'm honestly not sure why it's traditionally angelic since it seems more like glaives and other polearms intended to dismount soldiers, and mounts aren't used by angels, but that really doesn't matter. The art is beautiful, but in an army its use is limited. Anna always told me that was why it was so rarely used there, and even among the Holy Council's guards it was falling into disuse."

"Really?" Isalla asked, glancing at Rose curiously, and the other angel pursed her lips, looking like she was thinking. Kitania took the moment to admire Isalla, who looked particularly beautiful in the morning light.

The three of them were in the palace of the goddess Alserah, the patron of the Forest of Sighs, and numerous elves were observing from around the training field, though most of them were at least pretending to train. There were rather more of them than there had been a few days prior, which probably was due to the monsters that had assaulted the country only two days earlier.

Even the thought of the attacks almost ruined Kitania's mood, and her smile faded as she thought about the last couple of days. Ten hellfire worms and an equal number of storm phoenixes had assaulted the Forest of Sighs across its breadth, and the damage reports were *still* coming in. Alserah was doing what she could to help the recovery, but so far there were at least three thousand dead, and all of it because some angels had decided to make an example of the country.

"Anna is right, though I suspect she's even older than I

thought, if cloudpiercers were commonly used in the Council Guard," Rose said at last, her expression thoughtful. "I've known a few people who wielded them, but most of the practitioners were among the nobility, and especially those who didn't expect to see combat. It just isn't considered that practical of a weapon, even if you do extremely well with it, Kitania."

"That's perfectly fair," Kitania replied, slowly relaxing as she smiled at the two angels. She hesitated, considering what to say, then continued. "Based on what I've heard, she met Mother before she inherited her mantle, during the Blackstone War."

"Heavens! She's been in the hells for *four thousand years*?" Isalla demanded incredulously, almost dropping her practice sword, and Kitania couldn't help a laugh at her reaction and how Rose's jaw was hanging open. "That's the fourth crusade, when Anathiel was still leading the armies!"

"Something like that, yes," Kitania confirmed, smiling even more, and she carefully ignored the mention of the ancient archangel of war. She had her suspicions about what had happened to her, after all. "I don't know the details, mind you, but I know she's been in the hells for longer than most demons have been alive. I'm more impressed that she's retained her skill with how she stays in the spire most of the time."

"That's... impressive. And daunting, I'll admit," Rose said, straightening as she regained her poise. "I knew some of the other angels had been in the hells for around a millennium, but the idea of Anna having been there for four *times* that long never even crossed my mind. She seemed to know the heavens so well, or at least the orders."

"We're demons, and you're angels. Our societies change at a slow pace, if at all," Kitania pointed out, shaking her head as she smiled. "Anyway, enough of that. Shall we go see if there's any news from the captive?"

"We may as well, though I don't have high hopes," Isalla said, her smile fading. "We really can't wait much longer."

"Agreed," Kitania said, nervousness welling up inside her, though it wasn't just for what was coming.

Her relationships had gotten *incredibly* complicated over the last couple of days, and it was giving her a headache.

7

~

"I'm afraid that we haven't been able to get any further information out of the prisoner who's still alive," Alserah said with a grim expression. "The man has been extremely stubborn, and it likely will take a great deal of work to make him speak. Perhaps the others would have been easier to convince, but there's nothing to be done about it at this point."

"True enough," Rose agreed, her expression darkening, and Kitania's did as well.

They'd originally had three captives from the battle with Haral and her allies, after which they'd first focused on eliminating the remaining hellfire worms and storm phoenixes. Unfortunately, that delay had proven disastrous in some ways, as the afternoon after they'd returned to the palace two of the prisoners had fallen over dead. If it hadn't been for Vinara quickly dismantling the spell on the last captive, one whose wing Kitania had broken, he'd likely be dead as well. As it was, it was a rather depressing situation.

"It does mean that continuing to wait is a poor decision," Vinara chimed in, the green-skinned succubus's eyes dark and her arms crossed in front of her. "I informed Queen Estalia of what happened, and she told me that she has no new information, which concerns me. We don't have time to let the Society of Golden Dawn do as they please."

"No, we don't. Unfortunately, as much as I want to help, my absence would be counterproductive at this time," Alserah said, anger flickering through her eyes, then she shook her head as she continued. "We're having enough trouble keeping anyone from attacking some of the angels that live here. Part of me wishes that we'd been able to keep the involvement of angels in the attacks quiet, but then it would've been blamed on the hells."

"I do understand," Kitania said, wincing at the thought. She could barely fathom how many elves felt about the attacks which had come from nowhere, and at least they'd been rather visible in helping Alserah fight the monsters. That had blunted some of the suspicion where she and Vinara were concerned, but even if

Isalla and Rose had helped, they'd been on the receiving end of some accusatory looks.

"What are you planning to do, Your Grace?" Rose asked politely, exchanging a concerned glance with Isalla, which made Kitania wonder what they were thinking.

"I have a number of deities as allies, and this attack... they're likely concerned but keeping their distance since I haven't requested help. I'm going to ask them to come here and inform them of what I know," Alserah said, looking up at the angels calmly, her green eyes almost blazing with anger now. After a moment she continued, her voice soft, yet deadly. "I would like you to continue your investigation and keep me informed. When you've determined the source of this infection, I believe it's time to excise it."

For a long moment the room went quiet, and even Kitania felt her blood run cold. If multiple deities took the field against angels, *especially* if they were traditionally aligned with the heavens, it could be disastrous. She opened her mouth to speak, but it was Isalla who reacted first.

"Are you sure you want to do that, Your Grace?" Isalla asked hesitantly, her concern obvious as she swallowed hard. "I don't know what consequences it might have, but I know you've been allied with the heavens for... what, fifteen hundred years?"

"More, if you count my predecessor," Alserah said, sitting back in her chair as she looked at them, considering before she nodded gravely, her voice soft. "As to that... yes, I'm certain. I've never been comfortable with how the heavens seem to take our alliance for granted. The Holy Council often barely pays attention to mortal borders or desires, though at least they don't usually make *demands* for assistance. However, this? This is a betrayal on so many levels I cannot begin to express it. I will not let it pass, not when thousands of my people have died, and others have had their livelihoods destroyed. We can recover, and *will*, but I will not allow the infection to remain, even if it means an end to our alliance."

"I see," Isalla said, bowing her head slightly and hesitating, then spoke more firmly. "In that case, I won't try to dissuade you. However, our current leads indicate we need to travel to

Uthren, and possibly to Uthren's Throne itself. Dare I hope that your allies include their gods?"

"Uthren?" Alserah asked, her eyebrows rising, and Kitania couldn't help a wince.

Uthren was one of the oldest human kingdoms, located on the Harth Plateau on the far northern continent of Ness. Even in the War of Decimation the demons hadn't managed to breach Uthren's borders and had instead chosen to assault a gateway to the heavens well short of the nation. Kitania didn't look forward to trying to go there, especially since all three of the angelic orders had major garrisons there.

"Yes, that's right," Rose confirmed, letting out a soft sigh as she shrugged helplessly. "While Eziel couldn't give us a lot of information, she was able to give a few names, one of which was Rathien the Blue, a high-ranking officer in the Order of the Dragon, and he's stationed in Uthren's Throne, or was the last time we heard about him. On the other hand, there are a few officers in the Order of the Phoenix I believe I can trust there as well. The problem will be getting to them."

"I believe I understand, but unfortunately I'm not on good terms with any of the deities of Uthren," Alserah said, her smile fading as she shook her head. "It's unfortunate, but there isn't anything I can do to make it easier for you. However, I *can* provide transportation to Ness, and even a guide. I'm certain I can get you into the country, but nothing beyond that."

"Even that much would be an immense help, Your Grace!" Isalla said, her expression brightening as she smiled.

"I do see a problem, however," Kitania said, frustration starting to well up inside her.

"Oh? What's that?" Rose asked, looking at her curiously.

"Me. If I want to help... Uthren is famously dogmatic, to the point that even *I* know how dangerous it is for a demon there," Kitania explained, bottling her frustration as best she could, then continuing. "I want to help you, but with my tendency to throw off transformation spells, I can't really come along. I suppose I could send Eziel with you, but—"

"Fortunately for you, I have a solution for that," Vinara interrupted, just as the angels were beginning to frown.

10

"Really? What sort of solution might that be?" Alserah asked, looking intrigued.

"It's a simple one, honestly. The problem with Kitania is her appearance, but nothing prevents illusions from being used. As a matter of fact, I came up with one that would help some time ago, and made an illusion in my spare time back in Estalia," Vinara said, smiling broadly. "See, she has horns, fangs, *almost* claw-like nails, and a tail, yes? What if we were to overlay that with the illusion of her having draconic blood? Make her eyes slit like a dragon's, and her horns and fangs a little more draconic as well, while giving her a normal skin tone, and make the tail look like it's scaled, almost like a snake's."

"That… would probably work, yes," Kitania said, blinking as she thought about the idea, but she did see one flaw that made her unhappy. "My only issue is that if anyone touches my tail, it'll be readily apparent it *isn't* scaled."

"That's why you wear the tail armor in public, of course!" Vinara said, looking at Kitania with a smug smile. "The illusion will go over the armor, and it has the right texture to fit the appearance. It might not be incredibly comfortable, but it won't be too bad, not since the enchantments make the armor fit far better."

Kitania's worries eased at the explanation, and she smiled after a few moments, nodding as she murmured. "Yes, that *would* do it, wouldn't it? I'm assuming this would be an enchanted item of some sort?"

"That's right," Vinara said, nodding calmly as she added. "It's a bracelet, so you'll be able to keep it on pretty much constantly without worries. Hopefully no one can see through the illusion, but that's why it just changes the appearance of your body, instead of modifying you extensively."

The others looked at each other, and Kitania saw relief on Isalla's face, as well as how Rose had relaxed. It improved her mood, since that meant that they really *did* want Kitania to come with them.

"It sounds like you have a plan, then," Alserah said, sitting up straighter as she tapped the table, then added. "It will take a few days to arrange your transport, likely two but possibly three, considering the damage that Naer took, but I'm certain it will be arranged quickly. I'm not happy sending you away so quickly, but I see little choice."

"I don't think we blame you for that, Your Grace. If anything, I should thank you for the immense amount of help you've provided," Isalla quickly assured the goddess, standing and bowing deeply.

"You're most welcome. I look forward to seeing each of you at dinner tonight," Alserah replied, standing gracefully, and everyone else did as well.

As they prepared to leave, Vinara stepped closer and spoke brightly. "Now you just have to let Niadra know that you're leaving, hm? Maybe you'll even be nice and do it in person."

"Oh, shut up," Kitania retorted, glowering at her old friend.

Some days it was *really* hard not to punch the succubus.

CHAPTER 2

"*S*orm? What're you doing?" Haral asked, leaning against the doorway unsteadily as the rain drummed softly on the roof.

Looking up from the equipment spread across the table, Sorm's stomach tightened at the sight of Haral and his lips pressed together tighter. Haral was still paler than she should've been, and he didn't see more than the barest hints of her usual confidence and poise. While he was sure she'd recover, the hesitation in her voice was almost alien, and that made him angry.

It hadn't been long since she'd returned, missing half her left arm and right wing. Sorm was just relieved that he'd been able to get one of the society's healers to come regenerate Haral's limbs quickly, but that hadn't helped with the mental trauma she'd suffered. She'd been resting ever since, and this was only the fourth time she'd left bed in the last two days.

"Sorm?" Haral prompted, and he shook off his distraction, instead smiling at her, reaching up to rub his beard as his wings rustled.

"Sorry, I got caught up thinking. I'm glad to see that you're up, since you haven't been moving much the last couple of days," Sorm replied, clearing his throat as he straightened. "I was getting worried."

"I'd say you have good reason for that. However... *this* has me concerned," Haral said, slowly crossing the room to lean on the table. She picked up a wickedly barbed crossbow bolt with runes carved into it, studying it for a moment before looking at the other items on the table, her voice soft. "Explosive armor-piercing bolts, a stealth veil, incineration stones, a storm inducer... this doesn't look like the sort of items you'd need for your usual activities, Sorm."

"Of course they aren't," Sorm said, his smile fading as he sighed, then continued more solemnly. "I've requested permission to harry Isalla, Roselynn, and their companions. My request was granted."

"You did *what*?" Haral demanded, dropping the bolt as she looked up at him, her eyes flashing with anger and more of the confidence he remembered her having. That gave him hope, even if her outrage was directed at him. "What in all the stars do you think you're doing? You saw what they did to me, and they didn't even know that I was *there* until a few days before I was injured."

"I know. Believe me, I *know* what they did, and that's why I'm going after them," Sorm said, gritting his teeth for a moment as anger surged through him, but he forced it down, banking the rage for use later. Instead he continued after a moment, his voice soft but deadly. "I'm not going to strike anywhere that I think the goddess will be involved, believe me. My goal isn't to kill them all, Haral, it's to strike and run. I'm going to tear them apart one at a time and vanish into the mists before they have time to react. Or at least I'll try. If I have a good opportunity to kill them all, I'll take it."

Sorm calmly reached over and picked up the bolt that Haral had dropped, carefully placing it on the rest of the pile as he looked up at her, meeting her gaze as he focused on her, trying to share his determination as he continued. "They hurt you terribly, and if I hadn't been here you might have died. I will *never* allow that to pass, my love."

"I..." Haral blushed slightly, then looked away, her blonde hair shifting as a breeze wafted through the room. Eventually she spoke, her voice soft. "I'm happy that you care so much, but how are you going to do that, with the demoness able to regenerate? We don't know how to kill her!"

"No, we don't. But you said that the princess and several others were with her, including Alserah," Sorm said calmly, smiling more like a shark as he continued savagely. "I don't know if she *cares* about them, but believe me, if she does... I'm going to make her regret that. I'll destroy those around her, until she's the only one left. Then we'll find out just how far her ability to regenerate goes. And if all else fails, why kill her? Why not throw her off the continent into the void and let her fall endlessly?"

Haral paused, staring at him for a long moment, then slowly smiled as she murmured. "That... well, that *does* seem like it'd work, wouldn't it? It'd be a lovely way to punish her for what she's done, and I like it. I'm still worried about you, but if you're going to be careful..."

"Oh, believe me, I don't want them to catch so much as a *hint* of me at first. I want to destroy them without giving them the slightest chance to fight back," Sorm said, his voice flat now, his anger cooling ever so slightly at the smile on Haral's face.

"Mm, now I'm tempted to come with you and help," Haral murmured, looking like she was relaxing for the first time since she'd returned, at least while she'd been awake. Unfortunately, Sorm knew he had to refuse her idea.

"I'm afraid you can't, dear. I've received word from above, and they sent instructions for you," Sorm said, his smile fading as her happiness visibly faltered.

"Oh? I... well, what do they want me to do?" Haral asked, reaching up to toy with her necklace nervously. The teleportation charm had burned out, but he knew she had a replacement gem in storage.

"They've decided that, in case my attempts don't work out, we need to eliminate several avenues of assistance that Isalla and Roselynn might call on," Sorm said, taking a deep breath, then looked Haral in the eyes as he continued. "I've brought a supply of midnight shadow from them, and they've instructed that both the Emberborn family and Isalla's family be... dealt with."

Haral's smile faltered even more, and she paled for a

moment. It was only for a moment, but she regained her poise as she asked softly, "All of them? But the Emberborn family has been..."

"All of them. While the Emberborn family has an excellent reputation, the risk of Roselynn gaining the assistance of members of the family is too high for the society to risk. As such... well, you've heard their decision," Sorm said, understanding her hesitation. In fact, he paused for a moment before admitting, "I'm not terribly happy about it either, but... I think they're testing your devotion to the cause."

"I... see. Well, it seems I'll just have to show them that I haven't changed," Haral said, straightening and looking at Sorm decisively, gritting her teeth. "Even if I believe that such is going a bit too far... if it's what I must do, so be it."

Sorm nodded, the slight knot in his stomach easing. While he hadn't believed that Haral would refuse the order, he also knew that it was possible that she'd rebel slightly. She'd always had a soft spot for children, after all.

"Good. Well, I'm not leaving today; I'm just getting my things ready," Sorm said, glancing at the table, then asked a little more warmly, "I don't suppose you're feeling up to going out to dinner? After the last couple of days, I think fresh air would do you good."

"Even if it's raining?" Haral asked, glancing toward the window idly.

"Especially if it's raining. The air is never cleaner than during or after a good rainstorm," Sorm replied, his mood improving still more, and he smiled. "Besides, it'd be with you, and there's nothing as wonderful as that."

"Flatterer," Haral said, smiling warmly at him, then turned away, adding, "Let me get changed, hm?"

"Of course," Sorm said, and his anger eased even more as relief surged through him. His anger wasn't gone, but Haral was doing better, and that was something he'd needed more than he could express.

Even if he *was* concerned about the orders for Haral, she was devoted and clever. He had no doubts she'd do what she had to, even if she might bend the orders where she could.

16

CHAPTER 3

"Here you are, milady," Eziel said, offering Kitania a towel. The black-haired angel had a smile on her face, and she seemed far more at ease than she had been the last few days, likely because they were settling into their new positions at last.

Kitania was still a little disconcerted by the angel's presence, as Eziel *had* tried to kill her, but it wasn't as though Kitania would've been able to pick the angel out of a crowd afterward. In any case, it didn't make sense to hold a grudge after her mother had changed Eziel utterly. Now the only problem was how eager to please the angel was, since Kitania resembled Estalia somewhat.

"Thank you," Kitania said, having given up on telling Eziel not to treat her like a noblewoman. She took the towel and began drying off, thankful that *this* time Eziel hadn't started drying her off. It had been disconcerting the first time Eziel had done so, since Kitania hadn't had help in the baths in a very long time.

"It's a pleasure to serve you," Eziel said, instead moving to the attached closet where she'd put Kitania's clothing for the rest of the day. The angel spoke softly as she pulled out the dress on its hanger. "Is this dress still the one you wish for, or shall I acquire another?"

"That one's fine, Eziel. I'm not the type to change my mind

17

on a dress in only a few minutes, unless there's some event that necessitates it," Kitania replied, suppressing the urge to sigh as she dried her hair, which was the worst to deal with. "I haven't heard any alarms, so don't worry about it."

"As you wish," Eziel said, adjusting the blue dress with a critical eye as Kitania continued drying off.

In short order Kitania was done and allowed Eziel to take the towel, then to help her into the dress. As much as Kitania was loathe to admit it, it *did* help to have other people assist her with dresses, even if Kitania was extremely flexible. It was just too difficult to reach laces on her back most of the time and making them look good was even harder.

"Thank you for your help," Kitania said at last, swishing her tail to ensure the fabric wouldn't chafe, then nodded. "Yes, I think this will do nicely."

"There's no need to thank me, Milady," Eziel said humbly, carefully folding the towel and putting it in a laundry basket. "I'm entirely at your disposal."

"Perhaps, but I prefer not to take that for granted. It's rude, and as far as I'm concerned you're a different person than you were before you met Estalia," Kitania said, smiling at the angel. The overall situation they were in might be complex, but at least this was something she felt was easy to figure out.

"If you say so, Milady," Eziel conceded politely, though her body language indicated that she didn't agree with Kitania.

Shaking her head, Kitania left the bathing room, amused despite herself. Despite how eager to please Eziel was, the angel could be absurdly stubborn as well. It was probably part of what had made her a zealot, Kitania reflected. She was stubborn in her beliefs, which meant that it would've taken someone like Estalia or Anna to convince her of her errors.

"Have you heard of any plans, aside from lunch with the others?" Kitania asked, glancing back at Eziel. She'd arranged to meet Isalla, Niadra, and Rose for lunch today, and was looking forward to it. Alserah and Vinara had been invited as well, but both had been busy, so it would just be the four of them. Or maybe more with any servants, Kitania realized belatedly.

"No, I'm afraid not. Your schedule has been rather

inconsistent of late, but I've been arranging for proper supplies for the trip ahead as best I can," Eziel reported. "I also—ah, my apologies. Bright morning, Lady Cecilia."

Kitania saw Cecilia at about the same time, and smiled at Niadra's handmaiden, then paused as she saw how nervous the elven woman looked. Her blue eyes were filled with worry, even if her blonde hair was as elegant as always, and she was wearing a relatively mundane yellow dress. The handmaiden smiled back, but there was something forced about her expression.

"Bright morning to the two of you as well," Cecilia said, looking between them as she hesitated, then asked, "I... might I have a moment to speak with you in private, Lady Darkshade? I wish to speak to you about something. It's not on behalf of my lady, just myself."

Kitania blinked, then frowned as she asked, "I... perhaps so. How long will this take? I *do* have lunch fairly soon."

"I'm not sure, though it shouldn't take too long. I thought about trying to wait until after, but I don't know if I could work up the nerve again," Cecilia admitted, which confused Kitania even more.

"Hm... well, I suppose. Eziel? Would you go see if everything is coming along well for lunch?" Kitania asked, then gestured toward her room, adding, "If you'll accompany me to my room, Cecilia, we can speak privately while I finish my preparations."

"Yes, Milady," Eziel said, bowing her head and giving Cecilia a sidelong, curious look. However, the angel quickly moved down the hallway as she followed Kitania's orders.

"Thank you," Cecilia said, the relief on her face palpable.

"Not at all, it's fine," Kitania replied, her curiosity growing as she glanced at the woman, but led the way toward her room and opened the door. No one had been in since she'd left that morning, so she let Cecilia in, then closed the door behind them. Walking over to her vanity, she continued. "Now, what was it that you wanted to tell me?"

"It's... well..." Cecilia began, then hesitated, fidgeting visibly. Kitania could see her in the mirror and couldn't help a smile. It was a world of difference from how coldly Cecilia had acted just a few weeks before that it piqued her curiosity even more, but the woman took a deep breath, then spoke. "First, I wanted to thank you properly. You saved me and Her Highness from death the other day, and you really didn't have to. I... I thought I was going to die, and you saved my life."

"You're welcome. I... have mixed feelings about it. If it weren't for me, neither of you would have been targeted, but... that's water under the bridge. We had no way of knowing it might happen, and I feel terrible about it," Kitania said, shaking her head as she sighed.

"Yes, but even so... it made me feel guiltier because... well..." Cecilia hesitated, looking down. Past her, Kitania saw the door open a little, and Niadra poked her head in at that moment, her mouth opening. Before she could speak, though, Cecilia spoke quickly. "I hid the message that Isalla and Rose were coming."

Kitania froze in surprise, both shock and anger rushing through her, which she quickly forced down before she jumped to conclusions. The surprise on Niadra's face quickly turned to cold anger, but Kitania met the princess's gaze in the mirror and shook her head silently since Cecilia's gaze was downcast. Instead, Kitania slowly turned her chair to face the woman.

"That... is somewhat upsetting. Why would you do that?" Kitania asked, her eyes narrowing. Despite herself, Kitania felt anger smoldering within, and she tried to ignore it.

"I... well, it made more sense to me at the time, but..." Cecilia began, then stopped, inhaling as she looked up at Kitania nervously before continuing. "I saw how close you and the princess were becoming, and when I thought about how your relationship was improving her standing among the nobility... I was just selfish. I thought that if they *really* cared, they'd send another message, and what I did wouldn't matter, so discarded that one. But... it did matter, didn't it? You risked yourself for us, and I... I've been just trying to work up the courage to admit what I've done ever since. It wasn't right, and I shouldn't have done it."

Kitania stared at the younger woman, her anger flaring slightly for a moment, but then it banked as she thought about the situation from an outside perspective. It probably *wouldn't* seem like it was important to many people, even if it was to her. It frustrated her that she could have learned that Isalla and Rose were coming yet hadn't. Eventually she asked, "What did the message say?"

"It was from Isalla, and she mentioned that she had to keep it short. She said… she thought about you every day, and that they were coming for you. Nothing more than that," Cecilia said, hesitating before she admitted, "I burned the note, but I'm sure someone could copy it from the message book again."

"I see. That… would have made an enormous difference for me. I felt abandoned by them, and this would have told me that they hadn't left me alone," Kitania said, her voice quiet as she closed her eyes, taking a deep breath, then letting it out. "You… hurt me, by doing that."

"I know, at least now. I wasn't thinking about it at the time, and… well, I had to tell you now," Cecilia said. Kitania opened her eyes to see the young woman was shifting in place unhappily. "I don't expect your forgiveness, to be honest. I'd like it, but don't expect it."

"Mm… I will have to think about it," Kitania said, carefully not looking at Niadra, who was listening near the doors, her hands clenched at her sides. The demoness considered before asking, "Is Niadra aware of this?"

"No, I never said a word about it to her," Cecilia said, quickly shaking her head, a flash of worry flickering across her face as she spoke. "I'm planning to speak to her about it tonight, after dinner. I have no idea how she's going to react, but I… will accept the consequences. I made a mistake, and it's entirely possible that it led to the attack on us."

"There's no need to wait until this evening," Niadra interjected at last, her voice icy with anger and her blue eyes blazing.

"Your Highness! I didn't realize you were—" Cecilia began, but Niadra didn't let her continue, cutting the handmaiden off with a sharp gesture.

"No, Cecilia, you didn't. I heard everything just now and saying that I'm *angry* isn't the half of it," Niadra spat, her anger only seeming to grow stronger. She pointed at the door and continued harshly. "Get out."

"Niadra?" Kitania asked, but the princess ignored her, for the most part. For her part, Cecilia was as pale as a ghost.

"Out, and not out of the room. You're to leave the palace *immediately*, Cecilia. Gather your things and go home," Niadra said flatly, her gaze unwavering. "I doubt I'll forgive you easily, but I may. On the other hand, I may not."

"I... but..." Cecilia began, then her expression crumbled, and her shoulders slumped. The elf nodded, her voice tiny as she replied. "Yes, Your Highness. I... will go."

Kitania watched, a little stunned as Cecilia left the room, then looked at Niadra in concern. She waited until Cecilia was out of earshot, then asked, "Was that really necessary?"

"Of course it was!" Niadra snapped, then a flicker of guilt rippled across her face as she looked away, adding, "Sorry, I shouldn't have taken that tone with you."

"It's alright, Niadra, I'm just wondering why you reacted so harshly," Kitania said, though she was a little taken aback by Niadra's tone. She'd never seen the princess act like this before, so it was startling and a bit worrying.

"She overstepped herself dramatically. If she was entrusted with a message from Lady Azalea, that means that she was given it by Ethris or Hanrith, either of which have authority which far exceeds her own," Niadra explained, approaching slowly, her voice still taut with anger. "That means she didn't pass along a message that they entrusted to her, and *that* is beyond the pale. I'd have been angry with her in most cases, since she manipulated us, or tried to, but that is not something I can abide. If she withheld that information from you and I, what other information might she not pass along? What if she tried to keep something truly important from me?"

"I... well, that does make sense. I guess I didn't know that the message had to come from someone *that* important," Kitania said, frowning. A part of her was still troubled by how readily Niadra had dismissed Cecilia, but she didn't want to argue with Niadra, not now. It just... made her wonder. After a moment she shook her head and sighed. "I just... she admitted the truth and was trying to apologize. Everyone makes mistakes; what matters to me is that they learn from them. On the other hand, I might simply be more forgiving than I should be."

"Perhaps you're right. Maybe my anger with her will cool, and I'll give her another chance. However, that day isn't today. I can't trust her right now, so I'm not going to let her stay in the palace," Niadra said resolutely, shaking her head as her gaze darkened and she reached out to take one of Kitania's hands. "This isn't how I wanted today to go, you know. I wanted to relax with you, since you're leaving so soon."

"I know you didn't. It isn't how I wanted it to go, either, but... there's nothing to be done about it," Kitania replied, sighing softly. She squeezed Niadra's hand, then smiled as she asked, feeling like the expression was a little forced. "Would you like to help me get ready for lunch? Or was there another reason that you came here?"

"I'd love to! You're always interesting to help, with how different your skin tone is," Niadra said, a smile dawning on her face again at last.

Despite the smile, Kitania felt like she was ever so slightly more distant than before, and it sent a pang of regret through her. She hoped that the conversation with Cecilia wouldn't ruin what they had, but... Kitania wasn't sure what was going to happen in the future. With Isalla, Rose, and even Alserah herself involved... the future was just too murky for her to guess.

Setting the thoughts aside, Kitania turned to the mirror again, and smiled as Niadra eagerly began helping her with the makeup. It was entertaining how much fun the princess had with it.

CHAPTER 4

*T*he air shivered, and Alserah looked up, then smiled as she saw the yellow glow from the courtyard. Kitania and the others hadn't left yet, but she hadn't expected them to. What she also hadn't expected was for the first of her allies to arrive, but she certainly wasn't going to complain about it.

Standing, Alserah quickly stepped through the doorway and took flight, circling the tower as she approached the courtyard. The yellow glow was dimming as she moved, but it didn't fade too quickly, and she came around in time to see Gandar rolling his shoulders and tilting his head back and forth, as if to pop his neck. The dwarven god was stocky, like all his people, but was unusual in that he had no beard and was relatively slim, though his powerful figure was sheathed in ornate plate armor that had a great deal of gold engravings across it, and he had a similarly ornate double-headed axe slung behind him.

"Welcome to my home, Gandar. It's good to see you again," Alserah said, smiling as she stopped a few feet from the dwarf and bowed her head slightly.

"Eh, I was overdue for a visit anyway. It's been what, a decade? Then you went and got attacked by a whole host of beasties, and I'd have been surprised if you *didn't* contact me after that," Gandar said, his voice deep as he smiled, flashing his teeth at her, but his brown eyes were watchful, almost worried, she thought. It was hard to tell through the helm, plus they were in public. "How are you? Was it the hells?"

"I'm fine, in part because of my demonic visitors. As to visiting, you know you can stop by when you like and I'll host you, but..." Alserah shrugged, looking around the open courtyard as she took in the dozens of guards watching them, along with a few priests from the town outside the palace. Then she continued. "It wasn't the hells, but I'd prefer to have *that* discussion in private. Would you care to join me in the palace?"

"That bad, huh? Sure, let's go inside. I brought some of my private stock of whiskey, so if you want a nice drink, I'll be happy to share," Gandar said, his smile fading as he asked, "Who else is coming?"

Alserah led the way toward the palace at a sedate pace, amused to see that the gates opened well ahead of them. Obviously, the guards didn't want to be disrespectful in front of two deities, which she approved of. Gandar could be easygoing, but he also could be stubborn and prickly when he didn't know someone, which was why Alserah didn't plan on introducing him to any of the angels or demons in the palace.

"Let's see, I sent messages to Phillip, Ratha, Sidina, Ire, and you. You're the only one I could guarantee would come, though, even if I'm sure the others will make an attempt to be here," Alserah explained, walking a little more quickly as she realized Gandar looked impatient. He also looked worried at the list she'd rattled off.

"Alright, something is definitely up, then. I hope you'll tell me about it once we're in private, at least," Gandar said, falling silent as he eyed the guards, then asked, "How bad was the damage?"

"Several thousand dead, moderate damage to a dozen cities, and we lost a fort. It could have been much, much worse, too," Alserah told him, her tone almost flat. "If I hadn't found the person who was controlling the monsters, we couldn't have called them off as early as we did. I suspect we'd have lost at least three cities and five forts, in that case."

"Sandstone," Gandar muttered, shaking his head. "That's horrid. My condolences, Alserah."

"Thank you," Alserah said simply, leading the way into the palace and into a private meeting room.

She raised an eyebrow when she saw the tea set sitting on a table, resisting the urge to click her tongue. Even if it wasn't poisoned, which she wasn't going to rely on after the last week, it was obvious that whoever had tried to anticipate her requests didn't know Gandar very well. Alserah sighed, then pushed the tea set aside as Gandar sat in a chair, which creaked ominously under his weight. She doubted it'd actually collapse, but he had that effect on furniture.

Closing the door, Alserah ensured that the wards were active before taking a seat and letting out another sigh. She examined the teacups carefully, then nodded when she saw they looked perfectly clean, and not like anything had been smeared inside them. The tea was probably safe, but she wasn't taking any chances. Sliding a pair of cups toward Gandar, she looked at him.

"A bit of whiskey would be appreciated, especially after this past week," Alserah said simply, prompting Gandar's eyebrows to rise.

"It must be bad, if *you're* drinking. Alright, let's see here..." Gandar said, unhooking a gilded flask, then carefully poured whiskey into each of the cups, though not much.

"Thank you," Alserah said, taking one and sipping the liquor, taking a moment to savor it. It was smooth, exactly the way Gandar liked it, and oddly comforting, mostly because she knew that it meant she was with one of her friends.

"You're welcome," Gandar said, drinking from his own cup. It looked odd with him in his armor, but Alserah didn't laugh. Gandar was the staunchest ally she had, and she'd trust him with her life. More importantly, she'd trust him with the lives of her people as well. After a minute he asked, his voice soft, "What is it?"

"Angels arranged the attack, Gandar," Alserah replied, not looking at him as he inhaled sharply, and she smiled thinly as she continued. "They decided that since I didn't kill the demoness who appeared in my courtyard out of hand, my kingdom deserved to die. They unleashed the monsters throughout the kingdom, and if I hadn't had someone helping me when I went to deal with them, their trap would probably have killed me."

"Rust and ruin, what were the damned featherdusters thinking?" Gandar demanded, setting down his cup with a clatter. "We're their allies, damn it!"

"Ah, but this appears to be a splinter faction in the heavens. A group called the Society of Golden Dawn believes that the Holy Council has been too *accommodating* of demons and wish to strike out at any who would oppose them," Alserah said, her tone flat now. "We don't know the full details, of course. They've been keeping hidden for too long to unmask instantly, and the attack's leader managed to escape at the last moment. What I *do* know is that they've betrayed at least two angels who started getting hints of their existence, and would have killed them if they had the chance. They also attacked a princess only a few miles from here and were going to torture her to death and pin it on the demoness who was my guest, and they've been working on ways to try to trigger a war again. Why else would they create an arrow that, if my magi are correct, would have pierced my defenses and teleported me into the heart of Venadiel's defenses?"

Gandar flinched slightly at the last bit, shaking his head slowly at the mention of Venadiel, the god of darkness. Of all the deities on the side of the hells, he was one that Alserah would never challenge without having several other deities at her side, and that would only give her the confidence to draw even with him. When Ethris had reported where the arrow had been designed to teleport her to, Alserah had nearly lost her composure, and at the same time her relief that Kitania had torn it from the archer's string grew stronger. It was also why she'd supplied Eziel with arrows that were heavily enchanted, in case they ran into an archangel or the like.

"Ah. That..." Gandar began, then stopped. Finally, he shook his head and murmured. "That's worse than I thought it would be. I knew you had to have something big if you asked me to come here, but hearing that... Venadiel, really? He's one of the five most powerful gods of darkness, and he's *old*."

"Believe me, I'd rather not think about it, either," Alserah told him, taking another sip of the whiskey. It didn't taste quite as good with the subject of their conversation, but she continued anyway. "I wish I had better news for you, but there's nothing to be done about this. No, my concern is that we're going to be attacked again, and I'm not sure where or when it'll happen."

"That's bad, Alserah. Really, really bad," Gandar said, rubbing his chin unhappily. "I mean, I appreciate the warning, but how're we supposed to stop them if we don't even know when they might strike? I can't afford to piss off all the heavens by closing my borders to angels, you know."

"I don't expect you to. Mostly I'm contacting you because I want to arrange for your help," Alserah explained, and she smiled as she continued. "The angels who were betrayed are preparing to go into Uthren to find some of the conspirators they know the names of. They're trying to unmask the conspiracy, and when they do…"

"Ah, I see. You don't just want to warn us. You also want to tear this conspiracy out by the very foundation once they find it," Gandar said, smiling as he straightened, grinning at last. "If you were going to ask me for information, I'd wonder why you bothered. It isn't like many people tell my craftsmen much, especially since the angels do their own metalwork, by and large. Smashing enemies, though, *that* I can get behind."

"I'm glad to hear it," Alserah said, smiling as she relaxed a little at last. She continued a moment later, admitting, "On the other hand, we have no idea just how widespread the conspiracy is, so I want to have as many allies as possible. That's why I've made a few overtures to Queen Estalia in the hells, since she seems relatively reasonable."

"Really?" Gandar asked, looking at Alserah skeptically. "I wouldn't think you'd call a *demon* reasonable."

"Yes, but how many demons would hand over Sindria's Light as a gift for being nice to their daughter?" Alserah countered, and Gandar's face went purple.

"She did *what*?" the dwarf demanded, surging to his feet.

Gandar's reaction was comical enough that Alserah couldn't help a smile.

29

~

"I'm GUESSING that another deity arrived," Vinara said idly, polishing an iron wand and examining it critically.

"What makes you say that?" Rose asked, glancing up at the green-skinned succubus with a hint of a smile flickering across her face.

Vinara wasn't the best company in the world, yet at the same time Rose appreciated how calm the succubus tended to be. Even if she *did* like taunting Kitania and everyone else. At the thought of Kitania, some of Rose's pleasure faded into worry. Lunch with Kitania and Niadra the previous day had been unusually tense, and she wasn't sure why. Isalla hadn't known either, since she'd asked Rose about it later, but there wasn't much Rose could do without asking them directly, and Kitania's mood had been poor enough that Rose didn't want to do that.

"Mostly the glow I briefly saw, along with a subtle wave of magic that felt an awful lot like teleportation," Vinara said, shrugging as she smiled at Rose. "I'm not certain, but the sheer power in the glow indicates that it was a deity, in my opinion. If I'm to guess, it's one of Alserah's allies."

"A fair point. Your ability to sense mana is far beyond my own," Rose admitted, setting down her backpack.

"I think her senses are better than almost anyone's," Isalla murmured, running a finger down the edge of her sword.

"Mm, practice helps, and neither of you have a lot of practice sensing mana. It's a useful skill, but difficult to pick up," Vinara said, smiling a little more. Then she paused and added, a tiny bit grudgingly, "Besides, Kitania has a natural talent for sensing mana. If she was skilled at using magic, I suspect she'd surpass me, at least when it comes to sensing power. Speaking of which, what's she doing today?"

"Alchemy," Isalla volunteered, shrugging and smiling. "Last night she told me that she isn't going to rely on magical healing and wanted to get at least a few of her healing salves made before we left. A couple of the court alchemists overheard, and last I saw she had three elves watching her and asking questions. It's why I'm here, and not there."

"So *that's* why you came back," Rose said, her smile growing warmer as she looked at her lover and teased. "And here I thought you just missed us."

"I did, but I also couldn't understand more than half of what they were saying. It didn't help that Kitania kept having to snap at them when they tried to adjust the equipment, and I decided that discretion was the better part of valor," Isalla said, shaking her head in disbelief. "It was like a feeding frenzy in there!"

"I see. Well, at least she's getting some things done," Vinara said, setting down her wand. The succubus's smile faded as she looked at them, then sighed and spoke softly. "You know we're likely going to trigger a civil war, yes?"

"No, we aren't," Rose replied simply, forcing down any nervousness, leaving her feeling almost serene as she continued. "If there's a war in the heavens, it means it was already brewing. If this Society of Golden Dawn thinks that everyone in the heavens would go along with starting another war, they're delusional, and it'll lead to warfare. That's how the three great orders were founded, after all. They were founded in the aftermath of a war in the heavens, in order to try to keep the peace."

"Ah, I see. I think I heard something about that, but information about the history of the heavens is rather difficult to come by in the hells, or likely riddled with inaccurate details," Vinara murmured, shaking her head as she let out a soft sigh. "I understand My Lady's wish for peace, but I truly don't believe it's possible. People are too prone to creating controversies if there aren't any."

Rose nodded, her mood growing a little darker as she thought about Vinara's words. There was far too much truth to them to make Rose happy, and after a moment she sighed and shook her head, murmuring. "I believe you're right, but... at least she's trying."

"True," Vinara admitted, adding, "Too bad this is pretty much my last chance to relax in a while. Going to Uthren is going to be... nerve-racking."

"For you, maybe," Isalla said, grinning as her eyes twinkled with mischief that raised Rose's spirits again. "We'll be right at home."

"I *do* know where you sleep, you know," Vinara said, her eyes narrowing as she glowered at Isalla.

A moment later she laughed, and Rose and Isalla joined her. It was good to laugh, Rose thought, especially when they didn't know what would come on the morrow.

CHAPTER 5

*T*he countryside around Soaring Heights was beautiful, Haral reflected, glancing around in surprise. A gentle rain was falling, and the sunlight was bright enough that she could see at least four rainbows. Lush fields were interspersed between copses and hills, and she had seen several lakes further inland on her approach as well. With all the flowers and wildlife Haral saw, she was startled that the area hadn't become a popular vacation spot, at least for some of the nobility. It wasn't *that* far from the core of the heaven's, after all.

Regardless, Soaring Heights wasn't frequented by the elites of the heavens, and that made Haral's task both easier and harder. It was easier in that no one would really look too closely once she acted, but getting into place to carry out her task was slightly harder.

Isalla had told Haral a little about her background when they'd associated with one another, and it amused Haral how humble the young woman's beginning had been. The house Isalla had grown up in was perched atop a hill neighbored by a couple of fields, and as Haral watched she could see a pair of angelic men moving through the fields of vegetables, weeding them with brisk efficiency. The house was larger than she'd expected it to be, with two floors and fine planks for walls, though it didn't have any glass in the windows, just shutters.

"Mother, father, and brother... all of them are accounted for," Haral murmured, a pang of guilt rushing through her.

Haral really didn't understand why she'd been ordered to eliminate Isalla's family. The three angels were no one important, not even in the community where they lived. Seimal, Isalla's father, was a simple farmer who brought in crops that weren't exceptional in any way, but neither was he poor. The ruddy-faced angel looked cheerful enough from a distance, though Isalla and her brother took after their blonde mother rather than the brown-haired man. Unlike Isalla, her brother Anpiel was tall and muscular, the type that Haral would have expected to join the military, but he looked happy as he tended to the fields.

Not even Isalla's mother, Emmara, was exceptional. A pretty blonde woman, she briskly took care of work around the house. From Isalla, Haral had learned that her mother was the third child of one of the local merchants, and as such hadn't inherited much of anything. It just showed how unimportant they were in the grand scheme of things, which made Haral's guilt grow even stronger.

"I wish I didn't have to do this," Haral said, sighing as she continued standing in the forest, secure in the knowledge that her cloak would keep the angels from spotting her. It didn't make her invisible, but it helped her blend into the background, and that was good enough for now. Instead she simply watched the family go about their day.

If she was going to end their lives, the least Haral could do was watch them and remember them.

"I'M TELLING YOU, I think that learning to grow rice is a good idea. It's supposed to be getting popular in the cities, and we get enough rain that cultivating it shouldn't be hard," Anpiel said, leaning forward as he argued his point. "It could help us get ahead for once."

"You're not wrong about how popular it's getting, but you're forgetting something just as important," Seimal said, pointing his spoon at Anpiel as he smiled, shaking his head.

"What's that?" Anpiel asked, frowning unhappily. The idea of growing rice had him excited, yet his father didn't look nearly as thrilled, which worried him.

"The labor it takes. I've looked into growing rice before as well, and while it *does* have advantages, it takes a rather lot of labor to grow much of it. You have to create the fields that *don't* drain immediately for the seedlings, then there's taking care of them as well… no, I don't think we can manage that, Anpiel," Seimal said, shaking his head as he took another spoonful of food, smiling helplessly. "Not that I don't like the idea, mind you, but we can't, not with the two of us."

"Indeed. It was bad enough when your father decided to plant another field back when you were a child, then discovered that he just didn't have enough time to take care of all the crops," Emmara said, smiling slightly as she tore off a piece of her bread to dip in her soup. "He practically ran himself ragged trying to take care of them that year, then scaled back to just four fields until you were old enough to help. It was a really rough time and taught him not to overestimate himself."

"But—" Anpiel began, only to have Seimal cut him off.

"She's right, Anpiel," Seimal said kindly, shaking his head. "Now, if we have a good crop this year, we might be able to look at hiring a farmhand or two. It's a bit of a risk, but might be worth taking. I'm not saying we can't look at it, Anpiel. Just not right *now*."

"Alright, I suppose that makes sense," Anpiel said, sighing and going back to his meal. After a minute he murmured. "I wonder if they've managed to find Isalla yet?"

Seimal's smile suddenly went stiff, his wings rustling uneasily, and Emmara's smile vanished entirely, making Anpiel regret saying anything, especially as his mother looked down at the table, her hands trembling as she blinked rapidly, probably trying to force back tears.

"I haven't heard anything from the order yet," Seimal finally said, his voice heavy. "Some people are claiming desertion, but they don't know for certain yet."

"She'd never desert!" Emmara protested, looking up as tears shimmered in her eyes. "She was so *proud* to be chosen to join the order, she'd never just... just *abandon* it like that! Even if she was given a post that was considered bad."

"We know, Mother. I just... I wondered if they'd found her, since I worry about her," Anpiel said, sighing softly. "I can't imagine her just running away. It doesn't sound like my little sister at all."

"No, it doesn't. Still, I'm sure we'll find out what happened to Isalla eventually, so don't let it get you down," Seimal said, forcing a smile onto his face as he straightened. "Maybe you can even surprise her with a niece or nephew when she comes back!"

"Hey, I don't even have a girlfriend yet!" Anpiel protested, flushing a little.

"Not for a lack of trying," Emmara said, her smile slightly real this time.

Anpiel blushed more and shook his head, not seeing the faint mist that seeped under the front door.

THE HOUSE WAS QUIET, and Haral closed her eyes, trying to imagine what it was like for the people within. It was impossible for her to truly imagine, since midnight shadow didn't really have an effect on those who were awake. The poison lulled the victims into a deeper and deeper sleep, until they finally stopped breathing. She hoped that it was a peaceful way to go, but Haral couldn't be certain of that.

"You didn't deserve this. None of you were the ones that got in our way... you were just simple farmers living your own lives," Haral said at last, looking at the house as she took a deep breath, then let it out, shaking her head as she did so. "I... apologize. If I were able to take another path, I would, but when it's for the future, I will pay any price required of me. You have my apologies... and hopefully I can send Isalla to you relatively soon."

No one replied, but Haral hadn't expected them to. They should all be dead by this point, or well on their way there, which meant it was time for her to deal with the evidence. Haral tried to avoid thinking about the men and women in the house as she reached into her pocket, blinking back tears. She pulled out a small glass orb, one which flickered with faint orange light within. Haral examined it for a long moment, then murmured. "Mir's flame, I call to you. Heed my voice and obey."

The orb grew brighter and brighter, then dissolved as heat and light bloomed in front of Haral. A figure formed of pure flame took form in front of her, shaped like a small dragon that looked at her curiously. Mir's flame was a type of elemental that the Society of Golden Dawn used, just intelligent enough to follow orders, which was appropriate in this instance.

"Go down the chimney and reignite the fire. Cause the fire to escape the stove or fireplace so it can burn down the building, then return from whence you came," Haral told the elemental, cringing as she spoke the words aloud.

The elemental nodded silently, then winged its way up and over, then down the chimney. A skilled investigator would likely be able to figure out that something was odd about the fire, Haral knew, but the chances of someone like that being in the area were vanishingly small. Instead, she waited regretfully, watching the house for the first signs of flames.

It started as a soft glow, one which slowly grew stronger. Haral watched and listened, waiting for any cry of alarm, but didn't hear one go up. No, the house was quiet as the crackling sound of a fire grew. The first fingers of flame crept into Haral's sight, and at last she sighed, turning away. Soon enough a neighbor might notice the fire, and she didn't want to be in the area when that happened. Instead she spread her wings and took flight, winging her way away from the place where Isalla had grown up.

"I'm sorry," Haral murmured, blinking back tears as she did so.

Mortals were one thing, but murdering innocent angels who weren't directly in her way was... hard.

Nonetheless, she continued on her way, even as flames engulfed the house behind her.

CHAPTER 6

"*I*'m going to miss you, Kitania," Niadra said, hugging the demoness tight, her voice trembling ever so slightly, so slightly that most of the people present probably wouldn't hear it, Kitania imagined. Kitania thought the princess was almost on the verge of tears, and it probably wasn't helped by how she'd been looking for a new handmaiden. She'd probably settle for the innocent Breanne, since the young woman wasn't as prone to intrigue as many others would be.

"And I'll miss you," Kitania said, hugging Niadra gently as she looked around, smiling helplessly at Vinara's arched eyebrow, while Isalla and Rose were studiously ignoring them as they adjusted their clothing. It was strange seeing her friends without their wings, but even stranger in its own way was that Rose had hidden Ember and replaced it with a different sword.

Alserah was standing nearby, her arms folded as she watched them, and Kitania could feel her gaze even when she wasn't looking at the goddess. Kitania suspected she was in for a grilling from the others when they weren't around the goddess anymore. She wasn't happy about it but was resigned to it. In the meantime, she was just doing what she could to prepare.

"They *do* need to get going, Niadra," Alserah said at last, her voice patient as could be, but sounding slightly like a chiding parent. "I may be helping take them to the port, but that doesn't mean we have limitless time."

"Of course, Your Grace. I just... I worry," Niadra said, turning pink as she quickly let go of Kitania and stepped away, studying the floor in obvious embarrassment.

"I think that's reasonable enough," Rose said, smiling thinly. "We're all worried about what might be coming, and there's no way to know what it'll be, yet."

"Perhaps we'll learn soon," Eziel said, the woman's facial features subtly different than they had been, and the angel looked worried as she adjusted her leathers and bow. "I just hope we're moving quickly enough."

"You will or won't, that's the simple truth of the way the world works," Alserah said, taking a step forward as she looked around the room, studying each of them, then continued. "Now, a few of my guards are going to escort you to Uthren's Throne, but I dare not send many. That would put our opponents on their guard, so there are only going to be two of them. To keep rumors from flying too much, I've arranged for a different ship and crew to give you passage, *Dryad's Gift*. Her captain is skilled and loyal, but I cannot guarantee that her crew won't speak of things they overhear, so be wary."

"Thank you, Your Grace. Your assistance means an immense amount to me," Isalla said, relief flickering across her face, which Kitania certainly agreed with.

"You're most welcome. After all, if you hadn't informed me of the threat, I shudder to think on the consequences," Alserah said, then looked around as she asked. "Is everyone ready to depart?"

"I know I am," Kitania said, taking a deep breath as she adjusted her backpack. The weight of the tail armor was obnoxious, but she had to admit that the illusion Vinara had crafted was exquisite. With brighter violet eyes, pale skin, and the seemingly scaled tail, she'd have thought she was descended of dragons as well.

A soft chorus of agreement came from the others, and Kitania smiled at Niadra again. Alserah cleared her throat and spoke calmly. "Please step back, Niadra. I'm not taking you with us."

"Of course, Your Grace, right away," Niadra said, hastily taking a step back. As she did so, Alserah raised a hand and her mana spilled into the teleportation circle rapidly, the glow lighting up the room. Kitania waved as the glow grew brighter, and Niadra opened her mouth to say something.

Kitania never heard what she said, though. With a flash and a lurching sensation, like the floor had rocked beneath her feet, Kitania found herself in another room far from where they'd started. This room was wider and had heavily reinforced walls and arrow slits all around them, along with heavy iron doors blocking the way out. Kitania recognized the teleportation chamber of Mist from their previous visit, but Alserah didn't pause, her hand still raised as she charged the new circle as well. Kitania's stomach wasn't happy, but she braced herself for the second teleport just in time.

"Ugh. That was... urgh..." Isalla said, and when Kitania glanced at her, the angel was looking a little green. Kitania winced sympathetically, as she didn't blame Isalla for her discomfort.

They were in a room that was almost identical to the one in Mist, which didn't surprise Kitania much, even if her stomach was churning slowly. While the second teleportation had made her uncomfortable, it hadn't been nearly as bad as the one which had brought her to the Forest of Sighs to begin with.

"Ah, you haven't experienced consecutive teleportations before? My apologies, I simply didn't want to waste time," Alserah said, looking at Isalla in concern as she lowered her hand.

"It's... alright. I just feel a little seasick," Isalla said, breathing hard as she leaned over, placing her hands on her knees. "I'm sure I'll be fine soon, but it'll take a bit."

"Fortunately, it *is* about an hour from here to the port," Rose said, patting Isalla on the back, shaking her head as she smiled wryly. "That'll give you plenty of time to recover."

"Indeed," Alserah said, her smile fading as she looked at them seriously. "I can't go further with you, not without risking revealing your identities even more. I can't guarantee that agents from Uthren haven't already taken note of you, but we shouldn't make it obvious by appearing in public together."

"Very true. Thank you for everything, Your Grace," Vinara said, gracefully curtseying in a way that made Kitania think she'd been practicing it. In all likelihood she had, which prompted a soft sigh from Kitania.

"Agreed. I wish we could have stayed for longer, but… needs must," Kitania said, smiling as she added, "Thank you for being so reasonable."

"Thank you for saving my life," Alserah replied simply, then took a step toward Kitania.

The demoness only had a moment to blink in confusion before the goddess swept her off her feet and kissed her. Kitania stiffened in momentary shock, then felt her muscles relax as she returned the kiss, her mind grappling with what had just happened. Alserah was warm and her lips were slightly sweet, like the taste of apples. Then the goddess broke the kiss and straightened, setting Kitania back on her feet as she blinked in confusion.

"If *you* aren't going to take initiative, I will. Have a safe trip, all of you," Alserah said, stepping away as she smiled more broadly.

Kitania stared at her, blinking as her mouth opened and shut several times, utterly flummoxed by what had just happened. Rose was the one who shook off her surprise first, and she laughed, nodding respectfully as she said. "As you say, Your Grace. I hope that your realm remains peaceful. Come along, Kitania."

"I… okay…" Kitania said, shaking her head as she was led from the room, one hand held Rose.

The doors weren't locked, somewhat to Kitania's surprise, and Rose calmly walked past still more fortifications to exit the building. Kitania found it interesting that the teleportation circles had separate exits from the rest of the fortress they were inside, rather than going through the building like the ones in Estalia's domain did, but she supposed different groups would have different approaches to defending teleportation circles.

The smell of sea air greeted Kitania, though the scent was

relatively faint. Outside the building were numerous soldiers milling about, as well as a large group of workers by the wall, which had shattered stone around it, some of which looked like it'd been melted, which prompted a wince from Kitania. She hadn't realized that this fort had been among those attacked by the hellfire worms, but it looked like the workers had reconstruction well in hand.

A pair of soldiers approached them a moment later, each in unusually common armor, and it took a moment before Kitania blinked, snapping out of her shock as she recognized them. One was a vague memory at best, but the other she knew relatively well.

"Maura? What are you doing here?" Kitania asked, looking at the brown-eyed elf whose straw-blonde hair was pulled back in a ponytail.

"Yain and I were assigned to escort you to Uthren, since I knew you reasonably well, and Yain's been to Uthren's Throne before," Maura said wryly, staring at Kitania for a moment, then shook her head. "Sheesh, just a different coloration changes you a lot."

"Thanks to Vinara, mostly," Kitania said, glancing at her friend in amusement. "I didn't expect to have the two of you along with us."

"It doesn't help that neither of us have families, which makes it easier for us to go off on this dangerous lark," Yain said, the brunette's tone slightly harsher, but her eyes glittered as she glanced around, then asked, "Is it true we might be able to find the people behind the attack? I lost a cousin in Mist and would *dearly* like to make them pay for it."

"That's right," Rose agreed, glancing at Kitania as she asked, "Kitania, care to introduce us?"

"Certainly. Maura, Yain, I'd like to introduce you to Isalla, Rose, Vinara, and Eziel. I'd like the rest of you to meet Maura and Yain, two of the guards who kept watch on me after my unannounced arrival here," Kitania said, nodding to the elves and the rest of her companions.

"A pleasure, but we'd best stop using those names immediately, if you're trying to keep from being noticed," Yain said, folding her arms and glaring at them. "At this point I have to assume the people who're after you know your names and appearances, and even if you've hidden your wings, they'll be looking for you. We need to come up with a proper story for why you're going to Uthren."

"Ah, that's a rather good point. And one I hadn't thought of," Isalla said, looking a bit taken aback.

"I had. I'm going to go by Violet Carter and will be keeping this shape," Vinara said, gesturing down at herself in her guise as a brown-haired, shapely human woman. "As for why we're going there, I'm afraid *that* is more of a question. I don't know enough about Uthren."

"To be honest, most of the time we can get away without saying your names, but it's best to have them and the story figured out before we need them," Yain said, hesitating before she added, "Fortunately, neither of us is important enough to need to change our names."

"True… and you have a very good point about figuring out new names now. I was particularly bad about that when Isalla and I went to find Rose," Kitania said, hesitating for a long moment, then shrugged and said, "Kim, I suppose. I like names that start with a k, so that works. Kim Flametongue."

"As you like. For a story, I'd suggest that you're on a pilgrimage to Uthren's Throne, particularly to visit the high temple of their gods, as well as to seek the blessings of the archangels. It'll help you get close to those in power," Yain said, glancing at Maura as she continued. "We've discussed this a bit."

"Precisely. The two of us can be guards, but I'm not sure what sort of roles each of you will have," Maura said, nodding in satisfaction, then quirked an eyebrow at them.

"I think the simplest answer is mostly the truth," Isalla said, sighing as she hesitated, then said, "I'll go by… Isabel, I suppose. Rose and I can be old friends, both daughters of knights. Kit —*Kim*, would you mind pretending to be our healer, as well as a prospective knight?"

"I can do that. I'm guessing that Eziel can be a servant…" Kitania said, growing a little amused at the story they were weaving, her gaze settling on Eziel.

"Emma, and yes, most certainly," Eziel said, straightening slightly, a smile on her face. "Some noble families have servants who're also intended to defend their heirs, so I can play the role."

"Which means I'll be a mage who's hoping to ride your coattails to glory," Vinara said, smiling widely now.

"I suppose I'll go by Lynn. I'll come up with a surname later, but I hope that will suffice? We can pretend to be from a neighboring nation… Phenal, is it?" Rose asked, tapping her lip thoughtfully.

"That should be fine. I just want the basics in place before we reach Naer. No one gossips like sailors, and by the time we reach our destination they'll be ready to get drunk," Yain said, sighing heavily.

"I don't know about that; nobility gossip a lot…" Maura teased, grinning and dodging as Yain tried to hit her in the shoulder.

"Still, you have a point," Kitania agreed, letting out a soft sigh as she shook her head, a bit chagrined. "I probably wouldn't have thought of it until we were nearly to Uthren's border."

"Everyone has blind spots. You just have different ones than most people… which is amusing, since you spent a millennium hiding from your mother," Vinara said, grinning broadly. "Now, shall we go? Or we could discuss what happened in the teleportation room, if you'd prefer."

"Ah, no, I think I'd rather not," Kitania said, heat rising in her cheeks as she hastily looked away, asking, "How are we getting to the port?"

"A pair of carriages are waiting over there," Maura said, gesturing toward a corner of the courtyard, and it took Kitania a moment to spot the carriages past some carts of material for the wall. The elf asked curiously, "What happened in the teleportation chamber?"

Kitania ignored the question, quickly walking toward the carriages. Rose chuckled as she followed, embarrassing Kitania still further.

"I think it's best not to talk about that, Violet," Isalla said, her amusement obvious as she spoke. "While it's amusing to tease her, we *are* in the domain of a goddess."

"True enough," Vinara admitted, obviously following.

Kitania felt like her cheeks could be used as the beacon for a lighthouse at that point, and it only grew worse as Yain murmured, "Now I'm confused."

"You should be," Eziel assured the woman. "However, they really aren't wrong."

Kitania suppressed the urge to sigh, raising her gaze to the sky as she walked.

CHAPTER 7

*C*oral knocked on the door and opened it, smiling as she did so. "Lady Anna? I..."

The succubus paused and blinked at the woman standing in Anna's office, blinking in confusion as she did so. Coral was quite certain she'd never seen the angel before, since she was striking enough to stick out in the demoness's memory.

The angel was tall and powerfully built, her muscles distinct without bulging too much, and her skin was darker than that of most angels Coral had seen, a soft brown that was quite attractive and contrasted with her wavy silver hair. More surprising were the angel's wings, which had feathers the color of polished steel. The woman turned to look at Coral, and there was something familiar about her smile, blue eyes, and the woman's shapely figure, which was shrouded by a flowing white dress.

"Yes, Coral?" the woman asked, tilting her head slightly, and her voice was just familiar enough to make Coral's eyes go wide.

"L-Lady Anna? Is that you?" Coral asked, almost stammering in surprise. She'd never seen Anna looking like this before, and it was enough to put her off-balance.

"Yes, it is. Am I really *that* different?" Anna asked, smiling even more as she set a sheet of parchment on her desk casually. "This is what I looked like before I joined Her Majesty's faith, at least for the most part. I didn't revert *quite* all the changes... I mostly kept my figure."

"You're... I wouldn't have recognized you if it weren't for your voice!" Coral said, looking up and down the angel in shock. "You're stunning, but so *different* that I..."

"Good, then it did as it was supposed to," Anna said, her smile widening to show her white teeth as she explained. "I was deliberately trying to hide my identity when I changed what I looked like, Coral. If you were able to identify me easily, it would have shown that I didn't do a good job of it."

"I... I see. What brings this change, though? If you were trying to hide who you are, why did you change back?" Coral asked, shaking herself as she tried to focus.

There was something different about Anna, she realized. A sense of... not confidence, not exactly. Anna had always been confident and sure of herself, but this time it was different. It was that Anna didn't feel as *passive* as she had, Coral realized. The angel had a smile on her face that spoke of no fear, and of someone who wouldn't take no for an answer. It, quite honestly, was somewhat *exciting* for the succubus, and she licked her lips as she perked up.

"Mm... I changed back because the time for me to hide is coming to an end. I've rested for a very, very long time, and I may be needed. Her Majesty would never call on my services if she had another choice, and she has not called on them now, but..." Anna smiled and shrugged, her voice a little softer now as she spoke almost tenderly. "Things have changed a great deal. I used to be entirely weary of conflict and war, and I needed to rest, but I believe that I've rested long enough. When I'm needed... well, I'll just have to answer the call, won't I?"

"Oh," Coral said, swallowing as her pulse began to race, staring at the angel's confident smile, along with something else. It was an... an *aura* around her, Coral realized, and her eyes widened as she asked softly. "Um... Lady Anna... you feel... different. Are you... an *archangel*?"

Anna's smile widened even more at the question, and she focused on Coral as she replied, her tone surprisingly light. "Why yes, that I am."

Coral gasped, both at the confirmation and at the way her superior was looking at her. It took a moment, then she asked, her voice almost a whisper, "How... did I not notice before this? You're... you feel *different*."

"I know I do. I used some complex magic to... to *trap* much of my power elsewhere, at least until it was time to reclaim it," Anna said, sighing as she stepped away from her desk, smiling gently at Coral as she added, "Regardless, I'm still me, Coral. You can be sure of that much. In any case, you didn't come here to speak about that, did you? What did you need to tell me?"

"Oh, right, um..." Coral said, trying to bring her thoughts in order again. What she'd been thinking was completely gone or was for a moment. She took a deep breath, then spoke. "It's actually not for *me*, but apparently there's some debate on how to train the new knights, since a fair number of them are angels, while plenty of others are demons who don't have wings. That's causing a few problems, and I thought I'd let you know before it gets out of hand."

"Is that so? Well, I suppose I'll have to go nip the problem in the bud," Anna said, smiling warmly as she approached.

Coral stepped out of her way, but paused as the angel turned her head and leaned in to give her a gentle kiss. The succubus returned it eagerly, blushing as Anna broke the kiss off.

"I haven't changed, you know. This is just all of me, not only the part I let you see," Anna said, smiling warmly at Coral as she spoke. "I expect you not to try to hide your feelings, hm? It's not something which we're supposed to do here, after all."

"Of course, Lady Anna. I just am... shocked," Coral said, looking down as she hesitated, then admitted, "I just find your new attitude very, *very* attractive, and didn't want to overstep myself."

"You didn't. I'll see you at dinner, hm?" Anna said, and swept out of the room, moving at a brisk, purposeful pace.

Behind her, Coral blushed, reaching up to touch her lips. She had a feeling that something huge had just changed in Estalia.

CHAPTER 8

Kitania had never really liked ships, and *Dryad's Gift* wasn't an exception. It might be a beautiful craft, elegantly made from the dryad figurehead prow to the stern railings, but it still made her uneasy to be aboard. It was how confined she was aboard a ship, she knew, plus the deep waters below them. While Kitania couldn't die from drowning, that didn't mean that it was pleasant to constantly be on the verge of passing out.

It also didn't help that the sight of Naer had been shocking. Fortunately, the seawall had protected the city from the worst of the damage the storm phoenix could have inflicted, but large portions of the waterfront had taken heavy damage, the seawall had been in desperate need of repairs, and the uppermost parts of the fortress had collapsed in the attack. She'd heard that several hundred people had died, and most of the population had been singing Alserah's praises for rescuing them before it got worse. A few sailors had grumbled at how long it'd taken, but to Kitania it sounded like most people understood, since there'd been so many monsters assaulting the country.

That said, it'd been depressing to see so much damage, and Kitania had been careful not to say too much about it to others. As far as the captain was concerned, they were passengers who'd purchased passage, and the guards carried important messages to other nations. Considering the attacks, Kitania thought the woman wouldn't be too suspicious, though she *might* know who they were, with how her gaze had followed Rose. That or she was attracted to Rose, which Kitania could entirely understand.

"How're you doing?"

Kitania started slightly at Isalla's voice, not having heard the woman approach. The wind and waves made it difficult to hear someone coming, and an instant later Kitania relaxed and looked over to smile at her friend. Isalla was in human guise and wore the trousers and tunic of a traveler, along with a makeshift bandana copying a couple of sailors to keep her hair under control. Or to attempt to keep it under control, since the wind had already managed to tease several locks free.

"Not bad, Isabel. Not bad at all. I just… am thinking," Kitania said, looking out across the waves, pausing for a moment before she admitted, "I'm worried."

"Mm… I understand that. I'm just curious what you're worried about," Isalla said, stepping past Kitania toward the bow, staring into the breeze intensely. "There's a lot of worries to go around, after all."

"Very true. I…" Kitania paused, considering, then spoke again, a sense of guilt rushing through her as she held onto the railing a little tighter. "I owe you an apology, for how I treated you when we met. I was too harsh, and somewhat enjoyed putting you off-balance. After coming to the Forest of Sighs, and being in the same situation… I'm just sorry I did that."

"Wait, you're worried about *that*?" Isalla asked, doing a double take and staring at Kitania in surprise. After a moment she smiled and shook her head, speaking gently. "It's fine, Kim. I don't hold it against you at all, and you weren't entirely wrong about my attitude. It was… incredible how different things were from what I thought the truth was."

"Regardless of whether it was right or wrong, I still feel I needed to apologize. It wasn't right of me to do, and I should have known better," Kitania said, smiling a little at Isalla's reaction. It eased her mind, and it almost felt like a knot had loosened in her stomach. It took a few more moments before she continued quietly. "I'm also sorry that our relationship has had so many… problems. I pushed you away, then there was everything after we were separated… did you hear that someone *made* your message go astray deliberately, so I'd deepen my relationship with her lady?"

Kitania deliberately avoided Niadra's name, since she didn't want anyone to overhear it. Even if the sailors weren't that close, she knew sound could carry oddly over water or on the wind, and she didn't want to give everything away by accident.

"Say *what*?" Isalla demanded, her eyes suddenly widening. She looked shocked, then outraged as she continued. "Why would anyone do that?"

"The woman in question thought that the relationship couldn't be very deep if you didn't send another message, and that it would improve her standing if I didn't know," Kitania said, wishing she had an easier way of explaining. As Isalla's gaze darkened Kitania winced, almost regretting telling the angel anything, and quickly added, "She was rather heavily punished already, so try not to get too upset."

"Don't get *too* upset?" Isalla asked angrily, glowering as she gripped the railing hard with one hand, turning to Kitania with a fiery expression on her face. "She tried to ruin our relationship entirely! What could possibly make up for that?"

"No, she was trying to get me together with her superior, since I'd *said* that I wasn't sure if there was anything still between you and me," Kitania corrected, her tone growing slightly sharper as she looked back at Isalla, finally starting to get sick of the angel's indignation and possessiveness. "She lost her position, possibly permanently, and the trust of her superior. What more do you want her to lose? Her life?"

"I… no, of course not, I just…" Isalla visibly recoiled as she spoke, shock flickering across her face, along with guilt and worry. "I was just upset, and… why are you defending her, anyway?"

"Because *someone* has to. She was telling me the truth and apologizing for what she'd done, *trying* to make amends, and then she was told to leave. She never got a chance to properly apologize to everyone, including you, and that isn't fair. I've been on the receiving end of enough unfair judgments that I'm not about to let you talk without thinking," Kitania said, taking a deep breath as she calmed herself, trying to keep from overreacting as well. Even so, she knew her voice was colder than it necessarily needed to be. "Just… think about it, please. It isn't fair to pass judgment without fully considering the situation, even if we *have* had terrible luck with other issues of late."

"I… I guess you're right. I'll try to think about it, I just… I was upset, alright?" Isalla said unhappily, turning back to the railing again. She hesitated, then admitted, "We haven't really even had a good chance to *talk* yet, not just the two of us. I guess it's made me rather prickly."

"Perhaps so, but—" Kitania began, but stopped suddenly as she heard a cry from the top of the mast, one she couldn't quite make out. The sudden activity on the aftdeck worried her, though, and she frowned as she glanced back, murmuring. "That… doesn't sound good."

"No, it doesn't. It looks like our discussion might be delayed *again*," Isalla said, scowling as she looked toward the rear deck. "That's… annoying."

"Agreed, but we may as well find out what's going on," Kitania said, then paused and shook her head, a hint of worry welling up inside her. "No, probably not. We're supposed to be just passengers at this point. We'd probably best just wait until they decide to tell us. Or maybe let the others know that something's up, so they don't get surprised if it's important."

"You think it's bad, then?" Isalla asked, looking at Kitania in obvious concern.

"Not necessarily. It's more that, considering everything *else* that's gone wrong lately, I'd rather be cautious than not worry about something strange," Kitania said, feeling a little embarrassed despite herself.

"True enough. I'll go let the others know, though I suspect they'll find out soon enough," Isalla said, letting out a soft sigh as she headed for the forward hatch.

Kitania watched Isalla go, and as she did she looked up,

murmuring forlornly. "What did I do wrong? Everything seems like it's about to fall apart…"

Sighing, Kitania waited patiently, letting the breeze distract her, even if the activity on the aftdeck *did* worry her. She'd doubtlessly find out what was happening soon enough.

"LADIES, WE HAVE A PROBLEM."

Captain Riss's voice wasn't as smooth as that of most elven women Kitania had met, and the tone of her voice instantly put Kitania on edge as she turned toward the woman, her worry growing a bit stronger.

"I assume this has something to do with whatever's been worrying your crew for the last few hours?" Rose asked, looking at the captain calmly, an eyebrow partially raised.

"Yes, I'm afraid so. We spotted sails from atop the mast, and while the ship we saw is rather distant, it doesn't have friendly colors. We were hoping they'd keep going and leave us be, but it looks like not one, but *two* ships are chasing us. Probably members of the Fallen Kingdoms," Riss replied, and let out an unhappy, barking laugh. "Heaven's know why they're this close, but we're in an ugly situation. The fortress which guards the northern shoreline of the Forest of Sighs fell during the recent attack, which means our chances of getting drake riders to give us support are slim. It's possible we might run into an allied warship, but unlikely."

"That's… unfortunate. Very unfortunate. How likely are we to outrun them?" Vinara asked, frowning unhappily as she exchanged a look of concern with Kitania. "I don't know enough about ships to make an accurate guess."

"With our windstone it's going to be a long chase, but they're gaining anyway. They probably have more powerful windstones aboard their ships, which means that they'll catch up eventually. At a guess, mid-morning tomorrow to noon. If they were slower we could reach a port to take shelter, but we're too far from any major naval bases," Riss explained, her expression growing darker. "If it were just one I wouldn't be too worried, but two…

that's going to make this tricky at best. I hope we'll lose them after dark, but I can't guarantee that. We could be in for a bloody fight."

"Fortunately, we're all skilled combatants, so I think we can help defend the ship," Isalla said, glancing at Rose as she added, "Even Emma is rather skilled, and I know she has decent weapons. Nothing suited for a siege, but a relatively simple battle aboard ship..."

"I'm not sure about that. I've only seen her use a bow, and the rocking deck could play hell with her aim," Kitania chimed in, mentally placing Eziel as the one being discussed. It took a moment, but at least she was managing not to use the wrong names.

"She's not bad with a sword. Not incredible, but not bad," Rose said, smiling as she nodded to them, then told the captain. "If you have need of us, we're more than happy to defend the ship. It isn't like we've trained for years to sit back and watch others die for us."

The captain smiled broadly as she nodded, her tone much warmer now. "I'm glad to hear that. I'm afraid I don't know much about your skills, but every bit of help will help."

"Ah, well in that case... Isabel and I are knights, while Violet is a magister in training, and Kim is a healer, but also a quite skilled swordswoman. The weakest of our company is Emma, but... maids aren't generally expected to fight, hm? Still, *someone* needs to function as our shield-bearer," Rose said briskly, standing straighter as she considered, then admitted wryly, "Not that I'm happy about wearing plate on a ship. It's a trifle more dangerous than I'd prefer, but I'll do it when necessary."

"Heavy armor tends to do that, yes," Riss agreed and glanced behind them with a scowl as she continued. "It's why most of the crew prefers light armor, if anything. Still, unless they have a friend they signaled that's ahead of us, our pursuers won't catch up before dawn. I know these waters, and there aren't any sand bars or reefs that'll endanger us through the night. I'd recommend getting your gear ready now, though, just in case I'm wrong."

"That does seem like a good idea," Isalla agreed, glancing at

Kitania as she asked, "Shall we? I'm fairly sure that my armor is in good shape, but it's always good to check."

"Certainly," Kitania agreed, resisting the urge to roll her eyes.

Kitania knew her armor's enchantments, and a little sea air wasn't going to hurt it. She could sink it in the ocean for a century and it'd be fine, though Kitania suspected she'd need to detach barnacles and other sea life from it at that point. Maybe a crab would have claimed the helmet in the place of a shell, too, a thought which amused her enough that Kitania smiled.

"What's so funny?" Rose asked, glancing at Kitania curiously.

"Nothing, really. Just a random thought that has nothing to do with our situation," Kitania assured her, shaking her head, then glanced at Riss as she added, "My apologies, Captain, it isn't my intention to make light of our situation, my thoughts are just wandering."

"As long as you have them in order when the pirates catch up, I don't give a damn how you feel," Riss replied, her smile vanishing abruptly as she scowled at Kitania, then spoke bluntly. "Just no breathing fire on my ship, you hear me? If you do, I'm throwing you overboard."

The captain turned and left as Kitania stared after her in confusion. Looking at Vinara, Kitania murmured, "I can't breathe fire, though. Why would I breathe fire?"

"I suspect it's the draconic heritage," Vinara said, not even trying to suppress her smirk. "Come on, we have things to prepare."

"Alright," Kitania said, following the others as they started toward the cabin.

At least the interior of the *Dryad's Gift* was nicer than other ships Kitania had been aboard. Unlike many of the others she'd had the dubious pleasure embarking on, the bulkheads were polished smooth and reasonably well-lit, even if the passages were cramped. The room they'd been assigned was tiny, with six bunks, which she supposed were better than the hammocks that the crew seemed to use.

Eziel looked up from folding a tunic, smiling as she spoke.

"Welcome back, ladies. I presume you heard about the pursuers?"

"How did *you* hear about that? We were just barely told by the captain!" Isalla demanded, staring at the angel like she'd grown another head, and Kitania resisted the urge to laugh as she slipped into her bunk for the moment, since there definitely wasn't space for all of them to stand around. Instead she hefted the bag with her armor in it and opened it, planning to look her armor over even if she was sure it was in good shape.

"The crew's been discussing it for close to half an hour or so. I simply overheard their discussions, and thought you'd be back relatively soon," Eziel said calmly, slipping the stack of tunics into a cubby for the moment. "From what the crew's said, they're pretty sure these are corsairs or privateers in service to the Fallen Kingdoms or a demonic faction. Probably the former, but the latter is what makes them nervous, since demons usually have at least a few crew members that are capable of flying."

"Indeed, but that doesn't mean that they can't be dealt with. No matter who it is, we're going to have to deal with them," Vinara said, glancing at the angels with an idle smile. Kitania knew she wasn't saying anything about them not using their full capabilities on purpose.

Looking over her armor, Kitania frowned, a little annoyed despite herself. Vinara had cast a subtle, long-lasting illusion on it to make the armor look like simple polished steel, and part of her really disliked the change. She liked black, probably more than was necessarily healthy, and it bothered her. At least the others were in the same position, so it wasn't just Kitania having to deal with the simple coloration.

"I see you've been informed about our unwelcome guests as well," Yain said, the soldier appearing in the doorway rather suddenly, bracing herself against the bulkhead as she looked them over. "Getting ready for a fight already?"

"Mostly it's in case there's another ship ahead of us that could cut us off, since the captain suggested the possibility," Rose explained, looking up from her own armor with a slight smile. "I'm not happy about the idea, but there's nothing we can do but play the hand we're dealt."

"True, I suppose. I hope we don't have to deal with three ships... two is going to be bad as it is. The crew is military, so we're not defenseless, but privateers usually have oversized crews to take prize ships," Yain said, looking rather unhappy as she looked at them.

"Yes, but they also tend not to have skilled magi. I wonder if I can set their sails on fire when they get close... that'd ruin their day," Vinara said, smiling broadly.

"Most ships have enchantments to make that unlikely, I'm afraid," Yain replied dryly, shaking her head as she smiled. "Still, you have a good point. We'll just have to see what happens."

"True enough," Isalla murmured, and Kitania nodded in agreement.

Her armor was fine, Kitania knew that much, so her examination was entirely for show. The real question was whether they'd fight soon, and why the other ships were after them. It was possible that they were here coincidentally, but somehow Kitania doubted that. After the past weeks, she didn't believe that *any* of this was happening by chance.

CHAPTER 9

"*R*ight where my contact said they'd be," Captain Corbek said, grinning as he looked at the ship running from them.

Arrogance and *Vengeance* were slicing through the water more quickly than the elven ship, though they weren't gaining quite as quickly as Corbek would've liked. He'd hoped to catch the elves the previous night, but unfortunately they'd managed to get farther than he'd expected before they'd spotted the elves. It made for a longer chase, but they wouldn't get away in the end.

"What's the plan, Cap?" Evan asked, the big man looking at the elven ship suspiciously. "I know we're after the passengers, but how do ya want to go about this?"

"Aim for the rigging to slow them down, strafe their decks with the hailthrowers, then board from either side," Corbek replied instantly, looking at the elven ship for a moment before adding, "Be careful, though, that *is* a military ship. Even if we'll outnumber them three to one or more, they could always surprise us, and I'm told the passengers are probably warriors."

"Won't help them if they get mobbed," Evan said, shaking his head. "Why're we after them, anyway?"

"Because my contact is willing to pay a fortune for them, of course!" Corbek said, grinning broadly in return as he slapped

Evan on the shoulder. "Now, get to it! We'll catch up within the hour."

"Yes, Cap," Evan grunted, then stepped forward as he started bellowing at the crew.

Corbek just watched the elven ship with a hungry gaze. Whether the targets were aboard or not, he was sure they'd be able to capture a fair number of elves aboard the ship, and if the Forest of Sighs wouldn't ransom them, elves tended to go for a good price on the markets. He'd make a profit off this one way or another.

~

"MARREN CORSAIRS, SHIT," Captain Riss said, lowering her spyglass and cursing. Kitania winced slightly at her tone, though she could understand why the captain was upset.

Marren was a primarily maritime port, and it was located on a slightly larger island southeast of the Forest of Sighs, one with its own portal to the hells. Worse, the domains below that portal were some of the more unfriendly ones, in Kitania's opinion. Their influence had led to Marren becoming a haven for pirates, smugglers, assassins, and other extremely unpleasant activities. Like slavery.

"Well, that means surrendering really isn't an option. Does your kingdom ransom captives from them?" Isalla asked, not sounding very happy.

"No. His Majesty says that giving them money would only encourage them, so… if we're captured, at best we'll be sold on the auction block," Riss replied unhappily. "Worse, this has to be a wealthy captain, as the ship coming up to the starboard has two hailthrowers mounted on the aftcastle. Those will make defending the ship hell."

"No, I don't think they will," Vinara said, glancing at Kitania pointedly as she added, "I know a little about defensive magic, but I know Kim can do more. I'm fairly sure that between us we can deflect the majority of their fire, which should help on the whole."

"Thanks for volunteering me," Kitania replied dryly, folding her arms as she continued. "I don't make wards that large normally, and I'm not sure I can do it."

"You know how to use protective magic? I thought you were a healer," Riss said, looking at Kitania in confusion.

"I'm an alchemist trained as a physician. My magic is mostly defensive, because that's my strongest talent and a healer isn't much use when they're bleeding out on the ground," Kitania replied shortly, looking down the length of the ship unhappily.

Dryad's Gift wasn't enormous, but it wasn't small, either. The schooner was a bit under fifty feet long and cramped, especially with the oversized crew aboard. Thirty-odd sailors, the captain, plus their own company filled most of the deck, and Kitania glanced back at the other ships unhappily. She didn't like the idea of straining herself to put up a ward, but hailthrowers were dangerous. Kitania didn't know who'd developed the first one, but the magical weapons were used to spray hundreds of shards of ice in a cone, which allowed them to be used to clear the decks of ships relatively easily and without risking setting the ship on fire.

"Are you saying you can't do it?" Vinara asked, a smile flickering across her face.

"I don't *know* if I can do it, so if you'd shut up and let me think I'd appreciate it," Kitania retorted in annoyance but flushed slightly as several people looked at her in shock. Probably because she was taking such an angry tone with a mage, but Kitania didn't really care what they thought right now. Her worry was that she might not be able to defend the ship.

Kitania quickly ran through several spells internally but discarded each of them in turn as being impractical. Eventually she grimaced and spoke. "I think I have a method of defending the ship, but it doesn't make me happy. I have a spell which can deflect small, high-speed objects to some degree, but it's not one-way. If I cast it, we'll be hampered by the spell as much as they will, and it won't guarantee that all the attacks will be deflected, just the majority. The other options are worse or would take far too much mana to maintain as they approach."

"Goddess grant me strength..." Riss muttered, scowling as

she glanced back at the pursuers and added, "Just what we need, our bows to be taken out of play, too."

"If I may, is this spell supposed to be all around the ship or just along the side?" Vinara asked, tilting her head slightly. "If it's the latter, we could always hit them as they approach, then take shelter behind the spell without them knowing."

"Just along the side of the ship. I'm not an archmage, warding the entire *ship* for better than an hour with a spell like that? Please, that's far beyond my capabilities. Even making it travel *with* us is difficult enough as it is," Kitania said, shaking her head unhappily. "I'll be able to cast a couple of basic defensive spells beyond this one, but that's as far as I can go."

In truth, Kitania was understating what she could do slightly. She didn't have any other spells which could defend the ship, it was just too large for her to reliably shield it, but defending herself was an entirely different story. The thing was, these were just pirates, and revealing the full range of her defensive spells would be foolish and might even reveal her identity. Riss's worry seemed to ease a little, though it didn't fade entirely.

"That would be better, yes. I'm not sure how much good it'll do, but it's better," Riss said, glancing back as she considered the ship, then asked Vinara, "What about you? You're a mage, so how're you going to contribute?"

"Not at all, initially. I want to let them get close, then I'm going to try to drop a fireball on the second ship's main deck after they've assembled," Vinara said, her expression turning icy, and she glanced at Eziel as she continued. "Emma, Yain? Would the two of you assist me, and try to take out their helmsman? I'd like to keep them out of the fight for as long as possible."

"What? But what about the first ship? They're the one who's more dangerous!" Riss exclaimed, much of her unease returning suddenly.

"They have hailthrowers, so they're much more likely to have defenses against spells. That being the case, if we don't hit them with obvious magic initially, both ships will let their guard down a little," Vinara explained patiently, meeting Riss's gaze levelly. "I'm going to participate, don't worry, I just want to do as much damage immediately as I can. So as soon as they come alongside, I'm going to ice over their boarding planks."

"Ah, that makes more sense. Well, we'd best get to work, then," Riss said, glancing at Kitania, and the demoness suppressed the urge to sigh or bristle. She *really* didn't like being given orders, even implied ones, but she chose to obey. It wouldn't do to anger the captain at this point, and Riss had good reason for being upset.

Kitania settled down to cast her spell, weaving it as carefully as she could, and as she did she heard Maura speak to Rose softly. "Where do you want me?"

"You and Yain are our guides, so don't endanger yourself too much. Watch Isabel's back and try to keep us from being flanked," Rose replied calmly, the whisper of metal indicating that she'd unsheathed her blade to check it, then sheathed it again. "We're going to try to block as many of them as possible, so I wouldn't be surprised if they try to come around behind us."

"Alright," Maura agreed, not sounding very happy. Kitania couldn't blame her, since this wasn't the best start to their trip.

Unfortunately, while the others continued talking among themselves, Kitania couldn't participate due to the spell she was casting. The crew was unhappy, based on what she heard, and more than a touch scared. They'd seen close to forty people on the deck of the ship following them, and a quiet furor had rippled through the crew when they'd learned the ship was named *Arrogance*. They obviously recognized the name, and it demoralized them.

Channeling her mana into the spell took far too long, but at last Kitania finished, and she reached out to run a finger along the railing, willing the spell into existence. Unlike most of her spells, this one was almost silent, like a whisper in the wind as the air shimmered ever so slightly, then it snapped into being along the side of the ship and the majority of her mana rushed out of her.

"It's done," Kitania said, flicking her tail nervously as she glanced at Riss and the others, then smiled at Isalla as she added, "Hopefully it's an unwelcome surprise for the attackers."

"Agreed. We should be in extreme ballista range any

moment, so we'd best prepare ourselves," Riss said, glancing at Rose, then shook her head as she added, "I really don't envy you, with that heavy armor. I'd be afraid of drowning."

"Fair enough," Rose replied with a chuckle, and Kitania smiled as well. At least drowning wasn't something they needed to worry about.

Then the first enemy ship fired its ballista.

~

THE BALLISTA BOLT skipped across two waves before sinking, having come nowhere near the elven schooner, and Corbek resisted the urge to swear. Fortunately, Evan was on the foredeck, and he made his displeasure known vocally.

"Where were you daft sods aiming? Were you blindfolded or summat?" Evan roared angrily. "Reload and aim *properly* this time! We don't have ammo to waste."

Corbek chuckled, glancing up at the flags to ensure the windstone was working correctly as well. It should, with as much as he'd paid for it, then he glanced to the side, at the plain redhead standing there, her slit eyes deep crimson and calm as she looked at the ship ahead of them. The scars over her left eye and right cheek gave her a slightly more sinister look, and her black and rust-red armor accentuated the impression, even if the leather wasn't the best that she could afford. Corbek knew he paid the woman enough, but what she did with it was an entirely different question.

"What do you think? Do they have spellcasters?" Corbek asked, watching her curiously. As much as Corbek hated it, he was attracted to the sorceress, even if it was mostly because she wouldn't give him the time of day. The forbidden fruit always seemed so much sweeter, which was somehow maddening. He also wasn't about to ruin a perfectly good relationship because he was feeling randy. Not unless he was about to retire, anyway.

"I'm uncertain. We've only just reached a distance where spells could be used to attack, much like siege engines. I don't see any obvious casters, but that doesn't guarantee anything," Beatriz said, her voice slightly distant as she watched the ship warily. She never let her guard down, it seemed like, which Corbek thought was probably for the best, and she continued after a moment. "I cannot say, but I'll be ready to counter their spells if they attack us."

"As you say. At least we're not seeing a lot of magi, that would be… annoying," Corbek said, his mood improving as he looked at the elves. His ballista crew fired again, and this time the bolt came closer to hitting, which improved his mood.

That improvement vanished as the elves returned fire an instant later, and he swore as the ballista they fired glanced off the front of the hull. Scowling, he roared. "They scratched my paint job! Tear out their entrails and serve them for supper, already!"

Several crew members flinched at his roar, and Corbek couldn't resist a grin. It was good to have a reputation as a bloodthirsty captain sometimes.

Besides, it wasn't as if he was bluffing.

CHAPTER 10

*E*ziel held her bow and focused like she'd never focused before. Before she'd been captured in Estalia and met its queen, she'd always been fueled by her faith and conviction, which had allowed her to focus on goals to the exclusion of most other desires, but it hadn't been perfect even then.

After meeting Estalia, though, she'd been given a purpose, one which was more important than anything else. Pleasing Estalia was more important than her life, and it was what truly made Eziel happy. Then, wonder of wonders, Estalia had given Eziel a quest to make up for her horrid mistakes, entrusting Kitania's happiness and safety to Eziel.

A large part of Eziel had expected Kitania to kill her when they met, yet the demoness hadn't. Based on the activities she'd seen around Estalia's palace, Eziel had also expected to be asked to warm Kitania's bed for her. Somewhat more disappointingly, that hadn't been one of Kitania's requests either, and Eziel was perceptive enough to know that offering wouldn't be a good idea. It *was* something which a part of Eziel had hoped for, but she would never try to force the issue. It wasn't her place, after all.

Instead, Kitania was treating Eziel… almost like she treated everyone else. Oh, she gave directions and made the occasional request, but it was almost maddening to Eziel that most of the time Kitania did things herself rather than ordering Eziel to do it for her. All Eziel's being was wrapped up in making Kitania happy, since that would make Estalia happy.

That was why Eziel was focusing on her training with the bow. It wasn't her primary weapon, though she was almost as skilled with a bow as she was with a sword, but Eziel didn't care about that, not anymore. The privateers which were bearing down on them would try to kill Kitania and all the others. That would make Kitania unhappy, and if Kitania was unhappy, Estalia would be *very* unhappy. And that was a result to be avoided at all costs.

So Eziel slowly breathed in, her bow steadier in her hands than the ones in the hands of the elves around her, taking aim carefully. The rocking of the ship was nothing compared to adjusting to the winds of the heavens when flying, after all. She loosed her arrow suddenly, almost not realizing when she had, and watched it fly toward the aftdeck of the privateer unerringly.

"Drat. He ducked," Eziel muttered, disappointment rushing through her. The human didn't look nearly as happy as she'd expect at surviving, and his hat was pinned to the railing by her arrow.

Eziel didn't have much time to dwell on it, though, not when the enemy fired again, and *this* time the ballista came far closer.

SPLINTERS FLEW as a ballista bolt glanced off the rear mast, and Kitania ducked, swearing as a couple of them hit her armor. Several cries of pain came from the crew, which made her wince, then she glanced at the mast, relieved that it'd been hit at an angle rather than dead on. That could've dropped the mast, which would have been really bad.

"I *hate* naval combat. No room to maneuver as easily," Vinara said, her voice taut as she brushed herself off. "How soon will they board?"

"Just a couple of minutes," Riss said, scowling as she wiped away some blood from where her cheek had been grazed. "Why?"

"I'd like to ruin their day. Care to reduce sail and set things off early?" Vinara asked, grinning as she glanced at the others, adding. "I'm tired of being target practice."

"I think their captain is, too. I see someone casting a spell!" Yain called out, and Kitania's eyes went wide as she spun around.

"Oh crap, where... ah!" Kitania spotted flickers of light from the aftdeck of the ship, and based on the angle... she hissed and yelled, "Everyone, down!"

Fortunately, it seemed that people listened, though not everyone was in any position to duck when a deafening *crack* split the air and a lightning bolt blasted into the mast, leeching into a pair of unlucky sailors as well, who fell to the deck, writhing in pain.

The mast creaked and groaned, but Kitania ignored it as Riss began snapping out orders while climbing to her feet. Rose calmly spoke, her voice betraying her tension as she said, "Now would be good, Violet."

"As you wish, Milady," Vinara said, rising gracefully, her eyes glittering with malice as she added, "I'll keep the mage busy but will have my hands full."

"Right," Kitania agreed, taking a deep breath as she rolled to her feet. They were slowing down, probably because Riss didn't want to lose the mast, and that meant that any second the other ship would pull alongside. Losing the mast in particular would be bad.

An instant later Vinara snapped out the quick words of a spell, and a rippling orb of fire launched out from her hands, racing down on the second ship, then detonated over the deck with a muffled *boom*. Screams echoed across the water, but Eziel and Yain didn't seem to care about that as the two women stood to take shots at the helmsman of the ship as well. Kitania glanced over to see people on fire and scorch marks across the middle of the deck, and she winced. Obviously Vinara had impeccably aimed at the gathered crew, and she'd done enormous damage in her initial strike.

Kitania's attention whipped back to the nearby ship an instant later as it's ballista fired again. This time it was almost alongside, though, and the ballista bolt suddenly twisted in mid-air as it was redirected by Kitania's spell and went flying off ahead of the ship. Before she could do more than take a deep breath, the two hailthrowers fired, each looking like large crossbows without arms, but with numerous crystals across the front of them.

Hundreds of icicles spat out of the hailthrowers in a torrent that enveloped most of the deck of *Dryad's Gift*, and it would have been just as horrific as what Vinara had done to the other ship, at least if they'd struck home properly. Instead the spell did its job, and those icicles began flying every which way instead of being focused on the deck.

Screams of pain proved that Kitania's spell wasn't perfect, and six of the defending elves went down with injuries, though none looked like they were dead, and an icicle hit Kitania in the shoulder and bounced off, rocking her backward from the force of the blow. Kitania swallowed a curse as she saw the injuries, annoyed with herself. She'd hoped the spell would do better than that, but her unhappiness eased as she looked at the enemy ship.

At least ten of the privateers were down and screaming due to some of the icicles being thrown back, but the ship came in so quickly there wasn't any more time to prepare or change course. Privateers tossed grappling hooks as they pulled up next to the *Dryad's Gift*, and boarding planks came down hard, the spiked ends slamming into the deck harshly. The privateers surged up onto the planks with angry war cries.

"Ice to meet you," Vinara said humorously, her voice barely audible as she snapped her fingers, and a layer of ice suddenly covered the boarding planks.

The first privateers slipped and slid as their footing became incredibly precarious, and one man screamed as he fell between the two ships, followed by a sickening crunch. The remainder were off-balance as they came across, and the defending elves took advantage of their unsteadiness ruthlessly, as did everyone else.

Kitania stepped forward beside Maura, who had a rapier in hand and a grim look on her face as they rushed the first woman onto the ship. The attacker looked panicked, but Kitania tried to put that out of her mind as she focused solely on defending the ship.

The woman didn't have time to defend herself, not as Kitania and Maura cut her down in seconds. In her peripheral vision Kitania saw Isalla slam the lead attackers back on the plank with her shield, sending at least one woman off the edge to her doom, while Rose was wielding her sword with two hands and cut a man almost in two as she led the defense at the middle of the ship.

Kitania didn't have time to focus on her friends, though, not as a couple of opponents launched themselves from the railings to avoid the plank, and suddenly battle was joined in truth.

Fighting alongside others was an enormous change for her, and Kitania barely avoided overreacting several times as Maura and a male sailor fought at her side, the latter wielding a wickedly sharp cutlass. Her armor slowed her down, and the lack of room to maneuver was frustrating, though her armor quickly proved its worth as she took a pommel-strike in the helmet, then gutted the man in return.

Magic rippled back and forth in the air above them as the enemy mage tried to attack, but Vinara had her well in hand, it seemed, and Kitania occasionally glanced up as she and the others fought the attackers, at least until Kitania heard a roar of anger from her left.

Rose was staggering back, to Kitania's shock, and in front of her was a large man in surprisingly light armor, but in his hands was a massive maul-axe, and the dent in her breastplate indicated he'd hit her with the blunt end. It wasn't a large dent, but even so it was impressive. His attack opened a gap in their lines for his allies to spill into, and Kitania cursed, then *moved*, trusting Maura and the sailor to hold the line.

"Get them, you sorry maggots! There aren't that many, and —" the big man bellowed, but dodged just in time as Kitania lunged at him, his dark eyes flashing with anger. "Ah, a feisty one! Another sacrifice for the deeps!"

"I think not," Kitania replied shortly, recovering from her lunge and briefly regretting not being able to use her cloudpiercer. She mentally set that aside and struck again, aiming for the man's gut.

He dodged, roared, and swung his axe at her hard, almost completely disregarding his defense, something that startled Kitania. She hastily backed out of range, the axe-blade only inches from her throat, then surged forward to slam the man into the railing bodily, not using her sword or giving him time to recover.

"You little—" the man began, but at that moment a sword thrust past Kitania's head and into the man's throat. Kitania jumped slightly and recoiled as blood sprayed on her, and looked up to see Rose by her side, the angelic woman's face grim.

"Single combat has no place on the battlefield," Rose said grimly, blocking the attack of a pirate and kicking him in the stomach. "Shall we go on offense?"

"Sure, I'll watch your back," Kitania gasped, standing fully as she prepared to jump over the railing, hoping she wouldn't end up crushed between the ships as well.

The attackers were falling back quickly, Kitania saw, though they left numerous injured people in their wake. Just as Kitania was about to rush onto the enemy ship, she heard a man yell.

"Cut us loose!" the enemy captain bellowed angrily, and several privateers quickly cut the grappling hooks, while Kitania heard gears whirr and creak as the boarding ramps ripped free of the deck. The release rocked *Dryad's Gift*, and she swore as she almost lost her footing.

"Crap, they're getting away!" Isalla exclaimed angrily, fire in her eyes as she took a step forward.

"No, we drove them off," Riss retorted, and the captain looked much worse for wear, as she was bleeding from a couple of injuries and looked quite grim. "We don't have the people to chase them properly, anyway.

"That's... frustrating, but fair," Kitania said, taking a breath as she wiped her blade off on a nearby body and sheathed it. She'd clean it properly later, but she focused on the people groaning and bleeding out on the deck as she continued. "In the meantime, we should care for the injured."

"Agreed," Rose said, looking around as her lips pressed together.

Beyond the railing, the enemy ship was pulling away quickly, and Vinara snapped out the words of a spell as a fireball erupted from the aftdeck of the ship, only to be quenched by the succubus's spell. The other ship was there when Kitania glanced over, and it was slowly turning away as well, obviously devastated by the previous attack.

"How can we help?" Isalla asked, looking like she'd calmed down a little, and looked around in horror.

"Find the worst-injured and call me over, starting with our crew. If I can save them, that's the best option," Kitania said and glanced at Riss as she added, "If you have a healer, I'd deeply appreciate their help."

"Of course, let's get to it," Riss said and turned to yell belowdecks.

As she did so, Kitania got to work. The actual battle might have been short, but the conflict was far from over. Until all the crew were dead or stable, it would only continue.

So few people thought about the aftermath of a battle, just about the supposed glory of the fight itself.

"DAMNATION AND BRIMSTONE, what in the ever-living fires of the *hells* was that?" Corbek demanded as *Arrogance* limped away from the battle, shocked by the losses they'd taken. *Vengeance* had only managed a couple of ballista bolts in the entire battle, and had lost over two-thirds of its crew from the opening blast of the elven mage, which was bad enough, but then she'd been sniped by archers as well.

As for *Arrogance*, the crew was down to barely fifteen, and a quarter of them were injured, while Corbek had found himself dodging arrows from a particularly vindictive archer, even when the archer had been forced to shoot *past* Beatriz. It was infuriating, as was how the enemy mage had countered every spell his mage had thrown at them after the first.

"That was an extremely unfortunate encounter with a highly skilled mage, possibly two of them," Beatriz said, her tone flat as she glared back at the ship receding into the distance. "I don't think someone who could counter my spells could also have put up the barrier that shielded them from the initial barrage, though I could be mistaken on that. Either way, it was incredibly frustrating, and I'm not terribly happy with how things went."

"*You're* unhappy?" Corbek snarled, then cut himself short, growling under his breath as he shook his head, throwing his hands up in the air as he snapped at the helmsman. "We're going home. Hells take us if we're going to go after *that* deathtrap again!"

"Aye, sir," the man said, relief in his voice as he adjusted their course.

At least he wouldn't be having to pay most of the crew, which would make the trip a bit *less* of a disaster, Corbek reasoned morbidly, then perked up. They also might be able to spot a merchant ship on the way back, and that would be far more useful of a prize.

It was always good to try and find a silver lining after a nasty surprise.

CHAPTER 11

*I*t took most of the day after the attack for the crew to repair the mast, during which Kitania spent her time trying to save the injured, focusing entirely on the sailors. While a few of the privateers survived, it was mostly by chance and the occasional bout of pity on the part of the elves. Not that it helped, since they were promptly handed over to the first port they came across to be tried for piracy, which was a death sentence if they were found guilty.

Of the ship's crew of just over thirty, they'd lost eight entirely, another ten were injured, meaning that they'd been left shorthanded. On the other hand, Kitania's skills had done wonders for getting most of the crew back on their feet quickly, while Vinara had been able to help with some of the more heavily injured. Kitania had been forced to stock up on more herbs when they reached the port, but despite her frustration at using some of her alchemical cures, she couldn't convince herself that saving them and leaving the sailors with heavy injuries was a better idea.

Even so, they'd resumed their journey with only minor delays after that, though Riss had been even warier than before. Fortunately, aside from a bit of rough seas that had made the passage unpleasant, they managed to reach Port Hope, their planned destination.

"Thank you for your assistance, Captain. I wish that the trip had been uneventful, but we can't have everything," Rose said, offering a hand to the captain.

"It was my pleasure, Lady Lynn. It wasn't the most pleasant of voyages, but the company was pleasant, and we'd have lost significantly more people if you hadn't been aboard," Riss said, smiling warmly at Rose as she shook the woman's hand. "Hopefully we'll be able to have a more pleasant journey in the future, should our paths cross again."

"Indeed," Rose said, smiling slightly. "Farewell for now, however. Uthren awaits us, after something of a journey."

"As you say. May you have safe travels," Riss said, then turned to head back to her ship, where the quartermaster was waiting with an impatiently tapping foot.

"Ah, dry land again," Vinara murmured, stepping off the pier with a smile. "I do prefer not having the ground move under me."

"I just wish that I didn't always feel like the ground was moving for an hour," Isalla groused, glaring at the succubus. "I'm still not used to it."

"We learn to live with it or we don't," Kitania said calmly, looking around as she ignored her body claiming that the ground was moving. She wasn't going to let it slow her down, and Port Hope was a rather nicer version of the human ports she'd seen before.

Most of the city was made of wood, though it had a pair of towers with siege engines at the ends of the cliffs which encompassed the bay, and she could see the ends of a giant chain come up out of the water and into the base of the towers, likely indicating they could winch the chain up to block ships from entering or leaving the harbor. The piers were solid, even if they were somewhat weathered, and she didn't see any sign of the usual slums near the waterfront. There were plenty of warehouses and taverns, but there was also a fortress near the pinnacle of the city, while leaving Port Hope would require ascending a series of punishing switchbacks with gates along the way. There probably was more to the city above the cliffs, but

Kitania hadn't been able to get a clear look on their trip into the harbor.

"So, where are we going?" Isalla asked, looking at Maura and Yain. "You two have the best idea of what to do."

"We'll be resting here tonight, at a minimum, possibly for a day or two more," Yain said promptly, glancing at Maura as she continued calmly. "We have to arrange for a carriage or mounts to reach Uthren. By foot we'd be looking at close to a sixteen-day journey to Uthren's Throne, but if we get a stagecoach or use horses ourselves, we can cut that down to far less than that. I'm assuming you'd prefer horses, since it's easier to see an ambush coming."

"That's right. We're all soldiers anyway, so it'd certainly make me more comfortable," Kitania said, a shiver running down her spine as she remembered the attack when she was in the coach with Niadra. She'd been so helpless inside the carriage, which made her far less happy riding them now.

"Agreed," Isalla said, nodding firmly. Kitania was slightly curious why Isalla was so vehement but wasn't going to argue with someone agreeing with her.

"Everyone is agreed? Excellent. Then now for the climb," Yain said, nodding toward the switchbacks unhappily. "It's long, so be prepared for aching legs at the top."

"It does look unpleasant," Rose murmured, looking up and frowning. "I'd hate to think about what would happen if an army took the upper rim, though. The docks would be nearly helpless."

"Obviously you haven't seen the fortifications at the top before," Yain said, smirking back at the angel. "The walls and towers above are impressive, and for good reason. Port Hope is incredibly important to the country, and they have excellent defenses."

"Ah, much better than I expected. I'll admit that this cove makes me... anxious," Vinara said, looking around unhappily as she considered, then asked, "Has no one here ever heard of tidal waves? If one came in there's no way in all the hells more than a fraction of these people could get up that path in time."

"Um, maybe they have a solution for that? Probably

magical?" Maura suggested, blanching slightly as she looked around, and Kitania winced as well.

She hadn't thought about it until Vinara brought it up, but the port was just flat enough that there wouldn't be anywhere to hide from a tidal wave. It made Kitania even more uncomfortable, and also inclined to get out of the lower city as soon as possible.

"No, Maura, I don't think so. Oh, they could use magic to regulate the water, but unless they have a deity of water on hand, almost any barrier to slow water would shatter under the weight of a wave like that," Vinara said, her voice *almost* kind, but in a way that sent chills down Kitania's spine. "Water is immensely heavy, and enough of it can destroy nearly anything."

"Good thing we're leaving, then," Eziel murmured softly, and Kitania cracked a smile, looking up at the switchbacks unhappily.

"Agreed," Kitania said, inwardly thankful for her ability to regenerate. Without it, the climb would be *really* unpleasant.

Regardless, they headed for the entrance to the switchbacks, and as they did Kitania felt like her stomach was tightening still more. They were drawing closer to the heavens, and thus, closer to danger. She worried, but mostly for the others.

STANDING ATOP THE ADAMANT PINNACLE, Sorm took a deep breath, enjoying the cold wind that had his clothing billowing around him, while flags made snapping sounds above and behind him. In the distance above him was a pale, barely visible white glow, the portal to the heavens looking almost like a cloud. If it weren't stationary and perfectly circular, most people might consider it a cloud, or at least most mortals would.

Sorm preferred looking up to looking down, but despite that he allowed his gaze to slowly lower until he could see the multitude of mountains around him, much of their sides barren even over a millennium after the battle that had taken place here. Sorm didn't remember what the range had been originally named, but now they were the Scarlet Peaks. Even now there were craters here and there on the mountainsides, spots where the devastation that'd been unleashed had lasted far too long. At least there weren't many bones, as most of those had decayed, been removed, or been buried. On the other hand, it served as a reminder of why Sorm was doing this.

According to reports he'd seen, close to thirty thousand angels had participated in the battle, along with a hundred thousand mortals on their side. Opposing them had been a combined force of mortals and demons around a hundred thousand strong, possibly as much as a hundred and fifty thousand, though the records were uncertain of the exact numbers. While not as famous as the Siege of Rosken, the Battle of Scarlet Peaks had raged for nearly two weeks before the demons and Fallen Kingdoms had been driven back, but the cost had been incredibly high. More than half of each army had been killed in the battle, and so much blood had been shed that it'd led to the mountains being renamed.

It wasn't something Sorm liked thinking about, to be perfectly honest, but it did help reinforce his determination when he thought about it. Around fifteen thousand angels had died in the battle, and the thought of all the grieving families made him angry. The battle had also led to the establishment of the Adamant Pinnacle, and the society had been fortunate enough to essentially take over the fortress without anyone realizing what they'd done.

"Pardon me, Master Sorm, but we have the information you were asking for," a man said calmly, and Sorm turned away from the view, smiling slightly.

"Indeed? Excellent work, Adam," Sorm said, smiling warmly at the blond-haired angel, and the man smiled in return. Adam wasn't as handsome as many angels, but the man was fit and a fervent believer in their cause, which more than made up for that in Sorm's opinion.

"Would you care to come inside? I'm afraid it's a touch cool for these discussions, at least for me," Adam said, gesturing to the doorway.

Sorm really couldn't blame him, considering the sheer height of the Pinnacle. The structure was built for angels, not for mortals, and as such they'd built a tall, narrow fortress with heavy magical defenses, no ground entrances or ways through the tall, narrow walls, and numerous sally ports for their airborne soldiers. It *also* meant that the wind was powerful enough to cut through almost any clothing, but that was the price they paid for building a keep on the peak of a mountain.

"Certainly, if you'll lead the way? I'm not accustomed to the layout yet, and I doubt I'll have time for that to change," Sorm said, smiling wryly at Adam. "I *am* in a bit of a hurry."

"Ah, of course. Right this way," Adam said, nodding as his eyes twinkled with understanding. "I don't blame you, though. It isn't as though you were ever stationed here, and this *is* rather different than most other fortresses, especially in the heavens."

They started into the spire, the door cutting off the wind's chill as Sorm closed it behind him, and walked down wide, arched halls that were lit by orbs that seemed to glitter with a captured fragment of the sun's light. The floor wasn't large, but the halls didn't go directly where one might expect, either.

"No, it isn't. Most of the ones in the heavens are either built for show these days or are ancient enough that I wouldn't trust them to survive a single attack," Sorm replied, looking around curiously as he considered, then asked. "Speaking of which... have you heard anything from the Holy Council? Particularly about the Forest of Sighs?"

"Not much, unfortunately. They reported that there was an attack that could have been the fault of a faction in the hells, but that the details weren't certain," Adam said, a faint sneer in his voice as he shook his head and continued. "While they haven't come to conclusions yet, they've warned all fortresses to be on alert in case of an attack."

"I wish I could say I was surprised, but every time I hope that they might have learned better, the Holy Council only disappoints me more," Sorm said, letting out a soft sigh of frustration, following Adam into the angel's office.

Tapestries depicting the battle a millennium past adorned the walls, and a well-used desk sat in the middle of the room, mostly covered by papers. A scrying orb sat to the side, a flawless crystal ball that Sorm knew had been crafted via magic, and beside it were a couple of angel feathers.

"Agreed, but what can we do that we haven't already? We'll continue toward our goal, and in the end they'll either adapt or suffer a most unfortunate fate," Adam said, circling the desk to sit, letting out a sigh. "Now, let's start with the bad news. I've learned that the pirates were driven off in their attack on the elven ship, and every indication is that the renegades and their abominations survived the attack."

"Heaven's tears… well, I can't say that I'm surprised. If the pirates had taken them, it would have solved a great many problems, but there's nothing to be done about that," Sorm said unhappily, taking a seat as he resisted the urge to growl at the thought of Isalla and Roselynn. A part of him hated that they'd managed to get away, but a larger part of him was almost happy. If they'd been captured or killed, he wouldn't be able to make them suffer like they deserved.

"Yes, I entirely agree. However, they appear not to have taken heavy precautions against scrying. While they *are* warded, Isalla's feathers allowed me to pin down her location far more precisely than I'd hoped to," Adam said, nodding to the feathers with a smile that helped Sorm relax. "I couldn't actually *see* her and any companions she might have, but the traitor appears to have left Port Hope and is moving in the direction of the Harth Plateau."

"Uthren? She's going to *Uthren*?" Sorm asked, his eyebrows rising in surprise.

"I can't be certain, but that appears to be the case," Adam confirmed, frowning slightly as he admitted, "I'm not sure why, considering what a stronghold it is for the heavens."

"Yes, but it also has a large contingent from each of the orders. I wouldn't be surprised if Roselynn is looking to find allies there," Sorm said, his thoughts racing as he considered possibilities, then added, "Besides, even if it *is* a stronghold of faith, eliminating angels who've gone there would be… difficult to manage. The locals have enough reverence for us that they'd be far more likely to take them into custody. If that happened, they could even *talk*, and that could be disastrous."

"Oof, you have a point there," Adam said, wincing as he considered, then added a little more hopefully, "On the other hand, unless they're flying or taking a stagecoach, which didn't seem likely from my divinations, you have more than a week before they reach the borders. That gives some time to intercept them, since it's only a two-day flight to the route they'd have to take."

"Mm, true enough. However... do you know of any bandits we could tip off near Uthren's border? Ones who wouldn't have any idea we're behind the tip, I mean," Sorm said, looking at Adam thoughtfully. "If I could watch and figure out their strengths and weaknesses, it'd help a lot in dealing with our unwelcome guests."

"I think I can. If you can give me a few minutes, I'm sure I can track someone down who'd know," Adam said, smiling as he arched his eyebrows. "Would that be acceptable?"

"Please. They've gotten far closer to the heavens than I'd like, so it's time to nip this in the bud," Sorm said, nodding in satisfaction.

"I'll go speak to Reana, then," Adam said, rising from his chair and heading for the door.

Sorm sat back in his chair to wait, smiling thinly as he did so, a sense of anticipation rising along with his tamped-down rage. He was looking forward to making those who'd hurt Haral *pay* for what they'd done.

CHAPTER 12

*H*aral sat in the teahouse, brooding as she sipped from her cup. The tea was good, she *knew* it was, yet at the same time it seemed almost flavorless in her mouth. It shouldn't, but somehow she'd lost the joy that it should have given her, and that was worrying.

It'd started after she'd dealt with Isalla's family, she knew. Eliminating them had been necessary, she kept telling herself that, yet at the same time she wondered *why* it had been necessary. Isalla's family had been nobodies, they'd had no influence, and no one would have paid them any attention if they'd tried to claim that the Society of Golden Dawn existed. And now she'd scouted the area adjoining the Emberborn family's homes, and what she'd seen left Haral aghast.

While the Emberborn family was well-known in the heavens, that was mostly because of Ember itself, and the notable family members who'd wielded the blade. What she hadn't realized was how large the family truly was, or how wealthy they must be.

The Emberborn compound was huge, with at least four mansions she'd seen, and Haral had spotted a group of twenty or so children of various ages playing in the gardens, many of them with the bright red hair that Roselynn possessed. There were also dozens of adults, and she'd seen a luncheon among a

85

group in the garden as well. Some of the men and women had been in uniforms of soldiers, most predictably in the Order of the Phoenix, but others had been definitively non-military.

It had shaken Haral more than she cared to admit, and a few casual, quiet inquiries from merchants had led her to realize that she'd been directed to eliminate an ancient, noble family of more than two hundred angels, many of whom had little to do with the war. Oh, the Emberborn family was powerful, unlike Isalla's family, and they could easily make waves if Roselynn could convince them that something was wrong in the heavens, but killing that many of them would be horrifying. If she'd done it without investigating, perhaps she'd have been able to act without qualms, but as it was Haral wasn't sure she could go through with her orders.

Perhaps that made Haral a hypocrite, she realized, considering what she'd done to the Forest of Sighs, but she didn't care about that. They'd been mortal elves, without the potentially limitless lifespan of angels, and the kingdom had been corrupt. The heavens, though… angels were the epitome of what people should be, and killing innocent civilians who had no effect on what the Holy Council chose to do… bothered Haral.

"Pardon me, but is this seat taken?" a man asked, startling Haral into looking up from her teacup. A handsome angel with dark hair, shaved cheeks, and twinkling blue eyes stood across from her, his hand on the back of the chair. The man was wearing fine silk clothing, and the colors indicated he was from one of the noble families. Fortunately not the Emberborn family, but even so his presence disconcerted her.

"What?" Haral asked, taken aback. She looked around, then spoke further, her tone prim as she said, "I see plenty of empty tables, so why would you choose mine?"

"Isn't it obvious? You look depressed, which is a horrible situation for such a beautiful woman," the man said, smiling more broadly. "I'm simply trying to cheer you up."

Haral's temper flared suddenly at that, and her eyes narrowed as she looked at him. Still, she kept from snapping at the man immediately, instead speaking softly, her voice level. "I see. I'm afraid that I don't wish for company, so please find another table."

"Oh, don't be that way! Being alone and in a bad mood is just —" the man began, pulling out the chair he'd been holding, but Haral's fraying temper all but snapped as she interrupted.

"No. I am *not* going to have tea with you, sir," Haral said flatly, glaring at the man angrily, bile welling up in her throat. "Now *leave*."

The man looked at Haral in shock, then anger as his eyes narrowed and he spoke. "Well, if that doesn't ruin your appearance entirely. I suppose there isn't any point in trying to help someone like *you*."

Turning, the man all but stalked away, and Haral barely kept herself from clenching her fist tight enough to break the handle of her cup. Instead she closed her eyes and thought of Sorm and his easy smile, which helped for a moment. Right up until she remembered what he was doing, and her eyes snapped open at the sound of a pair of footsteps. A maid stood nearby, looking nervous as she looked at Haral.

"My apologies, ma'am, but—" the maid began, but Haral raised a hand to cut her off, standing suddenly as she glanced over to see the man who'd approached her speaking to the woman running the teahouse.

"Don't bother. Obviously, the good noble couldn't handle someone rejecting his attention," Haral said, her voice practically dripping with sarcasm as she shook her head. "I wouldn't have thought his ego was so fragile, but he certainly ruined my mood as well, if it hadn't been bad enough as it was. There's no point to staying if he's going to make life more difficult."

"Thank you for your understanding, ma'am. I wish this hadn't happened, but Lord Zelith can be quite determined," the maid said, a flicker of anxiety running across her face.

"I can imagine. Here, payment for the tea and your assistance," Haral said, pulling out a handful of silver, more than enough to pay for the tea three times over, and likely with room to spare.

The maid's eyes widened as she protested. "Ma'am, that's more than you need to pay, especially after being interrupted!"

"I know it is, but I'm not in poor enough of a mood to punish you for his actions. That would be the action of someone who's truly of low birth," Haral said, carefully pitching her voice to carry, and she could *see* Zelith suddenly stiffen, and how the other patrons looked in her direction, then at the angelic man. His cheeks colored slightly, but he retained his composure surprisingly well, in Haral's opinion.

"I... I..." the maid began, obviously floundering as she realized what had happened.

Haral simply took the maid's hand, pressed the coins into it, and headed for the door, ignoring Zelith as she did so.

If nothing else, at least his interruption had successfully distracted Haral from brooding over the Emberborn family. Haral still didn't know what she was going to do with them, but for the moment it really didn't matter. She'd figure that out later.

CHAPTER 13

"It's good to see you, Ratha," Alserah said, smiling down at the short human woman.

Ratha snorted, which made Alserah's smile only widen. The other goddess was smaller than most women and a bit on the chubby side, though she was fit enough, Alserah knew. Ratha had soft brown hair that she kept shoulder-length and bright blue eyes, and she smiled as she looked back at Alserah.

"That it is, Ally. You're looking better than the last time I saw you, too, which means that dream spider you told us about must have done a real number on you," Ratha said, an odd accent to her voice.

"Yes, well, it isn't like anyone exactly knew what the problem was. I feel... better. Much, *much* better," Alserah replied, leaning down to hug the goddess of harvests. Ratha might not be the most powerful of deities, but she was reasonably potent and had surprised a great many other deities. "Thank you for coming."

"I'm just sorry it took me so long. A host of nasty pests were coming over the border, and it took some time for the local deities to give me access so I could get the problem under control. Some idiot brought fruit from some of the eastern isles back that had... never mind, you don't care about the details," Ratha said, waving dismissively as she let go of Alserah and

89

smiled, nodding toward the gates. "Shall we? I feel other deities as well... what, is it a full conclave?"

"No, though it's closer than I like to think about," Alserah said, her smile fading slightly as she began leading the way. "You're the last to arrive of those I contacted. Besides you and I, Gandar, Ire, Phillip, and Sidina are here. I'm gratified that all of you came."

"That... is a rather select group, and a lot of power in one place," Ratha said, her smile fading as she considered, then asked, "How bad is it?"

"Likely worse than you think. Bad enough that I'm seriously considering taking the offer of assistance from a demon queen," Alserah said, pausing for a long moment as Ratha inhaled sharply, then added, "Estalia, to be precise."

"That's bad. That's *really* bad, considering how you've felt about demon lords for as long as I've known you," Ratha said, her voice grim. "Father said that you hated what they did during the war."

They were approaching the gates now, and Alserah nodded unhappily as she let out a sigh. "Yes, that's all true. However, I've since learned that some demons aren't as bad as others, so that's changed a bit. The other problem is what I've learned in the last few weeks, but that's why I called for all of you."

"I see, then I should wait to ask more until we can convene properly," Ratha said, her smile almost entirely gone by this point. Alserah completely understood why, since the news wouldn't have been pleasant if it'd been her hearing about it.

"Fortunately, the others should be waiting in the conference room, and Phillip put up wards to ensure our discussions are private. I don't think anyone is going to be overhearing anything we don't want them to," Alserah said, smiling as she led the way into the palace.

"That's good, at least. And it'd take someone with a *lot* of guts to eavesdrop on a gathering of deities," Ratha said, smiling again as she smirked. "Have the others been here for long?"

"Mm, Gandar's been here the longest, about a week and a half, while the others have been here for less. Ire got here the day before yesterday," Alserah said, passing a garden where she saw several nobles trying to be subtle as they watched her. Niadra was with a young woman, and Alserah resisted the urge to frown. Her descendant had been acting odd ever since Kitania had left, which concerned her.

"Not quite enough time for them to cause too much trouble, then. That's good," Ratha murmured, then her eyes brightened as she added, "That's the room, right?"

"That it is," Alserah agreed, smiling to herself.

The wards over the doors to the conference room weren't subtle, much as Phillip wasn't. Patterns of bright red light rippled across the surface of the door, and it'd take a blind man to miss them, in Alserah's opinion. It wasn't really a conference room at all, but instead was the room where Alserah had killed the dream spider that had infected her. It was large for even a gathering of deities, but Alserah had decided that she'd prefer the additional space.

Touching the doors, Alserah spoke calmly. "It's us, Phillip."

The spells rippled brightly, then the door audibly unlocked and swung open, allowing Alserah and Ratha to enter the room. The old ballroom was just as it'd been when Alserah had left it earlier, with a vaulted ceiling and newly polished floorboards, as well as all the other renovations it'd gone through after the dream spider had torn parts of it up. In the center of the room was a circular table with six seats around it.

Sitting in four of the seats were other deities, and Alserah closed the door after Ratha, then headed for one of the unoccupied chairs, studying her allies as she did so. Gandar was still in his armor, looking rather at ease, and next to him was Ire, a dark-skinned human man from the western isles who'd inherited the mantle of the ocean wind. His eyes were dark and his hair pulled back in dreadlocks, while his face was so expressionless it was almost unreadable.

Phillip sat opposite the chair Alserah was heading for, and just the sight of the blond human made Alserah want to cringe and her eyes water. Phillip had hazel eyes, but wore incredibly bright, flamboyant clothing that was eye-searing and clashed with itself horribly, making people stare in both horror and pain, in her opinion. Phillip was a deity of illusions and mirages, which helped explain the colors, but he was also a remarkable mage, on the level of an archmage even before he'd gained his mantle, which had improved his illusions to dizzying heights.

Last was Sidina, a human woman who was average as could be at first glance. Limp sandy blonde hair was pulled back in a ponytail, and her clothing was relatively loose without being too baggy, but Alserah knew better than to underestimate Sidina. The human woman was the goddess of unarmed combat and self-perfection, though several other deities shared the latter mantle, and as such she was probably the person present that Alserah would least enjoy fighting if they didn't start at range.

"Glad you could make it, Ratha," Ire said shortly, nodding at the woman as he smiled slightly. Alserah had always found it amusing how the man was reluctant to act on his feelings for Ratha, but she wasn't going to interfere, not since she knew Ratha was mostly waiting for him to make the first move. It *might* happen in the next century, but Alserah wouldn't put any bets on it.

"And I'm glad I can be here. My apologies about the delay, but there were some issues with the crops that couldn't safely wait," Ratha said, taking a seat between Alserah and Sidina as she looked around, smirking as she added, "It's been a while since I've seen this much power in one room, too."

"Quite, though from what I've garnered the caution may be necessary," Phillip drawled, smiling as he nodded to each of them. "Not that I've gotten the whole story while we waited, just bits and pieces. Care to tell us what's going on now, Alserah?"

"All will come in due time," Sidina said serenely, watching everyone with her hands folded in her lap. "I trust that we weren't called upon without need, after all."

"Believe me, I wouldn't have contacted you if it wasn't necessary," Alserah said, taking a deep breath, then spoke bluntly, sitting back in her chair. "The attacks on the Forest of Sighs were orchestrated by a renegade faction of angels who're seeking to reignite the war between the heavens and hells."

"What? Are you joking?" Phillip asked, his smile vanishing entirely. "I heard that there were angels involved, but I didn't hear anything about *this*."

"Oh, believe me, I'd love for it to be a joke," Gandar growled, crossing his arms in front of himself unhappily as he shifted in his chair, which at least was sturdy enough it wasn't threatening to collapse. "I was asked to examine the arrow they were going to use on her to double-check things, and these angels are vindictive. They would've teleported her directly into Venadiel's defenses, and coupling that with the attacks across the country... what do you think would happen, Phil?"

"Damnation. That's worse than I thought. The rumors were more along the lines of an angelic power play, not something leading to a damned *war*," Phillip said, looking far paler than he had.

"What else is known?" Ire asked quietly, his gaze locked on Alserah, which was always a little unnerving.

"The situation is more complicated than I'd like, and we don't *know* nearly as much as I'd like either. An angelic merchant named Haral has been the primary agent we've identified of this 'Society of Golden Dawn,' and they seem to be worshiping a supposed angelic god of light, which strikes me as worrisome in its own right," Alserah replied, pressing her lips together a little tighter. "Haral betrayed an angel named Isalla and cast her into the hells, then her friend Roselynn Emberborn was betrayed by others since she might have heard something from Isalla. It sounds like a portion of the Holy Council is involved in the conspiracy, but I don't have much information on them, yet."

"How did you get the information from this Isalla? You aren't anywhere near a portal to the hells, and this sounds troubling," Ratha said, looking at Alserah in concern. "Not that I doubt you, I'm just trying to put the pieces together."

"Ironically, Isalla was saved by Estalia's estranged daughter, while Estalia took in Roselynn for safekeeping, then they reunited, just in time for a group of angels to shoot Estalia's daughter with an arrow like the one Gandar mentioned. It was intended for Estalia, but instead her daughter was teleported into *my* defenses," Alserah said, smiling in amusement as Gandar winced.

"That... would be bad. Did you resurrect her?" the dwarf

asked, his voice pained. "I've seen those defenses go off, after all."

"There wasn't any need; she has a rather impressive ability to regenerate from damn near anything, so I just had to wait for her to rebuild her body a few days later. In any case, Estalia had the angels, and sent them to retrieve Kitania once she knew where she was. Kitania was the one who told me about the dream spider and how to kill it, and between them they helped fill in many of the gaps of our knowledge. Not enough, but some," Alserah said, frowning. "Unfortunately, Haral got away during the battle here, so we didn't have many leads."

"What leads do you have? Any group that's willing to kill deities to serve their own ends is far too dangerous to let move unchecked," Phillip asked, sitting back in his chair contemplatively.

"Unfortunately, the highest-ranking member of this society we know of is in Uthren's Throne," Alserah said, and all the others groaned, all but Sidina.

"Of course, where else but one of the most loyal bastions of angelic followers?" Sidina said, considering for a long moment. She focused on Alserah as she asked, "Where are these angels? The ones that gave you information."

"They're on their way to Uthren," Alserah said, relieved that her friends were taking this seriously. "They want to unmask the conspiracy if they can, since they have people they trust in Uthren's Throne as well."

"Isn't that dangerous? If they're your primary source of information, letting them go into territory where they could be killed seems risky," Ratha murmured, frowning deeply.

"It is, but there's no other way to get good information, from my point of view. I'm sure all of you know how difficult it is to get accurate information out of the heavens, and it isn't like *I* can investigate without giving everything away," Alserah said, smiling a little more now. "Besides, with the group I've sent I'm rather confident they won't get themselves killed, at least not easily."

All the deities looked unhappy, which was as Alserah expected. Getting information from the heavens was often like pulling teeth. In many cases it was hard to even get an idea of the geography, such as it was for continents floating in a seemingly endless sky.

"If you say so. The problem is, what can we do?" Phillip said, his frown pronounced as he considered. "It isn't like we can simply smite the angelic traitors, not without knowing who they are."

"That would also invite reprisals if we don't have evidence," Gandar added, nodding slightly in agreement.

"No, we can't. However, if a group is confident enough to risk reigniting the war, do you *really* think they're weak? I want to be prepared to act if they choose to move more overtly," Alserah said, hesitating a moment before adding, "Besides, this is why I've been seriously considering an offer of an alliance with Estalia. She doesn't want the war to start either, and she's somewhat invested in keeping the peace at this point. Additionally, she has information on the heavens… not as much as she'd like, according to her, but still more than I had."

"How does she have *that*?" Sidina demanded, her eyebrows rising. "Estalia is on the opposite side of the world, nowhere near any of the portals to the heavens."

"That's the question, isn't it? However… I *do* have a guess," Alserah said, her smile fading as she remembered Eziel, as well as Lady Azalea's reports of how overwhelming Estalia's presence had been. That wasn't even considering the numerous angels she'd seen in Estalia's palace, and it was that which had informed Alserah's suspicions.

"Oh?" Ire's inquiry was short, and his eyebrows rose as he examined Alserah closely, his curiosity obvious.

"Unlike many demon lords, Estalia doesn't kill or torment her captives. Instead, she seems to keep many of them for prisoner exchanges and buys slaves that other factions take. This includes angels, and when another demonic faction needs to exchange prisoners, they often contact her if they don't have captives," Alserah said, taking a deep breath to calm herself. Gandar interrupted at that point, to her mild annoyance.

"Yes, I'm sure we all know that," the dwarven god said impatiently. "What does that have to do with this?"

"Because, based on what my ambassador said, Estalia has *dozens* of utterly devoted angels in her palace, and she can convert them to her service incredibly easily due to her mantle," Alserah said flatly, pinning Gandar in place with her gaze. He at least had the grace to flush.

"Wait... you're saying she can convince angels to change sides *easily*?" Phillip asked, paling as the man put together what she was saying first. Ire cursed softly under his breath, and Alserah smiled, a tiny part of her taking glee in sharing her worries.

"Yes, and without magical compulsion, either. Her mantle appears to be primarily focused on social interactions, from what I can tell," Alserah explained, considering for a long moment before adding more softly, "She *can* convert someone more directly, but that version is extremely obvious. I don't think the person involved could hide the change easily."

"You're saying that Estalia has converted angel spies in the heavens," Ratha stated, her tone flat, and just a hint of disbelief in it.

"I think it's likely, yes. How many... I have no idea, but at least a few," Alserah said, nodding as she settled back, a sense of relief spreading through her now that she'd shared her concerns at last. She debated a little more before adding, "I honestly believe her when she says that she doesn't want the war to break out, but her long-term goals are more nebulous. Before her representative left, she gave me another message from Estalia, one which stated that if needed, she and a few of her allies would come to help fend off the Society of Golden Dawn."

"How? As said before, she's on the opposite side of the world. The number of ley lines between here and there, plus the portal to the hells makes such difficult," Sidina murmured, frowning ever so slightly. "By the time she could arrive, any battle would likely be long since over."

"No, it wouldn't," Alserah said, and she carefully reached into her belt pouch and pulled out a circular disk of gold, inscribed with mithral runes and with a large, flawless ruby atop it. At the sight of the disk Phillip inhaled sharply, sitting up suddenly.

"Is that a *teleportation beacon*?" Phillip asked, staring at it in shock.

"A single-use one, yes," Alserah said, looking at the beacon warily. "It can only be activated from this end, my magi told me that much. Her representative, a succubus named Vinara, said she had another with her."

"Damnation." Phillip breathed out, still staring at the beacon. The hunger in his gaze startled Alserah, and her eyebrows rose slightly.

"Alright, what's the big deal with a teleportation beacon? I haven't heard of them before," Ratha said crossly, folding her arms.

"Teleportation beacons are used to create an artificial ley line from the linked location to the beacon itself. They're *absurdly* difficult to make, and I've never been able to find records on how they're constructed," Phillip said quickly, sitting up straighter as he continued enthusiastically. "They require a huge amount of mana to function and burn out within an hour from what I've heard. I've never seen more than *pictures* of one before."

"Oh. *Oh*." Ratha's eyes went wide as she looked at the beacon, swallowing as she asked, "So *that* would allow Estalia to teleport here like it was a single nexus away?"

"That's right," Alserah agreed, letting out a soft breath as she looked at the device warily. "I've had my magi examine it, but they told me this has to be centuries old, and that they had no way of replicating it. It's simply too complex, and that in comparison to the arrow the angels were going to shoot me with, this is almost as difficult to craft."

"I believe it," Gandar said, examining the beacon with obvious interest. "The gem is nearly flawless, and the precision of the runes... it's an impressive piece of work."

"It's also dangerous, though how much aid Estalia would be is another question entirely," Sidina said quietly. "Even assuming she could be trusted, she's only a single demon queen."

"A demon queen who's been hiding her full capabilities for a long time, but yes, you're right. That's why I don't want to risk facing her without other deities at my side," Alserah explained, relaxing a little at their caution. "I think she's being honest, as I said, but that doesn't mean that I should take risks. I'd like your assistance in ensuring she doesn't take advantage of the situation should I have need to call for her."

"I will be here," Ire said, nodding slowly, and a rumble of agreement rippled around the table.

"Excellent," Alserah said, much of her tension easing as she looked at her friends.

"I don't suppose I could look at the beacon, could I?" Phillip asked hopefully, his gaze still fixed on it.

Alserah laughed, and beside her both Gandar and Ratha chuckled as well.

CHAPTER 14

*E*stalia stiffened slightly as she sensed a ripple of power behind her, pausing in putting on her necklace. The hesitation was only for an instant, then she spun, her rapier clearing its sheath silently before the necklace could hit the floor. The power of a god was unmistakable, and she wouldn't be caught off guard, especially if a deity or demon lord had somehow penetrated this deep into her palace.

The presence was on the other side of the door, and Estalia's eyes narrowed, bracing herself for whatever might be coming. She briefly considered ringing the bell to raise the alarm but abandoned the notion a moment later. If the intruder had made it this far without raising the alarm, the guards likely wouldn't be much use anyway. Tensing as the doorknob turned, Estalia braced herself to fight... then froze in shock as the angel stepped into the room.

"Anna?" Estalia breathed out, shock rippling through her.

"That *is* my name, isn't it? Or at least part of it, My Lady," Anna said, smiling in return as she closed the door behind her.

Anna was different than she'd been the last time Estalia had seen her, yet at the same time the sight of her sent a thrill of both worry and excitement through Estalia. The angel was sheathed in simple steel armor, but Estalia knew better than to underestimate that armor. It eschewed all adornments yet was better than anything her artificers had produced in the millennia of her rule. Anna's skin was darker, her feathers and hair the color of silvered steel… yet she was still the beautiful woman that Estalia had known for so long. Yet at the same time a sense of worry and guilt ran through Estalia.

"This is… unexpected," Estalia said, hesitating for a mere moment, then sheathed her rapier slowly. "I thought… I didn't expect you to come here so soon, my dear, let alone like *this*. I didn't mean to—"

"No, you didn't," Anna said, gracefully crossing the room and leaning down to pick up the necklace. The angel untangled the chain carefully, then reached out to put it around Estalia's neck, her voice soft as a morning breeze. "You were just warning me that you might have no other choice but to ask for my help, my dear."

Estalia half-closed her eyes as Anna effortlessly clasped the necklace despite her gauntlets, mixed feelings still rushing through her. Her guilt eased a little, but her confusion had grown instead, and she asked, "Then why…?"

"The time has come," Anna said simply, smiling gently at Estalia as she leaned forward to give her a gentle, chaste kiss. Estalia returned it, but Anna pulled away and continued, a note of conviction to her voice that was entrancing. "I've rested long enough, that's the simple version. If you need me, and *our* daughter does… well, I think that it's time to stop hiding."

"Are you certain?" Estalia asked, her voice trembling as she ran her hand down the front of Anna's armor, hope, wonder, and excitement running through her, even as caution tamped down her hopes. "This… this nearly *destroyed* you, once. It's why I never called on you, Anna, even when things were at their worst."

"Time may not heal all wounds, but it can certainly ease them," Anna replied, taking a deep breath, then smiled as she nodded slowly. "That said… yes, I'm certain. I feel like *myself* again, My Goddess."

"Your goddess? When you are more powerful than I am?" Estalia gently teased, slowly smiling as she murmured, "I wonder what the Holy Council would think of you if they heard that. The great Anathiel, calling a weaker demon queen her *goddess."*

Anna laughed and grabbed Estalia under her arms, picking her up and spinning the demoness in the air, prompting a squeal of laughter from Estalia, one which was far more real than any laughter Estalia remembered in the last few weeks.

"Ah, but their opinions don't *matter*, remember? At this point none of them were on the council when I was in the heavens," Anna replied, pulling Estalia in close to kiss her firmly, her eyes glittering brightly in the dim lighting of the room as she smiled. "Besides, with what their negligence has done to Kitania, why should I care? It's beyond time that someone cleaned house in the heavens."

"Fair, I suppose. I'll be *much* happier with you at my side, my dear," Estalia said, hugging Anna tightly as relief rushed through her. Despite everything she'd done to prepare over the last few weeks, nothing had made her entirely happy. There were just too many unknowns to be confident of success.

However, with Anna by her side that changed. Estalia would be willing to challenge the gates of the heavens with her beloved by her side, and that was important. Even better was that Anna wasn't wanting to hide, though it brought something else to mind.

Running a finger down the side of Anna's face, her right arm wrapped around the angel's back, Estalia asked softly, "Hmm… if you're done hiding, does that mean you're going back to Anathiel, then?"

"Mm, I don't know. We'll see how I feel about it, but it *would* come in handy when we face any archangels," Anna said, her eyes glittering even more as she straightened, pulling Estalia up with her. "Assuming they remember me, of course."

"And if they believe you're who you claim to be," Estalia murmured softly, breathing in the scent of her beloved as she smiled. "It *has* been a long time."

"If they don't believe me, I'll just have to beat them into submission, I suppose," Anna replied, her tone playful. "Now… how about you take me on a tour of the palace? It's been centuries since I last visited, and you've performed some renovations."

"Certainly!" Estalia said, smiling widely as she nodded, then teased, "Besides, it'll give me a chance to introduce you and explain why you didn't set off all the wards when you entered the palace. While I wouldn't mind the guards getting additional training, I wouldn't want you to disable all of them. We might need them, after all."

"A fair point," Anna agreed, smiling a little wider as she set Estalia down carefully. "As it is, they need to rely less on the wards and more on their eyes. I got inside *far* too easily, and my appearance isn't that subtle."

Estalia nodded, amused at the implications of that. The captain of the guard would *not* be pleased to hear about his people being lax.

On the other hand, Estalia honestly couldn't be bothered to care at the moment. She was too happy about *finally* having her beloved back.

CHAPTER 15

*K*itania thought Ness was a beautiful continent for the most part, though it wasn't truly that different than most of the others. The lowlands were predominantly deciduous trees, while she could see more pine trees on the upper reaches of some of the mountains they passed.

Ness was predominantly populated by humans from what Kitania had seen, which meant that most of their journey had been spent passing fields of various farmers, small towns that were almost as crude as some in the hells, and the occasional bits of wilderness. They were going through one of the latter, which Kitania found entertaining, in a morbid sort of way.

The forest they were passing through was darker than most of the forests Kitania had seen in the mortal world, and she could sense the hush pervading the forest. From what the people in the town they'd stayed in the previous night had said, the Southern Forest was the domain of numerous potent manticores and drakes, which the neighboring nations had set aside as a wilderness which they could send their knights into for training. Kitania simply found the name a terrible misnomer, since they were so far to the north.

"How close are we to the Scarlet Peaks?" Maura suddenly asked, her voice breaking the silence and almost making Kitania flinch. Mostly due to the content of the question than by speaking, though.

"Hm? Oh, not that close. See those mountains to our east?" Rose replied after a moment, nodding to their east, and toward the peaks barely visible through the trees. "Those are the outskirts of them. The war… well, the demons landed well to the east of Port Hope and moved north, avoiding most of the major strongholds on their way, until the Alliance of Light met them in battle."

"They used to be called the Moonlit Mountains, from the way the snows gleamed at night under the radiance of the heavenly gate," Vinara said, her voice musing, and Kitania could hear the note of sadness in her voice, an emotion that she shared. The two of them had lost a great many friends in the battle, and both of them had been injured before it ended. "The battle there was… bad. If it weren't for how violent Rosken was, and how it ended, I think the Scarlet Peaks would be far more infamous. I doubt anyone truly knows how many people were lost over the course of it."

"I've only heard legends, but it was enough to shake the heavens, from what I did hear," Isalla commented, looking around them as she did so, the angel looking a bit restless. "Lynn? Didn't you say they spent several years building the Adamant Pinnacle after that?"

"Yes, that's right. How close the army came to breaching a gate into the heavens shocked the three orders, since nothing of the sort had happened since Anathiel led the second crusade against the hells, and they chose to expend an enormous amount of resources to ensure that the gate was defended more thoroughly than it was before," Rose confirmed, wincing slightly as she shook her head. "I also heard that was why all the continents with gates near them had fortresses built or expanded after that as well."

"Interesting… I never thought of it that way, but the heavens never have really been under siege, have they?" Yain asked, tilting her head as she thought. "I know tales of the war, of course, but they primarily focus on what involved the Forest of Sighs."

"Unsurprising, as far as I'm concerned," Kitania said, shrugging slightly as she sighed, considering before she spoke again, a hint of sorrow rippling through her. "There're *thousands* of years of records about the war, and at a certain point... no matter how long-lived even angels or demons are, you can't begin to absorb the true weight of history which exists. It simply makes sense to focus on the parts that are most applicable to your life and experiences."

"Unfortunately, that same focus can be counterproductive as well," Isalla added seriously, looking at Kitania guiltily. "I certainly didn't know enough about demons until after I was betrayed, and it meant that I made all sorts of assumptions that I shouldn't have. I think the sheer amount of history behind the war breeds *more* misunderstandings, and that leads to people almost delighting in killing one another."

"Not necessarily *delighting*, but it can happen," Rose agreed, shifting in her saddle a little, and her horse whickered as she did so. "I certainly don't care for how things were portrayed to me growing up."

"Ah, Yain? Do you see that?" Maura interrupted before anyone else could speak, her voice soft and slightly tense. Kitania couldn't help the tension which suddenly began coiling inside her, not when the elf sounded like she was on edge.

"What... oh, yeah," Yain said, her voice turning grim as she looked at the road ahead of them, almost murmuring. "Let's see... four sniper blinds?"

"That's what I see," Maura agreed, and Kitania bit back the urge to swear as she glanced casually at the road ahead of them.

The trees extended branches over the road like huge green eaves, granting plenty of dappled sunlight and shadows around them, and most of the trunks were mottled with moss, as were the rocks that rested on the sides of the road. It was a tangled forest to say the least, and the environment was different enough from Kitania's home that it took her a moment to pick out anything unusual. The birds were quieter, though, and after a few moments she thought she caught a hint of movement from behind some rocks. They hadn't stopped moving despite the warning, though, as they'd discussed the possibility of an ambush a few days earlier. They also didn't want to give away the fact they'd noticed the attackers, since reversing an ambush could be devastating. Besides, they'd been traveling in full armor since bandit attacks were known to happen throughout this region.

"Our planned response, then?" Kitania asked softly, her tension growing a little more. It wasn't worry for herself, of course.

"Yeah, that sounds right," Maura said, glancing back as she asked, "You alright, Emma? You aren't saying much."

"I'm perfectly well, Ms. Maura. I simply don't have much to contribute," the angel replied politely.

"I wouldn't say that," Kitania murmured, trying to keep from watching the spots she could see too closely. She didn't want the ambushers to realize that they'd been spotted. It was foolish of them to try ambushing elven soldiers in a forest, in Kitania's opinion, but after an instant she shook her head internally. The soldiers escorting her and Niadra had been ambushed by angels, so it wasn't as simple as that.

"Perhaps, My Lady, but the simple truth is that I rarely have much to add that wouldn't be out of place," Eziel replied calmly, shaking her head slowly. "In fact, I often believe that any interjection would do more harm than good, so I choose to remain silent."

"I... think I understand," Kitania said, glancing at Isalla and Rose speculatively, but didn't say anything more. She'd noticed that Isalla held at least a mild grudge where Eziel was concerned, but her friend hadn't acted on the anger, so Kitania had left them alone. She wasn't sure how to fix it, anyway.

"Perhaps you do, My Lady. I can only do what I am able to," Eziel replied simply, her smile warm and brief. Unfortunately, Kitania didn't have time to continue the vein of conversation, as they were closing on the ambush site.

A few flickers of movement caught Kitania's eye, enough to have warned her of the ambush even without the earlier warning. The ambushers obviously weren't quite ready to strike yet, but she saw Vinara's fingers twitch, which was the signal.

Kitania's voice rose at the same time as Vinara's, each of them chanting the words of their spells as they drew the runes in mid-air. Vinara's runes were fiery red, while Kitania's were violet, and Kitania heard cries of shock from around them along with cursing, but the rustling of branches as they tried to move was just a little too slow.

Kitania's spell finished, and a glowing barrier of purple light snapped into existence just as the first arrows began flying, then bounced off the shield uselessly as a motley assortment of humans and a lone dwarf swarmed out of the forest. They'd obviously rushed their attempt to attack, as they were coming in dribs and drabs, but behind them Kitania heard a sonorous voice begin chanting in turn, and the demoness winced at his poor timing, as it was just as Vinara finished *her* spell.

A deafening *crack* exploded through the forest as a lightning bolt blasted from Vinara's hands and into the forest toward that voice, which cut off with a shriek of warbling pain, the man on the other end obviously not appreciating the blast, and neither did the three bandits who'd been struck by the bolt as well, as they were now writhing on the ground.

As the horses began panicking, Kitania quickly dismounted, as had everyone but Vinara. The succubus would be responsible for keeping the horses from running too far, and a bow twanged behind her, sending an arrow into the shoulder of one of the bandits while Kitania drew her sword. Eziel, Maura, and Yain would be using their bows, while Isalla, Rose, and Kitania took the bandits head-on.

Rose cut down the lead bandit mercilessly, her voice cold as she spoke loudly. "Bandits? Well, I suppose refuse can be found anywhere. Time to clean it up."

The following bandits hesitated slightly, likely due to the chilling effect of Rose's words, but it was only a moment before Isalla and Kitania reached Rose's side, and more bandits were pouring out of the trees as arrows plinked off her barrier. Kitania didn't have time to think about that, instead focusing exclusively on dealing with the ones who were already close.

Isalla took Rose's right, while Kitania rushed forward,

kicking back a bandit with a grunt as she blocked the woman's spear, then slammed her sword through the woman's gut when her guard went down. The woman fell with a cry of pain, and Kitania flipped the spear into the air with her foot, caught it, then threw it into the next bandit.

Beside her several more bandits went down, and still more screamed as they were struck by arrows. The bandits quickly began to waver, and Kitania couldn't help a sinister smile as a young man backpedaled in front of her, trying not to come into reach. Bandits weren't trained soldiers, and it often didn't take much effort to break their morale.

A man stumbled out of the bushes, his skin scorched with a spiderweb of black marks like lightning, and he roared. "Get them, already! Like they'll let us go, so *at them*, lads!"

Then the man began snapping out the words of a spell, even as the bandits started surging forward again. Kitania blocked a man's sword and riposted, cutting deep into his shoulder as he gasped and fell back. For her part, Kitania wasn't worried as she watched the enemy mage, since she knew Vinara—

Vinara cut off Kitania's thoughts with a single calm word, and a beam of fire the width of Kitania's hand ripped through the air at the man, striking him in the throat. Kitania winced and looked away as she heard sizzling, then the man fell to his knees. Several of the bandits screamed in horror, and those in front of Kitania hesitated, slowing their approach.

Rose and Kitania barely hesitated, stepping into the attackers instead as they ruthlessly cut into the men and women. Kitania regretted it, wincing as blood sprayed onto her as the hesitant young man fell, but she knew better than to stop. If the bandits had been able to, she and the others would die or be captured and abused, and she'd *never* allow that to happen.

The bandits broke and ran at last, many of them screaming as they scattered into the forest. A couple of final arrows bounced off Kitania's shield, but then they stopped too. Most of the bandits were running, but behind her the bows of the others still were rapidly firing, cutting down many of the fleeing bandits. In front of Rose and Isalla a pair of bandits threw down their weapons and fell to their knees suddenly.

"Mercy! Please, have mercy on us!" the young man said, blinking rapidly as a cut above his eyes bled. "We surrender!"

"Oh? And how many travelers have *you* shown mercy?" Rose asked, a predatory edge to her voice as she extended her sword so the blade was at his throat. "Do you cut them down mercilessly?"

"No! I mean, we let people go plenty of times, and... and..." the man stuttered, swallowing hard, then the woman interrupted, sounding a tiny bit calmer than he did, though her dark eyes were moving back and forth nervously.

"We normally raid merchants, and if they don't put up a fight we let them go with at least some of their things," the woman said softly, her hands clearly visible as she watched Isalla warily. "People like you, the boss rarely gave a chance to surrender, though. He said your type was too dangerous. I guess he was right about that much."

"Lovely. So you wouldn't have had mercy on *us*, but you expect it in return?" Isalla said angrily, her fingers tightening on the hilt of her sword. "That seems like a little much to ask."

"Perhaps, but perhaps not. I don't wish to kill them in cold blood, but we could always take them to the next city for them to face justice there. The sentence for such *is* often death, though," Kitania said and resisted the urge to smile as their faces paled. She wiped off her sword on a nearby body as she continued. "Or we could let them go without weapons if they tell us why they attacked *us* in particular. This has been a rather eventful trip, which is somewhat annoying."

"We were just told that some wealthy knights were coming through the area, that's all!" the man said quickly, reaching up to wipe blood out of his eye, then freezing as Rose raised her sword slightly. His voice was far more hesitant as he continued. "I-it was nothing personal, honest!"

"He's telling the truth," the woman added, glancing at Isalla as she spoke. "It's possible that whoever tipped off the boss had a different motivation for it, but I don't know. He didn't take any of us with him, so I have no clue who he talked to."

"Hm, that's an interesting claim," Kitania said, looking at the others as Eziel, Vinara, and the elves approached, the horses nervously following behind them. "What do you all think?"

~

Sorm frowned, watching the two bandits through the spyglass attached to his crossbow. He didn't think the bandits would have a clue about his involvement or that of the Adamant Spire, but that wasn't a guarantee by any means, and was moderately vexing as well. He really wanted to take shots at the companions of Isalla, Rose, and the demoness, but he only dared take a single shot right now.

The fight with the bandits had been short and brutal, much as Sorm had expected it to be. As deadly as bandits could be under the right circumstances, they were nothing compared to the soldiers he'd chosen to accompany Haral into the Forest of Sighs, and even without Alserah he'd expected them to be slaughtered. However, it'd also given him a chance to identify the mage in their company, as well as Isalla and Rose. The demoness had been obvious, disguised like a dragon-blooded human, and the others had been barely worthy of note. The barrier to block arrows was annoying, but he didn't really mind, as it gave him a better idea of the demoness's capabilities.

"Alright, let's deal with a couple of loose ends," Sorm murmured softly, replacing the bolt on the crossbow with one that was more appropriate. The tip of this one had softly glowing runes in blue and orange, which helped him identify it more easily.

Taking careful aim, Sorm targeted the female bandit, who was closer to Isalla, the person he knew was least resistant to fire among them. This would be interesting, he thought grimly, and almost gently pulled the crossbow's trigger.

The crossbow bucked against Sorm's shoulder as it launched the bolt, and Sorm hesitated only an instant, long enough to see the bolt shatter the barrier as it winged its way toward the bandit. Then he rose, slinging his crossbow as he quickly took flight, confident in his precautions for stealth.

A low *boom* echoed behind Sorm, and he smiled as his wings

beat. With any luck Isalla would be mortally injured, but the bandits should be dealt with at the least. If Isalla lived, she'd definitely be injured, which was at least the *beginning* of recompense for what had been done to Haral.

Sorm hoped the women would have many sleepless nights ahead of them.

∾

KITANIA SAW the streak of blue-orange light the instant before it struck her barrier, and there was no time to do anything more than begin to move. The barrier shattered where the bolt struck, sending a lurch through her stomach as the spell rippled, but the projectile didn't stop. The bolt slammed into the female bandit's chest as her eyes began widening with shock.

The world erupted with fire, and Kitania found herself airborne, at least for a moment, and her instincts took hold before she landed. Her tail whipped around, adjusting her flight into something slightly more controlled, and Kitania grunted as she rolled and sprang to her feet, heat flickering through her armor, but it didn't gain much of a purchase on her, only singeing her in a few places. Shaking herself, Kitania looked up and almost froze, though she didn't quite allow herself to do so as horses screamed and she heard people cursing, though with the ringing in her ears the sounds were indistinct.

Where the female bandit had been was just the lower body of the woman, which was heavily scorched, and Kitania flinched as scorched chunks of flesh hit the ground as well. The man who'd been next to her was a half-dozen paces away, severe scorch marks across his body. The burns were bad enough that Kitania doubted that he was alive, but even if he was, he wasn't the one she was concerned about.

"Is—" Kitania began, and only barely cut herself off before she said Isalla's name, rushing toward Rose and Isalla. Rose was pushing herself to her feet already, but Isalla was on the ground still, her arms splayed out beside her. Scorch marks and debris adorned both of them, and she quickly asked, "Are you okay, Lynn?"

"I'll be fine. I've always been a bit more resistant to fire, and my armor weakened the blast," Rose said, her voice slightly labored as she climbed to her feet shakily. "I'm hurt, but not too badly. How's she doing?"

"I don't know," Kitania said, quickly removing Isalla's helmet, and her breath hissed inward as she did so.

Burns scorched Isalla's face and hair, though they should have been worse, based on what had happened to the man. Obviously, Isalla's armor had possessed enchantments to protect from fire, just not enough to negate the attack. Still, some of the burns were slowly healing as Kitania watched, and her worry eased slightly. The armor also had the gem which powered healing spells, something Kitania hadn't known for certain. Rose's did, but Kitania hadn't had the chance to examine Isalla's.

"She's healing, so I think she'll be alright, but that blast..." Kitania said, then grimaced as she looked to the left. "Where'd it *come* from?"

"Maura and Yain are looking now. *You* focus on making sure she lives," Vinara said, her tone unpleasant. Kitania glanced back to see her friend's clothing was scorched, and she only had a single horse. Eziel was in sight, but the angel was trying to catch the other horses, which had understandably bolted after the explosion.

"Of course," Kitania said, hesitating only a moment before pulling out a healing potion. It wouldn't do a perfect job, but it'd help Isalla recover more quickly, and *that* was important. She really didn't want to think about how bad the burns might be beneath Isalla's armor, but she'd find out soon enough.

"Either way, I think that answers the question of whether or not the informant had a bone to pick with *us*," Rose said, wheezing softly as she looked around. "Why else would they wait until the bandits were talking before attacking with something like that?"

"You're probably right," Kitania said grimly, then looked up and asked, "Find someplace good to lay her down so I can get her out of her armor, please? I'm afraid this is going to be ugly, regardless."

"As you like," Vinara said and moved away.

Turning her attention to Isalla, Kitania murmured softly, "Don't you *dare* die on me. We haven't worked things out yet."

Isalla didn't respond, but Kitania was relieved she didn't seem to be getting worse. She *hated* burn injuries, but with Vinara there to help, they should be able to help the angel recover in a day or two.

CHAPTER 16

*I*salla was aching as she woke, though it wasn't that bad of an ache. It took a moment for her to remember what had happened, and she flinched internally as she remembered the sudden wave of fire that had enveloped her in the moments before she lost consciousness, and the searing pain had been horrible. It was something of a surprise that she wasn't in pain when she woke, and a sense of relief washed over her as she opened her eyes, the sound of birds chirping softly nearby.

"Ah, you've woken at last," Vinara murmured, looking up from her book. The succubus looked comfortable in her human form, which was a little disconcerting for Isalla. The succubus looked like she'd bathed recently from her damp hair, and her clothing was quite clean.

They were in one of the tents, each of them smaller than what angels preferred, but tolerable for those without wings, even if they were cramped. Each tent slept two, and Isalla flushed slightly as she realized that she was naked beneath the blanket. She doubted that Vinara had been ogling her, but Isalla was still embarrassed. She also felt like there was a yawning pit in her stomach, like she hadn't eaten in a long time.

"Apparently so," Isalla said, pulling the blanket a little higher. "What happened? I remember a sudden blast of heat, and that was it."

"I don't blame you, as close as you were to the explosion," Vinara said, licking a finger and turning a page of the book calmly, her gaze lowering to it again as she spoke conversationally, not like someone who was concerned about an attack at all. "Someone shot one of the bandits with a bolt that punched through Kim's barrier, then detonated like a rather potent fireball. I do wonder what they were thinking... the explosion was somewhat dampened by starting within her, though I suspect it *is* a rather deadly attack. In any case, she and the other bandit were killed, and while I was singed, you took the most significant injuries. Kim and Lynn were both burned as well, but nowhere near as badly as you were."

"Oh, that's... horrible," Isalla said, swallowing as she looked down at her arm, which seemed untouched. She hesitated, then reached up to run her fingers over her face in trepidation. She hated the thought of having scars, but half-expected them, yet a wave of relief rushed through her as she found only smooth skin.

"It was, but some people are quite ruthless," Vinara agreed, snapping the book shut so suddenly that Isalla jumped. Vinara was staring at Isalla as she spoke calmly. "If it weren't for the enchantments on your armor, you might have died, Isalla. The enchantments absorbed the brunt of the blast, and afterward it poured healing energy into your body to repair what damage it could. Even so, you had severe injuries across the entire front half of your body, and if we hadn't poured an immense amount of mana into the healing spells of your armor, as well as using Kim's healing salves and my magic, you'd still be unconscious and might have scarred. Instead you've only been unconscious for a day and a half."

Isalla's eyes widened enormously, and internally she flinched at the description of what had happened. She swallowed hard, then spoke. "Thank you. I didn't realize how bad it was, not really... what about the person who attacked us?"

"They got away. Maura and Yain found where they'd bedded down to watch the attack on us, and it looked like whoever it was flew away. Considering everything we've been through lately I'd assume we had an encounter with an angel," Vinara explained, her gaze almost boring into Isalla. "It's unfortunate, but I don't see any way to properly disguise us further. Unless we send Kim back, our options are incredibly limited, and if they spotted us *here*, I doubt we could easily throw them off."

"I... suppose you're right," Isalla said, hesitating, then asked uncomfortably, "Um, may I get up? I think I need to relieve myself, then find food. I'm famished, it appears... and thank you again. I'll thank the others later."

"Certainly, I think that'd make Kim and Lynn happier as well. We've been taking turns keeping an eye on you," Vinara said, pausing as she began to rise to add sternly, "Don't strain yourself, though. Our magic is *not* designed to help endurance recover, nor diseases or infections. You'll need to keep an eye out for any problems, though Kim *claims* she dealt with anything of that sort, as long as you aren't foolish."

"Ah, I'll keep that in mind," Isalla said, and watched as Vinara left the tent, half-stooped all the way. There was dim light outside, like that of sunset, but not much.

"She's awake and appears to be in full possession of her faculties." Vinara's voice was muffled by the tent, but readily audible. "I don't think she's sustained lasting damage, including mentally. It probably helps that she didn't *see* herself when she was in poor shape."

Isalla shook her head, pushing the blankets down to take a moment to look herself over. She obviously had been washed at some point, and her skin looked about the same as it had before the attack, which was a relief and a bit embarrassing at the same time. It was probably Kitania or Rose who'd been responsible for washing her, but she was more surprised that there wasn't any damage that she could identify.

Looking for her backpack, it took Isalla a minute to find her clothing, and she slipped it on reasonably quickly. As she did, she could hear other voices, primarily Rose and the elves, though there was also some clattering and the crackle of a fire in the background. Considering the time, they were probably working on dinner. The clothing was nothing special, just a simple outfit for traveling, and a moment later Isalla slipped out of the tent and looked around, blinking as she did so.

The campsite looked relatively normal, aside from a collection of large fangs and claws laying on a blanket near the fire, and the large charred circle to what she guessed was their south. The burble of a stream came from the north, while she could see the road just barely in sight to their east. Near the campfire were the elves, Rose, and Vinara. Yain was stirring a pot hanging over the fire, and Maura looked at Isalla with a smile.

"Welcome back, Isalla. I was worried when I saw you, but Kim and Violet assured me that you'd be fine. I'm glad they were right, especially considering how little time it took," Maura said, glancing at Yain as she added, "I wish that we had similarly skilled healers back home."

"They aren't *that* bad!" Yain protested, shaking her head as she glared at Maura. "The priests can do more healing than that, though they can't do it a *lot*."

"I believe that her point was more that none of us are magi skilled with healing magic," Vinara said mildly, settling down on a rock as she nodded at Isalla, adding gently, "If we had, you'd have been awake within hours at worst. Alas, we work with what we have."

"True. I'm just glad I *did* wake. What about Kim and…" Isalla paused, having forgotten Eziel's assumed name, which both embarrassed and frustrated her. At last she continued a little lamely. "Her servant, where did they go?"

"Kim and Emma went to take a bath in the stream," Rose replied, looking up at Isalla, at which point Isalla finally saw the relief in her lover's gaze. Rose took a couple of steps closer and enveloped Isalla in a tight hug. Isalla's eyes widened, then she hugged Rose back as the redhead murmured, "I thought I'd lost you for a time. Even with Kit… Kim telling me you'd be fine, you were so still. You *have* to stop doing this to me."

"I'm sorry. I didn't *try* to do it, you know," Isalla replied, embarrassment and contrition rushing through her. She hadn't really thought about how Rose would've reacted to her being unconscious for the better part of two days, and she should have. Certainly, she hadn't exactly had time to think about it, but it still wasn't good. She just hugged Rose tightly for a long minute, taking a deep breath, then let it out again as she murmured, "I'm sorry. If I'd known... well, I wouldn't have gotten burned at all. What about you? You were caught in it, too."

"I wasn't as close as you were, and my armor was made to protect against fire more thoroughly than yours was," Rose replied, letting go at last and letting out a breath, obviously relieved despite herself. "I was singed, nothing a night of sleep couldn't fix."

"I'm glad to hear it," Isalla said, smiling as she glanced at the others, and at how Maura and Yain were studiously ignoring them. She considered before asking, her curiosity somewhat roused. "What's with the fangs, and that huge scorched spot?"

"A forest drake decided that Yain would be a good meal and chased her. I'm pretty sure she'd have killed it eventually, though the swearing didn't help her acrobatics, but Kim decided to cut things short," Vinara chimed in, stowing her book and pulling out a packet from her belt pouch, which she offered to Yain.

Taking the packet, Yain opened it and took a sniff, then recoiled slightly, her eyes visibly watering as she gasped. "Oh, that's *potent*. A little in the soup, please? Just not much."

"Of course not," Vinara murmured, taking the packet and carefully adding a dusting of a red powder to the liquid. "I don't want my mouth to feel like it's on fire either."

"To continue her explanation, the drake was *far* quicker than the ones back home, so it was a right pain to try to fight," Yain said after a moment, stirring the soup more quickly now. "I probably could've killed it, but it wasn't fun. Kim, though... she seemed like she had *far* too much practice killing drakes, since she took it out in four or five moves at most."

Isalla blinked at the description, then smiled. She thought she recognized the powder, as Kitania had used something similar in the hells to give more flavor to their meals, and Kitania being practiced with killing drakes didn't surprise her. Drakes might be favored mounts for just about every airborne cavalry in the world, but they were still vicious, dangerous creatures when wild. Considering how dangerous the hells were, she wasn't surprised that the demoness had dealt with them before.

"That doesn't surprise me. Remember her upbringing, hm?" Isalla said, smiling as she considered, then asked, "And the fire?"

"Oh, that's where we dealt with the bandits," Maura said, her smile fading quickly as she looked at the black spot. "I initially suggested we just drag them off the road, but Lynn pointed out they'd draw scavengers over, and that would make the road more dangerous for travelers, so we built a pyre. It wasn't the most pleasant work, but better than drawing more drakes down on us."

"Ahh," Isalla murmured, looking at the scorched area much less happily. In the heavens, pyres for the fallen were the norm, since they didn't like the idea of graveyards, but they certainly weren't pleasant.

"It also ensured that they wouldn't easily rise as undead. Not a major concern this far north, but never discount the possibility," Vinara added calmly, looking at the spot and clicking her tongue. "I think it's why pyres are the norm where I come from."

"I'll believe that," Yain murmured, then looked up and asked, "Could someone go tell Kim and Emma that dinner is about ready? While it's hard to burn soup, I don't want to risk it this time."

"I'll go," Isalla said quickly, relieved to have an excuse to look in on Kitania and Eziel. No matter how much time had passed, she just couldn't help a nagging sense of suspicion where Eziel was concerned.

"I'll accompany you, since you just woke up," Rose said, smiling as she nodded at the others. "We'll be back shortly."

"You'd better, or we'll start eating without you," Maura chimed in cheerfully.

"Don't you *dare*," Isalla replied, glowering at the elf in mock anger. Or mostly mock anger, as much of a void as her stomach felt like. "I could eat just about *anything* right now, so if you eat my portion..."

"So hurry!" Maura replied, grinning in return.

Isalla huffed to herself, looking at Rose as she asked, "Lead the way, if you would? Since people are making threats, I don't dare take my time."

"This way," Rose said calmly, leading the way toward the stream.

The ground was mostly uneven, which made Isalla wonder why the spot they'd camped in was flat, but she didn't ask as they approached the nearby trees, their trunks often twisted into strange shapes rather than straight. A tiny part of her wondered why the forest wasn't named the Tangled Forest or the like, but it was mostly idle curiosity. The sound of water was growing louder as they approached, too.

"How'd the last couple of days go?" Isalla asked at last, startled to realize she was somewhat nervous. "While I was unconscious, I mean."

"The person who attacked us got away, the bandits scattered, and aside from the drake, things have been quiet and almost serene. I don't trust it," Rose said, shaking her head unhappily as she glanced to either side. "The bolt that was used was heavily enchanted, and I don't know why it was used on the bandits rather than one of us."

"It's possible that whoever attacked thought they might have some information and didn't want to risk it getting out," Isalla volunteered, wincing as she hesitated before reluctantly adding, "Plus, we were in armor, and none of the others were as close as the bandits. It's possible that whoever it was wanted to hit *us*, if they're an angel."

"That doesn't make me happy, but it's very possible," Rose agreed, leading the way past several trees. "Now, we found a decent spot where the water isn't flowing as much, and that's where we've been bathing. The water's cold, though, so *most* of us don't bathe for long. Kim seems to like using magic to mitigate the cold, though, which means she takes a lot longer than the rest of us."

"I'm not surprised. Remember her bathing room?" Isalla asked, prompting laughter from Rose, which made Isalla smile widely. Laughter was good for her heart, and Isalla's tension eased as she continued. "Besides, I can't say as I blame her, considering…"

Isalla's voice trailed off as they came into sight of the river and the pool in question. To Isalla it looked like there'd been a sinkhole next to the stream that it'd filled in, making a relatively calm area alongside the narrow stream, which was no more than twenty feet across and relatively shallow. It also looked quite brisk, sending shivers down Isalla's spine and instantly quelling any thought of taking a bath herself.

In the pool were Kitania and Eziel, both of them naked, but still in their disguises, while a glittering shell of blue sigils hovered around them. That was likely the spell to protect them from cold, Isalla realized, and she blushed as she looked at the two women, pausing despite herself. Their equipment was in easy reach on the shore, but neither appeared worried about anyone looking at them.

Kitania's skin was as flawless as always, though the human-like hue still disconcerted Isalla somewhat, as did the draconic tail behind her. A tiny part of Isalla wondered if the demoness was wearing the tail armor even now. The sight of Eziel next to Kitania sparked still more jealousy, though, and Isalla had trouble keeping from glaring at the angel. The dark-haired woman looked perfectly calm as she helped rinse Kitania's hair, her pale, athletic figure so much more solidly built than Isalla's was. Eziel was entirely unlike Isalla or Rose, who had petite and voluptuous figures, respectively, and a tiny, tiny part of Isalla feared that despite everything Kitania might find herself attracted to Eziel.

As she considered, Eziel glanced up and smiled slightly as she caught sight of Isalla and Rose, speaking just loud enough for Isalla to hear her. "Milady, it appears Isabel woke at last, and that we have company."

"What?" Kitania exclaimed, quickly trying to claw back the hair that was hanging in her eyes, then smiled brilliantly as she caught sight of Isalla, something which eased Isalla's jealousy immensely. Kitania's tone was enthusiastic as she exclaimed, "Why, it *is* you! How are you feeling, Isa? I wasn't sure when you'd wake, and it just figures that you'd do it while I was away."

"I'm well enough. Yain sent me to tell you that dinner was

ready," Isalla said, a little bemused as she saw Kitania obviously debating what to do. The demoness looked torn between rushing over to Isalla and staying where she was. "Isn't that cold, even with magic to mitigate it?"

"No, not really. I mean, it's a *little* cool, but you get used to it, and I've experienced worse. This isn't even snowmelt, which means it's not nearly as cold as it could be," Kitania replied and glanced at Eziel as she asked, "Are you done washing? I think this is good enough for me, but don't want to rush you."

"I'm ready whenever you are, milady," Eziel replied, stepping toward the edge of the pool and carefully climbing out, water dripping off her body quickly. The angel pulled out a couple of thin towels and stepped to the side, waiting as Kitania stepped out of the water, then began drying Kitania off. The demoness looked far more comfortable with it than Isalla expected, which heightened her unease, if only a little.

"Mm, good. Well, you're probably feeling starved, so I don't want you to have to wait too long," Kitania said, eying Isalla as she smiled warmly. "Do be cautious, though. You haven't had practically anything in your stomach for a while, so you'll probably want to take it easy at first. How're you, Rose?"

"Well enough, now that Isabel is awake. I'll admit to having been concerned," Rose said, but Isalla saw her cheeks color as Kitania snorted softly.

"Concerned? I suppose that's one way to put it," Kitania said, shaking her head and turning to pick up her things. Isalla tried to keep from staring at the demoness, but couldn't quite restrain herself, no matter how much she tried. "Either way, at least you're alright. I was a little worried at first, but once you made it past the first fifteen minutes or so, I was confident you'd be alright. I've seen you in worse shape before, after all."

"True enough. Not that I was aware either time," Isalla said, her pleasure fading as she remembered falling into the hells. Her smile faded as she murmured, "Haral has many things to answer for."

"That she does," Rose said, her voice soft, but her anger was obvious as she gripped Isalla's hand tightly. "I wouldn't be surprised if she was behind this attack."

"It's possible, but don't make the mistake of assuming that she's behind everything," Kitania cautioned, a frown flickering across her face. "They have to be a large organization to do everything that we know they've done, so ascribing everything to a single individual is rather shortsighted, I think."

"You have a point," Isalla admitted, chastened by the warning. She'd thought the same before, but at the same time, there was an emotional part of her that wanted to blame all the poor experiences she'd been through on Haral. It was simply easier to blame the people she knew about, not the faceless ones hidden in the shadows.

Kitania nodded slightly, slipping on her clothing with Eziel's assistance. The demoness didn't take much time to prepare, which Isalla regretted ever so slightly. She was probably just frustrated due to how long they'd been apart, plus her near-death experience, Isalla realized.

"Regardless, she does have much to answer for," Rose murmured, her eyes narrowing as she admitted, "I just worry about what she might be doing now."

"We can only deal with problems within reach. We'll get there, Rose," Kitania said, smiling encouragingly as she reached out to pat both Rose and Isalla's hands. "Now... let's go get dinner."

"That sounds *wonderful*," Isalla said, her stomach gurgling audibly.

Even Eziel giggled at that.

CHAPTER 17

A young boy turned the corner at a run and didn't stop in time, hitting Haral hard. Her breath left her all at once, and she barely managed to brace herself in time to keep from being knocked over.

"Oof!" the boy said, gasping as he bounced off Haral and fell onto the ground, blinking as he looked up, his blue eyes widening as he saw her. "Oh no! My apologies, milady. I didn't mean to run into you!"

Haral blinked at his surprisingly formal speech, taking in the young angel, his wings splayed behind him and his hair an unruly mop of red curls. He had a scattering of freckles, which she'd noticed was common to the Emberborn family, and his clothing was reasonably nice, though it was currently dirty and torn in a couple of places. She guessed that he was no more than ten or twelve years old, too.

"It's alright, though I *am* wondering why you were in such a hurry, young man," Haral replied mildly, raising an eyebrow as she rubbed her stomach where he'd hit her. "Your speech is also a bit more formal than I'd expect from someone your age."

"Ah, I was just… upset, I suppose, and not watching where I was going," the boy replied in embarrassment, clearing his throat as he stood, brushing himself off and fluttering his wings to get them back into order. He stood straight, then bowed before Haral as he continued. "As for my speech, I've been taught that a member of House Emberborn is to present as good of an image as possible to others. Alas, my behavior reflected poorly on me just now."

"I suppose so," Haral murmured, her smile widening ever so slightly, and her sense of guilt where her orders were concerned weighing on her. She should just cut off her discussion with the boy here, but at the same time, she really didn't want to. She'd always loved children, after all. After a moment of hesitation, she made a decision and spoke. "My name is Haral, originally of the Evergardens. What about you?"

"I'm Emanuel Emberborn the Fifth, Lady Haral," the young man said respectfully, his cheeks flushing as he hesitated, then asked guiltily, "I don't suppose you're going to tell my parents, are you? I'm truly sorry about what happened..."

"It isn't that," Haral quickly reassured him, smiling as she looked back toward the Emberborn compound, then asked gently, "I've heard of your family, so... what were you in such a hurry to get away from?"

"Oh, um... I just..." Emanuel hesitated, flushing bright red as he shuffled his feet, then gritted his teeth and answered. "It's just some of the other boys. They decided that we should have a contest to see which of us was best with a sword, and some of them were more violent than they should've been. They can be mean when adults aren't around."

"That doesn't sound good," Haral said, a frown flickering across her face. "I'd think your peers would support you, not be cruel."

"Oh, they aren't cruel, at least not on purpose!" Emanuel quickly protested, shaking his head as he gave a momentary smile. "It's just... well, I'm sure you've heard the rumors about my cousin going missing, along with Ember?"

"Ah... well, yes, of course," Haral agreed, only barely keeping her surprise from showing on her face. She had heard the rumors about Roselynn's disappearance going around the city, but she was startled that he'd bring it up. "I wasn't sure if they were true, but I've heard something about it."

"Yes... well, we're not certain what happened yet, but she

did go missing, and it has the house elders worried. They don't want the other houses to think that we've declined in strength, so they've been pushing all of us to improve ourselves," Emanuel said, running his fingers through his hair as he shook his head, sighing. "The problem is that they emphasize swordsmanship more than magic, and my talent is more with the latter than the former. All of us are trying to live up to our bloodline, but it's… it's hard, you know?"

"I can't say that I fully understand, since I'm not from a family like yours," Haral temporized, shaking her head in faint amusement.

Emanuel flushed and looked away in embarrassment, clearing his throat as he spoke. "Oh, I'm sorry, Lady Haral… I shouldn't have complained about all of this to *you*, not after running into you. It's terribly selfish of me."

"In all honesty, I find it interesting to hear about. While families like your own aren't *that* uncommon, those of us outside them don't really know what it's like for people who grew up there," Haral said, hesitating a bare moment, then smiled as she asked, "Would you care to accompany me for a bit, Emanuel? I can at least listen to you and give you a chance to unwind, hm? Perhaps I can even learn a little from you."

"I… well, I think that'd be nice, Lady Haral," Emanuel said, flushing slightly as he looked up at her, and Haral resisted the urge to smile. She'd learned long before that men, especially *young* men, had trouble denying the requests of a beautiful woman. The only question where Emanuel had been concerned was that he might be *too* young, but it appeared not.

"Would you care to accompany me to the park, then?" Haral asked politely, smiling now.

"Most certainly, Lady Haral!" Emanuel said more enthusiastically, and the young man offered his arm to her, much like an older gentleman would.

Haral resisted the urge to laugh as she took his arm, and he began leading the way toward one of the nearby parks. Fortunately, he appeared to be heading for a more secluded one, which made Haral happier.

"I am curious… why is your family so concerned about

Roselynn's disappearance? I know it's bad, but I don't understand why they'd be pushing you so hard," Haral said, frowning slightly to herself.

"Well, Ember has long been a very prestigious weapon for the family, as a powerful enough wielder is supposed to be almost on the level of an archangel. Sure, those who are chosen as its wielder make enormous sacrifices for the family, but it's also an immense honor," Emanuel said, and he hesitated before adding, "I met Roselynn once, you know. She wasn't what I expected... she was calm, polite, and gave me a few pointers. If she's dead, it's a huge loss for the family, and no one wants that. However, at the same time, we have to do our part to protect the heavens. For a long time that's been the responsibility of Ember's wielder, but now... well, we're all going to have to do our part, at least according to my father."

"I see. That's admirable of them, even if it's a little hard on you," Haral said, a ripple of surprise rushing through her. When she'd learned that it was a relationship between Isalla and Roselynn that had led to their disgrace, a part of her had believed that it meant that Roselynn's family was decadent as well. From what Emanuel was saying, that might not be the case, which made her feelings even more confused.

"It's supposed to be, but it doesn't help when all of us are being pushed to excel at once," Emanuel said, sighing deeply as he turned a corner to approach the park at last. It was a relatively small nook nestled between the manors of the upper class and was kept immaculate even when there weren't many visitors. There were several benches around the park, including one with a decent view over the city, and he escorted Haral over to it, allowing her to sit first as he spoke. "I think some of them are lashing out unconsciously because of it. I know I've been frustrated, and I've snapped at my sister a few times. It isn't becoming of me, but... what else can I do?"

"I think you just need time to adjust. Not everyone adapts well to change, and it can be hard for any of us, even those who should know better," Haral said, smiling slightly as she relaxed into the bench and he took a seat next to her. "Did you consider that your elders might be just as out of sorts as you? Ember has been part of your family legacy for thousands of years, hasn't it?"

"That... well, perhaps that's true," Emanuel admitted, frowning as he thought about it, then shrugged and smiled helplessly. "I just don't know what to do, aside from keeping going. If I don't compete, my parents will be disappointed in me. Besides, what else *can* I do? It's part of my responsibility to uphold the family's honor and protect the heavens, even if I'm young."

"That's an admirable goal, Emanuel," Haral said, her smile growing gentler as she came to a decision. Her voice was calm as she nodded to him. "I think you should keep that in mind whenever you get frustrated. You're the only one you can truly control, and you can always try to lead by example, hm? Make yourself into the best person you can manage, and from there things will work out how they will."

"Maybe so, but... it's daunting for someone my age," Emanuel said, flushing as he looked at the ground. "I feel strange even talking about it, honestly."

"Mm, then we should change the subject, shouldn't we?" Haral said, sitting back on the bench as she smiled. "How about you tell me about your family? I've always wondered what it's like growing up in a noble family, after all."

"Sure! I mean, it isn't that interesting, but if you want to know, why not?" Emanuel said with a shrug, looking far more enthusiastic. "I'm not from the primary bloodline of the family, but our family is pretty close on the whole. I mentioned I have a sister, and mother is a noted wind mage..."

The young man continued to talk enthusiastically, and Haral listened closely, filing away information and asking the occasional question, trying to keep them innocuous. She liked Emanuel, as the boy seemed rather sincere in his beliefs.

Besides, with the Lord of Light as her witness, she wasn't going to murder someone that could easily be one of their allies in the future.

∼

"EXCUSE ME, My Lord, but I have a message for you," Cilla said, her voice faintly accented, and Lord Ordath looked up with a smile at the elderly elf.

Her black hair betrayed a few threads of white, showing her age in a way that prompted sorrow to well up inside him. When an elf was in their final years, the collapse of their physical form came absurdly quickly, which meant she had no more than two years left at a guess. She was still vibrant for the moment, though, much like the young elven woman he'd rescued on the battlefield centuries before. Cilla was also one of the few people Ordath trusted absolutely, which was why she handled his correspondence.

"Oh? Who is it from?" Ordath asked, looking away from the sheet summarizing the forces available to the Society of Golden Dawn.

"It's Haral, and I'm afraid that she's chosen not to eliminate the Emberborn family," Cilla said, a frown flickering across her face as she entered his office, his orange-brown radiance washing over her as she did so, and Ordath's eyebrows rose in surprise. "I find myself torn, My Lord, even if she did refuse a directive."

"Truly? I didn't think she had it in her to *refuse* instructions," Ordath said, pausing to think for a long moment, his surprise and a flash of anger turning to curiosity.

If Cilla wasn't outraged, it meant that she at least partially agreed with Haral's decision, which made him wonder why. Ordath trusted her opinion, even if he didn't always agree with it.

"Yes, My Lord. She reports that Isalla's family is dead, but after investigating she chose to refrain where the Emberborn family is concerned, for several reasons," Cilla said, gently setting the letter on his desk, its seal broken. That was as it should be, since Ordath didn't open his letters personally, not when there was the chance of them being trapped somehow. Cilla knew she was protecting him, which was why she opened them instead.

"I see. If you'd summarize for me? I'd prefer to avoid her

flattery, and you're skilled at dissecting the essence of messages," Ordath said, smiling slightly more.

"As you wish, My Lord," Cilla said, a smile playing across her lips, then she straightened, growing far more serious than before. "During her investigation Haral met several members of House Emberborn, including several of the younger generations, and she learned that they're largely true patriots of the heavens, believing in defending it and living up to their ancestral honor, *especially* after Ember disappeared. While some of them may be less fervent than others, most of them appear to be closer to our beliefs than anything else, which made her wonder if she might have been too hasty in eliminating Roselynn. She believes that it's possible that she might have been able to convert her to our cause if she hadn't, and her family's fervor would likely prevent them from believing her if Roselynn tried to turn them against us."

"Interesting... and I have had little interaction with the family, so it *is* possible that she's correct. They simply have such deep ties with the Order of the Phoenix that we've been concerned that they could prove... *problematic*," Ordath murmured, sitting back in his chair as he considered, then raised an eyebrow at Cilla. "Still, I'm sure you have more to say about her decisions."

"Of course, though I'm not certain I entirely agree with her conclusions. A second aspect to her decision is that Sorm is hunting Roselynn and the others, though I'm skeptical that such is enough to keep them from interfering, personally. However, I am not an angel, and my grasp of angelic politics is imperfect," Cilla said, ignoring Ordath's snort of disbelief, since he knew far too well that she was quite well-versed in the political factions of the heavens. Her voice was steady as she continued. "However, her following point was quite relevant, in my view. She learned that the Emberborn family has in excess of two hundred members, if not even more, and that they have extensive holdings as well. She sincerely doubts that she could eliminate *all* of them, and with as deep as their relationship with the Order of the Phoenix are, the deaths of that many people would cause an extremely in-depth investigation that we may not be able to afford."

"Hm. I didn't realize they had quite *that* many members of the family," Ordath said, frowning deeply as he murmured unhappily. "When I acquired my mantle, there were only a few dozen of them... but it *has* been a rather long time. Longer than I thought, when I think about it, since you came well after that."

"I'm not surprised, My Lord. Immortality can lead to losing track of minor details such as that," Cilla replied, smiling gently in return, her expression softening significantly. "On a personal note, I've treasured my time with you since then."

"As it should be," Ordath said, pushing his chair back so he could stand, considering for a long moment, then asked, "Did Haral give any other reasons?"

"Yes. She said that while she's willing to destroy traitors without hesitation, she's realized that she draws the line at innocent civilians in the heavens," Cilla said, the warmth in her voice vanishing, almost with an edge to her voice. "She's willing to submit to any punishment the Council demands and will return if commanded to."

Ordath didn't respond immediately, though a part of him wanted to curse at Haral for making her own decision. Some of the other members of the Council probably would have her executed outright if she'd sent the message to them. When he thought about it, that was probably why she'd contacted him. On the other hand, she *did* have a few points, though her qualms about innocents seemed a bit childish to him. Ordath had long since steeled himself to the knowledge that defeating the hells would require sacrificing innocents of any species, not just mortals. Even so, he wasn't going to react immediately, he needed to give the message some thought.

"I see why you're conflicted, Cilla. I am as well, even if I think this is a bit late for her to hesitate," Ordath said at last, looking at the elf as he smiled. "What do you think?"

"I think that she's considered non-angels as lesser beings from the beginning, and that even a single innocent angel is more valuable than an entire nation of mortals," Cilla replied bluntly, shaking her head as she sighed. "I don't think she understands that sacrifices are required of *everyone* to make a difference, not just others. That said... My Lord, I think she may have made the right decision in this case. You didn't have the Emberborn family investigated before making the decision to send her after them, and knowing the other members of the council, I doubt they did, either. That or they didn't consider the potential consequences."

"Mm... so you think I should argue that she should get away with this?" Ordath asked, looking at Cilla curiously, probing the elf.

"Of course not, My Lord!" Cilla replied, looking scandalized. "I think she should be punished for it, but she's too useful to simply *discard*. I just don't know how you'd want to go about it."

"Fair," Ordath agreed, and the archangel smiled, nodding to her. "Please send Haral a summons. I'll see about contacting the rest of the Council so we can come to a decision."

"As you wish, My Lord," Cilla murmured, and she quickly turned to leave.

The archangel watched her go, then sighed as he took a seat again, murmuring, "So close, and things are starting to get precarious. Just a little further, though."

No one answered, but that was as it should be.

CHAPTER 18

*L*ooking through his spyglass, Sorm frowned unhappily as he saw the women approaching the Ascent of Faith, the primary route up the Harth Plateau. He was somewhat vexed at the sight of them, but didn't dare show it here.

Isalla and Roselynn appeared to be perfectly fine, which was stunning to him, and implied that one of their companions was likely a powerful healer. At his best guess, they'd been delayed a day, possibly two, and that was all. Worse, he didn't have a good chance to attack again here, as the Ascent of Faith was one of the most heavily guarded locations in Uthren. He'd rather attack them in one of the core cities of the nation than here.

Instead Sorm studied the others in the group, trying to decide who the healer could be, murmuring softly to himself. "Not the demon, obviously. Two humans and two elves… the elves look like guards to me, which means one of the humans. Question is, which?"

The two women each had dark hair, but the one farther back in the line looked more like a maid to Sorm, even if she was armed and wore leather armor. Conversely, the one in front had light clothing and what looked like a staff holstered beside her, which meant it was probably her. That didn't mean anything for certain, though, as Sorm had frequently seen healers learn to fight on the front lines so they could patch people up in the field. It was frustrating to not know, but he wasn't going to overreact, not yet.

"I could always let the authorities know that they had a demon infiltrating Uthren. That'd deal with them quickly enough," Sorm murmured after a minute, considering the idea for a long moment, then shook his head. "No, that wouldn't be *satisfying*. I want to see them suffer, not have an easy end."

It wasn't necessarily the wisest thing Sorm could do, he knew. It would be smarter to just let the knights know what was going on and ruin whatever plans Roselynn and Isalla had made. At the same time, though, he just couldn't bring himself to give up his personal vengeance.

"Soon. I'll get one of you soon... and make all of you suffer," Sorm said softly, his breathing slow and steady as he tracked them from his shadowy perch. He didn't want his spyglass to give him away, so he'd deliberately chosen a spot where there wouldn't be any direct light this morning.

Besides, he doubted he'd catch the women entirely by surprise this time.

~

"That is going to be *incredibly* unpleasant," Maura said, her disbelief obvious as she looked up at the plateau. "You didn't tell me we were going to have to climb something like *that*, Yain!"

"I said it was a plateau! It isn't my fault that you didn't think about what that meant," Yain replied tartly, and Kitania suppressed the urge to laugh at her indignation.

On the other hand, Kitania could understand Maura's complaint, as the ascent to the top of the plateau was even harsher than the one to get out of Port Hope. It looked like a small town was nestled at the foot of the plateau, just far enough away to avoid any falling rocks, and a series of waterfalls descended from above to form a river that ran through the middle of town. Another town was at the top, looking like it was slightly more heavily settled, though Kitania couldn't tell much from their angle and distance. Criss-crossing up the mountain were switchbacks, with numerous spots to rest along the way up, including what Kitania suspected were viewing points near the waterfalls, guard posts, and even an inn about halfway up. The last told her a lot about how hard the ascent was on most people.

"It's called the Ascent of Faith because Uthren considers all of the Harth Plateau to be holy ground, and pilgrims to the city are expected to take their time in contemplation on the way up. It's also difficult for many pilgrims, as high as the plateau is, so it's said to be something where the tradition came later, I think," Rose said, her voice calm as she looked up the mountainside. "There are two other ways to the top of the plateau, but each are less conveniently located, and none of them are easy to reach the top of. I seem to recall that they can redirect the river down the switchbacks if they need to."

"That would do a lot of damage to the trail, but anyone trying to ascend the mountain would be... upset, I imagine," Kitania said, looking at the upper town, then shook her head in wonder. "It's very different than most of the fortresses I've seen before, and impressive. *Really* impressive."

"We'll have plenty of time to admire it on the way up," Vinara said, her voice desert-dry as she looked at the mountain dubiously, sighing as she murmured, "Oh, to be able to fly to the top instead..."

"We could hire riding drakes to take us to the top, but that would mean abandoning the horses," Yain explained, her displeasure fading slightly. "On the other hand, we could always get a stagecoach or the like. After the attack, I don't like that idea, but I'm not going to say it isn't tempting."

"I definitely don't like the idea," Isalla said, shaking her head firmly. "If we get attacked again, I want the chance to go after whoever's behind it. Speaking of which, how's the spell, Violet?"

"Just as much of an annoyance to maintain as it was the last time you asked," Vinara replied calmly, smirking at the angel. "I fully understand wanting to deal with sniping, which is why I'm maintaining it, but it *is* a minor drain. There's only so much mana I can use in a day and still fully recover, you know."

"We're thankful you're willing to make the sacrifice for us,"

Rose said, smiling as their horses slowly meandered down the road, their hooves clip-clopping all the while. "I know that it makes me less worried compared to before."

"Agreed," Kitania murmured, nodding in appreciation at Vinara. The succubus smiled briefly, some of her distaste fading.

"You're welcome," Vinara murmured, obviously pleased by their attention.

The succubus had come up with a spell to hopefully deflect any bolt by creating a momentary, intense windstorm around them. While the bolt used before had penetrated Kitania's barrier, they'd reasoned that it likely wouldn't have the enchantments to completely ignore wind as well, which was why she'd been maintaining the spell, and was ready to trigger it at a moment's notice. Kitania didn't envy the effort it took and was amazed at Vinara's patience and ability to focus. On the other hand, Vinara always had been more skilled with magic than Kitania was.

Maura looked like she was about to speak, but paused, straightening in the saddle as she said, "I hear someone coming."

"Multiple someone's," Yain corrected, and Kitania again suppressed the urge to smile, as she wondered if they were getting closer, or becoming rivals. She *had* noticed Vinara smirking at the two meaningfully over the course of their trip.

"Likely a patrol, from what I can see," Isalla said, peering ahead of them, where a bit of dust was rising. "Does Uthren patrol this area often?"

"I honestly couldn't say. I don't remember encountering one near here last time I came through, but that doesn't mean that it doesn't happen," Yain said, peering ahead of them, while one hand went to the hilt of her sword. "Still, until I can see their colors, I don't want to make assumptions."

"What *are* Uthren's colors?" Kitania asked, a little bemused. "I never had reason to find out."

"Red and white, primarily a deep crimson," Rose replied, smiling as she explained. "They like to style themselves as the 'Blood of the Heavens,' which is a bit overwrought from my perspective. There seems to be some truth to it, as they've been some of the closest allies of the heavens for a very long time, and there are some angelic bloodlines among the humans in Uthren, but some traditionalists in the heavens bristle at the claim."

"Ah, I see. I understand the unhappiness that could prompt... and it *is* a rather arrogant claim, on the whole," Kitania said, watching the approaching soldiers, then smiled as she added. "It looks like their surcoats are close to what you described, so they're probably from Uthren."

"I think you're right. The dust makes it hard to tell, though," Isalla added, standing in her stirrups to get a better angle, which her mount didn't seem to appreciate as it pranced, and she exclaimed, "Hey, settle down!"

"Maybe you shouldn't try standing up like that," Rose said, smiling warmly as she exchanged an affectionate look with Kitania. "You aren't used to horses to begin with, so unsettling the poor thing isn't nice."

"Fine, fine," Isalla said, sighing as she sat back down, which seemed to calm the horse after a few moments. Kitania barely heard her murmur, "I can't wait to be able to fly again."

No one told her to be quiet, likely since there wasn't anyone nearby to overhear her complaint. Instead Kitania fell silent, moving to the right side of the road as they drew closer to the soldiers on the road.

The group appeared to be predominantly humans, though it was hard to tell with their armor and helms. Most of them were in full plate and had surcoats with different emblems than just the primary red with white trim. There were at least two dozen soldiers there, and two lightly armored men with a distinct aura about them struck Kitania as magi. As they came closer, she realized that about a quarter of their number were women, though it was hard to tell even up close.

"Hail, travelers!" the lead soldier exclaimed, his voice deep and with an undertone of arrogance to it. "What brings you to Uthren?"

"We're pilgrims heading to the capital, good sir," Yain replied respectfully, bobbing her head as she smiled at him, continuing as they brought their horses to a halt. Kitania's mount took the chance to graze on some grass alongside the road while they spoke. "To be more accurate, I'm the guide for the rest of these ladies, and this is my partner. What brings a group of knights of the realm out this direction?"

"I see! Welcome to the holy empire, then, and I hope you find yourselves properly inspired!" the knight replied, his voice growing even warmer and prouder as he spoke. "I highly recommend visiting the First Temple just before dawn, as the sight of it being first illuminated each day is glorious beyond measure!"

"We'll try to do that, sir," Rose said, bowing as much as she reasonably could from horseback. "I've heard tales of Uthren's Throne and wish to see it for myself at last."

"I'm glad to hear that. As for what we're doing here, reports have come to our attention that bandits are preying on travelers and pilgrims along the road, so we've been dispatched to deal with the miscreants before they become a serious problem," the knight explained, his good cheer fading as he spoke. "They've already killed at least a dozen travelers that we're aware of, which means more probably have simply vanished without a trace. How was your journey? Did you have any trouble in the forest, in particular?"

"As a matter of fact, we did. Four days ago, we spotted an ambush before it could close on us and had to fight our way out of it," Yain said, nodding back at Isalla as she continued. "Lady Isabel was injured and we were forced to rest for a few days while she recovered, but we managed. There were close to two dozen of them, including a mage, but we caught them off guard and had a spellcaster of our own. We managed to deal with the majority of them, then we built a pyre to dispose of their remains."

"Two dozen of them, against seven of you? Even if you have better armor than they did, you did exceedingly well to take on that many bandits and come out victorious," the knight exclaimed, straightening as the other knights began to murmur among themselves. From what Kitania could hear, they sounded both impressed and pleased that some of the bandits had been dealt with. Their leader wasn't done, though, as he continued. "Unfortunately, based on our reports I doubt that was all of them, even if it may have been a large batch of the bandits. Where did you build the pyre, out of curiosity? So we can investigate it and see if we can't track down more of the menaces."

"Of course, sir! It was just on the other side of the North Fork River that we rested, and I doubt you'd be able to miss the pyre, as recent as it was. The battle was no more than a quarter-mile past that on the road," Yain said, and Kitania couldn't help her relief that the woman was handling the talking. Yain obviously knew how to deal with the locals far better than Kitania would be able to.

"Ah, I know precisely where that is! Thank you, good lady, the information will be quite helpful," the knight said, bowing his head ever so slightly, then continued briskly. "Now, there's a long way to go and little light to spare! May the heavens shine on you and bless you always!"

"And may their wings shelter you from harm," Yain replied, bowing reasonably deeply.

The knight nodded, then flicked his reins as he led the band of knights past them. In the front Yain started forward as well, moving at a relatively sedate pace. Once they were past, the elven woman spoke dryly. "Well, that was certainly unexpected. Too bad the knights didn't come through a week ago, as it would've saved us a rather lot of grief."

"Possibly, or the bandits may have simply avoided them and attacked us anyway," Vinara said, her voice relatively calm as she glanced behind her. "The knights seemed reasonably skilled, but… they didn't seem nearly as skilled as the elven soldiers I met when in the Forest of Sighs. That seems odd to me, since from everything I've heard knights are supposed to be quite skilled. Am I mistaken on that?"

"That's because those were journey knights, not full knights of the realm. They obviously didn't expect us to know the difference, though it's obvious to those who've interacted with Uthren before," Isalla explained, smiling slightly.

"Journey knights?" Kitania asked, her eyebrows rising. "I haven't heard of those before."

"It's a rank commonly used in Uthren, but not in many other

nations. After becoming a knight, the men and women are considered journey knights until they've performed acts of sufficient valor and merit, and as such proved their value to the crown and gods," Rose said, shrugging as she added, "I think it also is their way of weeding out useless nobles, though it's only moderately successful, since that entire group was journey knights. I'll bet you that most of them were hired to help a couple of nobles become knights of the realm."

"Ah, the true nature of people. No matter how many rules you create, someone will *always* find a loophole they can slip through," Kitania said, smiling slightly as she shook her head, then nodded toward the switchbacks. "Given the look of that… are we stopping halfway, or going to the top before resting for the evening?"

"That depends on how tired we are by the halfway point," Yain replied, glancing back at Kitania as she continued. "Based on what I've seen, I suspect we'll be able to reach the top and rest at an inn there, but I could be wrong."

"In that case, let's find out, shall we? First one to admit they can't keep going gets to buy dinner," Vinara said brightly, grinning at she looked at Kitania and added, "Aside from you, Kim. Your body is unfair in contests like this."

"Spoilsport," Kitania replied, rolling her eyes and letting out an exaggerated sigh.

Everyone else laughed, including Eziel, though the angel's laughter was barely audible, and they continued on the road while Kitania relaxed and admired the scenery.

CHAPTER 19

*I*t took a while to reach the town, but as they did, Kitania realized there were several aeries for the riding drakes that had been mentioned, including a few larger breeds that looked more appropriate to carrying cargo to the top. They were limited in number and she doubted they could carry truly heavy loads, but they were probably useful and easier than trying to ascend the switchbacks with a wagon.

It took almost no time for them to enter the town with the documentation that Alserah had provided, which was a relief. This was the first town they'd reached that was officially part of Uthren, and the locals took their duty to protect the borders seriously. Even so, they didn't have the ability to see through Kitania's disguise easily, so their group was allowed through quickly.

Most of the people Kitania saw were human, though she was startled by the sight of a lower-built segment of the town nearest the plateau. Dwarves pervaded that section of the town, and after a few moments she realized that there appeared to be a mineshaft descending into the ground, though it was angled well away from the switchbacks.

"Are dwarves common in Uthren?" Kitania asked softly, watching a trio of the stocky folk chatting alongside the road.

Most people had the mental image of dwarves as being

almost as wide as they were tall and with thick beards, but actually meeting them had disproved that to Kitania long ago. Dwarves tended to be between four and five feet in height, and their bone structure did tend to make them broader shouldered than most humans as well as having stronger physiques, but that didn't make them fat or bearded by any means. The ones she saw were fit, while only one of the two men had a beard, which was trimmed short.

"Um, if I remember my history right, they originally controlled one of the biggest mountain ranges east of the plateau and had expanded onto it when Uthren was formed. After a lot of negotiations, they were integrated into the kingdom as a whole, though they're nominally independent," Isalla said, frowning slightly as she pondered, glancing at the dwarves. "I don't remember the full details, of course. I do know they're about a tenth of the population of Uthren, though, far ahead of elves."

"There aren't many forests on the plateau, which means there were never many elven communities there to begin with," Yain chimed in, nodding in agreement. "I didn't know the dwarves were independent, though. Honestly... I wonder if they do?"

"In the end it really doesn't matter," Rose said, looking at the dwarves curiously before she focused on their approach to the switchbacks. "It's been so long that I doubt either side can imagine doing without the other. I never really thought about how common they were in Uthren when I visited before... it just was."

"Fair," Kitania admitted, then flinched as she realized that Rose had slipped up in admitting that she'd been to Uthren before. Fortunately, no one seemed to have noticed, but she resolved to mention it in private later.

As they reached the base of the ascent, Yain slowed to a stop, explaining, "We'd best dismount here. While we could ride the horses up the Ascent of Faith, it'd unnecessarily exhaust them."

Kitania nodded and dismounted, patting her horse as she did so. She was thankful that it hadn't panicked at her scent, but a part of her wondered if others might find its relative calm surprising when she was supposed to have dragon blood. After a moment of thought she just shrugged, waiting for the others to be ready to climb the escarpment. Glancing at the gradual slope at the bottom of the switchbacks, which had both a footpath and a wider path for wagons, Kitania pursed her lips. Even if it was a gradual slope, it still would make it hard to talk before too long, especially if they kept a good pace.

In short order they started up the path, and Kitania quickly found her prediction came true, as they kept a steady pace that quickly kept anyone from easily talking, beyond which they were also constrained by the path forcing them to go single file so that people descending could pass as well. Birds sang, the crash of water descending from one holding pool to the next echoed through the air, and the breeze cooled Kitania even as the sun radiated warmth on her, bringing understanding of *why* this was called the Ascent of Faith.

With every step they took they were able to see more and more of the surrounding landscape, across the rolling hills and forests to their south and the distant peaks of mountains. It was a breathtaking sight, and the environment as one slowly moved upward was conducive to contemplation, especially with the wide viewing platforms that were at each end of a switchback. Kitania saw other travelers paused there, many of them raptly looking at the world stretched before them, and she could understand why. If it weren't for how much of a hurry they were in, Kitania would be tempted to linger on a railing herself, to feel the wind on her face as she mused.

Even so, the ascent was exhausting, and Kitania found herself breathing hard by the time they were only a quarter of the way up the switchbacks. They took a break at about that point, but only briefly before they continued until they reached the inn halfway to the summit. The inn was large, with an expansive stable for mounts and wagons, while plenty of rooms appeared to be available for travelers. They stopped for lunch and to water the horses, but no one suggested they stay the night, even if Maura looked a little more under the weather than the others, and Kitania suspected Vinara was hiding her fatigue.

They didn't linger long, and soon enough they continued the climb. It took half the day before reaching the top of the plateau, and when they did Kitania let out a sigh of relief, her legs aching ever so slightly as she looked at the town laid out in front of them. If her legs felt like this, she didn't want to *think* about how the others might feel, and Kitania resolved not to even hint at complaining.

The sun was also well on its way toward the horizon, so Kitania didn't complain when Yain led the way toward an inn wearily. As she did so, Rose slowly fell back until she was walking alongside Kitania, which prompted the demoness to blink, looking at the angel curiously.

After a minute Kitania asked, "Is something the matter, Lynn?"

"The matter? No, of course not, I was just considering what to say," Rose said, shaking her head as she smiled slightly, letting out a soft laugh as she murmured, "I'd have thought this would be easier after all the time apart, but it isn't."

"Distance isn't always a good thing. It can lead to people growing apart, and things have changed immensely since we first met," Kitania said, her curiosity growing stronger. "That said... sometimes it's best to just say something and damn the consequences. At least then it's *said*."

"I suppose you may be right," Rose admitted, looking at Kitania as she smiled, which sent a surge of warmth through the demoness. Rose spoke softly, her voice gentle. "Might you be willing to have company tonight? Possibly with Isabel, too. I know that things haven't been the best lately, but... if we don't talk and associate with one another, we can't try to fix things."

Kitania blinked, opened her mouth, then closed it again, looking at Rose in a little surprise, surprise that quickly turned into happiness as she smiled, murmuring quietly, "Now *that* isn't what I expected, after everything. I thought you weren't quite as sure about me as she was."

"Maybe, maybe not. I like to take my time to make up my mind. However, it *does* help that a part of me identifies rather strongly with you," Rose said, smiling even more as she continued, running a finger down Kitania's arm. "My time with Anna and your mother... well, let's just say that I've been *forcing* myself to keep my distance more than anything else."

"Ah, I... wasn't aware of that, though I suppose I shouldn't be *surprised*," Kitania said, her smile growing still warmer, but she glanced at Isalla, raising an eyebrow as she added, "I should mention, though... Isabel doesn't look like she's going to be up for anything but sleeping tonight."

Isalla was definitely under the weather, her skin flushed as she breathed hard, an ever so slight limp to her stride. As a matter of fact, Kitania suspected one of her salves was in order, to keep Isalla from being completely miserable the next day.

"Yes, but that's half the point, at least in this case," Rose said, her eyes glittering as she glanced at Isalla in amusement. "The idea is to make the two of you *talk*, instead of letting her brood on things more. She won't have the energy to argue as much as she might want to, which is rather important."

"I suppose you're right," Kitania admitted, smiling even more as she glanced around, then asked, "Yain, I don't suppose the inn we're heading to has baths, does it?"

"After *that* climb it'd better," Vinara muttered, prompting a chorus of chuckles and laughter.

"It does," Yain confirmed, smiling wryly as she added, "For *some* reason, baths are rather popular after the climb, so we're also going to be paying a bit more for them than I'd like, but that's the way it goes."

"At least they have them," Isalla groaned, wincing as she rolled a shoulder. "I'm *sore*."

Kitania laughed softly, smiling even more as she relaxed. Some days, life was good.

"Ugh... even after the bath I still hurt," Isalla groaned, slipping the key into the lock and opening the door of her room. Well, her room and Rose's, anyway. Her body was more relaxed than it had been, but the time she'd spent in a saddle, followed by the ascent, had not been kind to her body. She'd never even been *on* a horse before they left Port Hope anyway, which made her discomfort worse.

"It sounds like you need a salve massaged into your legs,

147

then," Kitania replied calmly, and Isalla stopped halfway into the room, blinking owlishly at the demoness.

Kitania was still in her disguise, but she was wearing light clothing and had a towel wrapped around her hair, showing that she'd gone to the baths as well. The demoness had a bag out and had several jars sitting on the nightstand next to the large bed, which confused Isalla, though not as much as Kitania's presence did.

"Kit—Kim? What're you doing here? I thought you were rooming with Violet?" Isalla demanded, then yelped as she was bumped from behind. Rose gently pushed her into the room and closed the door behind them.

"No, Violet is sharing with Emma. Kim is sharing with us, at my invitation," Rose said, smiling slightly as she glanced at Kitania in amusement. "That said… dare I ask if you're good at massaging? I have high standards, after all."

"I'm decent, though not as good as those you're familiar with. I learned as part of my studies as a healer and tried to keep reasonably in practice," Kitania said, smiling as she raised an eyebrow at Isalla in a way that made the angel flush in embarrassment, asking curiously, "Now… do you *want* me to leave? I was just planning to make you as comfortable as I reasonably could."

"No!" Isalla exclaimed, and blushed more deeply as Rose giggled, moving past her to set her clothing down on a small table. Isalla tried to regain her composure as she swallowed and cleared her throat, continuing as her cheeks felt like they were about to ignite. "I just… I didn't expect you in here, is all. I thought… well, what about Niadra?"

"I said we needed to figure things out, and we haven't really had time," Kitania replied, shaking her head. "Niadra and I… I don't know. The way she reacted to Cecilia makes me wonder still more, and I… well, I don't want to lose you. You or Lynn, for that matter. I can't let myself be stopped by wondering how she'll react."

"Besides which, we *aren't* on the safest of journeys," Rose added, her voice soft as she took a seat, letting out a soft, almost pained sigh. "Either way... Isa, either lay down or choose not take Kim up on her offer. If you won't, I will."

"Geez, just hold on a second! You spring this on me, then expect me to react quickly?" Isalla demanded, flushing brightly as she quickly stepped toward the bed, stripping off her clothing as she went. "Of *course* I'm taking her up on it! I don't want to be aching and groaning all night and tomorrow, too."

"That's what I thought," Rose murmured in satisfaction, and Isalla quickly got onto the bed to hide how she blushed still more.

"I intend to speak with Niadra when we get back," Kitania said mildly, her voice soft as could be. "Until then, I'm going to just go with whatever feels right. Now, try to relax. This is going to feel a touch cool, Isabel."

"I can deal with cool," Isalla said, relaxing at last as she realized that Kitania was almost back to how she remembered her in the hells, which was incredibly comforting.

A few moments later a cool liquid dripped onto her back, then Isalla almost melted into the bed as Kitania began to gently knead her muscles. It hurt a little, but it was a good hurt.

In fact, she almost fell asleep just like that.

CHAPTER 20

"*G*ently, don't be so firm," Niadra said, ever so slightly exasperated as she sat there and tried to be patient.

"I'm sorry, Your Highness," Breanne said, the young woman's nervousness readily apparent as she took a breath and tried to comb Niadra's hair more gently. The young woman was pretty much the only servant she was certain wasn't a spy who Niadra could take on, yet she wasn't as skilled as Cecilia had been, either.

The thought of Cecilia sent another surge of anger through Niadra, though it was nowhere near as strong as it had been when she'd first learned of Cecilia's deception. At the same time, Kitania's absence didn't bother Niadra nearly as much as it had at first, which was something of a relief. At the same time, it also meant that Niadra had more freedom to socialize with the other nobility, and with as restless as she was feeling, that made Niadra happier.

"Is this better, Your Highness?" Breanne asked hopefully, the brunette's voice hesitant as she gently brushed Niadra's hair. It wasn't perfect, but it *was* better than before.

"Yes, it is. You're learning reasonably quickly, Breanne," Niadra said, suppressing the urge to sigh. She wished that she could find a better handmaiden, but with everything that had been going on lately, she just didn't trust other servants.

Still, that didn't mean that Breanne couldn't be trained to become better at things. Everyone had to start somewhere, after all.

"After you're done with my hair, ensure that the violet dress is properly pressed and ready. I want to look as good as possible for tonight," Niadra said firmly after a minute, smiling a little, now.

"Yes, Your Highness," Breanne agreed, letting out a soft breath of relief.

Niadra nodded in approval, a sense of anticipation rising within her. She was curious what the other nobility were up to.

ALSERAH WATCHED the ball from her balcony, much as she usually did. The office behind her was dark and the night was just cloudy enough that the moon didn't provide much illumination, so she didn't think any of the elves and ambassadors involved in the soiree would notice her presence. That was half the point, after all, and a part of Alserah was relieved that she hadn't attended balls often over the past millennium, as it meant her absence wasn't notable.

It wasn't as though Alserah wanted to attend, anyway. The pomp and circumstance of balls wore on her, which was why she'd given the throne to others for generations. King Rayvan was simply the most recent of the monarchs she'd selected to take that duty, and unless Alserah perished in the coming weeks, he wouldn't be the last. That said, her gaze drifted from the handsome elven man who she was certain was reassuring some of the nobles to Niadra.

The princess was speaking animatedly with several other nobles and looked quite happy to be there. More interesting to Alserah, and slightly disappointing, was that she was gravitating toward eligible young women. That didn't bode well in Alserah's mind, and she let out the faintest sigh.

"Why the sigh?" Sidina asked so suddenly that Alserah almost overreacted.

If it hadn't been for Sidina not hiding the approach of her

aura, Alserah very well might have manifested her bow, and *that* would have gone poorly. Sidina had gotten onto the balcony seemingly effortlessly, and the human leaned on the railing gently, flicking a hair back from her eyes. She looked more comfortable without the other deities present, which was something Alserah could understand. Trying to talk with all the other deities around was difficult. As it was, the servants were acting jumpy with five other deities in residence, at least most of the time.

"I'm disappointed in one of my descendants," Alserah said, shaking her head as she did so. "I had some hopes for her, but she appears to be a bit shallower than I believed. Not that I'm going to settle on a conclusion instantly, mind you."

"Mm." Sidina didn't so much reply as hum, and the human looked more closely at the participants of the ball. Eventually she asked, "Why are you disappointed?"

"Niadra… well, she's the one who did the most to help Kitania adapt to being here. Kitania saved her life and that of her maid, and the two were doing so very well, on the whole. Kitania is a lovely woman, and one who caught *my* interest, of all things. Saying that… well, it's quite a change for me," Alserah said, a brief, mocking smile flashing across her face as she thought about how her attitude had changed, then the smile faded as she sighed and continued. "I thought maybe they'd do well with each other. Then Isalla and Rose came here, injecting uncertainty in the situation. Niadra threw away her handmaiden of years, Cecilia, for lying to her and Kitania, which troubles me. Yes, it was wrong of Cecilia to hide the information that Isalla and Rose were coming, but being banished the way she was? I feel the punishment didn't fit the crime… well, maybe it did. Who am I to judge? Regardless, I wouldn't be so concerned if it weren't for this."

Alserah gestured at the gathering with a sigh, looking as a young woman placed a hand on Niadra's arm and the princess simply smiled, moving closer instead of fending the woman off. Her disappointment was growing stronger, and her hands tightened around the railing as she continued. "She's *inviting* courtship, and that's disappointing. Kitania was already in a relationship before they met, even if she believed it to be doomed, and Niadra seduced her. Now, though? Kitania hadn't made a decision when she left, and hasn't been gone very long, so Niadra is knowingly choosing to abandon her, or worse, thinks she won't find out. Either way, I'm not happy with her. The least Niadra could do is send a letter or the like letting Kitania know what she's decided to do."

"Ah. That… is a thorny situation. Especially for you to be involved in," Sidina murmured, watching the ball with a good deal more interest. "On the other hand, I rarely interact with my worshipers, so I'm not one to talk. I also don't have a kingdom."

"You easily could have one. I know the monasteries that sprang up around your mountain are devoted to you, and there are entire communities dedicated to supporting them," Alserah pointed out, smiling as she teased. "In fact, last I heard even the neighboring nations don't really touch the locals there, since they're afraid you might take it poorly."

A flicker of annoyance flashed across Sidina's face, and the human sighed, murmuring, "I'm aware and want nothing to do with them. I found a remote peak for my training for a reason, and not because I wanted power over others. What the mortals around the mountains do is none of my affair, and I'll only intervene if someone or something starts slaughtering them wholesale. Or if the demons invade, I suppose."

Alserah resisted the near-overwhelming urge to snort at the reply. She knew that Sidina was far more attached to others than she liked to pretend, and she likely hid any assistance she might give as well. It was a trait that Alserah appreciated, since she did a few similar things as well.

"I just find it ironic that it isn't *demons* I'm concerned about right now. No new offenses have been reported, and it's almost peaceful on the front lines, or as peaceful as it gets," Alserah murmured, and a frown flickered across her face. "Not that I think that's going to last, even if not all demons are necessarily enemies."

"Mm. What do you think the angels behind this have planned?" Sidina asked, the hint of worry in her voice startling, if only because the woman rarely seemed worried about anything.

"I don't know. I really don't. However… I have to assume it's something big. I really, truly hope that they haven't come up with some way to give an archangel a deific mantle," Alserah said, taking a deep breath before admitting. "That… *that* would be bad."

"You have the most wonderful ideas, don't you?" Sidina murmured, prompting a chuckle from Alserah, though it was halfhearted.

Alserah didn't reply, instead watching the nobles dance and make merry in the gardens below, and doubtlessly continuing to do so in the ballroom as well. They were just recovering from the devastation that had been inflicted on the country such a short time ago, and she didn't have the heart to warn them that something far worse could be coming. Oh, a few people knew, but they were few and far between, and even they didn't have any concept of how bad things could truly become.

Only those who'd survived the War of Decimation and earlier conflicts had any idea what could happen, and that meant only angels, demons, and gods.

Alserah wasn't going to ruin the mood for everyone else, not when they couldn't do anything to prevent it. All she could do was insist that the military and priesthood continue preparing for the worst behind the scenes. Well, that and pray that Kitania and her friends would unearth the information they so vitally needed.

CHAPTER 21

*O*rdath watched Haral enter the chamber with a cool gaze, judging her as she slowly approached. The council didn't allow people to approach them often, and her presence would have been a great concession even at the best of times, which this most certainly wasn't. The only question was what her punishment would be, and if she acted inappropriately Ordath had no doubt that most of the others would cast aside their agreement to make her punishment harsher. For that matter, he would be displeased enough to agree with them.

Fortunately for her, Haral seemed to be well aware of that, and the angel fell to a knee a good two paces before she needed to and bowed her head, her wings stretching out and almost touching the floor in a submissive stance. It was the gesture of one who ranked far lower than she did, and Ordath noticed some of the anger of the others ease, if only slightly. Not that all of his companions were feeling quite as charitable, of course.

"Ah, *here's* the coward, then," Yimael said, her gravelly voice practically dripping venom as she glared at Haral. "You refused a directive, then you have the temerity to come back here begging forgiveness, after as many disasters as you've been responsible for?"

"Calm down, the lady has only just arrived," Ethan said, the thin angel's tone unruffled and almost cold. "I can't say that I'm happy about this either, but at least she didn't return after a failure this time. Instead she made a few points that had some merit."

"I'm glad that my opinions were of some use, My Lord," Haral said, holding her position with surprising grace as she continued. "My failures to date have been immensely frustrating on a personal level, and have imperiled our goal, so I am willing to accept whatever punishment is deemed fit."

"As you should. That said, your humility and willingness to come before us does you credit. It isn't as though you tried to go to the Holy Council, after all," Ordath said and saw Yimael shift uncomfortably out of the corner of his eye. One of her subordinates *had* tried that, and only the actions of a couple of alert sympathizers had prevented things from taking a disastrous turn.

"Please, there's no need to get worked up at this point," Sereth said, even her usual mellow tone betraying a hint of annoyance. "May we allow Haral to rise, please? Even seeing her in that position is making my back ache."

"Rise," Zithar rumbled, sitting back in his chair impassively, and Ordath felt relief rush through him. It was obvious that the only one truly holding what happened against Haral was Yimael, though the others might be upset. That was why they'd agreed on a punishment for Haral, though, and Ordath was grimly certain that anyone who heard about it would do their best to avoid upsetting the council.

"Thank you, Lords and Ladies," Haral said, carefully rising again, though she kept her gaze downcast as she folded her wings. That was probably for the best, in Ordath's opinion.

"Your thanks are unnecessary, as you're here for our judgment of your actions. After some discussion, I was chosen as the spokeswoman for the council, as I was the least biased for or against you," Sereth said, the blonde angel tapping her fingers against one another in front of her as she watched Haral with slightly narrowed eyes. "You were given a task to assure us of your loyalty after your failure in the mortal world, and you stopped with it only halfway done. Regardless of how many points in your favor there may have been, you still disobeyed us, which is most upsetting."

"I was aware that such might be the case, which is why I've come to accept whatever punishment you have decided that I've earned," Haral said, bowing her head slightly as she continued, her voice firm despite her situation. "I will do everything I can to support the society, but I've realized that I cannot convince myself to destroy those who believe themselves honest patriots of the heavens, and who aren't directly supporting the corruption of the Holy Council."

"Your fit of conscience was poorly timed, even if I believe that you were correct not to carry out the task in this case. If you had sent a message informing us of your concerns, I would have supported you, and would not have agreed to your punishment. However, our situation cannot afford those who lightly discard their tasks," Ethan said calmly, his gaze cold as he looked at Haral. "As such, I've agreed that you must be punished."

Haral inclined her head slightly but didn't reply, staring at the floor.

"Precisely. That is why you're to spend a week in the Chamber of Penitence, Haral," Ordath said, watching closely as the angel visibly flinched, resisting the urge to smile in response. He didn't blame her for being unhappy, as the punishment was rather more severe than he'd argued for, but when the others had insisted that an example be made, Ordath had ceded the point. He likely could have put his foot down and gotten it changed, but Ordath preferred to pick his battles rather than fighting over something relatively meaningless.

"A week?" Haral asked, her voice hesitant as she paled. "I... will I even survive that?"

"Since the last time we used the chamber, it's been adjusted so that it cannot cause permanent mental or physical damage," Yimael said flatly, her eyes narrowing as she smiled thinly. "Not that you're going to *enjoy* the experience. But that's the entire point you're going to be in there, isn't it? It's to teach you that you shouldn't treat your tasks lightly."

"As you say," Haral said, taking a deep breath and letting it out, obviously nervous. She didn't argue further, instead straightening as she asked. "When will the sentence be carried out?"

"Is there anything you need to arrange to avoid others noticing that you've vanished?" Zithar asked, his gaze focused on the young angel, and Haral swallowed audibly.

"A letter or two explaining that I'm delayed, perhaps, but that's all that would be necessary," Haral said, hesitating before she admitted, "I don't think anyone would notice, but I'd rather be certain."

"Then go draft your letters and ensure they're on their way. The sooner you begin your punishment the better," Zithar said, his smile cold as he added, "It isn't as though preparation will make the chamber easier to experience, after all."

"As you say, My Lord. May I withdraw to do so?" Haral asked, bowing again deeply. Only when she was given permission did the angel withdraw, and once the door latched Sereth spoke calmly.

"You're right about her attitude, Ordath. I'm not happy with what she did, even now, but I think eliminating her would do more harm than good," the woman said, sitting back as she frowned. Sereth was the only other archangel in the council, which gave her opinion far greater weight than most of the members. Still, Ordath knew that she took pains to not use that influence more than necessary to keep the council from fracturing, much as he did.

"Beyond which, she's right about the Emberborn family. After you informed us of her letter, I did some research and found that, if anything, her concerns were understated," Ethan said, shaking his head unhappily. "There are more of them spread through the Order of the Phoenix than I think any of us realized, and her chances of eliminating *all* of them would be incredibly small. If we didn't get all of them, the furor it raised would be intense, and I don't know that we could ward off all the investigations it'd cause. Even trying to focus it on demons would be risky in those circumstances."

"Which means we just have to be more careful about tasks we assign after this," Ordath said, and as Yimael inhaled he raised a hand and added pointedly, "I was one of the ones who suggested it, so yes, I'm at fault for this as well. I'm willing to admit it, so please stop sniping, Yimael."

"I'm not sniping," Yimael snapped, glowering at him. "I just think that she got off far too lightly."

"Lightly?" Zithar asked, his eyebrows rising as he looked at Yimael skeptically. "Would *you* care to spend a week in the chamber in her place?"

"Well, no, of course not," Yimael said, looking a bit taken aback, and more than a little uncomfortable. "I had a hard enough time testing it to get it right."

"Then it's an appropriate punishment, and it'll only increase her anger toward the traitors, rather than eliminating someone useful," Zithar said, letting out a sigh as he grew more solemn. "Now, what was this you mentioned about the Forest of Sighs, Ethan?"

Ethan shifted in his chair, and despite his attempts to hide his concern, Ordath saw the man's worry and sat up straighter. Anything that concerned Ethan was worth paying attention to, since Ethan was the most easygoing member of the council most of the time.

"Our reports from Alserah's domain have become… sporadic at best. The angels there are frightened, so we're mostly getting secondhand reports from sympathetic relatives of theirs, and I can't say how much of the information is accurate," Ethan said, his tone almost flat as he looked around the table. "Even worse, many of the sympathizers who live there have had a crisis of conscience *far* greater than Haral's after the attempt to destroy the Forest of Sighs. It's almost as though they didn't consider that they might be required to make the ultimate sacrifice for the greater good. As such, we have less than a tenth as much information about what's going on inside the country as we did even a month ago."

"We know, Ethan. You've commented about it enough in your messages that I'm fairly certain we all are aware by this point," Sereth said, a note of exaggerated patience in her voice.

"Perhaps you're intellectually aware, but I don't think you realize just how much of a problem it is. On the other hand, *maybe* this will change that," Ethan said, his voice sharp now, slapping a hand on the table as he continued. "Alserah has other deities in residence, now. A minimum of three are there, and rumor says that there could be as many as *ten* of them, and we have no idea what they're doing."

"What? How in all the stars can you have lost track of that many deities?" Yimael exclaimed, half-rising from her chair with her hands on the table. The anger in her voice was palpable, and Ordath felt shock ripple through him as well.

"Lose *track*? Just how few mortal deities do you think there are?" Ethan asked, sarcasm all but dripping from his voice. "I know of at least sixty archangels, and I'm certain there are more that are either obscure or who've hidden themselves away for ages, and we only have the support of eight of them, excluding Sereth and Ordath. Mortals are even more prone to gaining mantles than we are, and *they* have somewhere in the neighborhood of two *hundred* known deities. Certainly, about half of them are on the other side and they're fractious, but keeping track of hundreds or more deities is nigh impossible. Don't you *dare* give me grief about this, not when we're waiting on your artificers to finish their work!"

Yimael opened her mouth to speak, but Zithar interrupted suddenly, his voice cracking like a whip, and the other two at least had the grace to look abashed. "Enough! We don't have time to listen to you bicker. Ethan, do you have any more information about these deities?"

"The only one I *know* is there is Gandar, as he's a staunch ally of Alserah's. The lack of information is frustrating, and I can't do much about it," Ethan said flatly, shaking his head unhappily. "I've dispatched scouts to keep watch around their borders to see if they leave, but if they teleport it'll be hard to determine anything in time to act."

"Unfortunate, but there's nothing we can do about it. It won't be easy for them to act against us, though. They're not in the heavens, and we have no need to travel to the mortal world to continue our plans," Zithar said, shaking his head firmly. "Keep an eye on them as best you can, and we'll continue on our path. If anything, I'm more concerned about the other traitors, Isalla and Roselynn."

"Not much has been learned about them lately, though one of our best is after them, a man named Sorm," Ordath said, smiling slightly as he continued. "He's another reason I didn't mention for not punishing Haral, as they're in a relationship."

"Sorm... the one who was captain of the guard for the Holy Council?" Yimael asked, her anger seeming to ease slightly.

"That's right. Even with Ember, I'd confidently bet on Sorm over Roselynn, which should tell you a lot about him," Ordath confirmed, relaxing slowly. "I don't know much about the others, but I doubt he'll let them get in the way of doing his job."

"Excellent," Zithar said, nodding. "In that case, if you'd keep us informed? I don't want another surprise like this coming out of nowhere."

"Of course," Ordath agreed, and he pushed himself to his feet as the others began to disperse.

Things were going well, even if Haral would be regretting her decisions shortly.

HARAL SHUDDERED ON HER KNEES, hissing as pain seared through her body at the thought of her mistake where Isalla was concerned. She should have killed the angel outright rather than trying to blame her death on the hells, but she couldn't change that now. Not that the Chamber of Penitence cared.

The room wasn't large, a simple white-walled room with gold patterns on it to make it look more soothing, almost like a room for meditation and contemplation. That was what it was, in fact, though the enchantments over the room were far more sinister than its welcoming appearance might imply.

The enchantments worked their magic ruthlessly, and what they did was not only dredge up every mistake Haral had made for the last century one at a time, but they also forced her to examine the mistakes as pain racked her mind and body as punishment. In theory those who hadn't made mistakes could go into the room without being affected, but that was only in theory.

"Isalla. Roselynn." Haral whispered their names through

gritted teeth, her rage slowly burning higher as she was forced to examine her actions where they were concerned.

They were the reason for her pain, and it was only because of them that she was in this position. If Roselynn hadn't fallen for Isalla, the young woman would never have come to the Evergardens. If Isalla hadn't come to the Evergardens, she'd never have investigated the society's movements, and Haral wouldn't have had to deal with either of them. It was entirely their fault that she was in pain, and the angel hissed again, breathing hard as she clawed at the floor, her nails flexing painfully as they did so.

"Sorm, I hope they *suffer*," Haral said, her wings shuddering with every passing moment.

The worst part was, she'd only been in the room for a couple of hours, so this was going to be a horrifying week. Haral had her doubts that she'd come out intact, no matter what she'd been told.

CHAPTER 22

"*D*o you think it'll work?" Estalia asked, sitting on the edge of the bed as she watched Anna curiously, her eyes fixed on the amulet in the angel's hands. "It's been so *long* since that was made, after all."

"Oh, it'll work. Whether or not the building is still there is an entirely different question," Anna said, smiling as she looked up from the intricately carved amulet. The mana had leaked out of the device long ago, so she'd been carefully charging it again over the last few days, but the enchantments seemed to be as good as they had the last time Anna had used the amulet.

"Too bad we don't know about that, at least not for certain. I'd ask my agents, but I don't want to give anyone clues about your presence," Estalia said, letting out a soft sigh as she shook her head, and Anna couldn't help watching the way her midnight-blue hair stood out against the demoness's luminous skin. "Too bad it only works from the mortal world, and a single way. It'd be nice to visit the heavens far more directly."

"Even the most powerful magic has its limits," Anna replied philosophically, setting the amulet on the shelf gently. "Have you told Alserah about me?"

"Of course not!" Estalia said, sounding scandalized as she put a hand on her chest. "I know better than *that*. If they knew who you were, they might panic, and that's not something I want to happen. For all I know, the *society* would panic. They'd certainly try to kill you!"

"Very, very true. Or they'd try to *rescue* me, as if I needed that," Anna replied, rolling her eyes as she glanced at the teleportation amulet. She *was* curious if her old home was still standing, in ruins, or if it'd been repurposed. Probably the last, but she wasn't certain. It'd been far too long to be sure of anything.

She sighed softly, approaching Estalia and smiling warmly as she asked, "Do you mind that I've changed back, for the most part?"

"Mind? Of course not! Seeing you confident as you are... it sets my stomach all aquiver, almost like I was a girl again," Estalia said, her eyes glittering with mirth as she added, "Do you remember the look on Mother's face when I brought you home? I thought she was about to attack you!"

"It's almost like we were on opposite sides of the battlefield just a few days earlier, and I'd almost killed her. I'm more surprised that she let me stay without arguing much," Anna said, her mind drifting back to the day as she smiled.

The memories weren't all pleasant, as the bone-deep exhaustion that she'd felt at the time was terrible, but nowhere near as bad as her mental exhaustion. If it hadn't been for Estalia... well, her road would have been a much, much shorter one. Even so, she could still appreciate the shock on everyone's faces when she'd entered the throne room, and Anna took a moment to wonder what had happened to the others who'd been present. Her mood was dampened a little at the thought, though, as they were probably long since dust.

"She took me aside afterward and asked me what in all the hells I thought I was doing, since you could be a spy," Estalia said, grinning even more as she laughed softly. "I pointed out that of all the people to try pretending to switch sides, you would probably be the *last* one, considering how powerful you are. It was a terrible blow to their attempts to invade the hells, hm?"

"Oh? Well, I'm glad you managed to convince her I wasn't deceiving you. Not that I would have had much luck, as relatively guileless as I was at the time," Anna replied, sitting next to Estalia and pulling her close. The angel closed her eyes, enjoying the warmth and scent of Estalia for a long moment before continuing softly. "It was a dark time for me, though you made it much brighter."

"You aren't the only one whose life was improved," Estalia replied, her hand touching Anna's cheek gently, then the demoness slowly, insistently kissed Anna, who melted into it happily.

For a long minute the room was quiet, as they simply enjoyed the company of one another. Anna enjoyed it more than she probably should, but their decisions had kept them apart for far longer than either of them wanted, with only occasional, brief liaisons. A large part of it had been caution, Anna admitted privately, but it was also that she'd honestly come to enjoy her time in the spire. The work she did there was important and expanding the point of view of others was something she thought vital for the future.

"Are you really going to tell Kitania about us?" Anna asked suddenly, a thread of worry twisting through her as she opened her eyes again. She bit her lip for a moment, then admitted softly, "I... am worried about her reaction. It's been so *long,* and we've hidden her ancestry the entire time, cloaking it behind rumors about your brother."

"I'll remind you that he *agreed* to spread the rumors and not contradict them, even if he got himself killed later on," Estalia said, her smile fading as she let out a soft sigh. "That was... unfortunate. If he was around, all this would be easier, but fortune doesn't always favor us. But yes, I'm planning to tell Kitania. She deserves to know that she doesn't have a father and mother, but two mothers. And... well, I'm not *certain,* even now, but her immortality..."

"You think it's an angelic mantle," Anna stated, a tinge of grief rushing through her at the thought.

"That's right," Estalia agreed, leaning into Anna even more as she frowned, shaking her head sorrowfully. "It's the only possibility that makes any sense to me. She can't pass it on to demons or mortals, or at least she's never sensed how to do so, so either it *isn't* a mantle, which seems impossible to me, or it's an angelic mantle."

"You don't hear me disagreeing with you, do you? I've had plenty of time to think about it over the centuries, and I've come to the same conclusion," Anna agreed, hugging Estalia still tighter for a moment, then reluctantly eased her grip as she continued. "At least they probably can't *steal* it. Most mantles... well, it requires the person to be *dead* to absorb it, and that can't happen to her. So at least that's something."

"Very, very true. But that doesn't mean they can't hurt her badly, or the people around her," Estalia agreed, a flicker of pain crossing her face. Eventually the demoness admitted softly, "I... wish she was here. Where we could keep her safe."

"I know," Anna said simply, curling her wings around Estalia protectively, and the demoness went quiet, simply hugging Anna in return.

Nothing broke the silence this time, and after a long couple of minutes, Anna leaned down to kiss Estalia again, and this time they didn't stop at just a kiss.

CHAPTER 23

"You didn't mention how *cold* it is up here, Yain," Maura complained, clutching her coat closer as the horses plodded forward, her hair whipping in the wind. "It's summer, for crying out loud! It shouldn't be so chilly."

"It isn't always this cold, but the northern wind can be rather unpleasant," Yain said, not looking too much happier.

For her part, Kitania entirely agreed with them, since she was far colder than she'd prefer. Demons tended to be resistant to heat, not to cold. Only the angels seemed unbothered, and Kitania wasn't sure if that was because of their armor or if they were more used to the temperatures common in the north.

"Ugh, it's still unpleasant. I didn't pack clothing suited for late fall or early winter, after all," Maura grumbled, and Kitania resisted the urge to laugh at her. It wouldn't be nice, and Maura really didn't deserve to be mocked, since she and Yain had ended up doing a lot of the harder work on the trip.

The Harth plateau was truly immense, and Kitania was a bit taken aback by the sight of it, particularly at how flat the land here was. Stranger to her was how there were locals farming easily despite the apparent cold, though the crops were somewhat more unusual to her eyes. None of the others knew much about the plants, though, so all Kitania could do was glance curiously at the farmers working their way through the fields as she passed.

They'd passed a city as well, one which was lower-built than many human cities Kitania had seen, and the most imposing structure had been a broad, open-air temple which they'd been able to see from miles away. She didn't know an immense amount about the deities of Uthren, but Kitania did know that one of the major aspects of their faith was revering the sky, which was part of why they loved the heavens so much.

"Maybe so, but you'll be alright; the wind isn't always like this," Yain scolded, prompting soft laughter from Isalla. "You haven't been cold the last couple of days, so get over it!"

Maura just grumbled, and Kitania grinned, glancing at Rose in amusement, while the angel simply smiled in return, obviously about as entertained as Kitania was. Kitania was more pleased that the ice between her and Isalla had cracked, and Rose was slowly opening up as well, as they often talked quietly late into the night, feeling out each other a bit more carefully this time around. As much as Kitania liked Isalla and Rose, she didn't want to completely dive into a relationship that might go awry.

On the other hand, while Kitania had initially suspected that Maura and Yain were in a relationship or approaching one, she'd realized it was more of companionable banter. She still wasn't certain they weren't occasionally sleeping with one another, but if so it wasn't anything serious. She knew that sort of relationship, since Kitania had been in several similar ones in the hells, all the way back when she was living in the palace.

"How much farther is it to Uthren's Throne?" Kitania asked, quirking an eyebrow at Rose. "I don't see anything in the distance, but that doesn't mean anything."

"Ah, well… I'm not entirely certain. I'm not used to traveling on the ground, which makes it harder to tell, and the lack of easy landmarks is troubling," Rose replied, flushing slightly with embarrassment as she looked at Isalla. "How about you, Isabel? You were always better at geography than me."

"That's because I had to arrange travel more than you," Isalla said, laughing softly as she smiled. "As to that… I'm not sure if we'll make it there today, but certainly tomorrow. The distance is deceptive on the plateau, with several ripples in the landscape that can hide areas when you think it's flat, and the mountains in the distance are *way* farther away than you might think at sea level."

"Truly?" Vinara asked, looking at Isalla curiously. "How far away are they?"

"Well… look at those ones to the west," Isalla said, nodding toward a mountain range off to their left that looked no more than a handspan in height from their perspective. "Those are at least twenty miles away, if not even farther than that. I may be better than Lynn at geography, but I didn't pay attention to exactly where the mountains were, relative to our location. The thing is, line of sight is farther up here, and that makes it a little easier to overlook changes in the landscape. Sometimes, anyway."

"Ah, fair, I suppose. I wondered why they didn't seem to be getting larger as fast as I expected… well, you can learn something new no matter *how* old you are, I suppose," Kitania said, glancing at the mountains again, then stopped and blinked as she looked ahead of them, drawing her horse up short as she saw a man simply *appear* on the road ahead of them.

The others quickly stopped as well, and Kitania heard Eziel inhale sharply at the sight of the man. He was an angel, with brown hair and eyes, and cradled in his arms was a sleek, deadly-looking crossbow with an enchanted bolt loaded. He wore glittering chain without an emblem, which was immaculate, though the semi-transparent cloak on his back concerned Kitania a little, as did the smirk on his face. In her opinion that was a very bad sign.

"I thought about staying hidden for a while longer, but I'm afraid my patience is running thin," the man said, his voice a relatively pleasant baritone, but the harsh edge to his gaze told Kitania that he was anything but pleased to meet them. His gaze settled on Kitania for a moment, then he looked at Isalla and Rose, sneering slightly as he said. "Oh, how the mighty have fallen. Isalla and Roselynn… the two of you were long the dogs of the Order of the Phoenix, and now you're allies of the very beings you were supposed to stamp out. How very disgusting."

"Who are *you*? The bastard who attacked us when we fought the bandits?" Isalla demanded, her eyes narrowing suddenly.

Maura's hand was drifting toward her sword, but the angel obviously noticed as well, as his crossbow came up as quickly as a serpent could strike, taking aim at her as he spoke. "None of that, miss elf. I'd hate to kill you, but I'm more than willing to do so if necessary. My issue is with the demons and traitors. As for who I am? I'm not telling you that. I might be confident, but I'm not stupid. No, I'm here to give you a choice."

"What choice might that be?" Rose asked, and Kitania found her gaze drifting from side to side suspiciously.

The angel's confidence was unnerving, especially considering everything that Kitania and the others had been through over the past couple of months, and that made her wonder what gave him his confidence. There weren't any obvious spots on the sides of the road where other ambushers could lurk, and she also didn't see any sign of where they might be invisible, though that was harder to determine in general.

"You can kill the demon and surrender, or commit suicide yourselves, and I'll leave everyone else unharmed. If you don't, I'm going to go after *all* of you," the man said coldly, still aiming at Maura. "I have a few compunctions where you're concerned, but not many."

"Not a chance, you traitorous—" Isalla began, and at that moment Kitania's gaze fell to the road and her eyes widened as she saw where several points under the horses had been excavated recently. The signs were subtle, but the dirt had obviously moved, and a chill ran down her spine as she reacted.

As Kitania began snapping out the words of a spell, the angel switched targets to her, pulling the trigger to loose the bolt as everything happened so quickly it was almost imperceptible, his lips forming a word as well. Vinara flicked her fingers and a blast of wind roared to life around them like a whirlwind, raising dust and stray grass suddenly as the bolt left the crossbow. The wind deflected the bolt even as it continued to accelerate, though it came far closer than Kitania preferred as it raced past her shoulder. Even so, she didn't stop casting her spell, channeling magic quickly into it as the shield began to take shape, but Kitania wasn't quite fast enough.

Fire and stone erupted from the ground in a hail of shrapnel just as Kitania's spell began taking effect. It blocked some of the explosion, but nowhere near enough of it. The next thing Kitania knew she couldn't see through her right eye and was flying through the air as cries of shock, the rumble of the explosion, and the screaming of horses filled her ears.

The next instant Kitania hit the ground and felt multiple bones snap as the horse came down on her leg and hips, which caused *almost* enough pain to make her pass out. It still wasn't enough, and a moment later she realized there were other aches across her body, likely where she'd been hit.

"Then die, you damned—gah!" the man cried out in pain, cursing as he spoke. "You can all die!"

"Not while I draw breath." Eziel's voice was cold, and Kitania turned her head to see that of their entire group, only her servant was standing, with numerous cuts along her face and arms, and with her bow in hand as she fired several arrows in rapid succession, each of them glittering with magic.

Unable to see anything else, Kitania softly swore, trying to drag her mangled leg from under the twitching, writhing horse to try to help. She could hear some of the others as rubble pelted the ground around them, but it wasn't all of them, not even close.

The worst part of this was being unable to do *anything*.

EZIEL'S HEART felt like it was about to freeze, she was so terrified of what had happened. She was the only person who'd been outside the immediate zone of destruction when the ground had exploded, and Kitania's magic had shielded her from the worst of it. The blasts had caused her horse to bolt and she'd barely leapt free in time, and a couple of the others had as well, though all of them were down, injured. Rose had taken the brunt of the blast, and Eziel refused to look at her, instead focusing on the real threat, Sorm.

She'd already landed an arrow in his shoulder, and he swore loudly as he dodged another shot, his reflexes slower than they should have been. Eziel's arrows caused paralysis if enough of them hit, but she's only hit him the once. She *wanted* to help Kitania, but if he was allowed to act freely, they'd all die.

"Interfering mortal *insect!*" Sorm exclaimed, pulling out a glittering ruby stone with sigils burning across its surface, and Eziel's blood chilled still more at the sight of the incineration stone. If he hit the others, everyone but Kitania would die, and she couldn't allow that.

The angel spoke the word to activate the stone and threw it, and at the same time Eziel took aim, mouthing a prayer to Estalia as she loosed the arrow. For an instant she was afraid she'd missed, but only for a moment, as the arrow hissed through the air and bounced the stone back in Sorm's direction.

Sorm only had a moment to curse and dodge to the side before the stone detonated furiously, igniting plants near the road as a smaller crater was blasted into it, and Sorm emerged from the fireball scorched and limping. Eziel drew another arrow to finish paralyzing him when she realized he'd reached for his neck, then he flashed brightly and vanished without a trace, leaving behind only his crossbow and the smoldering ruins of the road.

Eziel hesitated a moment, then dropped the bow, turning her attention to Kitania and the others.

"Kitania out from under the horse, then everyone else. She'll recover, I know it," Eziel muttered.

The others were groaning and moving… all but Rose, so Eziel would go to her next. First she was helping Kitania, though.

CHAPTER 24

"Pardon me, Milady. I'm going to lift the horse, and I need you to drag yourself out from under it as far as you can," Eziel said, her tone surprisingly polite as she crouched, reaching under the horse as she braced herself. "The others are injured as well, so I need to tend to them, but once you're recovering I'll be much more at ease."

"What happened to him?" Kitania asked, breathing quickly as she braced herself, pain rippling through her as the body of the horse shifted slightly. Even if Eziel's strength was enhanced by years of training, she knew it was going to be difficult for her to lift the horse for long.

"Gone. Sorm—ugh!" Eziel gasped, her muscles standing out as she strained hard, lifting the horse a few inches.

Kitania bit back a scream as the pressure came off her leg and hips, allowing blood to rush through her lower body again in an incredibly unpleasant way. She didn't hesitate, though, dragging herself out from under the horse painfully, refusing to look at the damage. It was temporary, after all. Eziel let the horse drop a moment later, then continued.

"Sorm tried to finish the job, and I stopped him, but he teleported away, much like Haral did," Eziel said, then glanced away as she added. "Sorry, I have to go. Rose looks like she's in bad shape."

"Go, then! I'll be fine," Kitania told her, and Eziel nodded in relief, then darted away.

Kitania made the mistake of looking down at herself as she heard others groaning, and winced as she murmured, "I'll be fine *eventually.*"

～

ISALLA GROANED as she dragged herself to her feet, her left arm hanging uselessly by her side. She was afraid to think about what had happened, since she could barely twitch her fingers, and as soon as the world stopped spinning she'd be much happier. After a moment of hesitation, she reached into her belt pouch and found one of her healing potions, thanking the heavens that none of them had broken. Pulling out the stopper with her teeth, Isalla quickly drank the glowing vial, and let out a sigh as the world stabilized and her arm stopped hurting quite as much.

On the other hand, being able to see properly wasn't exactly pleasant, either. The road was a series of five overlapping craters, now, with a shallower one ahead of them, and plants alongside the road were smoldering, though it didn't look like the fire would last long. The first others she saw were Maura and Yain, with Yain trying to help Maura to her feet, even as she bled from a hole that'd been punched through her ear and several wounds across her upper body. Maura wasn't in much better shape, and didn't look like she was entirely focused, understandably from the way her hair was matted on one side of her head and blood slowly seeped through it.

Eziel was the only one who looked relatively untouched, and her horse was some distance away from them, though Isalla thought it looked somewhat injured. Vinara mostly looked bruised, though she was favoring a leg as she crouched next to Eziel. Kitania wasn't in sight, which prompted the faintest hint of panic, but that was overwhelmed as Isalla suddenly realized who it was that Eziel and Vinara were crouching over.

Rose's armor was still disguised, but it'd been covered in dirt and blood from the remains of her horse, making it almost unrecognizable. Worse, one of her legs was clearly detached, and Eziel was rapidly applying a tourniquet. As for Rose herself... the only way Isalla could even recognize her was by her hair, and even that was bloody and tattered.

"Rose!" Isalla exclaimed, almost tripping in her haste to approach. As she did so, Vinara quickly turned, her leg almost collapsing under her as she tried to rise. The succubus spoke bluntly, her eyes flickering with frustration.

"Stop!" Vinara said, her voice taut. "If you touch her, you could make things far worse, Isalla!"

"But... but..." Isalla gasped, almost hyperventilating as panic overwhelmed her. "I... is she going to be okay?"

"I don't know. It's a miracle she's still alive, and I'm not skilled enough with healing magic to be any help," Vinara said grimly, turning back toward Rose, her worry obvious. "If it weren't for the armor healing her, she'd be dead already, but I don't know how long that'll last, even if we all supply the enchantments with mana. The damage is so extensive that I just don't know, and Kitania isn't in a state to easily examine her."

"Heavens, where—" Isalla began, but her mouth snapped shut as she looked over to see Kitania laying on the ground near the back of the group and partly obscured by a dead horse, her leg at an unnatural angle and hips oddly flat. As Isalla watched, the demoness's leg twitched as a bone moved back into place, and Isalla felt her stomach roil as she gasped. "O-oh."

"Her mount landed on her," Eziel said, her voice grim as she straightened. "I helped her out from under it but helping everyone else was more important than Lady Kitania's comfort. Unfortunately, while I'm not as versed in healing as she is, I don't think we'll be able to save Lady Rose with what we have available. Healing potions will only delay the inevitable, and she'll expire the moment we run out of mana. If we were closer to Uthren, we might find a healer in time, but at this point... I don't know that there's anything we can do. She's just taken too much damage."

"No, no no no! She can't die like this, not after everything we've been through!" Isalla protested, taking quick steps forward as she grew unsteady, almost panicking again as her pulse raced and she grew dizzy. "There has to be *something* we can do!"

"There is," Vinara said flatly, and Isalla looked at the demoness as hope rose within her, hope that turned to worry at the grim look on Vinara's face. Vinara moved Rose's leg near the stump, and Isalla cringed as some of the flesh knitted together before her eyes.

"What can we do?" Isalla asked, desperation rushing through her. She hated to ignore Kitania, but under the circumstances she didn't see another real choice. Rose was the one in danger of death, not Kitania.

"*You* need to charge the armor so it doesn't run out of mana. If it does, everything we do will be useless," Vinara replied, taking a deep breath as she looked around, then nodded unhappily. "This isn't how I wanted to do this, but so be it. We need help *now*, not later."

"Vinara?" Isalla asked uncertainly, but she knelt next to Rose, her breathing coming in rapidly as she did so. The wounds across her beloved's body were terrible, and even as she watched blood was trying to ooze out of her wounds.

The succubus didn't respond, instead pulling a folded sheet of paper out of her belt pouch and unfolding it. Isalla reached down and felt across Rose's armor, trying to find the stone that held the mana beneath the illusion while she watched, seeing an incredibly intricate spell inked across the paper's surface.

"Here we go..." Vinara murmured, taking a deep breath, then began speaking quickly, and the letters across the surface of the scroll lit up as she did so. It took several seconds for the scroll to fully light up, and while Vinara invoked its magic Isalla found the gem at last, and teased mana out of her core and into the stone.

The scroll suddenly burst into blue flames, prompting Isalla to flinch away as she almost lost control of the thread of mana, but Vinara didn't seem either surprised or hurt by the fire. Instead, the fire took the shape of a songbird made of the fires, rippling in mid-air as it looked at Vinara patiently.

"We're nearly to Uthren's Throne, but Rose is mortally injured and unable to survive until we find help. We need assistance, Your Majesty," Vinara said simply. The bird paused for a moment, then flared and vanished.

"Her Majesty?" Yain asked, her voice taut with pain as she looked at them.

"My Lady, not yours," Vinara explained, shaking her head unhappily as Isalla felt her mana seeping into the gem. It was so *empty*, she realized, her fear growing stronger. No wonder Eziel had said that Rose wouldn't last until they reached the capital, not if the enchantments were barely keeping her alive after using this much mana. How bad had the injuries been to do that, she had to wonder, but still refused to look. That would just ruin her already shaky concentration.

"I see, but how—" Yain began, helping Maura sit down, only to be interrupted by a flash of blue light as the bird reappeared in front of Vinara.

"Activate the beacon, help will arrive as soon as possible." The bird spoke in Estalia's voice, and the queen didn't sound happy. "Hold on for just a few minutes."

With the message sent, the flames slowly evaporated, and Vinara let out a sigh of relief, smiling as she murmured, "Well, I suppose that's that."

She grabbed her bag where it was laying nearby, the leather remarkably intact after the explosion, and started going through it quickly.

"I hope she hurries," Isalla said worriedly, her eyebrows furrowing as her mana rushed into the gem. She thought she could fill it, but even so her mana was going to go fast.

"I'm sure she will," Vinara said, confidence in her voice as she pulled out a gold disk with silver runes across the top, then smiled. "Unlike what many people might think, Estalia *doesn't* abandon her agents. She'll act quickly, promise."

"Are you sure you want to do this? I have angels and mortals I could send instead," Estalia asked, but she didn't pause in handing over the satchel.

"They might be able to save Rose, but they wouldn't have the

BENJAMIN MEDRANO

authority I have. Herbert is still a deity, and I'm pretty sure he's not going to want to antagonize me," Anna said, smiling thinly as she added, "Besides, I'm sure my return out of nowhere will cause waves in the heavens, and a good deal of consternation among our enemies. Beyond which, they won't realize I was hiding *here*."

"Your Majesty, we have a lock on the beacon; it is *active*," Veldoran called out, and a glittering web of crimson runes overlaid the teleportation platform as he quickly wove his spell, grunting as he added, "We have two minutes, no more!"

They were in the teleportation chamber, and Anna was wearing her armor and armed, while the other angels in attendance were looking at her oddly. They had been since Anna had returned in her current shape, and Estalia knew they were wondering who she was, and why she radiated the power that she did, though none had dared ask yet.

"Well, I guess time's up. Go, my love. Make our enemies tremble before you," Estalia said and went onto her tiptoes to give Anna a kiss, bittersweet regret rushing through her at the thought of Anna departing so soon. Every time they were together, it seemed like they were pulled apart too quickly.

"I will. I'll *also* give Kitania your love, once I can," Anna said, smiling broadly, and she rested her cloudpiercer over one shoulder as she stepped into the middle of the teleportation platform.

"Good. Veldoran? Send her to them," Estalia said, nodding to the archmage as she breathed in deeply. The beacon Vinara wasn't as powerful as the one she'd given to Alserah, so it took a lot more work to prepare, unfortunately. Of course, that was why she'd given a proper one to Anna.

"Yes, Your Majesty! Brace yourself," Veldoran warned Anna, who nodded as he quickly chanted the spell to activate the teleportation, and the angel vanished with a thunderclap and a flash of red light.

The spells died down moments later, and Estalia looked at the spot where Anna had been standing moments before, ever so slightly forlorn. Then she sighed and murmured, "Well, it is done. *Now* the die is truly cast."

"Your Majesty? What do you mean by that?" Veldoran asked, the crimson-skinned demon wiping the sweat from his forehead as he nodded to his assistants, who looked far more bedraggled than him.

Estalia looked at him, then at the others for a long moment, considering. Then she smiled, realizing that caution didn't matter much at this point, and she asked, "Do you know who Anna is?"

"No, I'm afraid not. I thought she was just an angel, but the aura she's had the last few days makes me think she's an archangel. But that's ridiculous, as I'd think I'd have heard if you acquired the remains of an archangel," Veldoran said, his voice a little uncertain. "How else would she have gained the mantle of one since the last time I saw her?"

"Ah, but that is where you're wrong. She's an archangel, yes, but she's *always* been an archangel. She simply suppressed the mantle until it was undetectable, with a little help," Estalia said, her smile widening as she looked at the angels and added, "As to who she is… her *proper* name, not her nickname, is Anathiel. I do believe the realms will tremble at her coming."

"Anathiel?" Veldoran asked, blinking in confusion, and his face suddenly paled, much as the faces of the angels in the room did, and his voice rose as he protested. "*Anathiel* was *here*?"

Estalia laughed and turned to leave the room, smiling to herself. If nothing else, this would sidetrack all the spies for *months*.

CHAPTER 25

*R*ed lightning flashed above the disk, and Isalla flinched back slightly as a soft *boom* blasted across the landscape, blinking unhappily as she tried to regain her vision. She should have known better than to watch for the help that was coming, but it was better than watching Vinara channel her mana into Rose's armor, since that also meant looking at the ruin of her beloved's body.

The spots across her vision quickly faded, and as they did so a wave of pressure hit Isalla, one that was more mental than physical. She'd only been in the presence of an archangel a handful of times, and the sensation of their majesty was unmistakable, almost forcing Isalla to her knees. It was even more powerful than the others she'd encountered, Isalla realized, but the pressure retracted almost instantly instead of forcing her down.

"Who…" Isalla began, her eyes widening enormously at the unfamiliar figure who stood in the middle of the road, a surge of fear rushing through her as the possibility of someone having stolen the link to attack them rushed through her head.

The angel standing before her was beautiful, with warm brown skin, silver hair and eyes, and wore simple, functional steel armor, while her feathers were silver as well. She held a cloudpiercer which radiated power, though, and Isalla flinched

183

slightly, though the beautiful angel's smile set her slightly more at ease, as did the satchel slung over her shoulder.

"I'm Anna," the angel replied simply, her gaze focusing on Rose, and her expression abruptly turned grim as she added, "I also see you weren't joking about her being mortally injured, Vinara. It's a good thing I got here in time, then."

"Lady Anna? You... look very different," Vinara said, quickly moving out of the angel's way as she approached. "I wouldn't have recognized you!"

"This is close to how I originally looked, though with a few changes that I made over the years intact. I enjoyed them, and didn't see a reason to revert *everything*, even if I've decided to stop hiding who I am," Anna replied, setting her cloudpiercer aside and flipping open the satchel as she crouched next to Rose, her voice soft as she pulled out what looked like a glowing blue needle on a handle. "Rose, what *did* you do to yourself? Ah, well. I can't heal her personally, but I can take her to Uthren's Throne and get her tended to."

Without hesitation the angel stabbed the needle into Rose, and Isalla cried out in horror, at least until a shimmering barrier of blue light rippled over Rose's body. It took her a moment to realize Rose wasn't breathing, and Isalla demanded, "What did you do to her?"

"She's in stasis," Anna explained, relaxing slightly as she nodded, looking around at them and wincing as she pulled out a box. "Don't all of you look like you're in bad shape? Here, healing potions. What happened?"

"Sorm, a former captain of the Holy Council's guards, confronted us. He distracted us with demands, then set off at least five incineration stones that he'd buried beneath the road," Eziel said, her eyebrows knitting with worry as Vinara took the box from Anna, opening it to reveal several glowing vials inside it. "Lady Kitania attempted to block the blast but didn't have time to do so. I shot him once, but he teleported away after I deflected another stone back toward him."

Isalla winced at the explanation, a chill running down her spine at the thought of incineration stones. They were weapons of war among angels, and expensive due to the sheer power of the detonation they could invoke. The idea of five of them used to try to kill them... it terrified her.

"Well done," Anna said, nodding, then looked over at Kitania as she sighed, walking toward the demoness as she added, "Now, you look under the weather, Kitania. I thought I taught you to *dodge*."

"I was on a horse at the time and spotted where he buried the stones a bit too late," Kitania replied, her voice slightly strained, and she smiled unhappily, adding, "Thank you for the cloudpiercer. I'd thank you properly, but I'm afraid I'm in bad shape."

"I see that. However, I can't take much time here, not if I want to ensure Rose recovers sooner rather than later," Anna said, leaning over Kitania and brushing a few strands of her hair back. The gentle intimacy of the action startled Isalla, and she opened her mouth, then shut it again as Anna spoke. "I'm taking her to the city, so you'll have to catch up, I'm afraid. I can't carry *all* of you."

"Alright. How will we find you?" Yain asked, her voice unsteady as she drank one of the potions, and Vinara handed one to Isalla, who took it absently. As she watched, the hole in Yain's ear slowly began closing and her other injuries sealed themselves.

"Oh, that'll be simple," Anna said, walking back over to Rose while she unfolded a sling designed to allow angels to carry larger loads, then carefully shifted Rose into it, which Isalla knew had to be an awkward load, yet Anna handled her like she was weightless. The angel also picked up one of Rose's packs, specifically the one which contained Ember, and adjusted it to fit more easily. "Just come to the High Temple and request an audience. I'll leave instructions that I'm waiting for you."

"Ah... request an audience with *who*? I can tell you're an archangel, but I have no clue who you are," Isalla said, her voice a little nervous at this point. She'd never spoken to an archangel before, and she'd only been in their presence once or twice.

"Oh yes, of course... I suppose you *are* too young to recognize me," Anna said, her smile widening as she picked up her cloudpiercer. "Ask for an audience with Anathiel. Now, I have to go."

Shock froze Isalla in place as the angel's wings extended, then she took flight so suddenly the ground cracked where she'd been standing and dust blasted outward, sending Isalla into a coughing fit. She waved dust away, her gaze rising still more as she watched a silver streak head into the distance. Even so, Isalla's shock grew even more profound.

"Um, am I supposed to know the name?" Vinara asked, frowning deeply as she looked around. Isalla met Eziel's gaze, and the other woman looked like someone had dropped an anvil on her head.

"Just... well, maybe she isn't as famous among demons. I mean, she's history. *Ancient* history," Isalla began, swallowing hard as she grappled with the idea of who Anna was.

"As I thought," Kitania muttered, and her voice drew everyone's attention, including Isalla's.

"Wait, *you* knew she was an archangel?" Vinara demanded, her tone sharp.

"No, I *suspected* she was an archangel. I spent over a decade in her care, you may recall, and even as careful as she is, I heard a number of clues that made me suspect who she was. I just didn't know, and I wasn't going to pry," Kitania retorted, shifting slightly.

"Are you going to tell us, or make us figure it out for ourselves?" Maura asked, her voice slightly cross. "We've had a hard day, and I'm starting to lose patience."

"Anathiel, the third archangel of war... and the leader of *five* invasions of the hells," Isalla said at last, her tone flat with the shock rippling through her. "Slayer of more than fifteen demon lords, according to legend. She went missing during her fifth crusade, and her mantle was believed to be subsumed by the Archangel of Glorious War some thousand years later. *That* was over two thousand years ago. I don't remember exactly when she went missing."

Everyone fell silent at that, and after a moment Yain murmured, "Oh. Well... *that's* scary."

"Wait, *her*? I... of course I've heard of her! I just thought... oh, now I feel stupid," Vinara muttered. "I must have taken a rock to the head."

"She's rather nice, I'll have you know. If you aren't in a training salle with her," Kitania said, sighing as she added, "Vin? Would you give me a potion already? I'd like to have my bones healed, since we're probably going to be walking the rest of the way."

"Oh, right. I'm just used to letting you put yourself back together," Vinara said, and stepped around a horse as she approached Kitania with the box still in hand.

Shaking off her shock, Isalla uncorked her potion and downed it, feeling a wave of healing energy rush through her, soothing most of the remaining aches and pains as it did so. She wasn't in *good* shape, but she was doing better, now.

Besides, she was feeling much, *much* more hopeful now that she knew that Rose was in good hands. Even if the idea of Anna being the archangel of war terrified her more than a little.

"Uthren's Throne has changed," Anna murmured, mixed feeling surging through her as she shot through the air.

It wasn't surprising that the city had changed in the time since she'd last seen it. Empires had risen and fallen in that time, so with humans in charge it would be more of a surprise if the city *hadn't* changed. Even so, a tiny part of her was dismayed, and not just because it meant she was coming closer to her past.

Uthren's Throne had once been a fortress city, one which was dedicated both to their guardian deities and to the alliance with the heavens. It was large, yes, but protected by heavy stone walls that had been built by the dwarven kingdoms and built to withstand any siege. Most of those walls still stood, as did the massive temple at the city's core, but the city had grown far beyond the walls.

Now Uthren's Throne was nearly ten times the size it had once been, the old walls now circling the heart of the city, while farmland surrounded the unfortified outskirts to feed the people who lived within. There were manors and fine buildings in areas that had once held homes inside those inner walls, while most of the businesses must have moved into the outer city, based on what she was seeing.

The angelic fortress was also eye-catching, in part because it was the only building larger than the temple other than the castle itself, and also because of its sheer height. Even now Anna could see several dozen angels flying around it in patterns that looked like military drills, though they didn't look nearly as crisp as Anna would have expected. More annoying to her, she *still* hadn't heard an alarm go up by the time she'd crossed over the city itself, and she sighed as she banked toward the temple, and specifically for the uppermost chamber. That's where she expected to find Herbert, or where he'd show up once he felt her aura.

Finally, the first cries of shock reached Anna's ears, and she smiled slightly as she saw dozens of mortals stop in the streets to stare at her, some of them falling to their knees. It'd been so *long* since she'd seen that sort of reaction to her presence, even if she didn't necessarily like it. Being worshipped could be tiring, to say the least.

None of the wards over the temple activated to bar her way, showing that despite her time in the hells, Anna was still considered an angel where their magic was concerned. *That* was enough to make her smile, and she ignored the priests and alarm bells as she flew past the pillars of the chamber and landed, looking at the three thrones within as she raised an eyebrow.

"They've redecorated, too," Anna murmured, looking around and cringing inwardly.

Three thrones sat on a raised dais, one which was raised Anna's full height, and she didn't want to even think about how petitioners would have to crane their necks to look at the deities if they were in residence. That might be intentional, now that she thought about it, and all over the walls were engravings showing deeds from the deities pasts, most of them gaudily washed in gold, which was the main source of her distress. It lacked so much nuance, and made her feel even worse about leaving the Spire of Confession. At least most of the rooms there had been tastefully decorated, even when they were rather ornate.

The ripple of another deity's aura washed over Anna, and she turned as thunder rumbled over the city, just in time to see a stocky, brown-haired human land outside the room, his beard and hair crackling with lightning as he scowled, a flail that was wreathed with lightning as well in one hand, while he wore elaborate armor that made him look even more imposing, or at least she assumed that was the intent. He certainly didn't look happy to see her, though, and Anna didn't recognize him.

"Hellspawn, how dare you intrude into our sanctum!" the deity boomed, causing Anna's eyebrows to both rise. Unfortunately, she didn't have a chance to reply before he shot toward her, lightning crackling in his wake as he attacked her. Unfortunately for him, his movements were far too predictable.

Anna didn't bother dodging, a hint of derision welling up inside her, and she muttered under her breath, "Children."

Her free hand snapped up as the flail lashed out at her, and with her power flooding through her it was as easy as could be for Anna to catch it, and her arm barely trembled as a thunderclap exploded outward from the impact, lightning arcing uselessly down her gauntlet. Anna stopped the weapon in mid-air, her fingers half-curled around the head of the flail and using the spikes as handles as she looked at the suddenly shocked deity in front of her.

"Is *this* how Uthren greets guests these days? I must say, its standards have fallen," Anna replied coldly, and with that she ripped the flail clean out of the man's hands, tossed it in the air, and caught the handle on its way down. "As for calling me hellspawn, that was *quite* rude. I must assume you believe me to be ashborn, but nothing could be farther from the truth."

"What the... give that back!" the man demanded, lunging toward the flail with lightning speed, but Anna stepped out of the way, easily anticipating his movements as she clicked her tongue.

"No, no... I think I'll give it back when you've proven you deserve to have it. At the moment I'm afraid that you're more likely to destroy your own temple," Anna said, and her gaze drifted to the side as another deity appeared, this one *also* unknown to her, though the blonde woman looked a good deal more cautious, as her eyes widened at the sight of Anna and the man. Anna politely corrected herself. "Or, to be more accurate, the temple of you and your fellow deities. I can't say that I'm impressed at how things have changed."

"Who are you, and what are you doing here?" the woman asked, her voice cool as her hazel eyes narrowed, a hint of concern in her voice.

"I'm here to see an old friend and get the assistance a *young* friend of mine is owed," Anna replied, dodging again as the man took another swipe at the flail, a smile flickering over her lips. He had a lot to learn, and she could tell he was relatively new to his powers. "As for who I am—"

"What is the meaning of this commotion?" another voice interrupted, and a thinner man with brown hair and eyes landed in the entryway, wind swirling around him as he looked around, then almost froze as his gaze settled on Anna.

"Ah, hello, Herbert. Did your fellow deities pass on their mantles again?" Anna asked mildly, raising an eyebrow at him.

Herbert froze in place for a long moment, and Anna saw the woman give him a startled look as the deity's jaw worked, then he finally spoke incredulously. "You're *alive*? You've been missing for thousands of years!"

"I was not *missing*. I was *hiding*; there's a distinct difference," Anna corrected, clicking her tongue as she shook her head, then saw the thunder god's eyes shift just in time to dodge as he made another attempt to reclaim his flail, and she continued. "Also, the manners around here seem to have grown worse in the last few millennia. I was accused of being hellspawn and attacked without warning."

"Krath, stop that, you're just embarrassing yourself," Herbert said, reaching up to rub his eyes as he took a deep breath, then sighed. "As to that, I do apologize for your reception, but you must understand that almost no one knows of you personally anymore. I'd also appreciate it if you called me Cyclone; I struck my original name from the records before you disappeared."

The god stopped trying to reclaim his flail, looking at Herbert in surprise, and Anna couldn't help a smile, as well as wondering why he looked away when he was well within reach. The man was obviously inexperienced, which she thought foolish. The woman cleared her throat, crossing her arms as she looked between Anna and Herbert.

"May I ask who she *is*, since you seem to know each other?" the woman asked, her voice somewhat sharp. "I have no idea who she is, yet you seem wary of her, Lord of Gales."

"Ah, of course," Herbert said, shaking himself slightly as he took a deep breath, then bowed his head to Anna as he continued. "May I introduce Krath, Lord of Thunder, and Sanguine, Lady of Blood? Krath, Sanguine... this is Anathiel, Archangel of War."

"You're *who*?" Krath blurted out, the blood draining from his face as he stared at Anna in shock, and possibly a little horror. Sanguine had also paled a little, and Anna couldn't help raising an eyebrow.

"I prefer to go by Anna, as that was the name I used while I was in hiding, but *Cyclone* is correct. Did you all pick new names as deities? They don't sound normal to me, but I have been out of touch for a while," Anna said, a smile flickering across her face. "I *am* a little surprised that people remember me, though. It's been a good four thousand years, after all."

"Choosing names that we aren't embarrassed by has become something of a tradition," Herbert, no, Cyclone said, as Anna struggled to adjust to the new name. He let out a breath, shaking his head incredulously as he continued. "On the other hand, how in the blazes do you think people would *forget* you? You led five invasions of the hells, *five*, and are one of the most legendary generals in history! It's barely been a dozen angelic generations since you vanished, if even that. Why did you vanish, anyway? Hiding, you said?"

"I got tired of war," Anna said bluntly, her smile fading a little as she sighed softly, then looked at Krath as she asked, "Are you going to attack me again?"

"Ah... no, I don't think so. My apologies, Your Excellency, but your wings gave me the wrong impression," Krath said, with a sheepish look on his face that made Anna smile.

"I'm glad to hear that," Anna said, handing the flail back to him as she continued. "That said, you need to practice with your abilities; I can tell that you're new to them. Cyclone and his fellow deities were so respected because of how well their powers synergized, and between the three of them they could put up a good fight against me, even when my equipment vastly outclassed theirs. You simply need to get used to your powers so you can use them properly in a fight."

"That's about what I've been saying for the past few months," Cyclone said, smiling slightly as he looked at Krath, who had a thoughtful look on his face.

Sanguine shifted, frowning for a moment before the goddess asked, "Um, is she right? Did she really take all of you on at once?"

"Yes, but any explanation will have to wait. Give me a minute to go calm the guards and priests, then we can help you, Anathiel. I have to assume *something* happened to draw you out of hiding," Cyclone said, then he all but vanished in a rush of wind, leaving Anna with the two newer deities.

For a long moment they stood in awkward silence, and Anna studied the two. Based on what Cyclone had said, she knew they'd inherited the powers of the deities she'd known, which gave her a solid idea of their abilities. For their part, they were studying her in turn, their expressions betraying both worry and respect.

"The reason your predecessors could put up a good fight against me was simple enough, really. Cyclone handled ranged attacks and was incredibly mobile, while Ellis tangled me up in melee," Anna finally spoke, nodding toward Krath as she did so, and she smiled slightly as she continued. "That wasn't enough to deal with me, though, even outside of a city. That's why Ohsa was so helpful, as he used his powers to slow me down a bit while he healed the other two. As a group they were highly coordinated and skilled, people I respected."

"I've heard a little about them, but... what I find more startling is the idea that you could take all of them on at once. We're all deities, after all, and I've never heard that archangels are *that* much more powerful than us," Sanguine said, frowning slightly.

"Ah, but there are deities, and then there are *deities*," Anna replied, smiling a little more warmly now as she tilted her head. "Tell me, would you expect the deity of baking to be as powerful in combat as Krath?"

"Well... no, of course not. Their mantle isn't meant for fighting... oh, of course," Sanguine said, her confusion easing visibly as she nodded, then frowned. "A deity of baking wouldn't be good at battle. Yet our powers are heavily focused on things like that, aren't they?"

"They are. However that doesn't mean they're entirely focused on combat. Cyclone and Krath have weather control. You have the ability to manipulate all fluids to some degree or to seek them out. Each of you have aspects of your powers which aren't focused on battle," Anna said, her smile fading as she let out a sigh. "I, on the other hand... do not. I am the archangel of battle and war. The sheer breadth of my mantle means that I'm among the most powerful echelon of archangels and deities, and every single bit of my power is focused on combat. Beyond that, I have both a great deal of experience and the most powerful weapon and armor the heavens could forge. There are only four or five deities or demon lords who could fight me on a near even footing, and I'm not certain that all of them still live. Though I'll admit, I *am* a touch out of practice."

"Ah, I... I see," Sanguine said, looking shaken. Conversely, Krath seemed to be much calmer than he had been.

"Cyclone has said similar things before, come to think of it. I just didn't take them that seriously," Krath murmured, watching Anna thoughtfully. "But when you say it, well... you're a *legend*."

"She is," Cyclone agreed as he reappeared in a blast of wind, settling onto the ground as he let out a sigh. "There, the guards have been informed that we have a distinguished guest, so things should calm down. Now, why have you come, Lady Anathiel? If you've been hiding for so long..."

"That should be obvious, I'd think," Anna said dryly, looking down at the sling holding Rose's frozen form, and she continued. "This is a friend of mine who was traveling to Uthren's Throne with her friends, an angel you might have heard of, Roselynn Emberborn."

"Emberborn? I've certainly heard of the family, and have even known a few of Ember's wielders," Cyclone said, his eyebrows shooting up, and he looked at Rose in concern as he asked. "What happened to her? She looks like she's in bad shape, and that... is it a stasis spell?"

"It is. She was mortally injured, I'm afraid, so I placed her in stasis and brought her here so I could have her healed," Anna confirmed, letting out a soft sigh as she shook her head. "An angel was the one to do it to her, which is a... bad sign, to say the least. I'm afraid that there's trouble brewing in the heavens, and that's what made me finally decide to reveal myself."

"That doesn't sound good," Sanguine said, shifting from foot to foot, then asked, "Would you like my help with her, then? We have priests capable of healing virtually anything as well and could give her assistance quite simply."

"Thank you, but no. At the moment I simply need private lodging where I can wait for her friends, someplace where I can concentrate a little," Anna declined gently, shaking her head.

"Ah... I thought that your powers were focused purely on combat," Krath said, frowning. "If you're coming here for assistance..."

"Mm, perhaps that was the wrong way to phrase things, earlier. See, I have something with me which will allow me to heal her, most likely, and if it doesn't... well, it's always good to be somewhere I can get help. What I need for that method is privacy, mostly," Anna said, and smiled wryly as she added, "Honestly, that's why I came here rather than to the angelic outpost. They wouldn't be polite enough to leave me alone."

Cyclone's lips twitched, and Anna watched as he slowly failed to suppress his grin, and the deity chuckled softly before replying. "Well, I can understand that, and a private room... I think we can manage that. Do either of you disagree?"

"Of course not! I *would* like the chance to speak with you at some point, however... as we said, you *are* a legend," Sanguine said, her gaze moving between Rose and Anna curiously.

"And considering what you've said, I'd appreciate some pointers if you have time," Krath added, his tone slightly hopeful.

"I think I can manage that, assuming things don't go poorly. Might we get situated, then? I'll give descriptions of her friends for when they come seeking an audience later," Anna said, watching the three deities relax as she smiled at them. Almost no one else would get a reception like this, she knew, but there were advantages to being a living legend.

"That would be better communicated to the priests, but can be taken care of," Cyclone said, then grinned as he added, "I must say, your reappearance is liable to cause enormous waves. I can't wait to see how the other deities react!"

"I can only imagine, and the Holy Council is likely to throw a fit," Anna said, a bubble of mirth welling up inside her. "I'm sure it'll be good for them."

The laughter of the deities set her a bit more at ease, even if she *did* miss Estalia. Hopefully everything would end on a high note soon, and she could go home.

But for now, she needed to take care of Rose.

CHAPTER 26

Sorm finished downing the potion and set the vial aside, resisting the urge to curse again. The burns inflicted by the incineration stone eased still more as the healing magic washed through his body, and he let out a soft sigh as his wings began relaxing at last.

"Damned woman… who knew she would be that good of a shot?" Sorm muttered unhappily, wishing the brunette had missed, and not only because he hadn't appreciated the pain he'd gone through. He'd been so *close* to ensuring that all the loose ends except for the demoness were taken care of, only to be stopped at the last possible moment. *That* was galling, though he wasn't as displeased as he might have been.

"Roselynn took the brunt of the blast, and unless something went wrong, she should be dead," Sorm said, straightening as he looked around the room, noting that the house he shared with Haral was dustier than normal. She must still be out on a trip, as otherwise she'd have cleaned. Taking a breath, he nodded in satisfaction, his emotions hardening as he continued. "I suppose I'll just have to go back and finish off Isalla and the others. This is harder than I'd expected, but I'll manage."

Either way, he had to consider the attempt a success, by and large. He'd at least slowed down the group, and they'd have trouble getting in contact with anyone important with Roselynn out of the way. Things were looking brighter.

~

"WHO IS IN THE TEMPLE?" Rathien the Blue demanded, shock overwhelming any sense of complacency he might have had. A single angel flying to the First Temple shouldn't have been more than a footnote among his evening reports, not something that required a runner to urgently interrupt his afternoon.

"According to the priesthood, the archangel Anathiel has reappeared after her millennia away at last!" the younger angel replied, his blue eyes almost shining with hero worship as he continued. "Apparently, she's taken a room in the temple for the time being, and is ensuring an injured angel she rescued from the hells is healed!"

"I... well, this is most certainly a shock, Gabriel! I thought she was long since dead, since Lord Aelon is the archangel of glorious war, but I'm happy to hear that isn't the case," Rathien replied, regaining his bearings as he nodded. "Do you have more information than that?"

"No, sir. Unfortunately, we've only just received word of her presence, and I wanted to inform you immediately," the brown-haired angel said, straightening slightly.

"I see, well, I'm going to have to dispatch a message to the Holy Council immediately. I'm sure my counterparts will as well, but in the meantime, I'd like you to gather as much information as you can about her. If you can find out where she's been all these years, I'm certain they'll want to know," Rathien said, and the younger man nodded in acknowledgement, saluting as he did so.

"Yes, sir!" Gabriel said, and quickly turned to leave the room.

Rathien watched the man go, and once the door closed he felt a frown take hold, and he couldn't help murmuring, "Anathiel, really? What in all the heavens is she doing reappearing *now*?"

Part of him suspected that it had to be an impostor, after as long as it'd been since the archangel had gone missing, yet an impostor managing to deceive the deities in the temple strained his sense of disbelief. Cyclone was old and experienced and had risen to power during the fourth crusade in the hells, so he'd *known* Anathiel.

"Appearing just as things are reaching the final stages... that's worrying," Rathien said, distinctly unhappy about the news, but after a moment he sat down and pulled out a couple of sheets of paper. Regardless of *why* Anathiel had reappeared, if it was truly her it'd cause the balance of power to change throughout the heavens. She was simply too powerful not to cause changes, and he had no idea what would happen.

That was why he was sending a letter to not only the Holy Council, but also to the leaders of the Society of Golden Dawn. They wouldn't be happy about someone like Anathiel throwing their plans into chaos, but the sooner they heard about her the more easily they could revise their plans.

"Even if she's an archangel, she can't be allowed to change the course of the future. The heavens *will* prevail," Rathien said, his confidence surging as he quickly penned the letter. He might not be able to do what needed to be done on his own, but the society was stronger than any one of its members.

It had to be, to eliminate the hells once and for all.

ANNA TOUCHED the door and murmured the word she'd been given, and immediately felt the wards around the room seal it off. She'd still have fresh air, but it would take a battering ram to disturb her or breach the door, which would be difficult to get into the halls to begin with. She did approve of the quarters she'd been given, even if the colors clashed ever so slightly.

"They've taken to being gaudy, which is a shame," Anna murmured, then her lips quirked into a smile as she shook her head. "Or maybe they were *always* gaudy, and I simply didn't notice. That's a distinct possibility."

The room wasn't as bad as the deific audience chamber, but some of the ceiling had gilding, as did the posts of the heavy wooden bed against the back wall. There was a bathing room attached, which was a ruinous expense in Uthren's Throne, and a large walk-in closet that was mostly empty, along with the requisite table for tea, and an armor rack in the corner. Most important was the cot which had been brought in, along with a drop cloth for when Anna treated Rose. Not that she was planning to break the stasis spell just yet, not until she had things worked out properly.

"I suppose it's time to get to work, though. I can't believe that Herbert has had to train *five* fellow deities at this point. Is he a glutton for punishment?" Anna murmured, her smile widening a little more as she resisted the urge to laugh, then her smile faded. "Not that I can count on him for help. He's always trusted the heavens more than is wise, and his companions… well, they follow his lead, at least for now. We'll see about the future."

She sighed, then walked over to the armor rack as she began unbuckling her armor. It felt almost like a second skin with how easily it moved, but there was no reason to wear it when she was entirely in private. Besides, she was confident she could fight off most other deities even without the armor, though she'd be more likely to take wounds.

It took a few minutes, but at last Anna changed into something more comfortable and walked over to Rose's bag. She pulled out Ember without hesitation and looked levelly at the sword as she stated, "Burn me and we'll see how well you hold up against Infinity's Edge."

There wasn't a response, but she didn't hesitate as she unsheathed the ruby-bladed sword, and its blade blazed to life, flames almost dancing around it. It was beautiful, and Anna admired the weapon for a long moment, then gently propped it next to the fireplace, setting down the sheath as she smoothed her dress and sat in a chair, looking at it with a raised eyebrow.

For several minutes she just sat there, then finally spoke, her tone blunt. "How long are you going to keep pretending to be just a sword? I know the truth, and you know it too. I've even kept your little secret from Estalia, and *that* was a hard decision to make."

There still wasn't a response, at least for a minute, but just as Anna started to scowl, the sword shivered, then a male voice replied, his voice deep as the sword's light flickered with every word. "I suppose I *should* be thankful, but I find it difficult under the circumstances."

"There you are, Javan. I was beginning to think you'd gone senile or destroyed your mind when you transferred your soul into that blade," Anna said, smiling thinly as she shook her head. "How long are you planning to sulk, anyway? Not everyone has the opportunity to become an archangel, you know."

"And those of us who get the mantles sometimes aren't particularly thrilled to get them. I certainly didn't want to inflict it on anyone else!" Javan snapped back tartly. "Now, what do you want, Anathiel? I certainly hope you didn't bother me because you wanted a little *conversation*. Not considering everything I've heard about what's going on in the heavens."

"Why haven't you healed Rose?" Anathiel asked, sitting back as she looked at the sword. "For that matter, why haven't you chosen one of your descendants who *would* want the mantle and is worthy? Ember has gone through the hands of at least forty different members of your house at this point, and I know some of them would have been excellent recipients. Rose isn't even close to the most skilled wielder you've had, though I *do* like her well enough, so… what are you waiting on?"

"You can be an interfering, nosy bird, you know that?" Javan said, and Anna felt like she could *see* him hunkering down and sulking. "I haven't passed on the mantle because I don't think the family has deserved it, for the most part. Sure, a few of the wielders made me think they might be good archangels, but power corrupts too many of us, and once I make the decision it isn't like I can take it back. I'll be *dead* at that point, not just trapped in a sword, and inflicting something like that on the world… well, it doesn't sit well with me."

"Alright, I suppose I can understand that, though you did it to yourself, just because you didn't want anyone else knowing you were an archangel," Anna conceded, considering the ancient sword for a moment, then asked, "Why not heal her, then? Your power *is* that of the phoenix, not of fire in general. I've always been puzzled that Ember has only embodied the destructive aspects of fire, not the aspects of healing and rebirth."

"There are a few reasons for keeping that part of things hidden, mostly because I dreaded the thought of the Order of the Phoenix making Ember their signature weapon or some hogwash like that. It's not like they haven't worked my wielders to the bone *anyway*, as you know perfectly well," Javan said, and around Ember the flames began rippling more quickly as he hesitated. "As for healing Rose... I'm reluctant."

"Why?" Anna asked, her eyebrows rising in curiosity. She'd always thought that Javan's decision to hide his mantle and transfer his soul into a sword was odd, but not healing Rose made her more confused.

"Because if I heal her, others might figure out that I'm able to do so, and come to expect it. Worse, they might figure out that I'm *here*," Javan replied, his tone slightly more frustrated now. "I don't want that. This is the first time I've spoken since I hid myself in Ember, Anathiel, and I don't care to be revealed lightly!"

"Hm. I'm surprised... I always thought you were odd, but I didn't think you were a *coward*," Anathiel said, disappointment almost overwhelming her as she clicked her tongue.

"What did you call me?" Javan demanded, the fire suddenly blazing brighter around Ember, blackening the stone where the tip of the blade touched the ground.

"I called you a *coward*," Anathiel replied flatly, crossing her arms as she stared at the sword, her disappointment growing stronger. "You became an archangel, one of the most powerful beings in the heavens, and what did you do? Instead of helping protect others, you hid your mantle from all but the handful of us who witnessed your ascension. You could have passed your mantle down to those who would have used it, but instead you kept it and hid yourself in a sword. Certainly, you lent a fraction of that power to wielders, but only those you thought were worthy of it, and you've *hidden* for millennia."

"And you *didn't* hide? In the *hells* of all places?" Javan retorted hotly, the flames blazing intensely around his sword. "I've listened to everything that's happened around me, you know, and I know a *lot*."

"I hid, yes. But unlike you, I *used* my power, Javan. Do you want to try me? Do you want to *test* me?" Anna asked, her power billowing outward as she suddenly stood, flexing her wings as the feathers hardened until they were stronger than steel, her body's power increasing rapidly as it always did when she called upon her mantle. "I fought in *five crusades*. I can't count how many angels fought and died by my side, and they were *far* fewer in number than the mortals or demons who fell. I remember the death of Serin even if you don't, as her life's blood seeped out of her and her eyes went dark, even as you slipped from her grasp and did *nothing*. Do you remember that, Javan? Do you remember how your granddaughter died?"

"I…" Javan's voice trailed off, and Anna could see the flames weaken visibly as well, which didn't surprise her much. It disappointed her, but it didn't surprise her. For all his brilliance, Javan had always been a strange man, both stubborn and regretful at the same time. She hated to rub his failures in his face, but it seemed like the only choice she had.

"I remember," Javan said at last, a hint of loathing in his voice as he almost whispered in the quiet room. "I'd almost blocked it out, but yes, I remember that. It was the closest I ever came to intervening, and I've wondered why I didn't over the centuries. On the other hand, if I didn't intervene then, why should I now?"

Anna sighed, shaking her head and sitting back down, her expression turning cold as she did so, regret rushing through her as she murmured, "I suppose that if you're determined to be a coward to the end, there isn't anything more to say, is there? There are others who can heal her, though not as perfectly as you could."

The room was quiet again, at least for a minute, then Javan sighed loudly, sounding exasperated. "Fine, then! But I'm not going to do it *quickly*, I'll have you know. I don't want you telling anyone else what's going on, either. Lay me across Rose, and I'll fix her bit by bit. It isn't going to be too fast, though, and she'll be unconscious through all of it."

Anna's eyebrows rose, a little shocked that Javan had changed his mind. Yet at the same time she couldn't help a smile as she replied. "Truly? That's something of a surprise... but I can't say it makes me unhappy. Don't worry, I'm not telling anyone about your nature. My only question is how quickly you're going to work. We don't know how much time we have, you know."

"I'm well aware of that," Javan snapped, the fires growing more natural again as he spoke. "As for how long... I'm going to aim for a week, and I'm not planning on healing *anyone* else. My power isn't limitless, you know."

Rolling her eyes, Anna stood and nodded. "If that's what you want, so be it. Now, let's get to work, shall we? I also have a few young deities to put through their paces."

"For someone who was tired of war, you sure seem to take pleasure out of shocking young gods," Javan muttered, prompting Anna to laugh.

"True, true... but it *has* been a long time. Sometimes you just need a break to find who you are and to look at the world with new eyes," Anna said, taking Ember and carefully laying it on Rose's frozen form, the hilt over her breastbone while the blade went down across her legs. The fires grew stronger, and the shimmering barrier shattered, prompting her to tense slightly.

"If you say so. Now, I'm going to heal her, but I'll have you know that I have *no intention* of talking again this century or the next. If you have questions, I'm going to ignore you," Javan said briskly. "With any luck I can go as long without talking this time as I did last time."

"If you say so," Anna replied mildly, watching as Rose's bleeding slowly came to a stop, and she relaxed a little.

She had worried that Rose might not get the healing she needed from Javan, but no one could do a better job than him, not for the young angel. Even if Javan didn't realize why Anna had wanted him to heal Rose.

Turning away, Anna decided to read for a little while before going to speak with Herbert and the others. She couldn't have them thinking she'd managed to initiate Rose's healing so quickly, after all.

Hopefully the others would make it to Uthren's Throne soon as well, as that would give her a chance to properly talk to Kitania. *That* was something Anna had been looking forward to for a long, long time.

CHAPTER 27

*H*aral staggered out of the room, barely able to stand and her legs quivering with every step. In fact, she half-fell as her foot clipped the doorjamb, only for someone else to catch her midway to the floor.

"Easy, dear! You need to be careful after what you've been through," Sorm said, his voice warm and welcome after the horrible week she'd been through, and Haral blinked a couple of times, trying to focus on the other angel through her confusion.

"Sorm? But… why are you here? I thought you were hunting down Isalla and Roselynn," Haral said, her fatigue almost overwhelming her, as did her hatred of the two traitorous angels. If it hadn't been for them, she wouldn't have been in such a horrible place for what had felt like an eternity.

"I was. In fact, I just about got the lot of them, but had a setback. I *think* I took care of Roselynn but was forced to teleport away," Sorm said, a smile flickering across his face, but it was a little strained as he continued. "I was going to go try to finish the job, but then I heard about you, and I couldn't keep myself away. Why did you do it, love? You don't owe Roselynn's family anything!"

"No, but *they* aren't responsible for her actions. Nor are they responsible for the Holy Council's weakness," Haral replied, gritting her teeth as she forced her legs to behave and stood more fully, taking a moment to kiss Sorm gently, closing her eyes as she forced down the flicker of rage that the idea of Roselynn being dead sparked, and she sighed, murmuring, "If she's dead, I suppose it's for the best... even if I wish I could kill her with my own hands."

"That may still be possible." Ordath's deep voice echoed down the hall, and Sorm abruptly straightened, almost knocking Haral off-balance as he did so, but she quickly stood up as well, looking down the hall at the archangel.

Ordath glowed with faint orange-brown radiance, and he was a little stockier than most angels, with powerful, almost chiseled, muscles and brown hair and eyes. It suited him, as he was the archangel of strength and endurance. He was wearing elaborate white and gold vestments that suited him, and by his side was the elderly elf who'd served him for longer than Haral had lived, a woman whose name Haral could never remember.

"Your Excellency! My apologies, I didn't realize you were here!" Sorm said, giving a deep bow as he cleared his throat, and Haral followed suit with a curtsey, though she was more cautious due to her balance being off. "If I may, what do you mean by that?"

"The council recently received a most disturbing message from Uthren's Throne, followed by one with more detail. Apparently, a long-lost archangel has appeared once again," Ordath said, cracking a grim smile as he said. "You may have heard of Anathiel."

Haral swayed in place, feeling like she'd been hit over the head with a mallet. Anathiel had been one of the most influential archangels in history, and her determination had been an inspiration for most angels growing up. The idea of her suddenly reappearing, after everyone had believed that she was dead, was incredibly stunning, to say the least.

"A-Anathiel? She appeared in Uthren's Throne?" Sorm asked, straightening as he looked at Ordath in astonishment. The archangel nodded, and Sorm frowned, then asked, "Why would you say it's disturbing, then? Based on what I've heard about her, I'd think that she'd support us, not be a problem."

"I would have thought the same, if it weren't for several of the details in the subsequent message," Ordath said, looking surprisingly grim. "For one, she hasn't interacted with the angels in Uthren's Throne at all, and according to Rathien she's refused any audiences requested by angels. Even worse, supposedly she had an injured angel with her when she appeared in the city, and our best guess is that it's Roselynn."

"To be specific, rumor has it that Anathiel rescued an angel from the hells and took her to the temple for healing. According to reports, the angel had red hair and mostly normal-looking armor, but when I examined the timing I realized that it matched up with when your attack occurred, Sir Sorm," the elf said, her tone brisk and detached as she looked at them calmly, prompting dread to well up in Haral. "That being the case, the odds of it being Roselynn are fair."

"Which is a perfectly good reason to be concerned. Oh, Anathiel doesn't have much influence in the heavens these days, she's been gone for far too long, but if she tried to rally support, she'd be incredibly successful," Ordath explained, his tone and expression surprisingly grim. "Even some of the other council members are underestimating her, but I certainly won't. She's a blunt warrior, and always fought honorably. I think she'd *never* condone what we have planned."

"What can we do, then?" Sorm asked, his voice grim, and when Haral looked at him his face was ashen. Her face must not be much better, she realized as he spoke. "If she has Roselynn, she almost has to know what's going on, at least some of it."

"Agreed. Which is why we're going to start our plans early. The rest of the council has also insisted that we send a messenger to meet Anathiel and try to recruit her, but we're going to set things in motion so she *can't* stop us, just to be safe," Ordath said, his tone flat. "Sorm, which of the Holy Council's guards do you trust to assist us the most?"

"Aserial," Sorm said, not even hesitating as he frowned, then asked, "That said... don't we have a quarter of the Holy Council in the society? Why would you need the guards?"

"Because if the Holy Council is attacked, or even mostly destroyed, they need to honestly be able to say they had no idea what was coming," Haral said, the plans she'd helped draw up coming to mind instantly, and she winced slightly, looking at the others. "Do we have one of the gatecrushers ready, then?"

"We do. The plan is to use the prototype on the northern-most portal in Dolia," Ordath said, looking at Haral with a bit of approval in his gaze. "You realized what we planned quickly."

"I helped arrange for many of the supplies, so I know rather more than most people," Haral admitted, frowning as she thought, then asked curiously, a little dismayed that plans weren't going as expected, "May I ask why the portal so far north? I thought that we'd begin with the ones farthest away from Ness, not the closest."

"There has been a good deal of debate over that, but in the end, it came down to both convenience and relative safety," Ordath explained, obviously humoring Haral as he explained to Sorm as well. "The demons may be able to defend the portals farther south more easily, but even so they can't *stop* us. We can open the gates to the mortal world where we like, and the chances of them intercepting the gatecrushers if they're dropped are minimal. By comparison, they can strike back from the nearby portals more easily, so eliminating them first increases the safety of the heavens. A cornered rat is most dangerous, after all. Beyond that, the destruction likely to occur near the portal is liable to cause chaos, and if we time things to coincide with the attack on the Holy Council, it should lead many gods to think the demons are responsible."

Haral nodded, a bit relieved as she took in what Ordath was saying. If he was right, it meant that they were trying to take the safety of the heavens into account, which pleased her immensely. The mortals... well, she'd pray for the souls of the innocent, but there was little more she could do, while the demons weren't worth thinking about. As far as she was concerned, they could all die, and should if things went correctly.

"I see," Sorm said, rubbing his chin as he frowned thoughtfully. "I suppose it might work, but I worry that all it'll do is bring us farther into the open."

"If it does, so be it," Ordath said, then glanced at Haral as he added, "Regardless, I'd suggest getting some rest, Haral. If things go poorly, I expect you'll want to help fight off the traitors trying to stop us."

"Of course, Your Excellency!" Haral said, determination rushing through her as she stood up straighter, and Ordath chuckled, nodded, then went on his way, the elf at his side.

"Would you like some help, dear?" Sorm asked, concern beginning to work its way into his voice, and she could see the worry in his eyes. "I've heard horrible things about that room."

"It was terrible," Haral admitted, then smiled wanly as she added. "Some company would be lovely, though. It was a very hard week."

"Then company you will have," Sorm said firmly, and he helped her down the hall toward the room that Haral usually used, his solid, warm body more comforting than Haral could express, and she quickly found herself leaning into him.

Roselynn and the others could wait, at least for now.

CHAPTER 28

"This is more impressive than I anticipated," Kitania said, looking around the city as her eyebrows slowly rose. "I was expecting someplace smaller, and possibly more fortified."

They were inside Uthren's Throne at this point, though at least they'd managed to clean up enough over the previous three days that they didn't draw *too* many stares, though their group did seem to be garnering a lot of attention. That was probably at least partially Kitania's fault, though there were few enough elves in the crowds that Maura and Yain drew a fair number of gazes as well.

The city was rather impressive and at least four times the size that Kitania had expected it to be. She'd only been to two cities that were larger, and both of those had been major trade ports in human kingdoms to the south. Uthren's Throne was simply different, and she was impressed by how nice the buildings on either side of the road were, along with the rising spires toward the center of the city, along with a vast, raised area that she guessed was the temple grounds.

"It was smaller once, which you can tell by the old fortress walls. The problem is that the city grew too quickly, and eventually the government simply gave up on trying to expand the walls since the city hasn't been attacked in centuries," Yain said, pointing to the right, and Kitania strained her eyes for a moment before she realized that some of the stonework peeking over the edge of several buildings were old stone walls in the distance. "I really don't blame them, with as much work as building proper walls takes."

"I believe it," Isalla said, looking around unhappily, her hand clutching Kitania's tightly. The angel had been quite clingy the last few days, which Kitania really couldn't blame her for, not after what had happened to Rose. Isalla paused, then asked, "Where are you planning to stop?"

"There's a good inn near the walls that elves favor, called the Season of Light. It's run by elves, which is a large part of why we like it, and it'll give us a chance to clean up before going to visit the temple," Yain said, the worry in her expression easing slightly as she glanced back at them, hesitating before she continued. "I think that's the wisest decision, considering who we're going to be meeting."

"Entirely agreed," Isalla said immediately, and it was all Kitania could do to keep from interjecting again, and she firmly bit her tongue.

The others had been incredulous that she'd suspected that Anna had been an archangel and hadn't said anything. For her part, Kitania *was* slightly surprised that she truly was Anathiel, but not as much as everyone else had been, and they'd eventually accepted that she wasn't going to reveal someone else's secrets. She suspected her lack of surprise was at least partly because she'd spent so much time with Anna in her youth, and that experience was what made her think that Anna wouldn't be upset by them showing up in their normal clothing. Not that the others would be willing to hear that, so she kept her mouth shut.

"I'd almost be willing to kill for a hot bath… dare I hope that the inn has them available?" Maura asked, her tone betraying hope and just a hint of wariness.

"Of course, though you'd best be prepared for a wooden tub, not a bathhouse. If you're willing to risk those, there are several that you could pay to visit in the neighborhood, or there were last time I was here," Yain replied in amusement, leading the way down the street as they threaded their way through the crowd.

Eziel was following them with the horse carrying their things, so Kitania followed, secure in the knowledge their things would get there. If nothing else, Eziel had proven to Isalla that she was on their side, which helped ease Kitania's worries slightly.

A flicker of movement to the side caught Kitania's attention, and her hand snapped out reflexively to catch the young man's hand that'd been darting toward her coin purse. Her hand closed around his wrist with his fingers only inches from her purse, and a pair of hazel eyes belatedly widened as they rose to meet her gaze. The human boy had a slightly freckled face and dirty blonde hair, and he opened his mouth to speak, only to have Kitania interrupt.

"Don't even bother," Kitania told him bluntly, looking into his eyes steadily as she glanced down at his hand again and continued. "You were trying for my purse and failed. And if your *friend* doesn't back away from my companion, I'll call the guard."

The boy that'd been approaching Isalla while they were distracted froze, and her captive swallowed hard, then said, "I… I didn't… you're mistaken what I was trying for, milady, and—"

"I *said* not to bother," Kitania said flatly, glancing at the other boy with a mirthless smile that deliberately bared her fangs, prompting both of them to pale a little as she continued. "I have had a *horrible* week, and I don't have the time or patience for this. The two of *you* are going to go tell your friends to steer clear of us, because the next time I see a pickpocket, they're going to be explaining themselves to the city guard if they're lucky, is that clear? I'd also suggest trying to find a better way of making a living, as one of these days you're going to find someone far less forgiving than I am."

"Ah, um, yes, ma'am," the boy said, gulping audibly as he paled still more, and Kitania smiled.

"Good. Now go away," Kitania told him, letting go of his hand. She watched the two disappear into the crowd, then nodded to Yain and the others who'd stopped to watch her.

As they got moving again, Isalla asked, "Why'd you let them go? I mean, they *were* trying to steal from you."

"Because there really wasn't much point right now. From what I've seen of human cities, there are countless pickpockets who're young, and often the punishment for their crimes are… particularly harsh, in my opinion. I wish I knew a good way to prevent them from *needing* to be on the streets, or getting them jobs, but I don't," Kitania said, and bit back the urge to continue that such wasn't needed in the hells. The survival rate was low enough that there were *always* jobs to be had, but that was a problem in its own right.

"Well, maybe so. Aren't there thieves back where you're from, though?" Isalla asked, frowning unhappily.

"Of course there are, and many of them are more skilled than children like that. I don't like *them* either, and I'd turn those people in without batting an eyelash. They usually chose to be in a position like that, unlike the boys from before," Kitania said, guilt flickering through her briefly at the thought of being abandoned on the streets. At least she hadn't had to worry about that happening when she was young.

"I suppose that's true… I certainly wouldn't," Isalla admitted, following the others through the streets. Now she was keeping an eye out for pickpockets, Kitania noticed, suppressing the urge to smile. It was better late than never, she supposed. The problem was that as an angel, Isalla had probably never been targeted before, while as a human noble she was a much easier target.

Kitania didn't spot any more attempts to steal from them on the way to the inn, though she wasn't naïve enough to believe that she could spot anyone who might try. Most of them, certainly, but a truly skilled pickpocket would probably manage to avoid even her notice. On the other hand, she was sure there were far easier targets as well.

Reaching the inn, Kitania's eyebrows arched slightly, as it was only a street over from the old city walls, which were still well-kept from her point of view. Looking at the inn was the real reason for her surprise, though, since the inn was a nice enough building, but it was little different than any of the inns they'd passed on their way to it. The sign out front had two leaves painted on it, one red and the other green, and between them was a painted rendition of the sun.

"Here we are," Yain announced, a hint of relief in her voice as she glanced back, smiling as she said. "Emma? You can hand the horse over to the stable hand, and we can arrange for rooms."

"Thank you, but I'll go with and bring in our luggage," Eziel replied politely, smiling in return. "I'm sure it won't take long."

"As you like," Yain said, and led the way into the inn.

Kitania followed, and as she did her eyebrows rose even more for a moment, then her surprise settled down as she realized what was different about the inn.

The Season of Light was like any other decent inn she'd seen in the human kingdoms superficially, but that was only at first glance. Even the interior looked a lot like the others, but she expected humans would notice that something was off about it. The simple explanation was that the inn was in better repair and everything was higher quality to begin with.

Where most inns would get by with cheap, sturdy furniture, the chairs and tables Kitania could see were not just sturdy, but well-crafted to last for a long time. The walls were similar, with carefully planed boards that, while they might have stains, were obviously regularly cleaned and otherwise maintained. It was a subtle difference, but about what she expected from elves, with their longer lifespans and tendency to try to take care of their homes.

There were a decent number of people at the tables in the common room of the inn, about half of which were humans, while the remainder were a near even split between elves and half-elves. There were two maids serving as well, a pretty human and the other a half-elf, while behind the counter was a brown-haired elven man who looked up from the slate board in front of him. He smiled, looking much more handsome as his brown eyes twinkled at them.

"Ah, travelers! Welcome to Season of Light, how may I help you?" the man asked, pausing as he looked at Yain and asked, "As a matter of fact... I think I remember you, madam. Did you stay here once before?"

"Yes, I did, Master Dominick. It's been the better part of a decade, but I visited once before with a few family members," Yain said, smiling warmly as she nodded. "I'm Yain, and I'm surprised you remembered me at all."

"I have a good memory for faces, which is good in this business," Dominick replied with a chuckle, his gaze sweeping across their group, his eyebrows rising slightly as he saw Kitania's tail, but he didn't betray any further shock as he asked, "Now, what may I do for you?"

"We'd like three rooms for two, if we could," Yain said, her tone growing a little brisker as she continued. "I think we'll be here for at least three days, possibly more, and we'll definitely need baths. Unfortunately, we have an audience at the temple *today*, which makes things a bit tighter than I'd like."

"The temple? Today? Well, that's certainly going to be a problem for you," Dominick said, looking taken aback.

"Why do you say that?" Vinara asked, frowning as she continued. "I heard that it's always open for pilgrims."

"Yes, well, *normally* they don't have one of the most famous generals and archangels of the heavens in residence," Dominick replied, smiling wryly as he shook his head. "Anathiel arrived three days ago, and ever since the temple has been flooded with petitioners. Why, I even heard that she and Krath had a sparring match yesterday, which by all reports was glorious to behold! Getting inside isn't going to be easy for weeks, I expect. Still, you might be able to manage it."

"That means we'd probably better get those baths sooner, rather than later," Kitania murmured, glancing at Isalla as she asked, "Do you have the rooms available?"

"Certainly! Let's get you settled in while I have the baths drawn," Dominick said, pulling out a drawer with keys in it. "Do you need any luggage brought in?"

"Emma went to take care of that and to get the horse settled in," Yain explained, pulling out her coin purse. "Thank you for your help."

"I just hope you enjoy your stay in Uthren's Throne," Dominick replied, smiling broadly. "Now, as for payment..."

~

THE BETTER PART of an hour later, Kitania let out a tiny sigh as they headed down the street toward the temple, a tiny bit wistful. The bath hadn't been exactly *bad*, but bathing in a tub just made her remember her home in the hells, which spoiled the pleasure it caused, at least somewhat.

Isalla seemed to read her mind, as the angel glanced over and asked, her tone a touch wry, "Missing your hot spring bath?"

"Was it that obvious?" Kitania asked, looking back guiltily.

"Well, yes? I mean, *I* miss it, even if I could do without the scent of sulfur," Isalla said, a light blush rising in her cheeks. "It certainly was a nice luxury."

"Wait, what's this about a hot spring?" Vinara asked, her eyebrows rising suddenly.

"I built my home under a hill where a hot spring welled up," Kitania explained, keeping her explanation hopefully vague enough that bystanders wouldn't guess where she was from as she continued. "I gave it a separate room and set things up so that the hot water was filtered before coming into a large tub, then drained into the stream like normal. It was lovely, and every time I have to bathe normally, I miss it."

"That… oh, that would be *nice*," Maura exclaimed, her eyes widening a little. "There's only a couple of hot springs in the Forest of Sighs, and the people who control them charge others for access. I went once, and it was lovely, even if the water was pretty opaque."

"It certainly can be, if you don't filter the water right. It took some work to get the enchantments for that, but I think it was worth it in the end," Kitania said and smiled even more as Yain looked at Maura.

"I believe it," Yain said, letting out a soft sigh. "I can't remember having the chance to use a large, hot bath more than a handful of times in my life. It sounds absolutely decadent."

"I'm not sure about decadent, but certainly nice for those taking baths," Vinara said, eyeing Kitania crossly as she murmured, "I see you didn't suffer much in your absence. In any case, it makes me wonder why more places don't enchant pools to create warm water, and then charge for access."

"That would be the bathhouses mentioned before," Eziel said quietly. "They charge a relatively minor amount, which makes people more likely to make use of their services."

"I might have to give one a try after we're back to Dolia, and… oh my, I see Dominick wasn't joking," Kitania said, pausing as she caught sight of the plaza in front of the temple grounds, along with the steps leading up to the temple itself.

The plaza was larger than she'd expected to begin with, though when she thought about it Kitania really should have known better. With so many pilgrims coming to Uthren's Throne and the emphasis on faith in the nation, it only made sense to have a large plaza in front of it, and dozens of stalls had been set up to sell things around the plaza, mostly food from what she could see. The stairs ended at a gate that opened into the temple and its grounds proper, and to a degree the place looked like a fortress to Kitania, even if many of the buildings were airier and beautiful compared to most fortresses.

The problem was the sheer number of people she could see. At least a thousand people had to be crowded into the plaza or on the steps leading up to the temple, if not even more than that, and Kitania hated to think about what would happen if someone fell over in the middle of it. Most of the people looked like they were human, but a surprisingly large percentage were dwarves, and an even larger number looked like knights, mercenaries, or soldiers. On the other hand, Anathiel *was* the archangel of war, so it made some sense… though Kitania would've expected them to be more interested in the deity of war, whoever that was at the moment.

"Getting through that is going to be… interesting," Isalla said, sounding a little stunned.

"That's one way to put it," Yain said, eying the crowd unhappily. "I wonder if we can even *get* there before they close the temple for the night."

"There's only one way to find out," Maura said, and she led the way as she tried to forge a path through the crowd.

Maura's attempt didn't go as planned, mostly because she

simply wasn't large or strong enough to force her way through the crowd. Instead, they ended up slowly working their way through the mass of people bit by bit, and Kitania quickly regretted their choice to come there, as her nose was assaulted not just by powerful clashing perfumes, but also by the sheer mass of people in one place.

Slowly they made progress, though, and though she was separated from Vinara and the elves, Kitania, Eziel, and Isalla made their way toward the steps, where they managed to meet up with the others again. It'd taken a disgustingly long time, but none of them had the energy to try to shout over the crowd, so they instead moved to the side of the steps where people were ascending and got into the line of petitioners filtering up onto the temple grounds.

This time they were able to move faster, if only because half the stairs were intended to move upward, while the other half was going down, and they didn't have people loitering and talking. Still, it took a lot longer than it should have to reach the temple grounds, and Kitania's eyes widened as she took in the sight of dozens of buildings around the grounds, though they were behind fences that funneled everyone who was entering toward a set of gardens and a larger temple. The temple was probably for receiving guests, while the gardens were beautiful and likely for reflecting by the pilgrims, Kitania suspected, though right now everywhere was crowded, and frequent priests in light blue, red, or white and gold robes moved about, speaking to people while looking somewhat harried.

"Where to?" Kitania asked, having to raise her voice to be heard over the hubbub surrounding them.

"The temple!" Yain almost yelled, wincing as she did so. "If we want to contact her, that's where to do it!"

Kitania simply nodded, exchanging a pitying look with Vinara, as she realized that the keen hearing of an elf was probably unpleasant under these circumstances. Vinara considered, then Kitania saw her murmur something, drawing sigils in the air as she cast a spell. A shimmering, near-transparent bubble surrounded Maura and Yain's heads, and Kitania could *see* them visibly relax, then look at Vinara in relief.

She guessed that Vinara had dampened the sound which reached them, which was probably for the best.

Eventually they reached the temple, and after one look at the gaudy interior, Kitania winced and focused purely on following the others. She did notice that it looked like a couple of the three statues of Uthren's deities had been replaced recently, but it really didn't matter. Instead, she followed as Yain made her way to a female acolyte in red robes, and waited as the three people ahead of them went about whatever they were requesting. One received a blessing, and the brunette dealt with the other two briskly before focusing on them.

"Yes, how may I assist you?" the woman asked, a barely concealed note of impatience in her voice.

"We're here to request an audience with Lady Anathiel. She's —" Yain began, only to have the acolyte interrupt.

"No. Lady Anathiel isn't seeing *any* visitors, let alone random visitors who came in the front door," the acolyte said impatiently, her blue eyes flashing with irritation.

"But she's expecting us!" Isalla protested, inhaling to continue, but the woman didn't give her time to say anything more.

"You and half the city, by all estimations! No, she isn't seeing *anyone*, so if you don't have business in the temple to do with *our* deities, I'll have to ask you to move along!" the woman said bluntly, her eyes narrowing as she looked at them. "We're busy enough we don't have time to deal with common gawkers."

Even Kitania was taken aback by the woman's vehemence, and she promptly ignored them to start talking to the next person in line. On the other hand, Vinara looked around, then murmured, "I think it's time to send a message, hm?"

"An excellent idea," Yain said, and they pushed themselves to the side, ignoring the acolyte's irritated look as Vinara began casting another spell.

CHAPTER 29

"*L*ady Anna, my apologies for disturbing you, but when we requested an audience it was denied. We're currently standing in the outer temple next to what the inscriptions say is the Shrine of Blood." Vinara's voice was a whisper on the wind, and caused Anna to stop in mid-sentence, raising an eyebrow in surprise.

"Oh dear. My apologies, Anathiel," Cyclone said apologetically, and Krath blinked, looking between Anna and Cyclone in confusion. Anna shared the confusion for a brief moment, then she realized what had happened.

"Ah, I forgot that you can eavesdrop on wind-based message spells simply by being nearby. My apologies, Krath, but it appears that my *other* guests arrived and were turned away," Anna said, smiling wryly as she glanced toward the front of the temple, adding, "I suspect that it's chaotic enough that they're simply turning away *everyone* asking for an audience with me."

"That sounds likely, considering the complaints I've heard from my priests," Krath said, his confusion clearing up as he tugged on his beard gently, chuckling as he added, "I must say, having *priests* confused me for the first year with the mantle. I don't mind much anymore, but it's an awful lot of responsibility."

Anna nodded, smiling slightly as she murmured, "I never had many priests, not since angels don't generally worship archangels, but I had a few champions and the like. They're long gone, though. The nature of my mantle and the people they were... well, their deaths weren't unexpected."

Both of the deities fell silent at that, and Anna could understand why. Few deities liked being reminded the mortality of their trusted followers. It was why so many archangels and deities eventually passed their mantles to someone else and lived out the remainder of their lives quietly.

Suddenly Cyclone cleared his throat and sat up, changing the subject. "Regardless, if the people you've been waiting for are here, we should have them escorted into the temple proper. One moment."

Cyclone rang a small bell that was resting on the table, one which Anna knew was magically linked to a servant's room nearby. Moments later the door opened and a priestess in light blue robes stepped in, bowing deeply.

"You called, Your Holiness?" the priestess asked, maintaining the bow.

"Yes. A group of Lady Anathiel's guests just arrived in the outer temple and were turned away. They're near the Shrine of Blood, and require escort to the inner temple," Cyclone said, glancing at Anna as he asked, "What do they look like, again? I believe you told the priesthood before, but I'd rather she was able to identify them directly."

"Of course. The most obvious will be a woman with a dragon's tail and horns, but there are two elves among their number, as well as three humans, a blonde and two brunettes," Anna said, smiling slightly as she looked at the priestess as she straightened. Part of Anna was going through the suggestions she'd make for adjusting the woman's appearance if she was in the spire, though she knew that the woman would never end up there, considering the spire was on the opposite side of the world and in the hells.

"I will retrieve them immediately, Your Holiness, Your Excellency," the priestess said, nodding quickly as she smiled and added, "I will be back presently."

The woman turned to leave, and as she did, Anna went back to what she'd been saying before they were interrupted. "Now, as for your lightning, I've noticed that you tend to focus it too *much*, Krath. You need to learn to let it permeate your body, so even if something strikes from an unexpected angle it provides some defense. It won't work against everything, but..."

Krath leaned forward, listening closely, and Anna inwardly hoped she wasn't giving advice to a future enemy.

~

Kitania looked up as a back door opened and a priestess stepped into the antechamber. Despite the acolyte having pointedly hinted they should leave several times, their group had stubbornly stayed, though Kitania grew worried when the acolyte had spoken to a temple guard and several other guards had started gathering. It was likely they'd be forced to leave soon, which would be *very* annoying.

The priestess had pale blue robes, and at the sight of her the temple guards quickly snapped to attention, obviously startled. She spoke briefly to them as she scanned the room, then her gaze settled on Kitania and the others. The woman smiled slightly, then approached. As she did so, the acolyte caught sight of her, and the young woman's eyes widened.

"Mother Kora, I didn't know you were visiting!" the acolyte exclaimed, standing up straighter, and she was about to speak further when the priestess raised a hand to interrupt.

"I know you didn't, as I'm acting on the instructions of the Lord of Winds," Mother Kora replied calmly, smiling at her for a moment, then looked at Kitania and the others as she continued. "I believe that you're here for an audience, is that correct?"

"Yes, it is," Kitania said, relief rushing through her. A tiny part of her had been afraid that the woman was planning to kick them out, but it seemed their message had gotten through to Anna.

"Excellent. Just the six of you, yes?" the priestess asked, looking across them as the acolyte's eyes widened enormously.

"Yes," Isalla said, looking relieved as she smiled. "There was a seventh, but she should already be inside."

"Excellent. If you'd follow me?" Kora said, turning toward the doors again, and paused near the temple guards to add, "These six are allowed inside, but not any others."

"Of course, ma'am," the guard replied, bowing his head.

Kitania and the others quickly followed, and the demoness couldn't help a smile at the shock on the acolyte's face as they were led out of the crowded antechamber. On the other hand, the priestess's caution was obviously well-placed, as at least three people Kitania saw tried to follow Eziel through the door. Fortunately, the guards stopped them, and the door shut to give a semblance of quiet, though the noise still managed to filter through the door.

"Now that we're more easily able to speak, I presume you're here for a meeting with Lady Anathiel?" Kora asked, looking them over curiously.

"That's right. One of our friends was injured, and she took her away, then told us to ask for an audience with her here," Isalla spoke quickly, her voice a little nervous. "I... is our friend alright? Do you know?"

"I'm afraid I do not. I'm aware that she brought someone with her, but they have been sequestered in her chambers since her arrival," Kora said, her tone perfectly polite as she examined them, then nodded. "I must stress that you each need to be polite, as Lady Anathiel is currently in the company of the Lord of Winds and the Lord of Thunder. As the guardian deities of Uthren, they expect others to be respectful."

"Of course," Kitania said, a thread of dread rushing through her. Two deities beyond Anna didn't fill her with any sense of joy, just worry, so she took a deep breath as she tried to focus.

Murmurs of agreement came from the others, and Kitania noticed that Vinara had been unusually quiet lately. She glanced over, and she could see the concern in her old friend's eyes. Vinara met her gaze and flashed a smile, but it was quite brief and only increased Kitania's worries.

"Good, if you'd follow me? We'll have to go through the gardens to reach our destination," Kora said, her voice brisk.

The priestess swiftly led them out of the temple and into broad gardens that would be perfect for secluded contemplation, in Kitania's opinion. There were numerous acolytes tending to the gardens, both male and female, though there was a slight preponderance of men. As they walked Kitania noticed that their clothing was usually in one of three sets of colors; blue, red, or white and gold.

"May I ask what the different colors of robes mean? I'm guessing its which deity you serve, but I'd like to be certain," Kitania said, breaking the silence when they were about halfway to the largest structure on the temple grounds.

"That's right," Kora said, glancing at Kitania with a smile of approval. "Those of us who wear blue are the devoted of Cyclone, Lord of Wind and eldest of the guardian deities. You were at the Shrine of Blood, devoted to Sanguine, the Lady of Blood, whose colors are red and gold. As for Krath, the Lord of Thunder, his colors are white and gold. There are a handful who are devoted to more than just one of the Three, but it isn't common, and they usually wear a combination of the colors."

"Interesting," Kitania said, smiling as she relaxed slightly.

"I've always found it fascinating how stable Uthren is, even when the deities have passed down their mantles," Yain said, her voice musing as she looked around. "In some ways you've always seemed even more stable than those countries who haven't had their deities change over the millennia."

Kora nodded, slowing down slightly as she replied. "Indeed, it's something of a puzzle, isn't it? However, I personally think that it's because of the changes that we've been stable. None of the Three can make decisions without convincing one of the others, and the mantle being passed down means there's a chance for new ideas to come about, while My Lord is old enough that he has the wisdom of the past to draw upon. I believe it's a delicate balance, and one they've striven to keep over the centuries."

"Hm…" Maura murmured, looking intrigued, but while she opened her mouth to speak, she shut it without saying anything further.

"May I ask what your relationship with Lady Anathiel is? I'm startled that she'd accept an audience with any of you, after rejecting so many other requests, including those of the Heavenly Orders," Kora asked, looking back at them speculatively, curiosity in her eyes. "You don't have to answer, of course. I won't pry further."

"I believe I'm the only one with a lengthy history with her, but… I didn't know who she was at the time, mind you, but she taught me to fight," Kitania said and smiled slightly as she added softly, "I simply knew her as Lady Anna."

"I see," Kora said, glancing back at Kitania with wide eyes. "I wouldn't have expected that, and you've had an amazing opportunity."

"That I have," Kitania agreed, continuing to follow Kora toward the looming building ahead of them. At the very highest point in the back she could see a smaller building that was open to the air, and Kitania wondered what it was used for. The front was open, anyway.

They entered the buildings below that, though, and none of the numerous guards tried to stop Kora, leading Kitania to believe that she was either higher-ranking than she'd initially thought, or they knew she was on a task set by one of their deities. Possibly both, but almost certainly the latter. The hallways weren't quite as gaudy as the others had been, but there were numerous tapestries with different scenes stitched into them that Kitania had to assume were legends about the different deities of Uthren. Soon enough they came to a solid pair of double doors, and Kora slowed.

"Here we are. Please, remember to be on your best behavior," Kora warned them again, a flicker of nervousness in her expression, prompting pity to well up in Kitania.

"We'll do our best," Kitania promised sincerely.

"*I* certainly don't want to be smote by an angry deity," Maura murmured, prompting a titter of laughter from most of the others.

"Good," Kora said, waiting until they'd quieted down before knocking on the door.

"Come in!" a resonant voice replied, and even the sound of it sent a shiver down Kitania's spine. This wouldn't be the *first* she met a mortal god, but it'd be the first time she'd met one of those solidly on the side of angels. Alserah didn't count, not really.

While she was distracted, Kora opened the door and stepped inside smoothly, taking several steps forward before bowing deeply, her voice seemingly calm. "I have brought Lady Anathiel's guests, Your Holiness."

"Excellent," the man on the left said, the same one who'd spoken before, and Kitania only saw a glimpse of his brown eyes before she bowed as well, shivering at the aura of power that struck her.

The well-appointed room had a modest round table in the middle of it, as well as four chairs, though one didn't match the dark, polished wood of the others. Three of the chairs were occupied, and Anna sat in the one that didn't fit, smiling warmly as she relaxed in her white toga, her wings comfortably folded behind her.

In the other two chairs were other deities, both of them human men, and their power was obvious, though not quite as overwhelming as Anna's was. One was the man with blue robes and brown eyes, while the other was stockier, and Kitania thought she could smell a hint of ozone from him as he studied her.

"Ah, *there* you are! I'd expected you to arrive yesterday, not today," Anna said, her eyes twinkling as she looked at them. "I take it I underestimated how long the trip would take."

"I'm afraid that the attack killed all but one of our mounts, Lady Anna, so we had to walk once we received healing," Kitania said politely, holding her bow. "We arrived earlier today, and immediately made our way here. May I ask if Lynn is alright?"

"Ah, Roselynn was going by Lynn? Fair enough," Anna said, and paused.

A moment later the first deity spoke, his voice calm. "You may all rise. May we have some privacy, priestess? Thank you for your assistance."

"It was my pleasure, Your Holiness," Kora said, and Kitania

glanced over just in time to see the woman leave the room, while the others straightened cautiously, their nervousness obvious.

"As for Roselynn, she's doing well. It'll take a few more days for her to heal, but that's as I expected. To do it right takes a while, as the method I chose is more beneficial to her than simply using regeneration magic would be," Anna said, meeting Kitania's eyes with a hint of concern and... something else, something that Kitania couldn't quite identify, and she smiled. "Now, would you mind introducing yourselves to Cyclone and Krath? Cyclone is an old friend of mine."

"Of course," Kitania said, turning slightly to face the two men as she continued. "I am called Kim Fireblood and trained with Lady Anna when I was young. It's an honor to meet the two of you."

Isalla audibly swallowed, then spoke, her voice soft. "I'm... Isalla, formerly of the Order of the Phoenix. Yes, I'm an angel like Rose, Roselynn, I mean, and we were traveling in disguise together."

Kitania saw the expression of surprise cross Krath's face, though Cyclone was far more impassive. Despite that, they didn't say anything as the others introduced themselves. Neither Eziel or Vinara used their real names, and the succubus inserted a bit of nervousness into her voice, though that easily could be real, and the elves went by their own names. Maura and Yain didn't have to feign their nervousness, she knew, but she couldn't blame them. Even if they worked in Alserah's palace, it wasn't as though they interacted with her every day, and Alserah was *their* goddess.

"It's a pleasure to meet all of you, and a trifle intriguing. I'd ask why you were in hiding, Isalla, but my conversations with Anathiel have led me to believe that ignorance is better in this case," Cyclone said, and his gaze drifted to Kitania as he raised an eyebrow curiously. "That said... you truly trained someone, Anathiel? I thought you said that you were tired of warfare until recently."

"Just because I'm tired of war doesn't mean that I became naïve. The world is a dangerous place, Cyclone, and people should be able to defend themselves," Anna replied dryly, smiling as she glanced at Kitania warmly, her eyes glittering with mirth. It was such a different appearance for the angel, and yet at the same time it didn't feel wrong to Kitania. "As for training her, Kim was a gifted student for a mortal, even if she *doesn't* have wings. Have you been keeping in practice?"

"As best I can, yes. I was in a location where using a cloudpiercer was ill-advised, so used a sword for quite a while, but I've been trying to get my old form back," Kitania replied, resisting the urge to say anything more. She *really* disliked having to speak half-truths like this, particularly when deities could be far better at noticing inconsistencies.

"I see," Cyclone said, looking at them curiously, then let out a sigh as he murmured. "I take it you wish to speak with them in private?"

"Yes, but there's no need for the two of you to leave. I'm a guest in your temple, after all, and they're at least partly here to check on their friend," Anna said, standing up gracefully as she smiled at them and nodded. "I'll take them to my room so they can see how things are coming along."

"As you wish. I hope to speak with you again, Lady Anathiel," Krath said, standing quickly, and Kitania almost did a double take as she recognized the adoration in his eyes when he looked at Anna. *That* was unexpected, and she had no idea how to react to the idea, even if pretty much everyone in the Spire of Confession had loved Anna. They weren't gods, after all.

"I'm sure we will," Anna said, nodding graciously as she glanced at Cyclone and added, "I'll see both of you later. For now, I'll bid you a good day."

"And you as well," Cyclone replied, nodding but not standing.

Anna headed for the door, and without a word the others made a path for her, all but Eziel, who quickly opened it for the archangel. Stepping outside, Anna spoke calmly. "Thank you for getting the door. Now, would you follow me? I'd prefer to speak where we aren't going to be overheard."

"Of course, Your Excellency," Vinara replied politely, and Anna snorted softly, shaking her head.

"Oh, I don't want to hear that from *you*. Lady Anna is more than enough, and possibly even too much," Anna replied, pausing as they followed her out. Kitania resisted the urge to look back as she closed the door at last, letting out the faintest breath of relief at being out of the presence of the deities. She knew Anna and was far more comfortable with her, even if it'd been a long time since they were together.

"May I ask why it's taking time for Rose to heal? I've been really worried," Isalla said, her voice unsteady as she swallowed hard, and Kitania quickly took her hand and squeezed it gently. Isalla gripped her hand hard in return, which didn't surprise Kitania.

"That's one of those discussions for in private," Anna said firmly, gesturing for them to follow. "Come along, my rooms are warded fairly heavily."

"As you say, Lady Anna," Kitania murmured, and followed as Anna walked down the hallways, looking perfectly at home as she ignored the guards and priests along their path.

No one obstructed them, though the curious looks they received were frequent and Kitania could practically feel the scrutiny they were under. Anna wanted to speak privately for a good reason, obviously, and Kitania tried to pick up the pace a little, since she and Isalla were in the back.

Soon enough they reached an ornate hall with a set of doors which practically radiated magic, even if the runes of spells reinforcing the walls were fairly well hidden, and Anna laid a hand on the door. Kitania saw the wards dim, and Anna opened the door, speaking calmly. "Come in, all of you."

The others stepped into the room, and Kitania took in the room with a glance. The bed's sheets were perfectly folded, which some might think was done by a maid, but Kitania suspected that Anna had done it herself. The room was quite nice, and the only thing that was out of place was the cot next to the larger bed, resting on a drop cloth and with Rose's armor resting on an armor rack behind it, next to a rack holding Anna's equipment. Resting on the cot was Rose, and Kitania's eyes widened as she saw Ember laying across Rose, flames gently billowing around its blade.

"Rose?" Kitania asked, and almost jumped as the door clicked shut behind them.

The next moment Kitania froze as a warm pair of arms embraced her from behind and Anna almost picked her up, squeezing tightly as she spoke, and everyone else stared at her.

"Oh, Kitania, what *am* I supposed to do with you?" Anna asked, and Kitania blinked, startled and nonplused.

CHAPTER 30

"Um, Anna? What are you doing?" Kitania sounded stunned, which was about how Isalla felt as well, watching the archangel hugging the demoness. The relief on Anathiel's face was visible, which confused Isalla enough that her concern for Rose receded slightly.

Glancing around, Isalla realized she wasn't alone in her confusion, as even Vinara looked puzzled. The succubus was the one who should know the most about Anathiel besides Kitania, so if she didn't know what was going on, no one else would have a clue.

"I'm hugging you. Isn't it obvious?" Anathiel replied, a slightly teasing edge to her voice. "I know you were observant enough to figure that out before, but I suppose it's possible that a millennium in hiding might have dulled your mind."

"That isn't what I meant!" Kitania protested, craning her neck to try to look at the archangel. "I can *tell* that you're hugging me, but I'm not sure why."

Anathiel laughed and let go, taking a step backward as she looked at everyone in the room, then shrugged, folding her arms. The archangel's smile was almost infectious, and she looked at Kitania for a long moment.

"Mm… well, I suppose you *wouldn't* know, after how much

effort Estalia and I took to mislead others. Take off the illusion, Kitania. I want to look at my daughter properly," Anathiel said, amusement evident in her voice.

Her words caused the atmosphere throughout the room to practically freeze, and astonishment rushed through Isalla as she suddenly looked at Kitania, who wasn't moving, her mouth slightly open.

"W-what?" Kitania stammered, taken completely off guard for what was likely the first time since Isalla had met the demoness. Her reaction just made Isalla's sense of disbelief grow stronger.

"I said I wanted a proper look at you. Your mother and I agreed that it was time to reveal the full truth to you, even if she *had* intended to explain things when you got back to the palace," Anathiel said, clicking her tongue chidingly as she circled Kitania. "Now, off with the illusion, hm? I want a proper look at you… it's good you didn't take after any other ashborn, or our attempt wouldn't have worked at all."

"Wait, Kitania is half *angel*?" Vinara protested, her eyes huge. "That… wait, but I thought her sire was Her Majesty's brother!"

"A story which we came up with, and he agreed not to contradict. If people learned that Estalia had a child with an angel, it would have caused problems, likely with more dissidents trying to overthrow Estalia or to kill me… and that would have led to revealing who I was. That was something she was trying to avoid at all costs, so it was necessary," Anathiel explained, even as Kitania seemed almost rooted in place from shock, which Isalla couldn't blame her for. The archangel's eyes darkened as she continued softly. "That was why she sent you to me when you were rebellious, Kitania. She hoped I could do better with you, and I… I nearly told you many times, but I couldn't. I was too afraid to tell you, with how things had gone, and… well, I should have. I'm sorry I didn't, because if I had, maybe you wouldn't have joined the war."

"I… I just…" Kitania said, still looking utterly flummoxed.

"Kitania? Take off the bracelet," Vinara ordered, then paused, looking at Isalla as she added, "Or you take it off for her, Isalla. She's obviously too surprised to do anything."

"She's not the only one who's shocked!" Isalla protested, but reached for Kitania's wrist anyway, looking at Anathiel with wide eyes as she asked, "She's the daughter of you and Estalia? How? I mean, you're both women!"

"Magic is a wondrous thing," Anathiel replied, sniffing slightly as she smiled and added, "Though it was only used to let her bear Kitania to term, honestly. We discussed things, and she *did* need an heir. After we learned about Kitania's power, though… well, we decided it was best to refrain from having more children. It isn't as though she wasn't a handful all on her own."

"I just can't believe that neither of you *told* me before this!" Kitania finally managed, just as Isalla removed the bracelet and the illusion masking her appearance vanished. The demoness looked a little outraged and shook off the hand that Vinara had laid on her shoulder, her armored tail lashing as she said, "*Kingdoms* have risen and fallen dozens of times in the time I've been alive, and you led me to believe that my father was someone else entirely!"

"Kitty, calmly," Isalla urged quickly, grabbing Kitania's arm, and Kitania looked back at her, anger flashing in the demoness's eyes for a moment as she took a deep breath, but Anathiel spoke first.

"I'm sorry," the archangel said simply, regret filling her voice as she looked at Kitania. Isalla looked at her at the same time as Kitania, and the sorrow in Anathiel's gaze startled her.

"You're *sorry*?" Kitania demanded, her voice half-breaking. "That… that's…"

"Kitania, people make mistakes. They get set in their ways and go with what they know. It's all too easy to do, you know that," Isalla said, trying to calm her friend down, her concern growing stronger. Kitania's mood was impacting her own, and not necessarily for the better. Her steady presence was usually soothing, especially after what had happened to Rose, and to see her almost breaking down… well, it caused Isalla's stomach to knot up.

"That's—" Kitania began but cut herself off as she raised a finger in the air, breathing in and almost visibly counting to herself, then let out the breath as she forcibly steadied herself. When she spoke again, her voice was taut, and she reached over to squeeze Isalla's arm almost painfully tightly. "No, now is *not* the time to get into this. Not with so much company. I'm sorry to have made a scene at all, and I should apologize to Maura and Yain at the least. For now, you've seen me, Anna. I'm not going to pretend to be alright with things, but we can discuss that later. In private. For now, I'd like to know what in all the fiery magma of the *hells* is going on with Rose."

"Very well," Anna said, her disappointment obvious, but the archangel didn't argue, instead walking over next to Rose's bedside, where the angel hadn't stirred. She wasn't wearing her collar that hid her wings anymore, Isalla noticed, and the angel's wings were tucked carefully into the cot.

"As you can see, she's still unconscious, and will be until her wounds have finished healing," Anathiel explained, her voice calm as she reached down to touch the hilt of Ember. "As for why it's taking so long, it's because Ember is the one healing her. She's been attuned to the sword for so long that its help healing her is essentially ideal, improving her affinity for fire magic even as it restores her body."

"Um, why? I've never heard of Ember healing anyone before, not in all the legends of it," Isalla asked, frowning as she looked at her beloved, unable to shake her sense of unease. "This seems strange to me."

"Of course you haven't. No one in the Emberborn family has ever unlocked all its power, in part because the original creator of the sword didn't want it to become the symbol of the Order of the Phoenix," Anna said, her smile wry as she looked at Isalla, adding, "It was forged while I was still in the heavens, so I know a bit more about it than others. I knew the man who forged it, Javan Firewing, as well as several of its wielders. In any case, I was able to unlock the ability for it to heal Rose, and in three or four days she'll be fine."

"I see," Isalla said, slightly taken aback and chagrined as she looked down, admitting softly, "I... forgot that you were around that long ago. It's hard to believe... I've only heard *legends* of you, really. They still taught us about some of the battles you commanded when we joined the Order of the Phoenix."

"Mm, I wish I could say I was surprised, but I'm not," Anathiel said, her smile fading quickly as she shook her head. "Many people died for the sake of those tales of glory, and I doubt they pay them proper respect. Few of those who look back on history remember the countless people who died in order to allow others to succeed."

For a moment the room was quiet, then Yain cleared her throat and spoke nervously. "I... well, I hate to change the subject, but I have to ask... will you be helping us investigate, then? Or will you be waiting for Rose to recover before continuing the investigation, or...?"

"Whether you continue or wait is entirely up to you, but *I* wouldn't wait," Anathiel said, sitting on the bed as she looked at them all in concern. "Also, I cannot help you, not directly. My presence is too likely to draw attention from those we're investigating, and I've likely put them on edge. I'm an excellent distraction, but at the same time I bear many problems as well. For instance, look at the table."

"Hm?" Isalla murmured, looking over at the table, then blinked. She hadn't looked at it before, but now that she did, she found herself almost gawking. There had to be hundreds of letters on the table, sitting in numerous neat piles, and only half of them were open. She looked at them, then asked, "Ah, what's all of *that*?"

"Those are the letters that I've received over the last three days and exclude the countless letters from random citizens of Uthren's Throne or the heavens. I've only taken those from noble families, military orders, or similar groups," Anathiel said, her voice desert-dry. "As you can see, I haven't even gotten through all of them, and doubtlessly there are more waiting to be delivered. I've had demands for my presence from nobles, questions about where I've been, and even *orders* to present myself to a tribunal of the heavenly orders to answer questions. As if I answer to them... regardless, I haven't replied to any of them yet."

"Oh my," Vinara murmured, and Isalla had to agree with her.

The idea of Anathiel drawing that much attention so quickly was mind-boggling, though she had to wonder why the orders would dare try to make demands of an archangel.

"I see. So, you're going to stay here and distract them while we try to find out who's been plotting in the heavens?" Kitania asked, her voice cool, and her arms folded.

The archangel nodded, letting out a soft sigh as she shrugged. "Well, yes. I don't think I can do much more, yet, not without evidence. If some of my old friends come calling, I might try to get something of an alliance going, much as Alserah reportedly has been doing, but beyond that, there isn't much I can do without evidence. I can back you up and ensure that you don't simply disappear, but we're close enough to the heavens that I have my limits. I might suggest that you and Vinara take turns keeping watch over Rose until she recovers, Kitania."

"Unfortunately, I believe she has a point. If there's anywhere they'll be able to see through your illusion, or detect that I'm a demon, it'd be here," Vinara said unhappily, folding her arms as she looked at Kitania. "Agreed?"

Kitania hesitated, then nodded grudgingly, stepping over to the cot, and reaching down to stroke Rose's cheek gently. The sight helped soothe some of Isalla's worries, at least.

"That being the case, it sounds like the choice of how to proceed is up to you, Isalla," Maura said, and Isalla froze as everyone looked at her.

"Ah, crap," Isalla murmured.

Her response prompted a chorus of chuckles, though Maura and Yain's were a bit more nervous than Vinara's. Isalla took the moment to think, then sighed as she shook her head unhappily. Several of the plans she'd made for when they got to Uthren's Throne relied on Rose, and with her currently out of the picture it made things more difficult, and not just because Isalla wished Rose hadn't been injured. In the end, she didn't dare wait, which meant that she was going to be doing this almost entirely on her own.

"I think that I'm going to try to contact the current commander of the Order of the Phoenix. Rose was hoping it was still Janel Ironheart, since she trusts her, but I don't have much information about her, and don't know Janel personally," Isalla said, frowning unhappily as she added, "I don't think trying to bring anyone else with me is a good idea, either. That'd draw attention, while an angel seeking an audience with the current commander would be *relatively* innocuous."

"Mm, one moment, I seem to remember seeing a letter from the order…" Anathiel said, standing and moving to the table. She shuffled through the letters, and after a minute cracked the seal on one. Finally, she spoke in approval. "Ah, yes, this one is from Heavenly Wing Janel Ironheart, so I believe you're in luck. If you'd like, I can pen a short missive, which *should* allow you to approach her more easily."

"That would be very much appreciated," Isalla said, some of her tension fading at the offer. She considered, frowning as she looked at the elves, then asked, "Um, now that we're here, I was wondering… what are the two of you going to do?"

"We were primarily sent as guides, so I think our task is largely done," Maura said, frowning unhappily as she added, "Well, we were also supposed to be guards, but we *are* pretty far out of our depth. I think the attack on the road showed that rather pointedly, and we'd stick out like sore thumbs trying to investigate anything in the heavens."

"And Kitania and I wouldn't?" Vinara asked, raising an eyebrow skeptically.

"She didn't say anything about that. You two can at least fly, once you've used magic," Yain said, shaking her head and letting out a heavy sigh. "I think the two of us would be best left to guarding your things or something of the sort. I don't want to head back, not with so many things up in the air… besides which, I'm not *entirely* comfortable with what we've heard here."

"I can't imagine why," Kitania muttered, and Isalla couldn't suppress a smile at her slightly sullen tone, while Vinara simply laughed.

"Perhaps we should let Kitania stay here and talk to Lady Anna while she keeps an eye on Rose," Vinara suggested, glancing at Kitania with a slight smile as she added, "I imagine they have a lot to talk about."

241

"True enough," Anathiel said, glancing at Kitania, then let her gaze settle on Isalla. "Is that alright with you?"

"Of course. You've given me a lot to think about, and I'm not even the one who had the real surprises," Isalla said, looking at Kitania and hesitating, then asked, "Kitty?"

"It's a reasonable suggestion. Not one that makes me particularly happy at the moment, but I can't blame anyone else for that," Kitania replied, letting out a soft sigh as she looked at Isalla. It seemed like the demoness's anger had ebbed slightly, which reassured Isalla, but Kitania smiled faintly as she added, "Good luck and be safe. If you have to, use Anna's name to keep out of trouble, hm? They *might* consider you a deserter."

"A definite point. I'll write the missive and have it delivered to you a bit later," Anathiel said, setting down the letter from Janel as she smiled warmly at Isalla.

"Thank you," Isalla said, hesitating, then approached Rose.

Her friend was pale, and she could see the partially healed injuries across her torso, which made Isalla tremble internally. Still, Rose's face looked practically untouched and like she was in fairly good health, even if she was still. Anathiel had obviously been taking care of Rose, as the angel's hair had been brushed out and she looked like she'd been bathed, but even so it hurt to see her like this. Isalla tried to ignore Ember, though it was hard, with how the flaming sword laid down the length of Rose's body, billowing with surprisingly gentle flames that didn't burn Rose or the bed.

Isalla hesitated for a long moment, then leaned down to kiss her friend, murmuring softly. "Get better, Rose. Don't leave me, not again."

Rose didn't stir, which caused Isalla's heart to sink slightly, as a tiny part of her had hoped that Rose would wake, even if Anathiel had said she wouldn't for a few days yet. Instead Isalla stroked Rose's warm, smooth cheek gently as she straightened, then looked at Kitania sadly.

"Take care of her, please?" Isalla asked, surprised by the plaintive note in her voice.

"Of course I will," Kitania replied, her expression softening still more, and she pulled Isalla into a tight hug. Isalla felt tears welling up in her eyes as she forced them back, blinking rapidly as she hugged Kitania tightly for what felt like several minutes. Then at last she separated, giving Kitania a gentle kiss before leaving at last.

For some reason, Anathiel being an archangel just didn't feel as important, not with Rose injured.

CHAPTER 31

"*I* owe you an apology, as does Estalia," Anna said at last, now that they were alone in the room. Alone aside from Rose, at least, which suited Kitania just fine.

She couldn't express how much of a shock Anna's revelation was, and Kitania was startled by how much it'd shaken her, though she'd never admit that out loud. For centuries she'd been sure that she was purely a demon and that she was just a strange mutation, but now... now that assumption had been utterly destroyed. Worse, she'd learned that one of the few people that Kitania had ever truly trusted and respected, terrifying as her methods could be from time to time, had lied to her as well. That left a particularly foul taste in Kitania's mouth.

"Yes, you do," Kitania replied, crossing her arms as she stepped close to Anna's armor. The power radiating off the cloudpiercer resting on its rack made her skin crawl, and the mundanity of the armor puzzled her, at least until she realized that it bore as potent of enchantments as the weapon.

"You know... I never really expected this. For some reason I had an idealized idea of how things would go," Anna murmured softly, setting aside her ink pen as she finished her note, letting out a sigh. Kitania looked over in time to see the angel's eyes darkening in sorrow. "You and I got along so *well* in the spire. Oh, I made mistakes... I should have told Estalia no when she sent you to me. I should have encouraged you to fully find your path, but I didn't. I taught you duty because it was what I'd known growing up, and it led to... well, war. Yet somehow I thought that, as much as you seemed to adore me, you'd almost leap with joy at learning about our relationship."

"I probably would have, if I were still under a century in age, but I haven't been that young in a long, *long* time," Kitania admitted, shifting slightly as she considered her past unhappily, then continued. "I've thought that I knew who my parents were for a long time, and now you make me wonder... how many *other* things have you and Mother lied to me about? Not even direct lies, for that matter, but by omission? How much of my life was the product of still more manipulations?"

Anna reached up and rubbed her eyes tiredly, letting out a sigh as she shook her head and murmured, "Oh, what a *mess* we've made of things, haven't we? Well, there's naught to do but deal with the problem."

Kitania couldn't help a snort, turning away from Anna to look at Rose. She was concerned about the angel, but Rose looked healthy enough, and appeared to be healing fairly rapidly. How *Ember* was managing that was a whole different question, but not one that Kitania was going to voice at the moment. She had enough difficulty even looking at Anna.

"To my knowledge, we haven't deliberately misled you about anything else. Oh, I'm certain that there have been minor deceptions here or there, but that's normal. The day that someone goes their entire life without a deception of some kind is the day the world ends," Anna said, a trace of amusement in her voice, but her chair scraped against the floor as she stood. "No, we made mistakes, yes, but at least part of that is my fault, as I was trying to hide from the heavens. I didn't want to be Anathiel anymore, Kitania. I wanted to live a relatively normal life, and Estalia... she wanted to *give* me that. I'm so, *so* sorry."

Her vision was getting blurry, Kitania realized, and she blinked, trying to force back the tears in her eyes, but it was a losing battle. Instead she finally turned to look at Anna, meeting the archangel's gaze unsteadily as she murmured, "I... why couldn't I have had the same? Why did it have to come to what it did?"

Anna didn't reply in words, and instead she embraced Kitania again, hugging her tightly as her fingers ran gently through Kitania's hair. It took a little while before Kitania felt herself begin to relax into the comfortable embrace of the archangel. It wasn't easy to think of Anna as one of her parents, not after so long thinking it had been someone else. Still, she smelled oddly comforting, and Kitania slowly embraced Anna, holding her tight as a finger brushed one of the angel's feathers, which were soft despite their metallic hue.

As the tears began trickling down her face, Kitania closed her eyes and whispered. "If I'd known about you... if I'd known, I wouldn't have left for a millennium. I wouldn't have hidden from everything for so long."

"Oh. I... am such a fool. A damned fool, it appears," Anna said, and the shocked grief in her voice prompted Kitania to open her eyes. Anna looked like she'd been stabbed, and the angel blinked back her tears as she leaned forward to kiss Kitania's forehead.

"We made mistakes. Many of them, as it happens. However, there is *nothing* I want more than your happiness at this point, Kitania. Nothing at all," Anna said softy, almost rocking back and forth with Kitania in her arms. "Estalia... she truly *does* want peace, and I've supported her aims for all this time. Not because I think it's the best solution, but because it's the only one I've seen with a chance of working. However, if it means setting that aside for your happiness, I'd do it. I give my word, Kitania."

"Thank you," Kitania replied, her voice trembling slightly now. She was having a hard time seeing as she quietly cried, the tears tracking down her face to soak into Anna's shirt. After a moment she smiled hesitantly, teasing, "At least now I know why I've always been so attracted to angels. I must have gotten it from you."

Anna snorted, pulling away as she looked at Kitania skeptically. "Really? *That's* what you got out of all of this, when I ended up enthralled with a succubus? If anything, you take after *her* where that's concerned."

247

BENJAMIN MEDRANO

"I suppose. I just… it's so strange. I'm the daughter of an archangel and demon lord… no *wonder* I'm so weird. That much power is bound to cause issues," Kitania said, trying to joke, yet it almost fell flat as she looked at Rose sadly. "Immortality feels like a curse a lot of times."

"Yes, well… have you ever considered the possibility of your power being an angelic mantle?" Anna asked, drawing Kitania gently over to a chair, and only taking a seat once Kitania had settled into one, her expression turning thoughtful. "It was a possibility your mother and I considered for a very long time, though neither of us is certain. I can't say that I'm not relieved you were able to survive to this point, though."

"I… well, of course not! I'm a demon, not—" Kitania began, then stopped, blinking as she inhaled, then exhaled, murmuring, "I *thought* I was a demon. If it was a mantle, Mother said I'd know how to pass it down instinctively."

"That's right, but only if you *want* to pass it down, and are considering the proper individual for it," Anna corrected gently, frowning as she added, "I… probably should have passed down mine a long time ago, but I couldn't bring myself to do it."

"I see. So you're saying I might be able to die after all," Kitania said, a little mirthless at this point as she teased. "I thought you didn't want me to die."

"Death comes for everyone, no matter how powerful or insignificant. It's merely a question of *when* it'll happen," Anna said solemnly, a hint of grief in her voice as she looked back at Kitania steadily, taking her hands again as she let out a sigh. "I don't believe that anyone can be *truly* undying or eternal, and… well, would you really want it? Most deities pass down their mantles for a reason, Kitania."

"Of course I wouldn't, not in the end," Kitania said, letting out a sigh as she glanced at Rose and winced, murmuring, "If anything, I wish I could help her. I've felt so *useless* since I was sent to the Forest of Sighs."

"Who's to say you can't? The nature of a mantle means that you can grant divine gifts. Not to other bearers of mantles, for good or ill, but to those who're without," Anna replied, smiling and nodding at Rose. "Why don't you think about her? Honestly consider whether you *could* give her your power, Kitania. If you can... well, that'll mean that I was right, that it's truly an angelic mantle. And *that* would mean you could help her in truth."

"Well... I suppose it's worth a try," Kitania said, blinking a couple of times as she thought, surprised at how easily she'd gotten over her anger where Anna was concerned. Yet in the end, it really didn't matter that much, so she drew one hand from Anna's grasp and turned to look at Rose.

The angel was beautiful even in repose, and Kitania regretted every time she'd pushed Rose away. They hadn't had much time together since the Ascent of Faith, especially as dirty and tired as they were at the end of each day, but she'd enjoyed Rose's company, enough that she felt guilty. The memory of her time with Niadra plagued Kitania, as she hated the thought of doing something which would hurt someone else, and yet... yet it felt like she couldn't help herself. It was something she needed to address later, though, and Kitania took a deep breath, focusing on Rose and trying to truly *consider* attempting to pass her power to the angel.

For a moment there was nothing, and Kitania was disappointed. She almost stopped there, but her lessons with magic came to mind again. Magic was rarely something that could be done on a whim, so she took a deep breath and forced herself to truly concentrate on the possibility... and something deep inside of Kitania stirred.

It was something that had always been there, unmoving and silent for all these years, yet which Kitania hadn't ever noticed. Yet the moment it moved, Kitania almost stopped breathing, for the power was also immense. It almost felt like it blossomed within her, as a heat spread through her body. It would be so easy to pass it on, she realized, looking at Rose. All she'd have to do is touch the other woman, and it would gently slip into her body, granting her power.

"As I thought." Anna's voice distracted Kitania, and she looked back at the angel, blinking in confusion, at least until Anna gestured down at Kitania's hand.

Kitania looked down and blinked, her mouth opening, then shutting again. Her skin was glowing softly, almost like Estalia's did, though as she watched it slowly died down as the power within her settled back into place. This time it didn't entirely vanish from her awareness, though, because now Kitania knew it was there, and she could hardly believe that she'd missed the power within her for all this time.

"I… it's there. It's *always* been there, yet I didn't see it. It was like… like a boulder under the water, which I never even noticed," Kitania said, dumfounded as she shook her head slowly. "How is that even possible?"

"Most likely it's because it *has* been there all this time. Your power also appears to be something which acts mostly in a passive manner, unlike the powers of so many others," Anna said, looking at Kitania curiously, then she smiled as she added, "Take me, for instance. I am *war*. I am the clash of weapons, the thunder of cavalry, and the roar of war cries. When I call upon my power, I am steel. I am a blade which can break all foes."

With every word Anna spoke, her entire presence suddenly changed, almost like knives were touching Kitania's skin, and the demoness's eyes widened as she saw the table next to them tremble, Anna's feathers harden, and everything about Anna subtly changed to be almost harsh, sharp-edged and deadly. As the archangel had said, she was a *weapon* in that moment, and one that made Kitania tremble with a mere look. Anna held her power like that for a long moment, then relaxed, turning back to normal as she smiled again.

"My power is that of warfare, yes, but it's something which is called upon. Oh, I can defend myself instinctively, and my body is incredibly difficult to harm, but it isn't something that's always there and active, unlike your own," Anna explained gently. "That isn't to say you don't have other powers. You very well might have abilities you've never discovered, dear. However, that doesn't change the fact I'm not surprised that you didn't notice your power before."

"Maybe so. I just… how can this help?" Kitania asked, looking at her hands curiously, sensing the power within her and shivering. She didn't like the idea of Anna looking like that. It felt alien, like it wasn't the woman she'd known and trained with. The woman she was barely starting to believe might truly be her other parent.

"You know that deities of any form can give blessings to others, and despite what people may think, archangels and demon lords are simply another type of deity. The differences between our powers are minor at best, even if mortal deities can be slightly more powerful than us. Assuming they have a mantle that's strong enough, that is," Anna said, smirking at the last. "For instance, Krath seems to have a crush on me, after I disarmed him immediately after my arrival."

"You *what*?" Kitania asked, her eyes widening in shock as Anna distracted her. "I mean, I noticed that he seemed to like you, but... you disarmed him?"

"He thought I was ashborn because of my wings," Anna explained, then sighed as she nodded at Rose and continued. "However, we're getting distracted. A single angel, demon, or mortal can bear the blessing of only a single deity at a time, at least as far as I know, and they have to *accept* it. My blessing grants increased resilience and skill at arms, while Estalia's grants a measure of her aura and, ironically to her, improved skill with mental magic. Yours would likely improve their ability to heal, and I suspect a mortal with it might cease aging entirely. The problem with Rose is that you couldn't help her *now*. She has to be conscious to accept it."

"Ah," Kitania murmured, nodding as her mood improved somewhat. The idea of being able to grant additional healing to Isalla and Rose *was* rather appealing; the question was how to go about doing it. After a moment of hesitation she asked, "Could you teach me how?"

"Certainly," Anna said, smiling warmly as the archangel seemed to relax at last. "Now, first I need you to relax. This is going to take some work, at least the first time, and..."

Kitania listened closely, doing her best to relax and learn. Even if they were far away from home, this felt so much like being back in the Spire of Confession, and despite all her misgivings, there was a large part of her that just didn't care. She felt *safe* with Anna.

And that was as it should be.

CHAPTER 32

"There you are!" Isalla said in relief, standing up as Kitania entered their room at last.

It was well after dark, and Vinara had gone to keep an eye on Rose over two hours earlier, which had made Isalla even more concerned that something might have gone wrong. On the other hand, Kitania, back in her guise as a dragon-blooded human, arched an eyebrow skeptically. That was so much like Kitania had been like in the hells that a rush of relief washed through the angel.

"Where else was I going to go? I mean, I suppose that some priest or priestess might have invited me to their chambers, since none of the local orders practice celibacy, or a noble who wanted to learn more about Lady Anna could have, but you know me better than that," Kitania replied, and Isalla blushed.

"Well, that's not... I didn't..." Isalla began, then stopped, taking a deep breath before looking at Kitania sternly, speaking more bluntly. "That's not what I meant! Violet went to keep watch hours ago, and you barely got back, that's what I was saying!"

"Ah, well, I think you overestimated how much the crowd would die down as the sun set," Kitania replied, smiling as she hung her cloak on a peg and started taking off her tail armor. "When I left, I saw people setting up a bonfire and what looked like musicians getting comfortable on a platform. I wouldn't be surprised if there's singing and dancing by firelight this evening."

"That's... well, that does explain it. They're having a *festival*?" Isalla asked, shaking her head in disbelief, then a little amusement as she thought about it, then murmured, "Well, I suppose it makes sense. They've always been close allies of the heavens, so when a famous archangel of legend comes to visit their deities... they probably see it as adding legitimacy to their views."

Kitania paused, looking up at Isalla thoughtfully for a long moment, then continued removing the armor. It was rather involved, which didn't surprise Isalla much, considering how flexible the demon's tail was. If anything, she was surprised Kitania could stand to have the armor on all day to begin with.

"That would explain it, and I wonder if Anna knows? I doubt she'd be happy if she did... but it isn't like there's much to be done about it," Kitania said, a hint of amusement to her voice. "She doesn't seem to like the idea of worshipers, on a personal level. I can't say as I blame her, as managing a church seems like it would be hard work."

"Agreed," Isalla said, nodding and relaxing as she sat on the edge of the bed, a bit nervously.

The room in Season of Light was well-built and reasonably nice, with sheets that were nicer than most of the inns they'd stayed at on their way through Uthren, which made her happier in some ways. More importantly, the room was also built to dampen sound, which gave them a measure more privacy than in many rooms. Isalla was looking forward to that.

Kitania took off the last of the armor and let out a soft sigh of relief, stretching the tail for a moment, which looked a little comical with the illusion in place, then slipped a letter out of her belt pouch. "Ah, before I forget, here's the letter she's going to have you deliver. I'm told she's politely declining the request for an audience, since if she grants one, she'd have no time for the next year due to all the others she'd have to grant. She wanted me to let you know about the contents."

"Mm, I can't blame her. She seems to have gotten a *lot* of

attention," Isalla acknowledged, wincing slightly at the thought of the letters piled on Anna's table. She hesitated, then asked nervously, watching curiously as Kitania poured water in a bowl and slowly, carefully washed her tail, "So, did it go well? You weren't happy when we left."

"No, I wasn't. I also gave her a piece of my mind, and she apologized profusely. I also learned a few things which are… startling, to say the least," Kitania said, wiping a washcloth along her tail with a wry smile. "I thought I knew pretty much everything there was to know about myself, but I was wrong. It's a little embarrassing in some ways."

"Oh?" Isalla asked, her curiosity truly piqued by this point.

Kitania paused, considering for a moment before she finished washing her tail off and dried it with another cloth. She didn't speak immediately, instead waiting until she walked over to the bed and sat next to Isalla.

"I learned that my immortality *is* a mantle," Kitania murmured, her voice so soft that Isalla could barely hear it from right next to her. Isalla inhaled sharply, but Kitania hadn't finished. "In fact, it's an angelic mantle… and isn't that the height of irony?"

"What?" Isalla asked, her voice rising slightly, and she barely kept herself from shouting in her shock. Kitania quickly put her finger against her lips.

"Shh, we don't want other people to hear," Kitania cautioned, and Isalla couldn't help flushing. Instead she lowered her voice as she spoke.

"You're an *archangel*?" Isalla asked incredulously, shock roiling through her. "Are you serious?"

"Of course not. I'm not an angel, so I can't be an archangel," Kitania replied, looking at Isalla chidingly. "I simply have an angelic mantle, though that isn't exactly *simple*. I learned quite a bit from Anna, even if we initially had a few… disagreements."

"I see. That's… a little surprising, I'll admit, but fascinating as well. What can you do?" Isalla asked, looking at Kitania curiously. The idea of Kitania having an angelic mantle was startling, but it wasn't like it changed much unless Kitania could do even more than she'd thought before.

"Mostly? Heal from nearly anything," Kitania replied in a deadpan tone, looking at Isalla in amusement. "I've only had an afternoon to explore the idea, you know. Maybe I'll figure something else out eventually, but for now the only thing I know I can do now is give blessings to others. Not that I know what that would *do*, but... would you like one?"

"You... oh, wow!" Isalla said, blushing as excitement surged through her. She knew the tiniest amount about blessings, and those who received them were vanishingly small in number, as most archangels kept them as rare rewards for their followers, so the offer was shocking, and at the same time thrilling. Her voice trembled as she asked, "You really would do that?"

"Yes, unless you're holding out for Anna's. She might be willing, and at least *she* knows what hers does," Kitania admitted, an infectious smile on her face now. "It's really up to you, in the end."

"In that case... yes, of course I would!" Isalla said, blushing as she did so. The idea that Kitania was willing to do that helped her mood immensely.

"As you like. Close your eyes, Isalla," Kitania said, and Isalla did so, sitting there in eager anticipation.

For a long moment she sat there, waiting. She heard Kitania inhale, and Isalla couldn't help wondering how difficult what she was doing was. She knew barely anything about blessings, except—

The warmth of Kitania's lips pressing against her own was startling, and Isalla nearly opened her eyes. She suppressed the urge, though, and melted into it as she returned the kiss, wrapping her arms around Kitania as she enjoyed the demoness's embrace. As she did, though, she felt a strange warmth slowly envelop her, as if she were laying under the sun and its radiance was soaking into her. It wasn't incredibly strong, but neither was it weak, though she had some trouble focusing on it.

Slowly the warmth settled around her mana core, pulsing slowly with every beat of Isalla's heart, and she shivered, relaxing as it passed and she could enjoy the kiss at last. Which, of course, was why Kitania broke off the kiss at that moment. Isalla opened her eyes and glowered at Kitania in annoyance.

"You *stopped*," Isalla protested, trying to decide why she was really annoyed, then ignoring that as she looked at the demoness, who'd pulled a few inches back and reached back to pull off her hair clasp.

"I did, because you received the blessing. Did you not want me to?" Kitania asked, her voice calm and her lips betraying the barest hint of a smile.

"Would I be protesting otherwise?" Isalla asked, her glower deepening. "For that matter, why does a blessing require a kiss?"

"It doesn't. It requires touching you. I *wanted* to kiss you," Kitania replied smugly, and Isalla considered her for just a moment.

Then she reached over, grabbing the pillow, and swatted Kitania with it, prompting the demoness to yelp in surprise. Of course, that didn't last, as Kitania dodged Isalla's follow-up swing and snagged a pillow of her own.

It took a while before they went to bed, but when they did Isalla was smiling.

CHAPTER 33

"Good luck in there, Lady Isalla," Eziel said, respectfully standing next to Maura. They were in the market nearest the Heavenly Tower, and the two women were going to be shopping while Isalla delivered Anathiel's note, which didn't help Isalla's nerves.

She was in her full angelic form, partly because Sorm's attack had shown that the disguise she'd borne wasn't enough where the traitors were concerned, and partially because she was delivering a letter on Anathiel's behalf. Isalla was very carefully not dressed in the colors of the Order of the Phoenix, which made her a little unnerved, since *that* meant she also couldn't wear weapons to the meeting, and she wasn't going to wear armor, either. Someone might be able to tell it was forged in the hells, and that would be bad.

Instead she was in a relatively normal blouse and trousers, and her hair was pulled back by a blue ribbon Kitania had given her. A large number of the locals were slowing to look at her, and Isalla knew that the guards around the tower had seen her. She hoped it wouldn't cause things to go poorly for Eziel and Maura, but there was nothing she could do about that.

Shaking her head to clear it, Isalla looked at Eziel with an uncertain smile, nodding as she replied. "Yes, well, I *should* be safe. I doubt most of the people inside would stand aside if I were attacked."

"That isn't quite what I meant, but I agree with you. I'm hoping that your warning doesn't fall on deaf ears," Eziel said, and Isalla nodded, understanding what the woman had been implying at last, and her mood grew a little grimmer as well. She didn't like the idea, but it was a possibility she couldn't ignore. Janel Ironheart had been one of Rose's friends, after all, not one of Isalla's.

"A fair point, but if nothing else, Rose should be back on her feet soon. We just have to have faith," Isalla replied, her determination strengthening.

"Of course. However, faith doesn't fix everything," Maura said, smiling wryly. "Good luck to you. I haven't been a lot of help on the trip, but I'll do what I can. See you when you're done!"

"Agreed," Isalla said, and watched the two women move down the street, Maura with a relaxed, easy stride while Eziel took lighter, more precise steps. Perhaps there was something to be said for being able to tell angels apart from the way they moved, Isalla mused, remembering what Bell had said back in Silken Veils.

Turning away, Isalla spread her wings and took flight, beating her wings as she quickly ascended. Her wings hadn't gotten as much exercise as she'd like lately, so it was slightly more difficult to rise at a sharp angle than Isalla preferred, but she managed reasonably well, and approached the receiving platform on the first balcony of the tower, which she knew would be open to visitors.

The guards on flying patrol didn't challenge her, but as she landed two of the three angelic guards blocked the door with their halberds, each of them from different orders. The three orders were of the Dragon, Eagle, and Phoenix, though the Order of the Eagle primarily focused on matters in the heavens and were better known for their magic than the other two orders.

"What business do you have at the Heavenly Spire, daughter of the heavens?" the man in the uniform of the Order of the Eagle asked, his voice calm, but his gaze was watchful anyway.

"I come bearing a message for Heavenly Wing Janel Ironheart of the Order of the Phoenix," Isalla replied, bowing her head marginally as she looked at them and pulled out the letter.

"Ah, in that case, we'll happily take the letter and have it delivered," the member of the Order of the Phoenix said, smiling as he straightened.

"I'm afraid that will not be acceptable. Archangel Anathiel asked me to deliver the missive in person," Isalla replied, straightening and turning the letter to show the wax seal, which was of a winged sword. A tiny part of her was afraid they'd call her bluff, as she hadn't been told to deliver it by Anathiel, but rather by Kitania on Anathiel's behalf.

The guards all froze, and the woman in the colors of the Order of the Dragon swallowed visibly, her blue eyes brightening as she straightened, and before the others could say anything she eagerly asked, "You met her? I haven't heard of anyone meeting her since she arrived!"

"I did. A mortal friend of mine was trained by her while she was away, though she didn't know it at the time, and I was fortunate enough to meet with her afterward," Isalla replied, smiling a little at the woman's reaction.

"Oh, that's… you have a friend that was trained by an *archangel*? That's… I can't imagine how much of a blessing that must have been," the man from the Order of the Phoenix said, envy all but oozing from him as he jealously stared at the letter for a long moment, then sighed and shook his head. "I just don't know why she didn't come *here*, rather than the temple. She's an angel!"

"From what I heard when I met with her, it appears that she and the Lord of Winds are old friends," Isalla said, carefully picking her words as she looked at them, shrugging helplessly. "I suspect that if she's going to start associating with others again, it makes sense to first approach those she knows. I can't imagine what it's like to have been around as long as she has, after all."

"True enough, how could we?" the first man said, letting out a sigh and shaking his head, then looked at the man in the colors of the Order of the Phoenix. "Still, we need to get you to the Heavenly Wing. Would you go get approval for her to enter?"

"Sure. Not that there's any real question, considering," the man replied, nodding to Isalla as he smiled and stepped inside.

As the door closed, Isalla settled in to wait patiently, and the other guards glanced at one another. Isalla knew they were going to ask questions and braced herself, doubting it would take them long to work up the nerve.

"What was she like?" the woman asked after a minute, proving Isalla was right.

The woman's eyes shone with enthusiasm, and Isalla couldn't help a smile. A tiny part of her had wondered if all of the Order of the Dragon was bad, with Rathien being a member of the Society of the Golden Dawn, but the woman's hero worship was so familiar that Isalla realized she shouldn't paint the entire order with a single brush. That was what she'd done with demons, and Kitania had managed to disabuse Isalla of that belief in the end.

"Lady Anathiel is..." Isalla began, then frowned as she searched for how to describe the archangel simply, yet she failed. Eventually she settled on a simple term. "She's gracious."

"Gracious? The archangel of war?" the man asked, his eyebrows rising.

"I don't know how else to describe her," Isalla said, shrugging helplessly as she smiled at him. "Oh, she radiates power like I can't even *describe*, but at the same time it isn't directed at you. She's graceful, polite, and refined, and she always seems to have a smile for you. And yet... with how perfectly each movement seems choreographed, you can tell how much she's trained over the years. I have no doubt that she could have destroyed all of us who were there in the blink of an eye. Not that she would have... she seemed far too kind for that."

"Ah, I see. She may be the archangel of war, but that doesn't indicate lack of control," the man murmured, his gaze turning thoughtful. "Perhaps I should try to look at the records of her more closely. Assuming I can *find* any, with how many people have been obsessing over her for the last few days."

"As if you're an exception!" the woman said tartly, prompting a blush from the man as he cleared his throat.

"It's merely an academic interest," he protested, shifting from one foot to another, to Isalla's entertainment.

"Right, and I'm sure everyone believes that," the woman replied, her tone dry.

Before they could speak any further, the door opened again and both snapped to attention as a pair of men stepped out. One was the soldier from the Order of the Phoenix, and the other was a brown-haired angel who looked like he was the man's superior, with the insignia of a second sword on his collar. Isalla couldn't help straightening slightly at the sight, and the man raised an eyebrow, but didn't say anything as he looked Isalla over with a cool gaze.

"I'm told that you have a letter from Lady Anathiel to deliver to the Heavenly Wing. May I see it?" the man spoke at last, and while his words sounded like a request, there was a note in his voice that made Isalla suspect that if she said no, he'd deny her entry.

"As you wish," Isalla conceded, pulling the letter out again and handing it over politely.

The man took it and turned it over, examining the script on the front for a moment, then scrutinizing the seal on the back. For a moment she was afraid that he was going to break the seal, but Isalla relaxed as he didn't touch it, simply examining it closely for a long moment.

When he finally spoke, his voice was soft. "You're aware that this is the first reply she's sent, yes?"

"I am. She had a pile of over a hundred letters on her table when we met and told us that those were only from people who were of particular import," Isalla replied, a smile flickering across her lips as she added. "She hadn't had time to *read* all of them, let alone reply."

"Ah. I suppose that might be an issue, and one which I hadn't considered," the officer admitted, and behind him Isalla saw the guards exchange looks, understanding appearing on their faces as well. She suspected that none of them had considered that possibility, though as relatively common soldiers it wasn't a surprise.

Isalla waited patiently, suppressing the butterflies of

nervousness within her midsection and calling on all her training to try to look impassive. She doubted it fooled the officer, but it was the attempt that was important to her. He waited a little longer, then nodded and handed the letter back to her.

"It appears that your letter is genuine, so I will escort you to the Heavenly Wing. If you would follow me?" the officer asked, gesturing at the door.

"Of course, sir. It's why I'm here," Isalla replied respectfully, putting the letter away again. She suspected she would have had a significantly harder time getting in if she hadn't had the letter, though Rose likely wouldn't have had much difficulty.

One of the guards opened the door for them, and they quickly stepped into the wide, airy halls of the spire proper. Few other species built hallways that were truly intended for angels, as keeping their wings fully folded wasn't always comfortable, so she appreciated the space she saw, and let out the faintest sigh of relief as she let her wings relax a little.

"I'm Second Sword Anteroth. May I ask who you are so that I may announce you to the Heavenly Wing?" the officer asked, and at the question Isalla opened her mouth to reply, then paused, hesitating despite herself.

She had been using the Order of the Phoenix as her surname for so long that it almost felt wrong not to use it anymore, and yet at the same time it also wasn't appropriate, especially not here. Isalla struggled with herself, trying to decide what to do... then finally made a decision. Letting out a sigh, she replied softly. "My name is Isalla, of Soaring Heights."

"Isalla? The name sounds familiar, but I can't quite place it..." Anteroth mused, and Isalla's heartbeat quickened with near-panic at the thoughtful tone of his voice. She hadn't thought he might recognize her name, but fortunately he shrugged after a moment, continuing. "Ah, it doesn't matter, I suppose. There's plenty of people with the same names in the world, particularly among mortals. I must say, I'm impressed that you got to meet Lady Anathiel, after as many of our messengers as she's rebuffed."

"I was fortunate enough to have a friend who she trained

while she was away," Isalla replied simply, bowing her head as they ascended a staircase. "Otherwise, I suspect I'd *never* have had the opportunity."

"Ah, luck, that thing which can make all the difference in the world, yet which can only be hoped for," Anteroth said, chuckling softly as he smiled. Leading the way to down the hall, he came to a door and knocked, murmuring more softly, "Here we are."

"Enter!" a woman replied, her voice a little deeper than Isalla had expected, and Anteroth opened the door, stepping in.

"Heavenly Wing, May I present Isalla of Soaring Heights? She comes bearing a message from the archangel Anathiel," Anteroth said, standing at attention as he stepped to the side, allowing Isalla into the room.

Across the room from her was an angelic woman with black hair that had been cut short and a stocky, powerful figure. The woman was staring at Isalla with eyes almost as dark as pitch, while she wore the uniform of a member of the Order of the Phoenix.

The room was somewhat cluttered, but in the way that Isalla would have expected. A table next to a cabinet of maps had a large map of the north weighed down on it, while an armor rack sat next to a weapon rack, both bearing armor and weapons. The desk and chairs were scarred from where people in armor had sat or worked, and the only hint of more pleasant surroundings was the door to the balcony behind her, but even the windows there were small, and the door was heavily reinforced.

"Thank you for escorting her here. You may leave, Anteroth," Janel Ironheart said, and Anteroth saluted.

"Of course, ma'am!" he said, and the angel quickly left, latching the door behind him.

Even with him gone, Isalla stood there uncomfortably as Janel stared at her. There was something about the woman's gaze that made her uncomfortable, almost like Janel *disliked* Isalla. It didn't make any sense, since Isalla hadn't ever met the angel before.

"Isalla of Soaring Heights," Janel said, a definite note of

distaste in her voice as she looked at Isalla, almost sneering. "So *you're* the brat who ruined Roselynn's career."

Suddenly the pieces fell into place, and Isalla winced, wishing Rose were here more than ever before. At least now she knew why Janel didn't like her.

It still wasn't a good way to start their meeting.

CHAPTER 34

"*Y*es, that would be me, though I had no intention of ruining her career. Neither of us did," Isalla replied, her stomach almost churning as her mood sank. It was entirely possible that their hopes of convincing Janel to help or believe them were going to come up short.

"I don't *care* what you intended. What I care about is what you *did*," Janel replied, her tone almost spiteful as she looked at Isalla in disdain. "Drummed out of the order at last, though? At least there's *some* justice in the world, after Roselynn was disgraced trying to protect you. I wonder if you even care that she's gone missing."

"Oh, I *care*. I cared enough that I went to rescue her, even when it seemed like my chances of success were pretty much impossible," Isalla retorted, her worries suddenly vanishing as anger blazed to life within her, glowering at the Heavenly Wing in turn. The woman seemed slightly taken aback, but Isalla continued, her tone biting. "In fact, I even *succeeded*, I'll have you know. I rescued Rose from the plots of those who'd betrayed her, with the help of others. Then we decided to come *here* to get help, as you're one of the few people she trusts. Unfortunately, those same traitors decided to try to kill us again. They almost succeeded, as a matter of fact, and Rose is currently recovering in the care of Lady Anathiel."

"You *what*?" Janel asked, the shocked expression on her face turning to disbelief as she folded her arms and set her jaw. "Why should I listen to a word you have to say? Anyone could claim that."

Isalla bit back the urge to retort, and instead pulled out the letter from Anathiel and tossed it onto Janel's desk. When she spoke, she forced her voice to be cool and relatively calm. "How many of them could bring a letter from Anathiel? She gave it to me in part to make reaching you easier. As an aside, the answer is no, she will *not* grant you an audience. She doesn't have the time to grant everyone who wants to meet with her audiences, and she's not going to play favorites."

Scowling, Janel snatched up the letter and broke the seal, her eyes moving back and forth as she read the letter, while her scowl grew even more pronounced with every passing moment. Normally Isalla would have grown more worried at the reaction, but at the moment she couldn't find the motivation to care that much, not after the insults Janel had thrown her way. Worse, the insults had also been indirectly criticizing Rose's judgment, and after she'd been injured Isalla wasn't going to tolerate that.

Finally, Janel threw the letter onto the desk, her expression dark as she glared at Isalla, almost spitting as she spoke. "Fine, you at least were telling the truth about *that*. What do you want, that you used an archangel to reach me? Speak quickly or get out."

"Fine. I wasn't *kicked out* of the Order of the Phoenix; I was ordered to take a position investigating crimes in the Evergardens. I noticed some strange meetings by members of the Holy Council and started investigating, and for that a woman drew me into an ambush, cut my wings off, and dumped me in the hells," Isalla said flatly, taking a certain amount of pleasure in how the woman flinched, but continued bluntly. "I was rescued by a reasonably friendly demon, but at the same time they decided that since I'd sent a letter with my suspicions to Rose, they'd eliminate her as well. That's how she ended up *disappearing*, and I helped rescue her in the hells. Not that she really needed it at the time, but that part doesn't matter.

"If that weren't enough, they sent a group of angels to kill us.

They failed, but it was a near thing in the end. We managed to get further information and went to the Forest of Sighs... which I'm *certain* you've heard a bit about," Isalla said, her tone biting by this point, and she avoided looking at Janel at all, not wanting to see the incredulousness in her gaze anymore. "We helped Alserah fight the angels controlling the monsters, as well as killing the monsters themselves. Even so, we learned that a member of the conspiracy was here, so we tried to travel in secret. Rose was certain she could get help from you, so she suggested we meet with you once we got here. Unfortunately, just a couple of days outside the city our enemies struck *again*, and she was nearly killed. If it weren't for Lady Anathiel, Rose would have died long before we could have received help and is still healing."

Janel didn't reply immediately, simply staring at her instead, and it was all Isalla could do to keep from sighing in frustration. The skepticism in her gaze was obvious, and Isalla was quickly coming to realize that it would be hard to convince the woman of anything.

"Now, why in the name of the endless skies of heaven would they be doing all that?" Janel asked, her voice practically dripping with sarcasm.

"Based on what the captive we turned told us, it's because they want to *wipe out* the hells, and think the Holy Council is corrupt. They want to reignite the war, and that's why they tried to pin the attack on the Forest of Sighs on the hells," Isalla replied, trying to suppress the urge to yell at the woman. *That* certainly wouldn't help, and she gritted her teeth, then asked, "Would truthtelling magic help at all?"

"No, I don't want to pollute the ears of anyone else with this ridiculousness," Janel replied caustically, shaking her head in disgust. "Who did you think was a member of this conspiracy?"

"Rathien, the head of the Order of the Dragon here," Isalla said, dearly hoping she wasn't making a mistake.

Janel snorted again, turning away, and Isalla saw that her hands were clenched in fists, almost looking bone-white due to how tight they were. It worried her, but she didn't say anything, instead bracing herself for the possibility that Janel would call for the guards to imprison her.

"You are accusing a *Heavenly Wing* of another order of high treason. Without any evidence, based on what I've heard, but merely hearsay," Janel said, her voice taut. Isalla opened her mouth, but the angel spun and pointed at her, snapping out. "Don't you even start! I don't care that you claim to have a witness, or a captive, or anything else. *You* have caused more problems than I care to consider, and the *only* reason I'm not having you thrown in the dungeon to be put on trial for desertion is Anathiel and Roselynn! I don't believe you, put bluntly, but the archangel's letter gives you at least a *shred* of legitimacy. More than you deserve, really. Now, you can come back with either Anathiel or Roselynn and I'll *consider* what you have to say, but if you show your face again without them, I'm going to throw your arrogant ass in prison."

Isalla just stood there for a moment, stunned that Janel wasn't even stopping to ask proper questions. It was unbelievable to her, and yet, the expression on the woman's face made it clear that she wasn't going to listen to any protests. Instead, Isalla gritted her teeth and took a moment to bow slightly.

"If that's how you feel, then so be it. I'll let Lady Anathiel and Rose know, at least once Rose is awake. In the meantime, I do hope you'll at least keep a *slightly* closer eye out for any other traitors. In any case, good day to you," Isalla replied, straightening and turning to leave the room. She ignored the soft growl from Janel.

When she opened the door, Isalla almost stopped as she saw Anteroth standing across the hall, his arms behind his back. Suddenly she desperately hoped that he hadn't heard anything, as otherwise it'd be a disaster. Still, the door closing bumped her forward as well as jarring her wings, and Isalla took a step into the hall.

"I do hope the meeting went well for you," Anteroth said, his happy, easy tone putting Isalla more at ease, since she doubted *anyone* would have that tone if they'd overheard how Janel had been talking.

Isalla shook her head as she chuckled darkly, then murmured, "I'm afraid it could have gone much, *much* better. I don't think she likes me."

"That… is unfortunate. You have my sympathies, as the Heavenly Wing has a sharp tongue," Anteroth said, wincing sympathetically. Nodding toward the hall, he continued. "In any case, I'm here to escort you out. If you'd follow me?"

"As you say, Sir Anteroth. Thank you," Isalla replied, following as he began leading the way. Not that she really needed a guide, but she wasn't going to complain.

Now she just had to figure out how to explain the meeting to everyone else.

∼

ASERIAL PAUSED on opening the crate, frowning at the three bags inside it. She'd received the coded letter from the Society of Golden Dawn's leadership, and while she worried about the chaos it would cause, she wasn't going to object. Their goals were hers, in the end, and the letter had directed her here. However, it hadn't exactly led her to expect *three* bags inside the crate.

Reaching down, she opened one of the bags and her eyebrows rose slightly, startled by the sight of a dozen incineration stones inside it. Hesitating only a moment, she checked the other two bags, which each had an equal number of stones. She scratched her head, then shrugged.

"Well, I suppose they must know what they're doing, even if this is a *lot* of explosives," Aserial murmured, and she quickly grabbed all three bags before putting the lid back on the chest.

If she was going to plant the stones in the Holy Council's chambers, her best chance of doing so without being caught was in less than an hour.

∼

"WHAT THE… DID THEY MAKE A MISTAKE?" Isaiah asked, blinking as he looked into the empty crate. He'd been supposed to get some explosives to deal with some of the high-ranking officers of the Order of the Eagle here, only to find an empty crate.

The angel scratched his head, looking around the room, then shrugged and put the lid back on the crate, murmuring, "Maybe one of the other crates…?"

Isaiah checked all the crates, but none of them had the explosives he was looking for. In the end he gave up, planning to send a message to let his superiors know that he couldn't carry out their orders. He'd ask for replacement explosives, but there simply wasn't time for them to arrive.

Little did Isaiah know, nor the other agent who showed up still later, but the letter to Aserial had neglected to inform her she was only supposed to take *one* sack of incineration stones.

CHAPTER 35

"*I* can't say that I'm surprised," Kitania said, sitting back in her chair as she sipped the cup of wine, her eyes half-closed as she enjoyed the bouquet and flavors. They lingered in her mouth and made her feel much better about where they were.

Eziel and Maura had been thoughtful enough to get food on their way back, some type of baked pastry with a spicy filling of meat and tomato sauce, among other things, and Kitania found herself *very* intrigued by how it'd been made. If it weren't so hard to get flour and tomatoes in the hells, she might have been tempted to experiment with copying the pastry back home. The thought sent a pang of regret through her, as she found herself thinking of the house she'd likely never see again. *That* was depressing.

Regardless, everyone was there but Rose and Vinara, since the succubus was keeping an eye on the angel while she healed. Vinara was also catching up on her knitting, which had shocked Kitania a little, that her friend knitted to pass the time, but Vinara had said something about it helping with her precision.

"You aren't surprised?" Yain asked, her eyebrows rising as she paused to nibble on her pastry for a moment. "Did you know this Janel would ignore Isalla?"

"Oh, of course not. It's just that, now that I've heard Isalla's explanation, it makes sense that she wouldn't be likely to believe her," Kitania said, setting down her cup, thankful that they were allowed to meet on the temple grounds. The garden they were in was essentially deserted, which made it easier to discuss things like they were. She considered, then continued a bit more soberly. "Oh, I expected any explanation to be a difficult sell to begin with, don't get me wrong. Telling an angelic commander that a conspiracy in the heavens is trying to restart the war with the hells and has betrayed the Holy Council... you don't think that it would be met with at least a raised eyebrow?"

"True enough," Isalla admitted unhappily, having barely touched her food so far. "Even in the heavens we have a tendency to think the best of people on the whole. Sometimes even ignoring flaws because it isn't proper to pay attention to them."

"Mm, now consider this. If it's something you're *already* going to be skeptical about, and one of the people you dislike most in the world walked in to make the claim to you, would *you* be inclined to listen?" Kitania asked, her eyebrows rising slightly as she looked at Isalla, who looked distinctly uneasy. "I wouldn't be surprised if you'd been thrown in prison even *with* Lady Anna sending you there."

"I think you're right, as much as I hate to admit it," Isalla said, letting out a heavy sigh as she shook her head. "I didn't realize someone would bear a grudge against me, but... what angers me the most is that she seemed to ignore that it was what *Rose* wanted, too! Rose and I went into things knowing that it could cause problems, and she *deliberately* didn't defend herself to try to protect me. I didn't want that, but it was Rose's choice. How could she disrespect her like that?"

"Some people get jealous and wish to blame a single person for everything ill," Maura murmured, letting out a soft sigh. "Still, does this really matter right now? At the current rate, I'm not sure how much good we're going to do, and every day gives the people we're hunting more time to carry out their plans."

"There isn't much we can do. Not unless Lady Kitania wishes

me to unmask myself and use myself as bait to draw out our enemies," Eziel said calmly, taking a sip from her cup as she frowned. "My one concern is that it might lead them to destroy any evidence we might be able to find."

"No," Kitania said flatly, just as Yain was opening her mouth, and the elf shut her mouth, looking a bit guilty. She'd probably been about to suggest they take Eziel's offer, but Kitania wasn't going to allow that. It was too dangerous, and disrespectful to Eziel. After a moment Kitania continued, her voice calm as could be as she met Eziel's surprised gaze. "Yes, you were part of the Society of Golden Dawn, but that was before you met my mother. As far as I'm concerned, that was a different person entirely, and I will *not* sacrifice a perfectly good person just for simple expedience. Besides, it wouldn't necessarily work, and that would be a tragedy."

"As you wish, Lady Kitania," Eziel conceded, bowing her head slightly. "I simply thought it was an option."

"Yes, but not one we should seriously consider," Isalla said. Kitania did notice that the subtle dislike Isalla had possessed where Eziel was concerned had eased since Sorm's ambush, which was reassuring.

"Entirely fair. So, what do we do in the meantime?" Maura asked, eying Isalla's pastry speculatively. Isalla seemed to notice, as the angel snatched it up and began eating at last.

"I honestly think that we have little choice except to wait," Kitania said, shaking her head slowly as she sighed. "I doubt Anna will agree to go speak with Janel, considering what she said about drawing attention, so that leaves waiting for Rose to recover. It'll only be about two or three more days, so it isn't *too* much of a delay. If that's too long... well, I doubt we'd be able to stop the society from doing anything drastic in that time anyway."

"Maybe you're right," Isalla said, taking a large bite of her pastry. Kitania laughed as Isalla's eyes suddenly went wide and her cheeks reddened. The angel quickly swallowed and scrabbled for her cup, gasping loudly as laughter echoed around the table.

"Found a spicy bit?" Kitania asked, but Isalla didn't reply, as quickly as she was swallowing the wine.

On the other hand, Isalla could *glare* just fine, even if the tears in her eyes somewhat ruined the effect.

$\mathcal{T}$he night was quiet, which helped Anna relax a little, looking up to watch the stars. They weren't quite as brilliant as she liked due to the smoke in the air over Uthren's Throne, but that was the price of civilization. Even so, Anna loved watching the stars, as different as they were from the ones which shone in the hells. Others might not realize that many of the constellations were different in the hells, but she'd studied them often enough to know that they were.

It'd been a day since Isalla's unfortunate meeting with Janel, and Anna hoped that Rose would wake sometime the next day, since she seemed to be almost entirely healed at this point. Kitania was keeping an eye on Rose with Isalla's company, so Anna had decided to give the two some privacy. She found the subtle flirtation between the two adorable and didn't want to get in their way.

Fortunately, Anna didn't have to worry about Krath interrupting, as he was at some gathering among what passed for Uthren's nobility, so she could enjoy the night properly, though she *did* wish she had Estalia's company.

On the other hand, she knew the moment that someone interrupted her solitude. While the woman was trying to be quiet, it was quite obvious that it wasn't something she'd trained in, as her shoes scuffed gently on a flagstone and her breathing was slightly louder than most of the surroundings. While Anna didn't think it was someone trying to attack her, she also didn't let down her guard, instead waiting until the woman was a dozen paces away before she spoke.

"That's quite close enough," Anna said at last, looking over to see a woman in the robes of Cyclone's priesthood standing nearby, looking surprised. The woman was normal enough, with brown hair and eyes, along with a cute upturned nose, but she wasn't exceptional in any way. She *did* look a bit startled at Anna's words, and seemed nervous as she bowed. Anna spoke after a moment, keeping her tone mild. "What is it? Does Cyclone want to speak with me again?"

"Ah, my apologies, Your Excellency, but I'm not here on the behalf of My Lord. As a matter of fact, I'm here to speak with you about something else," the priestess said, holding her bow. Anna's curiosity began to stir, though she was annoyed as well. Obviously, someone had decided to try to get their audience in a very indirect manner, which was… frustrating.

"I see. You may rise," Anna said, keeping her tone cool as she watched the woman, turning to face her fully. "What's your name?"

"May, May Greer, Your Excellency!" the woman replied, straightening as she grew more enthusiastic, her eyes almost shining as she smiled, adding, "I simply have to add, it's such an *honor* to meet you! Your deeds are known throughout the world and are an inspiration to all of us!"

"I'm glad to hear that, even if that wasn't why I performed them. Now, May… why have you approached me, if it isn't on the behalf of Cyclone? I must assume you're here on behalf of another, as nervous as you are," Anna said, watching the woman steadily, trying not to let herself say too much. The woman did nod slightly at her statement, though, which was interesting.

"That's right. Not that there was much other choice, I should say! The people who sent me are in the heavens, and they don't have another way to contact you safely," May hastily explained, flushing a little as she looked to the side, admitting, "I work with a few angels who have extremely lofty goals, you see. Not that I do anything that would harm Uthren, of course. I'm just trying to help the heavens on the whole."

That gave Anna pause, and for a moment she couldn't believe what she was hearing, while her suspicions grew stronger. She doubted that it would be as simple as she was thinking it might be, but could the conspiracy *really* have decided to contact her? It didn't seem possible to her, and yet... at the same time she supposed it was feasible. It wasn't like anyone knew where she'd been hiding over the millennia, so she could understand them trying to contact her. She'd led enough wars against the hells, after all.

"I see. And just what did they have to say to me? I've been denying audiences with others while I determine what involvement I wish to have with other angels," Anna replied calmly, folding her hands in front of her.

"From what I understand, you're healing an angel who might be someone with... misinformation about the group I'm working with, so they didn't dare wait any longer. I'm truly sorry to force a meeting like this, but that's why I came to speak with you," May told her, standing up a little straighter, almost looking proud as she continued. "The group who I'm working with calls themselves the Society of Golden Dawn. From what I've heard, they have a number of archangels among their number, though I obviously haven't met any."

It took every ounce of control that Anna had to keep from reacting to that, mostly in disbelief. Instead she arched an eyebrow at the woman, murmuring, "Is that so? A lofty name, as well as impressive rumors of their membership, but what do they have to do with me? I've been gone for a very long time."

"That's precisely why they wanted me to contact you. See, the society believes that the Holy Council has grown complacent and corrupt. In the past millennium, the faith of mortals where battling the hells is concerned has waned, while the Holy Council has done nothing to combat it. With every passing day the hells appear to grow stronger, and that... that isn't something that can be tolerated. You've *seen* the horrors that the hells can unleash, so you should know better than anyone how terrible they are," May said, her eyes shining with zeal, and her conviction that she was right was obvious, to Anna's quiet dismay. "Since they won't act, though, the society has been working to take matters into their own hands. They would love to have your support, as you did more to face them than anyone else in the heavens, but they didn't want you to be misinformed."

Anna looked at the woman skeptically, a hint of rage beginning to burn within her, but she tamped it down to keep it under control. She'd never made the best decisions when enraged, so had tried to keep herself calm. Instead she spoke quietly, her voice almost unruffled. "I see. I don't see why I should involve myself with this group, not based on vague descriptions of what they *want* to do."

"Yes, they thought you might feel that way. That's why they told me to tell you something," May said, taking a breath as her enthusiasm grew. "Apparently, they're going to give a demonstration of their conviction and power tomorrow. What that entails, I don't know, but they told me it would be impressive."

Estalia would probably try to play along longer, Anna knew, just to get more information out of the woman and their organization. Estalia was good at deception and flattery and was far more focused on the end goal. Anna, on the other hand... she was *not* Estalia.

The thought flickered through Anna's head at the same time that she acted. One moment May was standing there, smiling hopefully at Anna, and the next her eyes bulged out in her head as she hit the ground, the air blasting from the woman's lungs, one of Anna's hands holding her throat.

"Unfortunately for you, I know significantly more than that, May. In fact, after your *society* attempted to murder my daughter, I've been searching for them myself. *That's* what brought me out of hiding, not simply the fact I'd been gone for so long," Anna said, resisting the urge to smile, since she *knew* it wouldn't be a pleasant smile. Instead, as the woman paled, Anna shook her head and added, "Oh, I'm not going to kill you. No, we're going to go speak to Cyclone, and then we'll see what your deity has to say."

"B-but... they're trying to do the right thing!" May protested weakly, barely having caught her breath. "You're an *archangel*!"

"They *think* they're doing the right thing. There's a difference between that and *doing* what's right," Anna said, bodily picking the woman up as she called on her mantle, looking around as she tried to sense where Cyclone was. "Now, then, where is he?"

When Anna found him, her wings snapped out and she took flight.

∿

"I REALLY DON'T UNDERSTAND why you're so upset about this, Anathiel," Cyclone said, glancing at the door which led to the room where May was imprisoned. It was a very *nice* prison, Anna had to admit, but the priestess wasn't being allowed to leave, even if Cyclone was a little skeptical.

"I'm *upset* because her so-called society tried to murder my *daughter* to keep any word about them from getting out. The only thing she knew was that a few members of the Holy Council had been meeting in private, and about some rumors of an angelic god, yet they decided she had to die," Anna said flatly, deliberately making it sound to others like she was meaning Isalla instead of Kitania. She stared the deity in the eyes, or tried to as he avoided her gaze, which told her a fair amount about his lack of confidence. "I was *trying* to keep from dragging you into all of this, since Uthren is such a staunch ally of the heavens and you don't need to be dragged into the heavens' internal problems, but *they* sent your priestess to me."

"She has a point. I don't want to admit it, but she has a definite point," Sanguine said, the goddess's arms crossed in front of her as she frowned unhappily. "I've noticed that Lady Anathiel has been very careful not to try to drag us into whatever she's been investigating since she got here, at least until now."

"And the idea that a group of angels has been recruiting *our* priesthood without telling us... well, I don't know about you, but that makes me uneasy," Krath said, shaking his head slowly.

It'd been the better part of an hour since May had

approached Anna, and she hadn't been present as Cyclone questioned the priestess, to her annoyance. Not that she suspected the woman knew much in the end, but the unhappy look on Cyclone's face had been telling. Somewhat to her surprise, the two younger deities seemed far more accepting of Anna's claims, and more worried about the potential consequences.

"Perhaps so, but it isn't like May knows much. She's just passed along information about demon movements and the occasional bits of information about other deities," Cyclone said stubbornly, crossing his arms as he took a slightly more defensive stance. "I don't see what she can do to help you, even if you question her."

"The easiest thing would be if she told me who it was that contacted her. Then I could track down these miscreants myself," Anna said calmly, trying not to corner the deity. That wouldn't end well, she knew that for certain. No one really *wanted* to take on a deity on their home ground.

"No. Oh, I'm going to ask, but I'm not telling you immediately, not without making some inquiries of my own. Besides, if they're going to make some sort of *demonstration* tomorrow, it'll be obvious to us as well," Cyclone said, his eyes narrowing even more. "If it's obviously bad, *then* I'll tell you. If it's bad enough, I'll even let you do what you want, assuming Krath and Sanguine agree, but I'm not letting you hustle me into a decision."

Krath nodded, obviously reluctant as he looked at Anna apologetically. "I can't say as I blame him, Lady Anathiel. This is too complex and came at us all at once. If we had evidence they were trying to do something bad to us, maybe I'd be singing a different tune, but I need to at least sleep on this."

"As if you could carry a tune in a bucket," Sanguine murmured, prompting a flush from Krath, and the faintest hint of a smile from Anna.

"As you wish. I just desperately hope that this demonstration isn't too destructive. I... worry about what they may have planned," Anna said, trying as hard as she could to keep her disappointment hidden. She doubted that she succeeded, but it was worth the attempt. Even so, she paused only a moment before inclining her head and continuing. "In any case, I believe I need to go speak with the others and let them know what happened. Whatever happens, I want to be ready."

"Very well. Would you care for company on the trip to your room?" Krath asked politely, though Anna could tell he didn't expect her to agree.

"Thank you, but there's no need for that. I'm sure the three of you have things to discuss privately," Anna replied, nodding to them, then turned to leave. She could feel their gazes on her back, which wasn't comfortable, but she could handle it, at least until she was out of their sight.

Anna headed back to her room, where she knew Kitania would be waiting for her. The others wouldn't be, but soon enough Kitania would be heading back to the inn, and she could let the others know whatever she found out. Still, it wasn't exactly an ideal situation, from Anna's perspective. For a moment she'd hoped that she'd found a way to crack open the conspiracy, only to be brought up short.

As the door opened, Kitania's voice rang out softly. "Welcome back, Lady Anna."

"There's no need for that. I'm on my own, this time," Anna replied, closing the door and glancing at Rose as she asked, "Any change with her?"

Kitania was sitting in a chair next to Rose, a book in her lap as she rested in her guise as a dragon-blooded human. The disguise amused Anna, even if she wished that Kitania could look like she was supposed to. Her daughter wasn't as far into the book as Anna had expected, though she belatedly realized that was probably because Kitania wasn't truly fluent in angelic, let alone in reading and writing it. A medical text in angelic was probably difficult for her to parse, when Anna thought about it.

"Not really. Oh, she breathed a little more quickly for a little while, which made me think she might be about to wake, but she didn't," Kitania replied, setting the book aside as she reached out to take Rose's hand gently. The demoness paused as she looked at Anna and frowned, then asked softly, "You... look out of sorts, at least slightly. Is something wrong?"

"I'm mostly frustrated, because..." Anna paused, then smiled wryly at Kitania as she admitted, "The Society of Golden Dawn just tried to recruit me, not even an hour ago."

"They *what*?" Kitania demanded, almost shooting to her feet, and if the book hadn't been sitting on the nightstand next to her, it'd probably have fallen on the floor. Kitania stared at Anna with shock and excitement in her eyes. "What did you do? Did you catch them?"

"Slow down, dear. You're getting ahead of yourself, and I don't want that," Anna said, then stopped to wait as Kitania visibly took a breath and let it out.

"Well, if you're acting like *that*, obviously we don't have a target yet," Kitania murmured, her voice calmer as she glanced down at Rose, adding, "I wish they weren't being so damned careful."

"Yes, we all can wish that. If they weren't, Estalia's spies would have already ferreted out *something*. Believe me, she has more agents than you think, even among the heavens," Anna said, sighing as she glanced at the door and scowled. "They were careful here, too. They'd recruited one of Cyclone's priestesses, and she was the one who carried their message. He's being... difficult."

"Unsurprisingly," Kitania murmured, prompting a nod from Anna.

"Indeed. He's old and set in his ways. It sounds like she didn't have much information to begin with, but even what little she could tell me was incredibly worrying," Anna explained, frowning as she did so, wanting to pace a little. "She said that tomorrow they'd be giving a demonstration of their 'conviction and power'. *That* is a poor sign."

"You're telling me," Kitania said, chewing her lip nervously as her eyes narrowed. "Do you think they might attack here?"

"I doubt it. I'm far more concerned for Estalia and the Forest of Sighs. I was going to message Estalia with a warning, which hopefully she can pass on to Alserah," Anna explained, rolling her shoulders and half-stretching her wings in an attempt to relax the knot she felt forming in the middle of her back. She scowled, murmuring unhappily. "I hate being on the defensive."

"I think they think the same thing. That's why they're attacking *us*," Kitania said, reaching down to stroke Rose's cheek as the demoness's gaze hardened. "In that case... why don't you go warn her, then? I think we'll need every advantage we can get."

Anna nodded, reaching over to ruffle Kitania's hair before she added, a bit more pointedly, as she looked at Rose and Ember, "Agreed, which is why I'm *sure* Rose will be healed by morning, hm?"

There wasn't a response, but Anna was fairly sure she saw the flames around Ember flicker just a *bit* more quickly at her words.

∾

ALSERAH FROZE with the teacup halfway to her lips as light flashed in front of her and a tiny, bird-like creature of blue fire appeared. She tensed briefly, then relaxed as she recognized the creature as a magical construct, and a weak one at that.

Phillip sat up in his chair curiously as he asked, "What's this?"

The bird spoke before Alserah could decide how to respond, though, its voice that of Estalia, though there was no humor in the demoness's voice. "Alserah, my apologies for contacting you this way, but it's urgent. Anna, who I sent to assist Kitania and the others when they were attacked, was indirectly approached by the conspiracy this evening. They attempted to recruit her and said that there would be a demonstration of their power tomorrow. I don't know what that will entail and neither does she, but both of us have been targeted by them before. I recommend you reinforce your defenses."

With its message delivered, the construct collapsed into nothing a moment later, and Alserah frowned, then looked at her fellow deities in concern, replying simply. "Trouble, obviously."

"So I heard," Gandar said, frowning slightly as he leaned forward in his chair. "Do you believe her?"

"I don't see any reason *not* to believe her. Besides, I've been hearing a few rumors from the north that indicated something was happening in the heavens, but I haven't gotten any solid information yet," Alserah said, shrugging slightly. "I mean... what harm does reinforcing my defenses do?"

"True enough, I just had to ask," Gandar said, raising an eyebrow as he asked, "Would you like some help with that? I don't know about the rest of you, but I'd rather be safe than overconfident."

Phillip nodded, smiling slightly as he agreed. "Oh, most certainly! I'm also interested to meet whoever it is that casts those fascinating spells of hers... while not unique, there's a certain flair to them, and communicating messages like *that* in the heart of your palace is impressive."

"Mm..." Sidina said, slowly climbing to her feet, and Alserah couldn't resist rolling her eyes. Phillip had been a problematic guest since he arrived, in part because of how he'd harassed the magi about their spells, along with significant amounts of flirting. She was sure he'd managed to seduce at least some of them, but at least he appeared to have kept it quiet. More annoying was how much he'd begged to study Sindria's Light, but *that* request had been quite firmly denied, since she had no way of knowing that he'd be able to resist the urge to make off with it. Alserah might trust Phillip with her life, but she didn't trust him with her things. Particularly not valuable magical artifacts.

"I will go rest," Ire said, pushing back his chair to stand, taking a moment to bow to them before he straightened. Alserah resisted the urge to sigh, as she'd like his company, but it wasn't as though he could do much. Ire wasn't the best with wards, after all.

"If you would, could you let Ratha know? She's in the field, and it'd be good to have her back early, if possible," Alserah suggested and smiled as Ire straightened more and nodded.

"Of course. I will be back shortly," Ire agreed, looking more enthusiastic as he headed for the doors.

"I wonder when the lad is going to admit his feelings to her," Gandar muttered, rubbing his chin thoughtfully as he watched Ire go.

"Lad? I'm fairly certain that he's older than you are," Phillip said, grinning broadly as Gandar raised an eyebrow.

"Age doesn't have anything to do with maturity. Why, you're living proof of that!" Gandar retorted, grinning evilly in return.

Phillip stopped, blinked, then glowered at Gandar, his expression briefly so comical that Alserah couldn't suppress a chuckle, which prompted laughter from Gandar as well, and a smile from Sidina. Phillip looked at her in betrayal, spreading his arms.

"Alserah, is that any way to treat an old friend? You heard what he said!" Phillip exclaimed dramatically.

"That doesn't make it any less true," Alserah replied, then nodded toward the door. "Come on, let's get to work. There isn't much daylight left, so let's make the most of it."

Phillip slumped slightly, but Alserah knew it wouldn't last. While Phillip's ego deflated easily enough, it *always* recovered.

She was far more worried about what the angels might have planned.

CHAPTER 37

"You know what to do?" Yimael asked impatiently, tapping her foot as she watched the angel adjust the harness. Ordath resisted the urge to sigh at the woman's attitude when *she* wasn't the one taking an immense risk.

"Of course, My Lady. I fly over the portal while invisible, and when I'm certain I'm close enough the wind won't blow the device off-course, I drop it into the portal," Phina replied, the freckled angel looking up with a smile as she patted the harness. "Then I fly back up through the portal to give a report."

The young blonde was an enthusiastic, relatively new addition to the society, which gave Ordath some pause about giving her such an important mission, but Yimael had insisted that the woman was ready for it. He wasn't about to argue with her, so instead he examined the gatecrusher again, resisting the urge to frown, as it wasn't particularly impressive. Of course, this *was* the prototype, not the ones which the artificers had been spending most of their time on for the past months.

It was primarily steel, which made the small artifact rather heavy for its size, which was about as large as a child's head, and it had additional protrusions that made little sense to Ordath, though each was engraved with carefully formed symbols that someone had lined with platinum. The device was in its own harness, and all it would take to drop was Phina pulling two of the straps of her own harness, so it wasn't like it was terribly complex.

"Just remember that we don't know how violent the reaction will really be," Ordath said, surprising himself as he looked at Phina calmly. "Don't get any closer than you have to, just to be safe, and the moment you drop it, try to get through the portal again."

"Of course, Archangel! I'll do my best to get the job done," Phina assured him, bowing her head deeply, even as Yimael glared at Ordath.

Ordath just returned the look impassively, as she hadn't been exactly looking out for the young woman's health. He didn't think that Phina would be in much danger, but he *did* prefer to take precautions where possible. It was hard enough to recruit members to the society even without sacrificing them unnecessarily.

"Well, we're pretty much ready here. Do you think everything is going well elsewhere?" Yimael asked, huffing unhappily as she crossed her arms in front of her, obviously still displeased with Ordath interfering.

"Ethan's in charge of things there. If anything doesn't go as planned, it'll be because other people changed plans, which will definitely annoy him," Ordath said, his smile growing a little more. "I'm sure it's going fine. We just need to do our part."

"Good. In that case, let's open the portal," Yimael said, looking over at the five angelic magi waiting patiently. She smiled grimly as she nodded at them. "Alright, open the gate. I want to ensure this is done as efficiently as possible."

"As you say, milady," the leader of the magi replied, bowing deeply.

Then the magi turned to begin their ritual as Ordath slowly walked toward the edge of the continent.

The endless skies of the heavens were always soothing to him, though he *did* frown when he saw the darker clouds slowly working their way in their direction. It looked like it'd be raining, which wasn't appropriate for the day that was going to be one of the society's greatest triumphs.

"Ah, well," Ordath murmured, looking downward instead. The weather didn't matter, just the results.

$\sim$

BELLS TOLLED OVER SKYHAVEN SLOWLY, filling the air with their music. The sound reverberated even deep within the Hall of Wisdom, where the Holy Council was preparing to meet, and the first of the councilors were already present.

The chamber was large, carefully designed to make it easy for a speaker's voice to be heard throughout the room, and all around it were desks and chairs for the four-dozen angels who made up the Holy Council. In the center of the room was a raised platform for whoever was speaking, while lights illuminated exquisitely carved and painted walls. Few places in the heavens were more richly appointed, and the councilors certainly reflected that.

Half a dozen councilors were present, and the men and women wore robes and dresses made of the finest materials found in the heavens, from the hides of rare beasts to enchanted fabric that would have fed a village for a year or more just for a tunic, and all of them were immaculately poised as they spoke with one another. Even the representatives of the heavenly orders practically oozed wealth and confidence, though only the woman who headed the Order of the Dragon was present, sitting in her chair as she went over a few documents.

Other than the councilors, a dozen guards were stationed around the room, each in enameled white armor with gold trim, swords at their sides and with cloudpiercers in hand. They were ignored by those in the room, by and large, but when they moved, each showed the grace of a highly trained soldier.

"Any word on Anathiel?" one of the female councilors asked, sounding distinctly unhappy.

"Nothing," another said unhappily, shaking his head in annoyance. "From what I've heard, she's been ignoring all the letters other people have sent her as well, but I've seriously considered going to try to speak with her myself."

"How rude! She went and vanished for an incredibly long

time, leaving us in dire straits for the entire time, then she returns and doesn't have the common decency to come speak with us?" the first woman snapped, her eyes narrowing. "We're the ones who've been protecting the heavens for all these years; she should show some respect!"

"Calmly. She's an archangel, and one of the more powerful ones at that. If she wanted to, she likely could form an alliance that would threaten even our power," another man said, shaking his head as he frowned at her. "I'm no happier with what she's done than you are, but there's no point in getting upset yet. She could simply be getting her bearings after being absent for so long."

The woman scoffed at that, but didn't verbally disagree, instead ruffling her wings a bit as she scowled and changed the subject. "What about today? What's our agenda, since you said there was something new."

"I've received some worrying news from the Forest of Sighs. When Alserah closed her borders to angels we lost many of our usual information sources, but some has been getting through anyway. Apparently, she's blaming the attack on a faction of angels and even has a prisoner!" the second man said, a note of shock in his voice as he looked at his companions. "I've noticed that she isn't blaming *us*, but even so it's inconceivable!"

"How dare she?!" the woman snarled, her lips curling as she continued. "We're the only reason the hells didn't overwhelm the mortal world ages ago! Her little nation wouldn't even exist without us, so she shouldn't make wild accusations!"

"Regardless, it's a worry, particularly since she's called several other deities to her side. I have no idea what they're planning, but—" the man continued, but paused as the doors opened and more councilors began pouring into the room. He sighed and shook his head as he changed the subject. "Alas, it appears we'll have to wait. I see that it's about time to call the session to order."

"Very well. We'll just have to consider how to put her *properly* in her place for those accusations," the woman muttered, heading for a chair, while the other men gave each other nods, then headed for their own seats.

It took a few minutes for all the councilors to filter their way into the room, and a low rumble of conversation filled the room as they spoke with their neighbors, talking about everything from crops to the most recent events in the borderlands between the Alliance of Light and the Kingdoms of Darkness, but the most common subject was Anathiel. Not all of the councilors were as upset as the first group, but many of them were, and others were simply suspicious of her motives.

Eventually, the second man looked around and nodded to one of the guards, who closed the door as he stood and adjusted his clothing slightly before stepping up on the platform. Most of the others grew quiet as the man looked around and nodded to them.

"Thank you all for coming today!" he said, speaking loudly so his voice would clearly be heard throughout the room. "I call to order the seventh session of this year's Holy Council meetings, and—"

The man never finished his sentence, as at his words, magic sparked to life. Incineration stones placed below the platform detonated in a near-simultaneous ripple of fire and death that ripped him apart instantly, sending stone and wood shrapnel flying across the room. Yet that wasn't the end of it.

All around the room, desk after desk exploded almost as one, instantly killing the councilors sitting there before they could even react. Most of the angels didn't have time to do more than flinch before the fiery waves hit them, and screams echoed in the chamber with the explosions that mercilessly enveloped its inhabitants, even as the room's shape channeled the blast upward to weaken the roof's supports.

The doors were blown off their hinges, and before the guards outside could begin to react, the walls creaked, groaned, and the roof came down on the smoldering remains of the Holy Council.

CHAPTER 38

*P*hina took a deep breath, excitement rushing through her despite the weight of the device she was carrying. It was incredibly heavy, making her flight labored at best, but it was all worth it in her mind. She was going to be striking the first of the blows necessary to eliminate the hells at last, and *that* was an immense honor. Ordath's presence before she took flight simply thrilled her even more, as it meant an archangel would be watching as she did it. Phina descended carefully toward the portal to the hells, trying her best to avoid breathing in the stench rising from the volcano-like mountain.

The continent below her was Dolia, from what Phina understood, and she admired it for a moment. Even from her height she couldn't see the oceans in the distance, the air wasn't clear enough for that, and the portal mountain was a decent distance from the nearby mountain range. The lands were green and verdant for the most part, and Phina looked on the fortifications around the portal in approval.

Once the volcano rim might have been simply a road up out of the hells, but the defenders had gotten rid of *that* ages ago. All the interior roads leading up to the rim had been demolished, and they'd carved the rim itself into a gigantic circular fortress, with siege engines in place to deal with any flying creatures that came through, and a gigantic net in place to keep them from getting away easily. Even now she could see the ant-like figures of soldiers patrolling the walls, and she nodded, hoping the blast wouldn't be too big. They were fighting the good fight against the hells, after all. Still, getting past the net was why she'd been told the device created blades of air which would cut through it on its way down.

Not that she could see the device at the moment, with the invisibility spell in effect. Still, it wasn't *too* windy, so Phina descended a little more, beating her wings quickly as she took a position near the center of the portal, if far above it, and glanced upward. She could just barely see the portal to the heavens, and only because she knew the pale circle of radiance was there. It was beautiful, compared to the inky darkness of the portal to the hells. So after a moment she looked down, doing her best to hold her position as she took hold of the straps to drop the gatecrusher.

"May the Lord of Light's radiance purge all evil!" Phina said, smiling widely as she pulled the two straps hard.

There was a sound of metal rasping on metal, and the gatecrusher was suddenly visible as it fell, leaving her invisibility spell. The sound had been a rod leaving the device and activating it, and the sudden loss of its weight caused Phina to surge upward abruptly. She only glanced at the device as it began glowing, then she quickly beat her wings as she headed back toward the portal as quickly as she could. It was a long climb, though, and she wouldn't have time to reach it before the gatecrusher reached the portal to the hells.

Not that she wouldn't try, though.

"WHAT'S THAT?" Norman asked, and Josh blinked, looking over at the dwarf.

"What's *what*?" he asked, letting out a breath in annoyance. Josh *hated* being paired with the dwarf, since they were similar heights, but his superiors and squad mates thought it was hilarious seeing them next to each other.

"That!" Norman said, pointing toward the center of The Pit,

as most people stationed at Dolia's portal to the hells called it, and Josh looked up, blinking in confusion.

A golden light was falling toward the portal incredibly quickly, and he couldn't make out any details, but Josh couldn't help frowning in worry. Still, there was an easy explanation, in his opinion.

"Maybe it's a falling star? Hell, nothing we can do is going to stop it, though. I doubt the net's going to stop it, and—see? It went right through it," Josh said, gesturing as they watched the light barely slow as it hit the net and continued downward. "Let's let the captain know when we get back. I'm sure he'll want to—"

The light reached the portal as he was talking, and the world suddenly lit up as the inky black portal turned brilliant white. Josh cried out in pain as he suddenly couldn't see anything, and beside him he heard Norman curse.

"Earth and stone, what in all the—" the dwarf began, but he didn't have time to finish. Before Josh's vision could begin to clear, the earth convulsed, and then he was falling sideways for an instant before everything went black.

"HEAVEN'S TEARS!" Ordath cursed, raising a hand to mute the sudden glare of light from below.

It was like the sun had suddenly risen through the portal, and the sheer strength of it worried him, since it meant that other people would probably see it, too. They'd been planning to keep the attack at least *somewhat* hidden, but this was far more obvious than he wanted it to be.

Relief rushed through him as the light vanished a moment later, but his relief was short-lived as he saw that it'd been replaced by a sphere of pitch darkness. That sphere seemed to be sucking everything in, and Ordath's eyes widened as he realized that he couldn't see the crater the portal had been in at all, and it was *collapsing* on itself.

"That's not supposed to happen," Yimael said, cursing in her rough voice as she rubbed at her eyes, scowling downward. "And what is *that*?"

"Close the portal," Ordath said, fear rushing through him suddenly, as a sense of crisis enveloped him. "Close it now!"

"What? But we won't see what—" Yimael protested, only to be cut off as he glared at her, unleashing his mantle ruthlessly.

"*Now*, Yimael!" Ordath thundered as his glow washed over her, and she paled, then gestured at the magi.

"You heard him," Yimael said, and the five magi nodded, ending their chants. The portal faded away below them, as did the vision of the mortal world as Ordath relaxed. Yimael turned to him, scowling as she asked. "Now why—"

IN THE HELLS, the mountain looked the same as it always did, at least at first. The summit of the mountain was buried in a black portal, but unlike Hellmount, this one was rarely used these days. The portal in Dolia was simply too heavily guarded, and multiple demonic fortresses dotted the landscape around its base, as did villages, most of whom hoped to find some hardy mortal world seeds that'd been blown through the portal.

Still, some of the people there looked up, sensing that something had changed just as the first cracks of white spread through the portal. Moments later the cracks spread, and then there were monstrous groaning and popping sounds as the mountain abruptly fractured, cracks ripping up and down its length, immense amounts of mana pouring out of it ceaselessly.

Animals and monsters instinctively began panicking, but it was far, far too late, for at last the portal that had been there for countless years suddenly detonated, and with it exploded the mountain as well.

The earth shook like an immense volcano had erupted, and the shockwave destroyed everything within a hundred miles of the mountain, flattening forests and cities without pity, even as a hail of lava and molten stones pelted the region. Where the mountain had been was an immense geyser of magma erupting upward like the rage of the gods themselves, and earthquakes wracked the land.

Nothing was left to see it, though, as the sheer violence of the eruption destroyed everyone and everything as well, save for a few tattered foundations of particularly sturdy buildings.

～

IN THE MORTAL WORLD, the black sphere collapsed on itself just as the portal to the heavens closed. Phina never made it near the portal, and the angel only had a moment to look down as she wondered what she was supposed to do, fear rippling through her at last. Of course, it was far too late, for at the same time that the mountain exploded, so did that tiny black sphere which was hovering over the near-perfect spherical hole where the mountain and portal had been a moment before.

The shockwave it unleashed killed the angel instantly, mangling her unrecognizably as it shattered the ground around itself, the blast wave shredding the towns that'd supported the garrison as well as the fields and forests, turning a lush, peaceful region into a desolate wasteland in an instant.

If that had been all, it would have been bad enough as it was. Unfortunately for everyone, the blast wasn't merely *physical*.

～

JUST AS YIMAEL was demanding an explanation, the ground beneath Ordath's feet trembled, then bucked, staggering the archangel. A thunderous *boom* split the air a moment later, followed by more bucking that caused Ordath to sway in place, while Yimael fell to one knee.

Ordath glanced down and paled suddenly, as he saw where the portal had been. A wave of black and white energy was fading as he watched, while he could also see a vortex beginning to form where it'd been. Far worse were the crackling, *popping* sounds he was hearing.

"Take flight, *now!*" Ordath snapped, even as he was following his own advice. He barely had a moment to feel guilt for Phina's sacrifice, as he was far more concerned with his own safety at the moment.

Yimael managed to take off a moment later, as did a couple of the magi, but before the others could react, the entire continent lurched in front of Ordath's horrified gaze, and a vast, miles-wide section of the continent began sloughing off into the void. The ear-splitting sound made conversation impossible, and Ordath felt like his ears were going to bleed as the vortex tore the shard of the continent into pieces, swallowing the stone and trees mercilessly.

All but one of the magi made it off, as even so the process was slow, but one of the men screamed as a tree toppled onto him, and Ordath's guilt grew as he saw a tiny angelic village was on the land being consumed. He circled higher, fighting the turbulence as he looked down and saw a handful of angels staggering in the village. One spotted him and reached out as if calling for help, their figure so tiny he couldn't quite make out more than the fact the man was blond, and it was far, *far* too late.

With earth-shattering cracking sounds, the village and land it'd been on was pulverized and consumed by the vortex, which spun for a minute or two more, then collapsed on itself. At the same time, it felt almost like the very world itself was convulsing around Ordath, making it hard to breathe at times, and he gasped, his stomach shuddering with every passing moment.

Ordath stared downward, then turned toward Yimael, who was now as pale as a sheet. He suppressed the urge to grab her by the collar and shake the woman as his anger surged higher, as he couldn't anyway, not while flying. Instead he snarled loudly, not bothering to hide his shock and rage. "Yimael, what in the name of the *ever-burning sun* was that?"

"I... I don't know! That wasn't supposed to happen, the device shouldn't have hit our portal at all! It was *closed*, and it was designed to destroy the portal it fell *into*!" Yimael protested, looking at him with wild eyes. "It was supposed to direct all the damage into the hells! It might've hurt the mortal world, but it wasn't supposed to affect *us*!"

"Well, obviously you were wrong! Now a section of the *heavens* has been destroyed, and—" Ordath began, then stopped, cursing under his breath as he saw flecks of white beginning to rise into the sky in the distance. The other angels would be investigating, so he hissed, then ordered as the convulsing sensation began settling down. "Other angels are coming! It's time to get out of here, Yimael, but this isn't over! We need a *proper* explanation, not excuses!"

Yimael gritted her teeth but nodded, her voice unhappy as she replied. "Yes, of course. Come on, all of you! We need to go!"

The group quickly flew back toward their headquarters, keeping low to try to avoid being spotted. They didn't have time to take a roundabout route, unfortunately, and Ordath simply hoped no one would notice them, as he suppressed his aura once more.

CHRISTOPHER'S EYES were fixed on the angels he saw fly overhead, his stomach still settling after the horrifying sensation, one which had felt like the world itself was in pain. More important, though, were the six angels barely flying over the top of the trees, the only ones he'd seen who were flying *away* from the area which had been devastated.

That made him suspicious to begin with, but he'd also seen a glow like the power of an archangel from the direction not long before. Coupled with the messages he'd received from Estalia's agents over the previous couple of weeks, he wondered if these might be the ones they were looking for.

So he looked at Irene and smiled at her nervously, murmuring, "I think those might be members of the group Our Lady is looking for. I'll follow, you try and let others know? Whatever's happened, I think she was right."

"Of course," Irene said, smiling warmly. His wife was one of the handful of converts to Estalia's beliefs that Christopher had recruited over the years since he'd been repatriated to the heavens, and he trusted her absolutely. She gave him a quick kiss and spoke sternly. "Be *safe*, though. She'd want you to be."

"Yes, dear, I will be," Christopher promised, and he quickly took flight. Fortunately for him, he obviously knew the area better than the suspicious group who'd just passed by, so he was sure he could tail them safely, at least for a while.

In the meantime, he had to wonder what had just happened. The rumbling in the distance, lurching of the ground, and the feeling of the world itself in pain did *not* bode well.

CHAPTER 39

"What in the name of all the stars was that?" Rose asked, wiping the bile away from her mouth and looking distinctly unhappy.

Kitania couldn't blame Rose, since there'd been multiple crashes from outside, almost instantly following the sensation like the world itself had spasmed around them. Worse, it'd happened *just* after Rose woke up, and her friend's stomach wasn't settled, though at least she hadn't had anything in her stomach to throw up.

"I'm not sure," Kitania replied, breathing in and out slowly. Anna had left the room before the incident, which made Kitania nervous, to say the least, and only Eziel, Isalla, and Vinara were present. They'd made the decision to leave Maura and Yain out of this, which was why they weren't here, but everyone else had their weapons and armor.

"I can guess," Vinara said, looking far more haggard than she normally did, and her skin was pale. "That was the ley lines, I could tell that much… something must have damaged them on a massive scale. I couldn't say what, though."

"The ley lines? I didn't know anything could damage them!" Eziel said, her eyebrows rising as she looked at Vinara in horror.

"Oh, they can. It was a practice banned by both sides millennia ago, since it led to a few barren areas," Vinara said

303

grimly, shaking her head firmly. "No, this feels worse than even the descriptions I read about in books. I have no idea what the society did, but it's not good."

"You can say that again," Anna said, opening the door as she looked at them unhappily, her eyes dark. "The portal to the heavens just spat out huge chunks of debris across the city, some of them dozens of feet across, and the temple and many other areas have been damaged. The temple is in chaos, especially since the mangled bodies of a few angels were found in the wreckage, and they're investigating what in all the hells just happened. Worse, Cyclone's intercepted messages that something terrible happened to the south and took off. If anyone can figure it out quickly, it'll be him, and—"

Anna's voice cut off as a tiny bird of blue flame appeared before her, putting Kitania's teeth on edge, considering how dangerous sending a message like that *here* was for them. Estalia wouldn't have done it without reason, though, so she listened, bracing herself.

"Anna, I have no idea what they did, but the results are obvious enough. The world just tried to shred itself, and there's a black cloud to the north like nothing I've seen in my life, so Veldoran scryed for the source." Estalia's voice was flat with anger. "Black Mountain and all the nations around it are *gone*, Anna. The portal is gone as well, and there's an expanding lake of lava over ten miles across where the mountain used to be. I don't think anything's alive within fifty miles of the explosion, so I *think* we know what their little demonstration was. I'll inform you if I get any more information."

The bird vanished, and Kitania felt like someone had punched her in the stomach with all the strength they could muster. Vinara's horror was obvious as well, and Anna pinched the bridge of her nose, closing her eyes as she slowly breathed out. Only Isalla and Rose looked relatively bewildered, though still horrified.

"What's Black Mountain?" Rose asked, her voice soft.

"Remember Hellmount? Black Mountain is the mountain that leads to Dolia," Kitania said flatly, and both women abruptly paled.

"Oh, no, you can't possibly... they destroyed the portal?" Isalla asked, her eyes going huge, horror dawning on her face fully. "I didn't think that was possible!"

"They destroyed the portal and *every living thing* within a massive distance of it," Vinara corrected, her voice almost a snarl as her nails bit into her palms. "It *shouldn't* be possible, and to even do so is madness! Those idiots don't realize how interconnected the ley lines are, and the portals are *part* of the network! If anything, they're core parts of the ley lines, and if those are destroyed, I can't even imagine the consequences!"

"Which is why I dread learning what else it is they've done," Anna said, her voice surprisingly soft and calm, and she looked at Rose coolly, then the others. Despite her apparent calm, the look in Anna's eyes sent a chill down Kitania's spine, and she couldn't help straightening as Anna spoke again. "Kitania, would you help me with my armor? I'd ask the rest of you to help Rose into hers as well, as I want all of us ready to move. I think it's time and past for us to have a rather *pointed* discussion with Janel and Rathien. The time for subtlety is *past*."

"As you wish," Kitania agreed, her stomach tightening still more, which didn't quite feel possible, but at the same time her horror was quickly being replaced by anger.

Those who were behind this would pay for what they'd done.

"WHAT HAPPENED?" Alserah asked, resisting the urge to rush over to Gandar. The other deities weren't present, as each were contacting their own homelands, all but Sidina, who had quietly withdrawn to practice in private.

Gandar stood in the middle of the plaza where he'd teleported in, looking grim as could be, even as he stepped toward her unhappily, his voice blunt. "The Pit is gone, as is pretty much everything important within twenty miles, including some of *my* people. It's worse in Phenal, since they owned most of the territory around it, but what I've seen is quite bad enough. The portal is completely gone, and the land... mana is suffusing everything, and I think it's almost half as bad as Rosken."

Alserah flinched at the description, as to her knowledge Rosken was *still* half-molten in the center of the crater. Plenty of magi had tried to come up with a way of repairing the damage, but nothing had worked as of yet. She paused, then replied, her voice about as blunt as his was.

"I see. You got the better of things, from what I've heard. Estalia contacted me, and her magister scryed on the area in the hells. They lost about fifty miles at a minimum, and the mountain is entirely gone," Alserah said, and Gandar almost froze, a flash of incredulousness crossing his face as he stared at her.

"They *what*? I thought that the surface was bad enough, but they unleashed something like *that*? Are they out of their feather-brained minds?" Gandar snarled, his anger mounting quickly enough to worry Alserah. "Where are the bastards, anyway?! I want to crush these traitorous, arrogant, *shit-eating* angels in person!"

"I don't know, not yet. But this? This could easily lead to open war. Hopefully they'll figure out what happened, and soon," Alserah said, and grimaced as she looked at him, then admitted, "I've set up the beacon Estalia sent us. After *that*, we need all the help we can get."

"Fine. I just hope that she gets off her little throne and does something *useful*. I lost more people than I care to think about today," Gandar said, storming off toward the building.

Alserah followed him, her emotions like ice now. Despite everything, even the angels' willingness to sacrifice her and her people, she'd never expected them to do something like *this*. It was so far beyond the pale she had to wonder why even their members would be willing to put up with it.

CHAPTER 40

The sound of shouting caused Ordath to pause, looking at Yimael with a scowl, but he didn't say anything. The other members of the council were obviously displeased, and he figured it was probably her fault, at least in part. Not that he could truly blame her now that he'd had time to think more, it wasn't as though they'd had a chance to test the gatecrushers before this, so there'd been no way to know what the consequences would truly be.

Taking a breath, Ordath opened the door, and the angry shouting suddenly stopped as the others looked at him and Yimael, the frustration on their faces obvious. What surprised him more was the traces of *fear* he saw as well.

"So, just how badly did *your* task go? We felt the continent shudder from *here*, Ordath," Zithar stated, his deep voice unusually unhappy.

"It worked!" Yimael protested, crossing her arms defensively as she looked away, hesitating before she admitted, "Some things worked differently than expected, but it worked... I think."

"You think. Absolutely wonderful, as if we needed another disaster on our hands," Sereth said caustically, slamming her hands on the table, to Ordath's surprise and worry. Anything that could discomfort the other archangel worried him.

"What do you mean, *another* disaster?" Ordath asked, frowning heavily.

"First, what happened, Ordath? Not you, Yimael," Ethan said, shaking his head slowly.

"The gatecrusher was dropped as planned, and it appeared to do as it was intended to. However, something about the design appears to have been... flawed. It caused severe destruction in the mortal world and felt dangerous enough I ordered the portal closed," Ordath said, crossing his arms as he hesitated, then continued unhappily. "The explosion came through the closed portal anyway and ripped off a section of the continent several miles across and consumed it, somehow. Not all of us escaped in time, unfortunately, and we quickly vacated the area, hopefully avoiding anyone spotting us."

"Light preserve us... no *wonder* we felt it," Ethan said, rubbing his forehead.

"What's happened here?" Ordath asked, looking around the room. "Initially I thought you were upset because of what happened with us, but now it seems like something else has happened."

"You might say that," Sereth said, her smile almost mocking. "The Holy Council is dead. *All* of them."

"What? But the plan was to—" Ordath began, but Zithar interrupted.

"To kill enough to give us a majority, we know! The *problem* is that the explosions were too powerful, and Ethan received messages that the incineration stones for dealing with the commanders of the Order of the Eagle and the Order of the Phoenix were missing when the agents got there," Zithar said, scowling as he shook his head. "Our best guess is that the idiot who planted the stones in the council chambers used *all* of them, three times what was needed! Last we heard, the council chambers collapsed and the leadership of the heavenly orders are fully on their guard!"

"Tears of heaven," Ordath murmured, reaching up to rub his eyes, shocked at the disaster that had occurred.

The entire point of decapitating the command structure of the two orders they didn't have full control of was so the remainder of the Holy Council could appoint the society's members as new successors. That would have allowed them to declare war and crusade against the hells properly, and they *might* have even managed to blame the destruction of part of the continent on the hells, too.

"You see the problem, obviously," Ethan said, his voice deadpan as he shook his head. "We came all this way, only to screw up now. Still, the heavens are in chaos. We still have a chance to spin things the way we want, and should be able to drum up enough support from the populace if we act—"

The angel was interrupted by pounding on the door, as a man called out. "Lady Yimael, Lady Yimael! Come quick, it's urgent!"

No one spoke, and Ordath's sense of foreboding simply grew worse as he looked at Yimael, who growled, then turned and threw open the doors, snapping, "What is it?"

The angel on the other side of the doors was sweating and had a wild look in his eyes, his hair looking almost stringy and his clothing smudged with dirt. He looked at Yimael in relief as he spoke quickly. "It's the artificers, milady! Things were going fine until they heard what happened over on the continent rim, and an argument broke out! I don't know who started it, but it turned into a fight, and when the dust settled, we realized that a bunch of them ran with the completed artifacts!"

"They *what*? Where were they going?" Yimael demanded, seizing the angel by the collar as she picked him up, her face turning almost purple with rage.

"I'm not sure, a couple of the other guards went after them, but they were heading east, and that means—" the man began, only for Zithar to cut him off.

"The headquarters of the Order of the Eagle. Damnable *cowards*!" Zithar said, straightening as he looked at the others and spoke bluntly. "I think the time for subtlety has passed. We can blame them for the destruction of the Holy Council, but we have to keep word about our role from getting out! Who's with me?"

Ethan swore under his breath but nodded grimly, looking at

Yimael unhappily as he said. "Agreed, for all the good it'll do. I think we need as much assistance as we can get, though."

"It's good that we warned the faithful to be ready today, isn't it?" Sereth said, smiling thinly as she nodded. "I'll send a message to the Adamant Pinnacle and other major forces for reinforcements, but I think we'll need more than that. Ordath, shall we contact the Lord of Light? If there was ever a time for him to intervene, I believe it's now."

Ordath hesitated only for a moment before nodding, taking a deep breath before he spoke softly. "You're right, I suppose. His light will illuminate and purge the darkness. Let's do this, then."

The others all nodded as Yimael dropped the angel, speaking bluntly. "Prepare for battle! It's time for *us* to lead the heavens to a glorious new dawn!"

"Yes, milady!" the angel said, relief evident on his face as he turned to run down the hallway.

The other council members nodded grimly to Ordath and Sereth, then they headed out at a brisk pace, each probably to get their own gear. As they left, Sereth looked at Ordath and asked, "Do you think the others are ready?"

"They have to be. As Zithar said, it's time to act more openly," Ordath said, his jaw tightening slightly as he shook his head. "I just hope our preparations were enough."

"We'll see," Sereth said, and she quickly headed into the back of the compound, while Ordath followed.

If nothing else, Ordath was confident that *no one* was prepared for the Lord of Light. The only question was whether or not he'd be enough.

CHAPTER 41

$\mathcal{T}$he guard's eyes were wide with shock and fear as he held the halberd in front of the doorway, his hands visibly trembling. "I-I'm sorry, Your Excellency, but we're in a state of emergency, and everyone is to be denied entrance, no matter who—"

"Young man, you can either move out of my way or I will move you. I've been patient before this, but no more," Anna interrupted, and Kitania winced at the icy tone to her voice, pitying the poor member of the Order of the Dragon. He obviously wasn't prepared to deny an archangel entrance into the fortress.

"B-but..." the young man began, looking at the two other soldiers for support, only to find them edging out of the way nervously, one of them tugging on her belt to adjust it, and their reaction finally caused his brave front to crumble. "V-very well. But I need to make clear I do this under protest."

"Of course you do," Anna said, shoving his weapon aside with her cloudpiercer as she impatiently stepped past the guard and opened the door.

The sound of rapid footsteps echoed through the tower halls, and Kitania quickly followed, glancing around nervously at the sight of an angelic redoubt. It had been a long time since she'd been in one, and at least there weren't the sounds of battle this time.

Behind Kitania the others quickly followed as well, and Kitania had to admire Rose's resolve. Despite having barely woken up after nearly being killed, Rose was in her armor and fully composed, as though she'd never been gone at all, and the woman obviously was attracting attention from others as well. Isalla was in her own armor, while Vinara had taken the form of a green-haired angel in robes to infiltrate the tower more easily. Eziel could almost be missed in her relatively drab leathers, but the angel was in her own form at last, which almost looked alien to Kitania at this point. She rather looked forward to all of this being over and being able to keep their own forms at last, though.

"Isalla? Lead the way, please. I don't know where the Heavenly Wing's office is," Anna said, ignoring the several angels that slowed at the sight of their group. One of them, likely an officer, started toward them as she spoke.

"Of course, Lady Anathiel," Isalla said, bowing slightly, and the officer abruptly stopped, the blood draining from her face, then she beat a hasty retreat.

Kitania resisted the urge to laugh, and instead glanced at Vinara as she murmured, "Useful to be with her, hm?"

"As if we could get in here easily any other way," Vinara replied, her monocle placed over one eye as she looked around. "This is pretty heavily warded."

They followed Anna and Isalla down the hall and up the stairs as they spoke, with many angels quickly making way for Anna. That helped, considering the building practically looked like it was in chaos. Part of Kitania desperately wanted to know why the angels were so panicked, since it didn't seem like they should be worried about a few dozen houses and buildings being damaged or destroyed.

Soon they found themselves in front of a door, and Isalla motioned to it. "We're here, Lady Anathiel."

"Excellent," Anna said, and didn't even knock as she opened the door, her gaze frosty as she stepped inside.

"Who—!" a woman began, only to stop suddenly, and

Kitania waited for Isalla and Rose to step inside before she peeked in, only to be surprised by the sight of Janel Ironheart. She hadn't expected the woman to be quite as short as she was, though the woman looked dangerous in her armor.

"It's good to see you're well, Janel. Even if it sounds like you've also been unfairly accusing Isalla of ruining my career. I did that myself, thank you," Rose said, her voice cool. "I thought you had better judgment than that."

"Roselynn? What in all the heaven's happened to you?" Janel asked, just as Eziel closed the door, and the woman's voice grew a sharper edge as she continued. "For that matter, who are all of you, and what are you doing in my office?"

"*I* am Anathiel. Archangel of war," Anna interrupted, her voice surprisingly mild, even as her aura rippled outward, prompting the angelic commander to stiffen. "As to who everyone is, that doesn't matter. What *matters* is that yesterday I was approached by the conspiracy that Isalla told you she was investigating, and they told me that today there would be a demonstration of their power. I've already learned that they've destroyed a portal to the hells in Dolia, with catastrophic consequences below and likely in this world as well. However, *that* is not enough to get this sort of reaction. What else have they done?"

"Why should I tell you?" Janel retorted, the woman's back stiffening as Kitania's eyes widened. If nothing else, the woman certainly had a backbone, even if it was rather foolishly misplaced. Especially as she continued. "*You* have been hiding for millennia, while the rest of us have been actually working to defend the heavens, and I don't see—"

The butt of Anna's cloudpiercer came down on the floor hard enough that one of the fine stones shattered instantly, and the dark expression on her face sent a thread of fear through Kitania, one which she suspected Janel shared, based on how the woman fell back a step.

"You have no idea what I sacrificed. How many friends I lost, all on the damned, foolish quest to destroy the hells the Holy Council of the time had set me on. Rest? Hah! That was something for common soldiers, not for *archangels*. I was thrown into battle again and again, like an unthinking, unfeeling *weapon*. Don't even start, child," Anna said, her voice uncharacteristically cold as she stared Janel down. "I've also lost patience. You will tell me what you know, or I will find out by the simple expedient of finding Rathien myself and getting it out of him, no matter what it takes. No matter *who* gets in the way."

"Don't try her, Janel," Rose said softly, shaking her head. "Please?"

For a long moment the room was quiet, then Janel let out a breath and spoke, her tone ever so slightly less combative, though she was looking at Anna warily now. "Fine. It isn't as though it won't be all over soon enough, but not only did a portion of the continent south of Skyhaven rip away earlier, about the time everyone felt that horrific *pulse* through the world, but the Holy Council was killed in a massive blast that brought the roof down on them. There were no survivors, so needless to say there's a good deal of chaos in the heavens! We've been warned to be on guard, as it could be a prelude to an invasion or the like, but we have no idea what's going on."

"Oh, hellfire," Kitania muttered, closing her eyes. No one spoke for a long moment, which was fortunate.

"I think it's time to pay Rathien a visit," Anna said, her voice taut with anger. "I want *answers*."

"What are you talking about? Why would *he* have answers? How could he even be involved in this... this *plot* you claim exists?" Janel demanded, glowering at Anna as she almost laughed, adding, "In fact, he's never even come close to the Holy Council!"

"He wouldn't need to. Rathien was one of the leaders I took orders from before he sent me to Sorm, and *he* was formerly captain of the Holy Council guard." Eziel spoke calmly, her voice drawing Janel's attention as well as everyone else's. The angel's gaze was haunted as she continued softly. "If anyone could convince a member of their guards to assist them, it would be him."

"Hellfire and brimstone," Kitania muttered unhappily, the pieces falling into place at last. She'd been told that Sorm had headed the Holy Council's guards, but it had been long enough before that she hadn't made the connection immediately.

"Regardless, he'll have answers if anyone will, and I think I know how to convince him to implicate himself," Isalla said, smiling as she looked at Vinara, asking, "Vin? Would you mind making my armor look like I was in the Order of the Phoenix again?"

"Now see here, I won't have you masquerading as—" Janel began snarling, only to be cut off by Rose.

"Isalla was betrayed and thrown behind enemy lines while investigating the Society of Golden Dawn, and this is just a continuation of her duties. Regardless of what the order may have decided since she vanished, until she receives official notice from the grandmaster of the order that she's no longer a member, she's entitled to the armor and position," Rose said, her tone almost bored as she looked at Janel. "As she's in a different branch of the order, *you* have no authority over her, Janel, nor do I, and the investigation of those believed guilty of high treason takes precedence over all other crimes and directives."

The room was silent for a moment, while Janel's mouth hung open, then Vinara snickered softly, turning to Isalla as she replied. "Certainly, Isalla, especially after that lovely bit of legal weasel-wording. One moment and I'll have you as the very image of a member of the Order of the Phoenix again... though admittedly with nicer armor than most of the others I've seen."

Kitania couldn't resist a smile, especially with how put out Janel looked, and she smiled wryly at Rose, who smirked as she told her, "All that time dealing with stodgy rules growing up had to count for *something*, didn't it?"

"I suppose so. Eziel? Do you know where Rathien's office is?" Kitania asked, looking at the angel expectantly. At about the same time Vinara finished her spell, and Isalla's armor shifted colors to match those of the Order of the Phoenix.

"Of course," Eziel said, pausing to look at Anna as she asked, "Is it alright if we do this, Lady Anathiel? You were taking the lead before this."

"No, go right ahead. My approach would be to simply kick down his door and confront him about this, which wouldn't necessarily be the best approach at the moment," Anna said, looking slightly more relaxed as she watched them curiously. "My *other* method would take far too much time, so if you can get the information out of him more easily, go right ahead."

"Excellent. Thank you for your information, Heavenly Wing," Isalla said, far more politely than Kitania would have been to the caustic woman. "Now, Eziel? Would you care to lead us to his office? I'd also like people to be prepared for him to react poorly."

"Sure," Kitania said, calmly pulling out the hairpin which would turn into her cloudpiercer as she followed Isalla. She thought she heard Rose say something to Janel, but the clatter from outside the room distracted her.

The hall circled much of the tower, and Eziel led them to a door, stepping aside as she said calmly, "Here we are."

"Thank you," Isalla said, looking back as she took a breath and smiled. "Here we go."

Kitania moved forward, just to the side of the door as she waited as calmly as she could manage, the hairpin in one hand, and Isalla knocked. Vinara was just behind her, but Kitania's ears perked as she heard a soft curse from inside the room.

"One moment, I'm rather busy!" a man snarled, footsteps approaching the door, which opened abruptly as he demanded, "What is it now?"

Rathien was a handsome angel with black hair and a close-trimmed beard which was marred by a scar that ran down his chin at an angle. His blue eyes were intense, and he wore the silver and blue armor of the Order of the Dragon. Behind him Kitania could see a room that was decorated more than Janel's had been, though she could only really see one wall. On the other hand, Isalla spoke immediately.

"Rathien the Blue, you are under arrest for your involvement in the Society of the Golden Dawn and its involvement in the assassination of the Holy—" Isalla began, but midway through her speech Rathien cursed and reached for his sword as he stepped back.

Kitania smoothly took a step past Isalla and through the door in that moment, willing her cloudpiercer to extend to its full length as she instantly began spinning it. The weapon snapped out to its full length in mid-spin, and the backside of the butt caught Rathien's right leg and pulled it out from under him, sending him crashing to the floor. Kitania quickly stepped forward, one foot on his chest while the other planted on the hand near his sword, putting the blade of her cloudpiercer against his throat. The man froze, his eyes huge as he stared up at her, and Kitania smiled at him, revealing her fangs in the process.

"Very nicely done, Isalla. I think that shows he's not on the side of *good*," Kitania said, not looking away from him as she spoke softly. "I *suggest* you not move, lest I carve you a second smile."

Rathien stayed perfectly still, and Isalla stepped into the room, patting Kitania on the shoulder as she said, "Thank you, Kitty. I thought it'd do the job, and… there're some letters on the desk. That might help give us information."

"Whatever you think you're doing, you're not going to get away with this! Assaulting an officer of the Order of the Dragon is—" Rathien began blustering, though he kept still and was starting to sweat, but Anna stepped in at that point and interrupted.

"That's minor, compared to conspiring with a private group of angels to start a war without the authorization of the Holy Council. According to the strictures of all three heavenly orders, doing something like that is grounds for life imprisonment in *mild* cases, while severe cases are punishable by death," Anna said, looking down at him coldly. "I think you'd best explain yourself, unless you'd prefer the latter."

"I'm not telling you *anything*. I won't succumb to your threats!" Rathien retorted, then shut up as Kitania pressed the blade against his throat gently.

"Not that he needs to. He *just* got a letter, and it doesn't look like he even had time to read it yet. A rather hasty one, in fact," Isalla said, smiling as she added, "It isn't even in *code*, of all things! Let me read it off."

The angel cleared her throat, then spoke, loud enough that even some of the soldiers outside could hear, Kitania suspected.

317

That was good, since she suspected they'd just been working up the courage to try to interfere.

"Rathien, things have gone awry. Immediately distract the other orders and see that they don't return to the heavens, as the destruction was more severe than we expected. Dissidents have taken artifacts to the Eagle Citadel, so we must immediately deal with them in the heavens. Our brethren in the Adamant Pinnacle are coming to our aid, so you must keep our opponents from being reinforced. Destroy this letter immediately. The dawn shall come for all." Isalla stopped, looking up from the letter with a harsh smile, adding, "Rather telling, isn't it?"

"That it is," a man said, his voice grim as he stepped into the doorway, only to be stopped by Rose, who was blocking it. "May I pass, please? I'm Heavenly Wing Tagan, leader of the Order of the Eagle, here. I want to read the letter myself."

"Let him in, Rose," Anna said, and Rose let him by.

"As you wish, archangel," Rose said, looking at Kitania and smiling. "At least we found *some* confirmation, finally."

"Agreed," Kitania said, tensing a little as the angel passed her, then relaxed as he didn't do anything, and simply took the letter Isalla handed him.

The blond angel read through the letter quickly, and as he did his expression grew darker and darker, then he cursed under his breath and glowered at Rathien, obviously upset. Even so, he didn't say anything for a moment, and when he did speak his voice was cold. "Rathien, I always thought of you as a friend, even if you were hot-headed at times. This, though... how could you do this?"

"Tagan, you can't let them deceive you like this, I—" Rathien quickly protested, swallowing hard as a drop of blood welled up where Kitania's blade pressed against his throat, but he was interrupted as Tagan slapped the desk hard.

"No, that's enough. *You* are going to prison for a proper investigation into your loyalties. My guards will keep an eye on you," Tagan said, glowering at the letter, then setting it down as he looked at Anna. "Lady Anathiel, my apologies for not greeting you sooner, but I'm afraid this is getting out of hand,

and I don't have time. Will your companions hand Rathien over to us?"

"Certainly. We don't have the resources to keep him captive at the moment, and it sounds like the heavens need our assistance more than anyone here," Anna replied, looking at Kitania with a raised eyebrow. "Kitania?"

"Of course. As soon as his guards are present, I'll let them take this... *filth* off my hands," Kitania agreed.

"Excellent. Fortunately, I have something of a shortcut to the heavens on hand. Once we're done here, we can leave," Anna said, and she smiled as she added, "I imagine whoever has taken over my old home is in for a shock."

CHAPTER 42

The rumble of thunder across the training ground caused Alserah's eyebrows to rise more and more, and not just because of the scale of what she was seeing. Mass teleportations were rare even in warfare, simply due to the amount of mana they required, so this would have been surprising enough even with just that, but it was who was accompanying Estalia that surprised her more than anything else.

No one would mistake Estalia for any of her companions, for the demon queen was a glorious beacon that drew the eye in her midnight plate armor, luminous in the middle of the training ground, but beyond that she was also the only demon present. Instead of demons, the men and women snapping into existence around her were *angels*.

Over a hundred angels had appeared so far, all of them in midnight-blue armor that matched Estalia's, though some were obviously magi, and the sight was shocking, especially since they practically *radiated* magic from all the equipment they were wearing. Minor enchantments on the equipment of elite soldiers were common, in Alserah's experience, but she'd never known of a nation that could afford to use powerful ones on a large group. Not that she knew that this wasn't an elite unit, but Alserah didn't dare assume that the angels were the most powerful unit in Estalia's domain. She'd never heard of them before, after all.

"Alserah, I'd say that it's a delight to meet you in person, but the circumstances couldn't be much worse," Estalia said, glancing at the other deities flanking Alserah almost casually, then smiled thinly as she added, "Things have changed still more since I messaged you, in fact."

"Oh?" Alserah asked, deciding to dispense with pleasantries, since the demon queen had already done so. Even with having seen her through Vinara, Alserah was having a hard time fighting off the urge to stare at Estalia, which was *very* disturbing.

"Among those who I've repatriated to the heavens are those who had chosen to follow me. I often gave them the ability to send me messages in the case of an emergency. One of those people sent me a message indicating that he believed he'd found the headquarters of the Society of Golden Dawn," Estalia explained briskly, her eyes narrowing slightly. "He gave me the location, and it's on the same continent as Skyhaven, but I don't have further information as of yet. Unfortunately, the methods of receiving information I have are... limited. Am I right to believe that the mortal world didn't come through the *incident* unscathed? I was also informed that even the heavens were damaged by it."

"Damned right," Gandar grunted, his arms folded as he stared at Estalia unhappily. "We lost an area about forty miles across to whatever those featherdusters did."

"Featherdusters? An amusing insult if I've ever heard one," Estalia said, laughing softly, her voice enchanting enough to distract for a moment, but her amusement faded as she nodded. "Indeed. It seems my initial estimates were wrong, in any case. We haven't determined the full scale of destruction, but my magister hasn't found an intact city within eighty miles of Black Mountain yet. I've informed Anna and the others, and she informed me she's on her way to the heavens, where she'll set up *her* teleportation beacon for us."

"Ah. Is that why you have angels with you, then? I... must admit, I'm startled to see so many of them in your colors,"

Alserah said, frowning as she looked across the angels, then realized the sea of white wings had a few oddities in it, with a handful of black, gray, or even blue or red wings among them, and after they'd reached about two hundred in number the teleportations had slowed, then stopped. After a moment she asked. "Unless... are they disguised demons?"

"Demons? Oh, no, of course not. Bringing demons into the heavens would be far too close to an invasion, and prompt those who *aren't* the society to jump to the wrong conclusions. That's why I asked for volunteers from the many angels who'd taken refuge in my domain," Estalia said, smiling again as she looked at the angels affectionately, adding, "I will say, they're all skilled in battle, I didn't bring anyone who couldn't defend themselves properly, and I ensured that all of them had the best gear I could provide. It won't be enough against archangels, but against angelic soldiers they'll hold their own."

"Just hold their own?" Phillip asked, arching an eyebrow skeptically as he folded his arms in front of him. "If that's all they can manage with *that* kind of magic, they're not that good."

"I prefer to be modest about their chances rather than appearing to be overconfident," Estalia replied, her smile widening still more as she looked at Phillip and the others, nodding slightly as she murmured, "Let me see... Gandar, Ire, Ratha, Phillip, and... Sidina, yes? I hadn't expected *quite* this many deities to be present."

"You know who we are?" Ratha asked, looking a little taken aback as she glanced at Alserah nervously. If they hadn't been in front of the angels, Alserah suspected that her friend would have backed away.

"Of course I do. I make a point to keep an ear out for information on deities, especially for new ones or those who've handed down their mantles," Estalia said, shrugging as she looked back at her soldiers. "It simply makes sense, as powerful as you all are."

"I think I should be more worried about your spy network than anything else," Alserah murmured, eying Estalia warily, a little concerned despite the intense aura of attraction she felt toward the demon queen.

Estalia laughed, her voice ringing out beautifully despite the situation, and Alserah could see how all the angels straightened at the sound, looking happier despite themselves. She couldn't entirely blame them, with how riveting the sound was, and Estalia looked at her with twinkling eyes.

"Oh, Alserah... believe me, that's the *least* dangerous thing about me," Estalia said, her mirth obvious as she grinned widely.

HARAL MADE sure her vambrace was properly in place and nodded to herself, glancing down at her whip to ensure that it was coiled properly on her belt. She didn't like using it indoors, which was why she had a sword, but it was her favored weapon and even having it on her person helped soothe her nerves.

Now fully armored, though not as heavily as so many other members of the society, she quickly stepped out of her room and into the chaos. Members of the society were rushing down the halls, likely heading for the Eagle Citadel to reinforce the vanguard. Haral longed to rush after them, but Sorm had told her they'd been ordered to gather in the council's antechamber.

Moving against the flow of angels slowed her down more than she liked, so Haral was a touch late, at least based on Sorm's voice as he spoke to a group of a dozen other angels, most of them heavily armored, though there was a priest and mage among them.

"...our task is to guard the council members who're coordinating messages. Chances are that no one will strike here, but there's no guarantee that we'll go unnoticed," Sorm told them grimly, his hands folded behind his back, while he had a sword at his side. Haral had half-expected him to use a cloudpiercer, but she supposed that just because he'd trained with it didn't mean he liked it. He continued steadily, ignoring the echoing boots in the hallways. "I want all of you to be on your guard, as things have gone too far awry already, and I will *not* let them go wrong here."

"Sir?" one of the angels spoke up, her voice betraying a touch of nervousness. At Sorm's nod, she continued. "Why are we staying so far inside the complex? Wouldn't it be better to keep anyone from entering?"

"If we had more people, we could. Unfortunately, every angel we can spare is going to assault the Eagle Citadel, and there're too many halls to guard with a force our size. No, we have to focus our defense on somewhere we can ensure no one is getting by us, and that's here," Sorm said, gesturing around the wide antechamber. Haral looked around, and she had to admit that he had a point.

The room was large, with a couple of sofas and chairs for those waiting to meet with the council, and it had plenty of space for them to spread out, yet there were also only three exits, the two that led into the halls of the rest of the building, and the one that led to the council chambers. Haral would be astonished if the council didn't have some way of escaping from there, but getting in wouldn't be easy.

"Besides, I'm sure that the wards will slow down any attackers," the mage said, his deep voice oddly soothing as he folded his arms. "Hopefully there won't be any, but…"

"Agreed. That's why your first task is to secure the room. I want spells in place to at least weaken any common attack spells launched into the room, *especially* fireballs, and other defenses as well. Archers, feel free to grab tables from other rooms to use as cover if you want them. I'm not taking any chances," Sorm said, scowling as he looked at them. "Now, get to it."

"Sir!" the soldiers rumbled, and the priest and mage quickly got to work, while the two archers discussed things, then left the room for the moment.

Haral hesitated, then approached cautiously, waiting until the others were out of earshot before she spoke to Sorm quietly. "Sorm… do you know why we're in here? I would've thought that we'd be with the attackers, especially you."

"Mm, we might've, if Aserial hadn't screwed things up. I hear she managed to not only kill the *entire* Holy Council, but in so doing she also kept attacks on the commanders of the heavenly orders from happening," Sorm replied, grimacing ever so slightly as he shook his head, sighing. "I don't know how it happened, but I can't believe she'd do it intentionally. As it stands, though, I suspect they're keeping us here because they don't want us making a mess of the attack on the Eagle Citadel."

"Deadly winds," Haral murmured, stunned enough to just stand there for a moment in shock. She'd known most of the members of the society who were, no, *had been* on the Holy Council, and the idea of them being dead was an enormous shock to her. After a few moments she shook off the shock, though, taking a deep breath and letting it out. "Well, I suppose I understand why, even if I'm not happy. Still, it's an honor to guard the council, isn't it? The people in charge of relaying communications are important too."

"That's the right way to look at it," Sorm said approvingly, smiling at last as his worry seemed to ease at last. "We'll get through this, love, then everything will be done."

Haral nodded, resisting the urge to lean in and kiss him. As much as she wanted to, it wasn't the time or place for that. They had their task, and it was time to carry it out.

Kitania barely flinched at the lurch of the teleportation, and the thunderclap of their arrival echoed through the room around them. The world felt different, and Kitania looked around curiously, a bit surprised by their surroundings.

Anna had revealed she had an amulet that would allow her to return to the heavens, and she'd used it to bring all of them with her. Kitania had been expecting to appear in a temple or field, not in a building, and what surrounded her was somewhat amusing.

The room they were in smelled of wood shavings and the somewhat fouler scent of lacquers, prompting Kitania to wrinkle her nose, but she wasn't upset about it. Woodworking tools surrounded them, and she could see carefully made violins hanging from racks along the ceiling. Some were quite complete, while others looked like they were in the early stages of construction.

More amusing than anything else to her was the blond angel

sitting on a chair only a few feet away, his mouth open as he stared at them, a brush in one hand as he paused in the midst of applying a coat of lacquer to the violin in front of him.

"Hm, this is something of a surprise. I suspected that my home had likely passed to another, but I didn't expect it to have been turned into a craftsman's workshop," Anna said, looking around for a moment, then smiled at the man. "My apologies for the intrusion, good sir, I'll endeavor not to repeat this, but there are no guarantees. I'm afraid this was a bit of an emergency."

"Um, I... are you A-Anathiel?" the man asked, his voice and hands trembling.

"That's right," Anna confirmed, tilting her head slightly, and the man's eyes seemed to light up as he smiled widely.

"So rumors were true; you *did* live here!" he exclaimed, looking relieved. "It... it's a surprise, but it's not a problem, if you aren't going to do this often. I'm just glad you didn't show up when I was working on something delicate."

"Thank you for your understanding," Anna replied, then looked at Kitania and the others, adding, "That said, we have to go. This *is* an emergency, after all, and we need to get Kitania and Vinara's gawking over with."

"Why would I gawk?" Kitania asked, a little miffed that Anna had singled her out, but she followed as Anna opened the door to leave the workshop and headed down the hall of the house.

Kitania was surprised by the width of the doors and windows at first, after having spent so long in the mortal world, but she supposed it made sense with everyone having wings. The house was filled with examples of woodwork, and was a nice, homey sort of place, which she certainly appreciated.

"Because neither of you have ever been in the heavens, and I *know* you," Anna replied, brushing past a lady angel who'd come from the kitchen to their left, adding, "My apologies, ma'am. We'll be out immediately."

The woman stared in shock, obviously taken aback as the six of them proceeded through the home, then out the front door. Kitania opened her mouth to speak, but when she finally got outside she almost froze, mouth agape as she looked at the sky.

Kitania felt like she could see forever, at least until the clouds got in the way, but the clouds... *those* were like nothing she'd ever seen before. The enormous clouds over the oceans of the mortal world had astounded her when she'd first seen them, but even they were dwarfed by the immense white and gray clouds that towered upward to incomprehensible heights. They made her feel so much smaller, it was practically impossible for Kitania to describe, especially with how dark some of them were.

Beyond that were the mountains Kitania could see in the distance, many of them floating in the sky, serenely ignoring gravity or wind as they just *hung* there, like they'd been fixed in place on a pole or something. Those mountains hung over a land of lush forests and fields, ones that reminded Kitania of the Forest of Sighs, if even greener, and the air was incredibly refreshing.

On the other hand, they were also in what looked like a small village, standing on the doorstep of a shop in the main part of town, and Kitania quickly shook off her astonishment. She looked around, blinking as she saw how angels going about their business stopped to look at them curiously.

"See? You gawked, even if not for *quite* as long as I expected," Anna said, glancing back at Kitania with a smile. "It also looks like the village has grown since I was last here. Not unexpected, since it's been a long time, but strange to me. In any case, let's go. We need a good place to set up the beacon, and in the middle of town seems like a poor idea."

"True enough," Rose agreed, looking around and frowning, then pointing to their right. "If I'm not mistaken about where we are, the Eagle Citadel is that way. We probably should go that direction, since we'll be heading there anyway."

"Most likely, yes," Anna agreed, and her wings extended as the archangel took flight, and was quickly followed by the others.

Kitania hesitated only a moment before channeling mana into her armor to take flight as well, glancing over at Vinara as she did so, commenting, "This is different than I expected."

"Mm, I agree. I never expected the heavens to be like this, even if I read some books that described it several times," Vinara agreed, still in her angelic disguise, looking down at the village with brief glances as she added, "I suppose it only makes sense that they wouldn't have walls, but I would've thought they'd have dangerous animals here."

The lack of walls was something Kitania hadn't noticed, and she looked around, pursing her lips as she took in the sights of the different buildings. They were all different than what she'd expected, a little closer to the flowing elven style than the blocky dwarven, human, or even demonic construction she'd seen. If anything, the angelic structures seemed to be designed to allow the wind to pass them by. That was probably for a very good reason, though, and she glanced upward at the sky, trying to imagine what it would be like to live in a supposedly endless sky.

"The heavens are relatively safe, especially compared to the hells, but even the mortal world is more dangerous," Isalla chimed in, flying alongside them as Anna led the way upward over the trees, which seemed to grow far taller than others Kitania had seen, though many of them were growing at angles, probably due to the wind. "There are a couple of continents with more dangerous creatures, and they're mostly kept that way, as both game preserves and training grounds for soldiers. There's never really been a need for walls, since any invaders would presumably be capable of flight, and the heavens have never really been threatened by others."

"Not until the Battle of Scarlet Peaks. That came far closer than the heavenly orders liked and prompted them to fortify areas near the portal there," Rose added, her voice relatively quiet as the wind buffeted them.

"I believe it. A lot of people died, and the commanders of the hells thought they'd succeed in getting through the portal at first," Kitania agreed, noticing that Anna was now angling toward a broad field, one which didn't look like it was a farmer's to her.

"Not surprising, considering the fears that were likely on the other side," Anna said, swooping down for a landing, then turned around, grinning as she added, "Speaking of which, I don't see a point to keeping your disguises, you two. It's going to be *very* obvious that something is amiss here in a few minutes, after all."

"A fair point," Kitania said wryly, reaching over to pull off her gauntlet so she could get to the bracelet. It took a few moments, and as she did so Vinara returned to the shape of a succubus for the first time in what seemed like months to Kitania. It was a bit of a surprise, but when Kitania pulled off the bracelet she felt relief surge through her, like a weight had been taken from her shoulders.

"Now let me see..." Anna murmured, pulling out a teleportation beacon, and this one surprised Kitania, since it was composed largely of adamantine and platinum, and she saw several glowing diamonds set into it.

"Um, Anna... is that what I think it is?" Kitania asked, eying the beacon in worry.

"Most likely, though I can't be certain," Anna replied absently, smiling slightly as she glanced at Kitania as she set the beacon on the ground. "Your mother is bringing an entire military unit with her and can't afford to drain their mana to get them here, so she sent this with me."

"Oh. Well, she *definitely* is taking all of this seriously," Kitania said, relaxing ever so slightly, while Vinara took a step forward.

"Indeed. I've never seen one of this type of teleportation beacon... I wish I had time to study it," Vinara said, a hint of longing in her voice.

"What exactly is it, Lady Kitania?" Eziel asked curiously, a hint of worry in her voice. "It sounds like it... negates the cost of teleportation or something of that sort? I didn't believe that was possible."

"That's because it isn't possible to *negate* the mana cost. No, that beacon is designed to draw the mana from itself to form a link to its twin, creating a much stronger connection, then each teleportation takes much less mana than normal, and is drawn from the beacons themselves," Kitania said, shrugging as she smiled. "I suspect we'd better step back. I have no idea how many soldiers Mother is bringing with her, but we don't want to get in their way."

"Agreed," Rose said, following Kitania as the demoness

retreated. The others came along as well, though Vinara hesitated for a long moment.

It took Anna a minute before she was happy with the placement of the beacon, and Kitania saw the gemstones glow a little brighter as she nodded in satisfaction. Then Anna pulled out a green gemstone and murmured something, causing the gemstone to evaporate into green flame, turning into another of the bird-like messengers Kitania had seen her make use of lately. It vanished after listening to her message, and Anna walked toward them calmly, her cloudpiercer resting over a shoulder.

"How many of those gems do you even have? It can't be easy to make them," Kitania asked, raising an eyebrow at the archangel, who laughed softly in response.

"I had ten, originally. I have… three left, I think," Anna said, looking at her belt pouch speculatively. "Your mother will be displeased, likely as not, but what's the point of having them if they aren't used?"

"True, I suppose. How long do you think—" Kitania began asking, only to fall silent as the beacon began glowing more brightly.

"About that long," Isalla said helpfully, and Kitania glared in response.

The first person appeared with a cracking sound almost like thunder, if on a far smaller scale, and Kitania raised an eyebrow slightly, but wasn't really surprised by the sight of the angel in her mother's colors. She was a bit more startled as one after another began to appear, not a single demon among them, while the first angel approached and bowed before Anna deeply.

"Lady Anathiel, Her Majesty instructed me to inform you that one of her agents found the headquarters of the Society of Golden Dawn as well, so it appears that we will have to split our forces. She is going to arrive shortly, accompanied by Alserah and five other deities," the soldier said, not rising from her bow.

"Rise, I don't expect you to stand on formality under these circumstances," Anna said, frowning slightly. "Splitting our forces… that doesn't strike me as a good idea under these circumstances. Doubtless the society has at least a few archangels on their side, and it sounded like they wanted to take out the Eagle Citadel badly."

"True, but if we know where it is, a group could function as a scouting party, couldn't they?" Kitania suggested, considering for a moment before adding, a little dryly, "If there are six deities coming along, I'd almost say *we* should look into it, since I don't think you'll miss us."

"I'll *always* miss you, but you may have a point. We'll discuss it briefly once everyone has arrived. I wonder what wave Estalia is going to—ah, there she is!" Anna said, her face lighting up with a brilliant smile as Estalia appeared in the midst of the angels, looking as poised as always, though significantly less happy, comparatively.

That lasted all of a moment, though, as the demon queen smiled at the sight of Anna and Kitania, and Kitania's breath caught in her throat as the weight of Estalia's mantle and pleasure struck her, staggering the demoness hard. She almost didn't notice the appearance of Alserah and several other non-angels behind Estalia, the attraction was so strong.

"Anna, Kitty! Oh good, you both look fine... not for lack of trying on our daughter's part, of course, but what else can we expect from her?" Estalia exclaimed, coming toward them at a brisk pace.

Anna laughed and folded Estalia in a hug, causing a clatter since both of them were armored, and kissed the demon queen briefly before nodding to Kitania, smiling as she teased, "Well, yes, but she's intact right now, no matter what the day might bring."

"Oh? You got yourself injured *again*, Kitania?" Alserah asked, striding forward in her armor, a wry smile on her face. The elven goddess was in full armor and had her bow in hand as she looked closely at Kitania. "I would've thought you were trying to avoid that."

"Yes, well, I didn't have much of a chance to avoid it. An angel buried incineration stones below the road, and all of us were injured to some degree. Besides, *this* time I didn't take the worst of it," Kitania replied, shifting from one foot to the other as she tried to decide how she should react to the goddess's presence. She mostly felt relief and a little happiness, which surprised her a little.

"I was the one who nearly died, I'm afraid. If it weren't for Anathiel's timely aid, I would have been in need of resurrection, assuming it even worked," Rose added, pausing before she continued. "Also, Maura and Yain are fine, they're currently holed up in an inn."

"Excellent, though I'm sorry to hear about your close call," Alserah said, and her gaze grew far more complicated as she turned to face Anna, hesitating for a moment before she bowed her head and spoke humbly, a hand on her chest. "Lady Anathiel, your reputation precedes you, and it's an honor to meet you at long last. I am Alserah, goddess of the Forest of Sighs."

"Ah, so *you're* the one who ended up with Kitania for a while! Don't be overly formal, Alserah, there's no point to it. As far as I'm concerned, we're equals at worst," Anna replied with a grin, glancing at the other deities as she added, "I don't immediately recognize any of your companions, though I suspect I knew the bearer of at least *one* of their mantles, but I'm glad to see we have assistance. I think we're going to need all of it, even if we *did* manage to convince the leader of the Order of the Eagle in Uthren's Throne to send reinforcements."

"Proper introductions can wait," another deity said, one with his hair in dreadlocks. "What do we need to do?"

"Apparently the Society of Golden Dawn is attacking the headquarters of the Order of the Eagle, called the Eagle Citadel. I'm not sure why, but their letter to Rathien indicated it was important and said something about artifacts," Anna said briskly, straightening as she looked at them. "That's about twenty miles east of us, and if they're planning to take out the citadel it'll take a huge force. I fully expect we could run into a few archangels in the process, along with the bulk of their troops. Fortunately, the Order of the Eagle won't take that standing down. They're the masters of magic in the heavens, and I doubt the attackers are going to be able to break in quickly."

"We also have the location of their headquarters, or at least a hideout on this continent," Estalia added, her expression far more focused now as she looked around the group. "I'm not sure of the exact location relative to us, but some of those I brought with should have figured that out by this point."

"It's about sixteen miles to the northeast, Your Majesty," one of the female angels reported. Behind the deities the angels were organizing themselves into combat units, Kitania noticed, which she definitely approved of. They were all in potent magical armor, which she thought would serve them well in the coming conflict.

"Thank you, Karakel," Estalia said, smiling briefly, then continued. "The question is, how do we deal with this?"

"If we could have one or two of the message stones Anna has, I think we'd be willing to investigate the hideout," Kitania said, folding her arms in front of her as no less than *eight* deific gazes came to rest on her. It was intimidating, but she continued as if they weren't looking at her, or as close as she could manage to it. "If it looks heavily guarded, we can let you know and watch to see if anyone tries to escape. If it *isn't* well-guarded, we could try breaking in to see if we can't sabotage more of their plans."

"That... isn't a bad idea. If they're careful they wouldn't be in much danger, and it isn't as risky as splitting our forces," the dwarven god said, stroking his chin. Kitania *thought* he was Gandar, who she'd heard about during her stay in the Forest of Sighs.

"We don't have time to debate, not really. Any objections?" Estalia asked, looking around the group of deities, and when there weren't any raised, she looked at Kitania with a worried smile as she spoke. "Then go for it, Kitty. Just try not to take too many risks, hm? I don't want to lose you *again*."

"I don't intend to," Kitania replied, hesitating before she hugged Estalia. Her mother hugged her tight, and Anna smiled at Kitania over Estalia's shoulder, though she seemed far more at peace with things than Estalia did.

"Karakel, take your squad and support them. You know the way, and I don't want them on their own," Estalia ordered, breaking off the hug after a long moment.

"Yes, Your Majesty!" the brunette angel acknowledged with a salute.

"Sorry for volunteering us," Kitania said, looking back at the others, and Vinara rolled her eyes while Isalla and Rose laughed.

"Let me think, we can try to investigate an angelic stronghold, probably from a safe distance, *or* we can get sucked into a massive war zone with angels on both sides who probably wouldn't mind torching obvious demons... you know, I think I prefer the former," Vinara said, mock indecision in her voice.

"While I may not think of it in *quite* the same way, I don't mind, either. We're trying to bring down their organization, not gain personal glory," Isalla added, looking at Rose in amusement as she said, "Besides, neither Rose nor I are going to be getting any sort of glory, since we left our order."

"I wouldn't be so sure of that, though it *does* make glory rather unlikely, I'll agree," Kitania said, taking a step back as she looked at Alserah, hesitating for a moment before she spoke to her. "Do be safe, Alserah? With what's coming... well, this could be even worse than Rosken."

"A distinct possibility, and one that's run through my mind several times," Alserah agreed, relaxing ever so slightly as she looked back at Kitania, a hint of a smile on her lips, yet also a bit of some other emotion in her gaze. The goddess's voice was surprisingly calm as she continued. "There are already more of us with mantles than last time, after all. With any luck, there won't be as much destruction, but... if we all get through this, I'd like to invite you and your friends to stay in the Forest of Sighs for a time. Isalla commented on wanting to see the country, and I think it'd be good to give you a chance to relax."

"I'd like that. I'll have to talk to the others about it, but I think it would be good to rest without something terrible looming over us," Kitania said, heat trying to rise in her cheeks, but she fought it down firmly. Instead, she bowed her head slightly and added, "I'll see you later."

She turned away at that point, unwilling to delay any longer and looked at Karakel. The angel had gathered a group of eight other angels, one of whom was in leather armor and carrying a staff. Karakel looked at Kitania and bowed her head, asking, "Are you ready, Lady Kitania?"

"I am. Is everyone else?" Kitania asked, looking at the others. Each of them nodded in turn, and as they did, Kitania inhaled deeply, then let it out as she murmured, "Then let's go."

"Follow me, if you would. We'll be traveling swiftly and low to the ground," Karakel replied, and the woman quickly extended her wings and took flight, her soldiers almost instantly behind her.

Kitania willed mana into her armor, and as she did so the spectral black wings took form behind her. She left the ground almost effortlessly, while the others followed. Even so, the sound of wings beating the air was louder than she'd expected, and Kitania glanced back.

Nearly two hundred angels were taking to the air almost as one behind her, and the sight of them in the midnight-blue armor of Estalia sent a shiver down Kitania's spine. In the lead was Anna, her glowing cloudpiercer almost as radiant as Estalia herself, and beside them were the glittering figures of the deities Alserah had brought with her.

Kitania desperately hoped that they would be enough.

CHAPTER 43

"*T*ornado off the fourth tower!" Baradiel snapped, pointing at the location, and one of his magi immediately began casting his spell, even as the commander swallowed a curse.

The Eagle Citadel was relatively remote, in keeping with the order's tendency to avoid the limelight, unlike the orders of the Dragon and Phoenix, which usually meant that the scenery outside the citadel was calming and beautiful. That was only normally, however, and today was anything but normal.

The eight outer towers of the citadel were sparkling with magic, the crystals at the pinnacle of each spire shining as they maintained the glowing purple shield that surrounded the citadel, a shield which looked like a faceted jewel. That was unusual enough, since running the shield at full power normally would drain its mana reserves faster than anyone was comfortable with, let alone Baradiel, but fortunately that wasn't a concern. Far more important were almost two thousand attacking angels, and Baradiel couldn't be certain that they didn't have items to breach wards on them, hence his orders.

Where he'd pointed the air swirled, then a tornado roared into being, sucking a half-dozen attacking angels into the vortex savagely. One was dashed against the shield, but Baradiel was under no illusions that it would *kill* any of them. It took a powerful mage to create tornados strong enough or long-lasting enough to kill most angels, and he only had a handful of magi capable of that present. Most of his skilled magi were unfortunately elsewhere.

A blast of lightning ricocheted off the shield, but Baradiel barely flinched, instead staring at the motley assortment of attackers, more than a little flabbergasted at the sight. Many of them were in relatively drab armor more like those of the common folk, but among them he saw members of all three orders, including members of the Order of the Eagle, but predominantly they were formed of members of the Order of the Dragon. He'd even seen a large woman who he would've *sworn* was in the armor of a smith of Skyforge. The only way to tell their faction for sure was by the yellow sashes that all of the attackers wore, and he didn't dare let *anyone* inside. Especially not after the traitors struck earlier.

Arrows shot outward through the shield at the attackers, and as they did so, Baradiel considered the day unhappily. It had started normally enough, right up until the shockwave had rippled through the ley lines along with what people in the mortal world would consider an earthquake. Then word had arrived about the Holy Council, which caused a large panic throughout the citadel. His magi had begun investigating what the ripples might have been, but they'd only had a couple of hours before his guests arrived… a couple of hours in which Baradiel had dispatched several teams to look into the quake and reinforce security in the capital, something he was deeply regretting now.

Twenty-three angels had arrived at the gates, carrying large metal devices and babbling something about their research being wrong, and that some 'Society of Golden Dawn' was risking everyone's lives. Baradiel had been skeptical, but even with his somewhat weaker grasp of magic compared to his fellow members of the order he'd been able to see the massive amount of mana in the ten devices. His questions had been interrupted when several members of the garrison had suddenly attacked him *and* the guests, shocking Baradiel and nearly killing him, while they succeeded in killing five of the guests before the other guards had managed to stop them.

That had been enough to make Baradiel take the men and women seriously, and those hadn't been the only traitors so far. He'd had reports of nearly two dozen residents of the citadel trying to aid the attackers, and Baradiel was grimly certain that more were biding their time, which made securing the citadel tricky. Worse, the artificers who'd taken refuge had quickly explained that they couldn't simply destroy the devices they had, they contained too much mana for that to be safe, so they had to slowly drain them before they could destroy the apocalyptic devices. They were using some of the mana from them to power the shield, which was the only bright spot Baradiel could see about their current situation.

"Sir, we've received a message from Uthren's Throne!" a soldier exclaimed, rushing up to Baradiel and taking a moment to salute, breathing hard as he did so.

"What is it?" Baradiel asked, frowning as he saw a group of enemies gathering on a hilltop, including the one who he thought was in Skyforge's armor. They worried him, but there wasn't anything he could do at the moment, they were too far away to easily target, and getting rid of the attackers who were close was more important.

"Heavenly Wing Tagan reports that Anathiel unmasked Rathien of the Order of the Dragon as a traitor, and he was under orders to prevent reinforcements from being sent here. The Heavenly Wing reports that he and the bulk of the military stationed in Uthren's Throne is moving to our aid as quickly as possible," the soldier reported, looking far more hopeful than most of the other soldiers had been. "The message ended there, sir!"

"Good, at least *something* is going right," Baradiel growled, his worries easing slightly. "Now we just have to hold out for a few hours before we get reinforcements. Assuming that these blasted traitors don't keep showing up, that is. Now back to your post, soldier."

"Yes, sir! I'll get right—" the man began, but at that moment the group spread out again, revealing a long, thin crystal shaft with the Skyforge woman behind it. The sight of a starlance was unmistakable, and Baradiel's worries spiked, *hard*.

"Everyone down!" Baradiel bellowed, grabbing the soldier and dragging him downward as the crystalline shaft glowed like a star.

The starlance emitted a beam of blazing white light that slammed mercilessly into the citadel's shield, which went opaque as it tried to block the blast. An instant later the shield around the blast shattered completely and the lance of light ripped through the parapet just to Baradiel's left, sending a shower of rubble flying as it bored a hole into the side of the citadel itself.

Beside him the soldier had frozen, staring at the hole just in front of where he'd been standing, several thin cuts on his face from rock chips oozing blood as Baradiel climbed to his feet, swearing all the way. The shield had blocked most of the blast, keeping the lance from penetrating into the citadel's heart, but an opening large enough for a dozen angels to fly through had been cut through the shield, which was slowly rebuilding itself.

The attackers weren't waiting, though, and dozens of angels charged, themselves enveloped in a shield projected by one of their number. Behind them Baradiel could see more angels closing on the starlance, obviously planning to recharge the siege weapon, which did *not* make him feel better.

"Repel the attackers! We have reinforcements coming, and the citadel will *not* fall!" Baradiel exclaimed, unsheathing his sword and raising it high. The other soldiers of his order rose as well, and the melee combatants who'd been biding their time took flight to join Baradiel as he charged toward the breach.

The attackers descended on Baradiel and the others with war cries, and furious, mid-air combat ensued. Instantly Baradiel realized that most of the angels had never fought alongside one another, though, as only a handful of them were properly cooperating with each other, and *that* was disastrous under the circumstances. His soldiers worked together like a well-oiled machine, and one after another they cut down the angels trying to breach the shield.

Baradiel's hopes began to rise again as they fought, seeing

the shield rapidly closing the breach, and he called out in mid-clash, blocking the sword of one of the attackers to let one of the others cut the woman down. "That's it, drive them back! They're not as skilled as us, so let these traitors have it!"

"Really?" a deep voice came in response, and Baradiel looked up and instantly paled, fear rushing through him.

Three angels were above the citadel, and any one of the three would have been enough to make him concerned on their own, while all three of them radiated the immense mental pressure of archangels. In the lead was a blond man, his hair trimmed short, while his heavy armor was washed gold and gleamed almost like the sun with his power, a massive claymore in one of his hands. He was Aelon, Baradiel knew, the archangel of glorious war, and was one of the more powerful archangels in the heavens. Worse, he was the one who'd spoken.

Beside Aelon were Halith and Nuriel, and the sight of them made Baradiel's heart sink. Halith was an icily beautiful brunette with cold eyes, and was the archangel of stone, as evidenced by the rock armor enveloping her body, and she had a stone maul in hand, while Nuriel was a burly red-haired man with a bushy beard. He was the archangel of the hearth, who most people underestimated. Worse, Baradiel could see hundreds of angels approaching over the tree line behind them.

"Lord Aelon! You aren't joining these traitors, are you? This isn't—" Baradiel began, only to be interrupted when the archangel struck.

The archangel's movement was a blur, but Baradiel managed to get his sword up just in time to block the downward swing of Aelon's claymore. The impact numbed Baradiel's arms and he kept his grip barely, but was sent flying downward as pain blasted through his arms, then his back where he hit the ground.

"Sir Baradiel!" several soldiers exclaimed in horror, and for the first time since the assault began, Baradiel saw their unity break. Two descended toward him, three attacked Aelon with expressions of anger, and the other seven retreated toward the wall. Worse, Baradiel couldn't gather enough breath to tell the attackers to back off.

Blazing light gathered on Aelon's body for a moment, then

erupted outward in a blinding wave of heat, and screams echoed through the sky for a moment. The three angels fell from the sky as charred corpses, while the two who'd been coming to Baradiel's aid almost fell, their feathers scorched by the heat. The archangel spun, his claymore flashing as he shattered large parts of the shield, then he paused, looking down arrogantly at Baradiel as he spoke, his voice booming loudly over the battlefield.

"Traitors? The only traitors here are you and those who've held power for so long… and those who've taken refuge inside your walls, I suppose," Aelon said, extending the claymore to point at Baradiel as he smiled. "Your kind have allowed the depredations of demons to continue for too long. For centuries we've dealt with the shadows of their evil, but that time is past. The Lord of Light has come, and with our own angelic *god* we shall purify the heavens once more and destroy demonkind once and for all. For the Golden Dawn!"

"For the Golden Dawn!" the other attackers echoed Aelon's shout, making the ground practically rumble under Baradiel, to his horror. He struggled to breathe, gripping his sword with trembling fingers as he started to rise, just as Halith and Nuriel shattered other sections of the shield, though it looked much more difficult for them than it had been for Aelon.

Three archangels *and* the starlance were much more than the citadel had been meant to repel, Baradiel knew, especially not after dispatching half the standing garrison to other locations. He was probably going to die, but he took a breath and prepared to die on his feet, glaring up at Aelon as he spat out, "I have no idea what you're going on about, but you're insane if even *half* of what I've been told is true! I may fall, but you *won't* win this battle!"

"Oh, really? Well, you can die and we'll see how your army's morale crumbles," Aelon sneered, a barrier of light around him bouncing several arrows away, and he prepared to dive, causing Baradiel's stomach to involuntarily clench as the two soldiers raised their shields next to him.

A light flashed, and an instant later there was an explosion outside of the citadel, distracting Aelon and Baradiel for a moment. He looked for only an instant, and gaped as he realized that there was a crater where the starlance had been, and the woman using it was staggering to her feet. The next moment rapid wingbeats echoed across the battlefield, before something hit Aelon and the other archangels, the sound of metal clashing on metal splitting the air.

Aelon went flying back through the breach as sparks flew from his claymore, the man reeling as he struggled to regain his balance, while Nuriel was simply sent staggering back and Halith struck the ground like a meteor. Baradiel gaped for a moment, looking up in shock.

"You must be the current archangel of... what was it, *glorious* war? A misnomer if I've ever heard one, considering how brutal war actually is, but who am I to judge? I'm also told that you've claimed that your mantle subsumed my own, which is patently false," Anathiel said, the woman's wings beating as she smiled at Aelon, her glowing cloudpiercer held in an easy grip. "On the other hand, given all the other falsehoods and betrayals that your organization has perpetrated, I suppose I shouldn't be surprised."

Near the archangel were two others, a dwarven man whose armor shone with a dull light, and whose massive double-bladed axe had smashed Nuriel back, and a plain blonde woman in a flowing outfit who'd spun Halith like a discus before sending her flying into the ground. Baradiel vaguely recognized them as deities from reports he'd read but didn't know much more than that.

"Anathiel, you've joined these traitorous gnats as well? After all the wars you led against the hells, they squandered your successes, and—" Aelon began only to shut up as he hastily blocked when Anathiel lunged forward.

Her cloudpiercer struck like thunder that echoed across the battlefield, then spun as she used the butt of it to launch him upward, and Anathiel's voice was calm as she spoke. "Enough talk. I've heard quite enough already. Why don't we take this to the skies, away from those who can't withstand our battles, hm?"

"How dare you—argh!" Nuriel bellowed as he was hit by the

dwarf again, then a glittering arrow of energy flashed out from the side to slam into his shoulder.

"It's not just three gods, they have at least *six* of them!" Baradiel muttered in shock, looking up as more deities rose from the forest, and an instant later he realized that the unit of dark-armored angels he'd seen coming weren't reinforcements for the attackers, but people coming to support the citadel. They slammed into the rear lines of the attacking force, causing many of the angels to pivot, but even so, much of the damage had already been done.

Angels were pouring toward the breach in the wards, even as the human goddess threw Halith into the air, avoiding the blows of the archangel, and Baradiel shook off his shock, downing a healing potion, which sent a surge of warmth through his body.

As rumbles of weapons striking armor echoed down from the skies above, Baradiel exclaimed, hope rising through him at last, "Everyone, for the Order of the Eagle! For the heavens!"

He rushed to defend the citadel, hoping that the reinforcements would be enough to help, even if he *did* wonder what the strange urge to look at the blue-armored reinforcements was coming from.

CHAPTER 44

"*T*hat… is surprisingly well hidden," Rose murmured, and Kitania's eyebrows rose as she glanced over at her.

"Oh? What do you mean?" Kitania asked after a moment, since Rose didn't elaborate.

The building in front of them looked like a monastery of some kind to her, with a sign she couldn't read in front of it, and it was built into the side of a mountain. At the moment the doors were closed, which made her worry a bit. If they'd come to the wrong place it would be rather frustrating, especially since they could hear the rumble of what sounded like thunder from the direction of the citadel.

"Angels aren't particularly well-known for mining, for some odd reason, and most of our buildings are on the surface for a reason," Rose explained and nodded toward the doors as she continued. "*That* is masquerading as a winery and place to rest away from the rigors of the world. It isn't something particularly common in the heavens, but it's not unknown."

"It also explains why they were able to have plenty of people visit without drawing too much attention… if anything, I'd think they would have trouble with people wanting to visit who weren't part of their organization," Isalla added, nodding in agreement.

Kitania simply exchanged skeptical looks with Vinara. The

succubus didn't look very impressed, which only made sense to Kitania. She thought it was far more likely that the angels had been too self-absorbed to notice the brewing rebellion, but she wasn't going to annoy Isalla and Rose with a comment like that at this point.

"Either way, Karakel should be back any minute, once she finds the informant," Kitania said, simply hunkering down behind the tree to wait.

Fortunately, they didn't have to wait long. Shortly, Karakel returned with a plain, nervous looking angelic man with brown hair and eyes, whose clothing was rather drab compared to what Kitania might have expected. His eyes widened at the sight of Kitania and Vinara, but he simply nodded to them rather than saying anything.

"This is Christopher, our contact here and the one who told us about the hideout," Karakel said, nodding to them as she added, "Christopher, these are allies of Our Lady, as well as Kitania, her daughter."

"Her daughter?" Christopher said, his eyes widening as he focused on Vinara, then Kitania and hesitated. "Err, which one? I'm not entirely sure…"

"I am," Kitania said, resisting the urge to smile, then nodded toward the plain entrance as she asked, "Are you sure that this is where the society is headquartered?"

"Um, well, I can't say they're *headquartered* here, but it seems likely, milady," Christopher answered nervously, tapping the trunk of a tree as he leaned against it. "What I did see was an archangel heading away from the spot where everything went wrong, along with some others, and I followed them here. Then, about an hour and a half ago, I saw a bunch of angels flee, carrying a bunch of devices that were really heavy, then they were followed by other angels in armor, including some heavily enchanted gear, with a ton of other angels boiling out of there like they were in a panic afterward. And if *that* wasn't enough, I just saw a golden light go flying by a couple of minutes before you arrived. I think it came from higher up the mountainside."

"Well, that's good enough for me," Isalla said, reaching down to her sword hilt and hesitating, then asked, "Do you know if anyone is left inside?"

"I'm not sure… a *lot* of people left, more than I would've expected to be inside, to be honest," Christopher replied, looking at the building as he explained. "I haven't seen anyone, but that doesn't necessarily mean anything. If it could hold a few hundred or more people, there could be plenty who just haven't revealed themselves."

"Ugh, I love it when asking a question just raises more," Isalla murmured, then straightened, looking at Kitania, Rose, and Vinara as she asked, "What do you think?"

"I think we should bid Christopher farewell and go in," Rose said immediately. "If there are people there, so be it. I'd be startled if there weren't, honestly."

"Entirely agreed," Vinara murmured. "Nothing ventured, nothing gained. Besides, we could always retreat if it looks like we're heading into a meatgrinder."

Kitania laughed and nodded, not seeing the need to verbally add her opinion, since it pretty well matched the others. Instead she looked at Christopher and spoke gently. "Thank you for your help. If it weren't for you, we wouldn't know to come here. That said… I'd suggest heading back home or such. I wouldn't want you to get dragged into a battle if things go poorly."

"Um, thank you, milady. All I did was follow them when they flew overhead… it wasn't really anything at all," Christopher replied, his cheeks coloring a little as he cleared his throat, but Kitania interrupted before he could say anything more.

"That's where you're wrong. You put yourself in danger to investigate, and it'd be remiss of me to ignore that. Thank you," Kitania said firmly, trying to view herself as Estalia's representative.

"Well, thank you, milady. Thank you very much," Chris said, fidgeting, then took a breath and added, "I will go, then… I wish you luck."

Kitania smiled and nodded, watching the man leave, then glanced at Karakel as she murmured, "Now then… I assume you don't have any objections?"

"Of course not. I'll just remind you to check all the doorways and halls for spells before traveling down them. Angels tend to prefer setting wards over physical barriers, and I have no idea how extensive they'll be inside," Karakel said, glancing at her mage.

"Is that so? Well, I have just the thing!" Vinara said, grinning as she pulled out her monocle again and put it on. "This will be quite... wait, what is *that*?"

"What's what?" Kitania asked, looking at the succubus, who was staring into mid-air with a dumbstruck expression on her face. Seeing the confusion on Karakel's face, Kitania explained. "The monocle allows her to detect mana far more easily via sight."

"Ah, I see," Karakel murmured, nodding in understanding.

"As for what I'm seeing, it's an *incredibly* powerful mana stream between somewhere deep in the mountain and... the battlefield, I'm guessing," Vinara said, frowning slightly as she looked back and forth, concern growing much more visible on her face. "As powerful as it is, it should be practically visible, yet it's been hidden somehow. That's... worrying."

Kitania blinked, worry welling up inside her, but before she could speak, Isalla did.

"In that case, I think our mission here just became *much* more urgent," the angel said, her determination obvious as she looked around. "If they're channeling a lot of mana, it can't be good for the others."

"Then we should go," Rose said, calmly standing up fully and drawing Ember. The blade blazed to life, but the flames were oddly muted, as if they were trying not to give them away, which Kitania found rather odd.

"Right," Kitania agreed, shrinking her cloudpiercer to where it was almost a sword, since she didn't want it to catch on anything.

They quickly headed for the front door, and as they moved, Kitania hoped that there weren't too many traps or other things that would slow them down. More importantly, she hoped they wouldn't run into too much danger, either. If it was a trap... well, that didn't bode thinking on.

~

I_T'D BEEN MORE_ than an hour since the others had left, and aside from those in the room with Haral, the halls of the building were silent. It was eerie, after years of visiting, yet at the same time Haral knew she was probably just imagining things. Even if there had been members of the society living and training here for decades, they'd rarely been loud enough that much noise would reach here, the antechamber to the council chambers.

Yet at the same time, Haral couldn't help the nagging feeling that everyone else was missing. It was frustrating to just be sitting here, when her comrades were fighting, and possibly dying, for the future of the heavens.

"Nervous?" Sorm asked, his voice breaking the silence at last. Some of the others looked at him, almost jumping at the sound, and Haral smiled and shook her head.

"Nervous? Not really... I'm more anxious. Being left here while everyone else is trying to deal with our enemies... it's just a little frustrating, honestly," Haral said, surprised by how calm she felt. "We've been working for it for so long, so being sidelined like this is... annoying. Even if it's an important task."

"Entirely fair. You aren't the only one who'd like to get out there and do something, but... well, it isn't like we have many other choices. Besides, while this may not be as glamorous, it's certainly safer. It isn't like the Order of the Eagle will go down without a fight, and I'm sure a battle with the Order of the Phoenix will come soon enough," Sorm said, letting out a soft sigh as he shook his head unhappily. "I wish they'd come to their senses, but you know that won't happen."

"I suppose that's true," Haral said, letting out a soft sigh as she considered, then asked, "Do you think it's going well?"

"Honestly? I have no idea, but I *also* know that the security in most of the order strongholds doesn't tend to be that good. They've never been attacked, and that makes people lax," Sorm said, considering for a moment, then shrugged. "In any case, unless Yimael has some sort of secret weapon, which she may, they'll probably have to wait for one of the archangels to arrive. Once they do, though... that'll be it for them."

"Good. The sooner this is over, the better," Haral murmured, and the others voiced their agreement as well. That made her happier, since at least Sorm knew the other guards reasonably well.

Being accepted was a nice change of pace.

THE BUILDING WAS VIRTUALLY SILENT, and it worried Kitania, making her thankful she'd already cast her defensive spells. No guards or servants were roaming the facility, and it was much larger than any simple winery, either. Vinara had disabled several wards designed to detect or attack intruders so far, and Kitania was sure she'd disable more in the future.

She'd returned her cloudpiercer to its normal size, since the halls were easily large enough for her to make use of it, and it was all Kitania could do to bite back sarcastic comments about angels overbuilding their structures. Even if they had wings, she saw no reason they should make them wide enough for an angel to have their wings almost at full extension. Well, that might be an exaggeration, but only a slight one, since three angels could easily walk abreast down the halls.

Even so, the building was far more functional than she'd expected. There was less ornamentation than in most of the buildings she'd seen before this, and the rooms they'd peeked into had been relatively sparsely furnished and task oriented. It was obvious that the inhabitants had left in a hurry, since she'd seen half-chopped vegetables in the kitchen, dirty clothing sitting next to a wash basin, and more signs that people had suddenly abandoned what they'd been doing and left.

"This worries me. Maybe we won't find much of anything?" Isalla whispered, her voice barely audible.

Karakel's troops were scouting, and they seemed far better suited to it than most of the others, except maybe for Kitania. She was happy to let the angels take the lead, though, since they were marginally less likely to cause people they encountered to raise the alarm.

"I doubt that. I trust Vinara to be right, even if she's annoying at times," Kitania replied softly, ignoring Vinara's grin as she looked around, continuing. "They left in a hurry, which means I'm sure we'll find *something*. We've already proven this isn't a winery and resort of some type."

"I suppose, it's just—" Isalla began, then fell silent as Karakel suddenly stiffened and stopped.

One of the soldiers slipped around the corner and the man spoke quietly. "One of the hallways turns just after reaching a wider, more ornate doorway deep in the complex, and we heard voices near it, sir. We listened, and it sounded like they were talking about the battle. They didn't expect it to take long, once their own archangels entered the fray, and apparently they're guarding something which is supposed to be important."

"Really... *that* sounds promising," Vinara said, straightening as she grinned. "They're in for a surprise due to our reinforcements, then."

"Most likely, Magister," Karakel agreed, then frowned. "Still, considering everything else they've done, I don't dare leave them be. That mana conduit you sensed concerns me."

"Agreed. That's why we'll go take out these people, and deal with whatever they're guarding," Rose said firmly, glancing at Karakel, and the woman nodded in agreement.

"I'd recommend letting Lady Vinara go first to check for traps, though," Eziel commented quietly, almost making Kitania jump in surprise. Eziel hadn't said more than a few words since coming to the heavens, and the complicated look on her face was concerning, but they didn't have time to deal with it right now.

"Very true," Kitania agreed, raising an eyebrow at Vinara, who rolled her eyes and looked at the man.

"Lead the way, then. And you might want to get the rest of your soldiers back together, this could go poorly," Vinara said, pausing before she added in amusement, "Though hopefully it *will* go poorly for them. That would be rather nice."

"True, Magister," Karakel replied respectfully, and they quickly headed down the hallways, taking pains to be silent.

The complex seemed to be even bigger with every minute, making Kitania wonder how anyone had failed to notice it being excavated. Were the locals blind? Or... possibly a mage had excavated it, which would make more sense. Either way, at last they came to a hall, and Kitania peered around the corner to look at the doorway.

Double doors that were carved with images of the rising sun were down the hall, with gilding over the suns themselves, and she could hear the soft sound of voices as well, mostly because the doors were cracked open slightly. Vinara tapped Kitania on the shoulder and motioned her aside impatiently, the succubus scowling in apparent annoyance.

Moving, Kitania watched Vinara examine the room with narrowed eyes, and due to how quiet everyone was she could hear the succubus barely murmur under her breath. "Ah, wards... but a touch sloppy, since they can be seen on this side of the doors. Let's see..."

For a long moment the succubus studied the door, then she turned to look at Isalla. "Have you progressed enough to shove open the doors with an air spell?"

"Ah, yes, of course. That's pretty simple, really," Isalla replied, blinking in confusion.

"Good. Now... can *you* either throw a curved fireball to launch it through the doorway, or dispel a particular ward?" Vinara asked, looking at the mage among Karakel's soldiers.

"I'm not skilled with fire, but rather with metal," the mage replied, who had a slightly odd accent that Kitania couldn't place. "I should be able to dispel a ward, though."

"Right. Come here, I want to show you the ward I want removed," Vinara said, removing her monocle and offering it to the angel. The angel put it on, and Vinara murmured, pointing. "The ward I need you to remove is the one with the purple-ish glow that looks like a net. It mitigates fire spells, which would impede Rose as well as a fireball. No, not yet! We need to all act at the same time."

"Of course," the mage said, sounding a little chagrined as she returned the monocle, lowering her hand.

Turning to the rest of them, Vinara's expression grew more

solemn as she spoke softly. "The room is heavily warded, so most combat spells won't work, thus my request. I have no idea how many people are within, but if we're going to hit them, I suggest we strike hard and fast. I'll throw a fireball into the room, but it's likely that I won't do more than injure a few of them, depending on the size of the room or what defenses they have. When we hit them, I want the rest of you to rush the room."

"Fair. There's something to be said for the element of surprise," Rose said, glancing around. "Who goes first?"

"Me," Kitania said, and as Karakel frowned she added rather bluntly, "If someone's going to take the brunt of their defenses, it should be me. I'm effectively immortal, and my defensive spells and armor make me incredibly hard to hurt. We also don't have time to discuss this."

"As you wish, Lady Kitania," Karakel acknowledged, but quickly added, "My people will be right behind you, however. The safety of your group was an explicit priority."

"Fine, but let's get this going," Rose said, and Isalla nodded, drawing her sword. A tiny part of Kitania suddenly realized she'd never offered Rose her blessing, but it was a little late for that now.

"Alright. Isalla, start casting right after her, then I'll begin my spell," Vinara instructed and looked at Kitania wryly as she added, "Kitania, try not to block my aim, hm?"

"I won't," Kitania promised, suppressing a smile.

"Alright. Here I go," the mage said, taking a breath, then she began her spell as softly as she could, her fingers tracing symbols through the air. Isalla began casting an instant later, then Vinara, and Kitania braced herself to move.

Everything happened all at once. First was a sizzling sound from down the hallway, followed by a gust of glowing white wind that slammed the doors open. The tiny orb of flames left Vinara's hands just behind the wind, and the instant Kitania saw it, she charged forward, half-closing her eyes to be safe as the orb's path twisted and rocketed into the room as cries of alarm rang out. The fireball detonated with a flash of light and a dull *whump* that almost knocked the doors closed again, just in time for Kitania to kick the door open and confront a pair of staggering angels blocking the doorway.

The butt of Kitania's cloudpiercer hit the ground and she vaulted over the pair, spinning in mid-air to slash into the back of one of them, and her tail hit the other in the head, almost knocking the woman over. Her blade glanced off the man's armor, but he screamed as her blade caught his wing, half-severing it at the base.

The room was smoldering, and Kitania took in the dozen of angels at a glance, then smiled darkly as she spotted the two in the back.

"Ah, Haral, Sorm! I've been looking forward to seeing you again," Kitania purred as they picked themselves up off the floor.

That was when the others caught up, and the battle began in truth.

CHAPTER 45

*E*stalia smiled at the angel nearby, throwing her mantle's strength into it, and the man hesitated, looking at her lustfully for an instant too long. The soldier he'd been about to cut down took advantage of the opening ruthlessly, stabbing the man as he recovered and nodded to Estalia. She didn't have time to do more, though, as she was dealing with her own admirers, such as it were.

The four angels attacking her were well-coordinated, Estalia noticed, parrying the blade of one with her rapier, while she used her gauntlet to almost gently push the thrust of another aside, clicking her tongue in annoyance.

"You don't *have* to be so forward, you know. If you put down your weapons and were reasonable, you'd not only have a chance to live, but I'd be happy to chat with you," Estalia told them, riposting savagely, stabbing perfectly through the gap in the armor over the woman's inner elbow.

"Silence, harlot of the hells!" one of the men snarled, but the undertone to his voice made her want to roll her eyes in disgust. "You have no place here, and need to be punished!"

"She needs to *die*, you idiot!" a woman retorted, to Estalia's amusement.

The problem with her mantle was quite simple, in Estalia's view. Her mantle was that of desire, and it attracted attention and could even overwhelm minds, if she had the time to focus it on people, which made for excellent distractions in combat. The problem was that people reacted differently to desire at times. Some wanted to turn her into a servant, which would *never* end well for them even if they succeeded, while others hated her beauty and how others were attracted to her. It tended to draw entirely the wrong sort of attention, in her view... though it *did* help draw attention away from her subordinates.

"Now, now, you really shouldn't be fighting over me, not when we're in the middle of combat," Estalia said, distracting the two again as she took a step back, effortlessly avoiding an attack that was aimed at her throat.

"Shut up, you—agh!" the woman began, only to scream as one of Estalia's soldiers stabbed her in the back.

The others screamed as well, not having noticed how Estalia had led them deeper into her army, giving ample opportunities for her soldiers to deal with them. Estalia could have killed them on her own, but she was trying to conserve her energy.

"You really should have watched where you were going, rather than focusing *just* on killing me," Estalia chided the woman belatedly, then looked at the soldiers and said, "Thank you, now to deal with more of them, hm?"

The smiles that they gave her eased Estalia's heart, and they quickly moved back into the battle, which didn't just rage on the ground, but also in the sky above her.

Estalia's force was dealing far more damage to the renegade angels than most others might have expected, anyone but Anna or Estalia herself, at least. Oh, they'd taken casualties so far, but including a priest or priestess in each squad had hopefully kept most of those injuries from resulting in death, as had the incredible expense Estalia had made in making them the best armor and weapons she could manage. Few other realms of the hells could boast equipment like Estalia's elite forces possessed, and it'd taken her thousands of years to build an economy which could afford it.

Coupled with their equipment, the soldiers had drilled together for years in private, knowing that if they had to they'd be facing enemies beside Estalia, so they cut through the majority of the angelic rabble far more easily than even the soldiers of the Order of the Eagle could manage. The biggest problem was ensuring that the Society of Golden Dawn didn't surround them, which was a definite issue with more dribs and drabs of their organization showing up with every passing minute.

Blood soaked once-beautiful fields around the citadel, and Estalia was staring across a battlefield of angels, watching the blue-clad defenders protect the spear-like structure and its surrounding towers savagely, obviously trying to push the attackers into Estalia's army, such as it was. That amused her a little, since the Order of the Eagle had at least two to three times as many soldiers as she did on the field, and between them they had less than half what the society had possessed initially. Of course, it helped that Ratha had chosen to help in the battle, the goddess of the harvest calmly throwing out seeds that sprouted into immense roots in seconds to mire and impede their enemies.

Thunder rumbled from above, and Estalia glanced up calmly, then smiled. Another archangel had arrived to help the society's supporters, but the battle wasn't going well for them.

Anna struck the golden archangel yet again, sending him flying backward with another deep dent in his armor, which was battered and scarred by this point. Estalia had to admit he was tough, with how much of a beating he'd taken. The female archangel's stone armor was cracked, and she was bloody, defending herself from Sidina and Ire as best she could, while the new blonde archangel just barely managed to deflect an arrow from Alserah, defending the hurt other archangel. The arrow vanished into the distance and exploded, sending a shockwave through the earth. If their battle had been on the ground, Estalia knew that there wouldn't be anything left of the army.

A sudden sense of danger struck Estalia, and she dodged without even thinking about it just as a crossbow bolt hissed past her, crackling with holy energy. Estalia turned and blinked as she saw a trio of angels bearing down on her, all of them in heavy armor that practically crackled with enchantments. One was wielding a sword and shield, and his armor glittered white, while a woman wore armor that was heavier than anything Estalia had seen an angel wear before, one that was deep brown with gold trim. She also had an axe slung on her belt and a crossbow in hand, while a thinner man took her left flank with a two-handed sword, his armor relatively normal compared to the others.

"Ah, you must be the leaders of this little uprising... or at least the ones who aren't archangels," Estalia said, smiling at them, and she visibly saw the three hesitate at least for a moment, though the woman suddenly dropped the crossbow and raised her gauntlet, and a glittering shield snapped up the instant before a lightning bolt hit.

Electricity arced off the shield uselessly, which Estalia was certain would dismay her mage, but she was more impressed by the woman's reaction time and device. Instead she simply smiled more widely as the thin man spoke.

"We're not going to fall for your foolish mind control, not like all these deluded fools," the angel said coldly, a slash of his sword ringing off the armor of one of Estalia's soldiers. The woman's armor held, but she likely would need healing, judging from how she went flying. "We'll kill *you*, then they'll despair when they realize you're merely mortal."

"Mind control? You think I control them with *mind control*?" Estalia asked, shock rippling through her, along with more than a little anger as she moved forward deliberately.

"How else could you corrupt this many angels? You're a despicable—" the woman began in a rough voice, snatching a rod off her belt, but Estalia had had quite enough.

"*Kneel*," Estalia snarled, and *this* time she didn't hold back, as she allowed her power to release fully for the first time since the battle had begun. She felt the power billow out of her in waves, and she struggled to focus it solely on the three in front of her, yet she knew she failed.

Her power rippled across the battlefield, and an expanding wave of angels suddenly fell to their knees, including many of her own soldiers. The wave of power was ruthless, and many angels struggled to make it to the ground under the weight of her words, while some fell from the sky entirely. Estalia did hope that all her people were alright, but she kept her glare focused on the three as their knees hit the ground almost simultaneously, while the man with the sword and shield almost choked.

"W-what…" he gasped, struggling to rise, yet unable to do so.

"*This* is mind control, you imbeciles," Estalia replied coldly, approaching them with her rapier in hand. "Given time I could destroy an *archangel* with my power, but I don't do that sort of thing, not without great need. No, I convinced all those angels around me with something incredibly simple. The truth. It's amazing what you can do via honesty, something which all of *you* seem to have forgotten."

"You… you think we'll succumb to your lies? We're not so weak-minded that we'll allow you to turn us against our allies!" the woman growled, starting to resist enough to start standing, but it was far too late for that.

"Turn you? You seem to be under a mistaken impression," Estalia said coldly, taking a step forward and thrusting her rapier directly through the eye-slit in the angel's helmet. The two men's eyes went wide at her smile, as Estalia spoke calmly. "See, I've long since learned that once battle is joined, I shouldn't use my power to turn people. No, I simply *kill* my enemies. It would've been different if you'd surrendered, but…"

Estalia withdrew her rapier, watching the woman's body hit the ground, then stabbed the thin man through a crease in his armor, directly through the heart. The third man quickly spoke. "Wait, I surrender, don't—"

"Too late," Estalia interrupted with both word and blade, flawlessly slipping her rapier under his gorget, and watching red spill down his throat. She withdrew much of her power as she flicked her rapier clean, murmuring, "Much too late, you murderous bastards."

The armies began to recover from the impact of her power, and Estalia looked up again, wistfully wishing her power was more useful in a battle like this. The most she could really do was disable both sides, and that wasn't really the sort of thing that Estalia wanted.

Then she saw a brilliant glowing light shooting toward the

battle in the distance, and suddenly Estalia stiffened with a hint of fear as she felt the wave of power radiating off the figure, murmuring, "Uh-oh."

～

"COME NOW, is that all you can do?" Anna asked, savagely slamming Infinity's Edge into the joint of Aelon's right arm. His armor was good, as it managed to keep her from cutting clean through his arm, but the battered archangel cried out in pain as he nearly dropped his sword, and she continued derisively. "I thought you were supposed to be my *successor*. What I'm seeing is nowhere near acceptable."

"I don't want to hear that from a damnable traitor!" Aelon snarled, his wings beating hard as he tried to open the distance between them. "You're working against the heavens, which disgusts me!"

Anna resisted the urge to roll her eyes, since she was wise enough to not take her gaze off her opponent. She could see his arm healing slowly, which told her a bit about his powers. Much like Kitania's power, he must have accelerated healing, if not full regeneration. In all honesty, if she'd had to take on the four archangels present on her own, she might have been in trouble, but with the deities taking on the others it was simply a matter of dividing and conquering. As it was, he'd only managed to land a couple of glancing blows on her, which her armor had easily absorbed.

"Working against the heavens? Coming from an organization who murders those who've come to suspect that you're trying to ignite a war again? You're *pathetic*," Anna retorted, but she saw the glow around his left hand increasing as he gathered power, and she kept any further commentary to herself, instead rushing forward like lightning.

The archangel tried to dodge, but his reaction was a just a bit too slow. The butt of Anna's weapon struck his left shoulder unerringly, and Aelon went flying back with a scream of pain and the tortured peal of shattering metal. Anna followed him, catching a glimpse of the three other archangels trying to regroup, but they were being harried by the deities.

Catching up with the falling archangel, Anna caught him by the throat and spoke calmly, looking into his pain-filled eyes. "Do you have any last words? I'll give you at least *that* much respect."

Aelon looked like he was about to spit at her but paused as a gold radiance played across his face, the source behind Anna, and he grinned. His voice was almost gloating as he spoke savagely. "You're going to die, Anathiel. The Lord of Light has come, and you are nothing compared to him! I'll watch him destroy you, and—"

His reaction told Anna enough, and with his ability to heal she didn't hesitate at all. With a single slash she cut Aelon's head off just above his armor, and he had the time for his eyes to widen in shock as she murmured, "No, I don't think you will."

Anna dropped the archangel's head as his body fell, only her gauntlet stained by his blood. Someone would start claiming his mantle before the day was out, she was certain, but it didn't matter that much to her. A tiny part of her regretted killing the man, but it was only a brief thing, considering what he'd been doing. Instead she spun to face the coming threat, and when Anna saw the oncoming foe her eyes went wide and her hair felt like it was standing on end.

The figure approaching them shone like the sun itself, not with the relatively minor golden glow that Aelon had possessed. It was hard to look at the man, but Anna could still make out some details.

Four wings extended from the man's back, each feather on them a flawless white that radiated light, while he was sheathed in armor seemingly cast of solid gold and carried a hand and a half sword in one hand easily, the blade bearing powerful enchanted runes. She couldn't make out his face under the helmet he wore, but brilliant golden eyes glowed like stars within the helmet. Worse, the degree of power he was radiating was like nothing Anna had ever sensed before, not even when going up against the most powerful demon lords in the hells.

The man didn't even slow down as he aimed directly at

Anna, and she recovered from her shock, calling on all her power to reinforce her body and weapons, waiting until the last moment to dodge to the side and strike at him.

Light flashed as she did so, the man changing course as though momentum meant nothing to him, and Anna barely had time to block his strike, shock rushing through her, along with more than a little fear as she braced herself, but it wasn't enough.

The blow hit harder than anything Anna had ever experienced, her arms feeling like they were almost going to shatter under the force unleashed. One moment she was in mid-air, and the next the wind blasted past her and she felt an immense impact as she hit something. That something shattered as Anna went straight through it, and she blinked. It took an instant to realize that he'd hit her so hard that she'd smashed right through the shield over the Eagle Citadel *and* into the main tower, and she was looking back through the tunnel she'd made in a momentary daze.

"The time for a new dawn has come, and all those who oppose it must be purged, that the heavens may shine with the glory they *truly* deserve," the man said, his voice a deep rumble that echoed across the sky as he looked down on the battlefield arrogantly, his wings beating slowly. "I am the Lord of Light, and all those who fight my followers will *die*. Lay down your arms and you will be granted the peace of an easy death."

As he spoke, motes of light like dust drifted down from his wings and onto the battlefield. Where they touched his followers, Anna saw the injured healing, and their blades begin to glow with a similar light. She staggered to her feet, trying to remember the last time she was so sore, but unwilling to back down.

"Ah, shut up, you damned featherduster!" Gandar roared, and the dwarf brought his axe down on the archangel with all his strength, only to be blown backward by a wave of pure energy.

An arrow ripped through the air at him, and the Lord of Light deflected Alserah's arrow with his sword, his eyes narrowing as he spoke. "So be it. Children of the Golden Dawn, destroy the heretics to light the way!"

"For the golden dawn!" the army below exclaimed fervently, attacking with renewed spirits.

"This... isn't good," Anna murmured, worry rushing through her, but she didn't have time to delay, not as the other deities attacked the Lord of Light, only to be beaten back seemingly effortlessly.

If they were going to have a chance, *all* of them needed to be in the fight, and with the other archangels... well, she was just glad she'd dealt with Aelon once and for all.

CHAPTER 46

*S*creams echoed through the room as angels fought one another, metal echoing on metal and blood splashing on the ground. Well, *mostly* angels fighting one another, Kitania reflected, her cloudpiercer spinning as she almost danced, sparks flying every which way as Haral's golden whip bounced away and she deflected Sorm's sword. The frustration on their faces was palpable, which almost made her laugh.

"Why won't you damned well *die!*" Sorm demanded, bouncing back to snatch up a crossbow and firing it at her from point-blank range.

Kitania dodged pretty much instinctively, and her spells helped deflect the bolt as she *did* laugh, sweeping her blade around to hit the ankles of an angel fighting one of her mother's soldiers. It distracted the woman a little too much, which ended that combat brutally.

"You know, I *do* believe this is the first time we've had an honest fight. Every other time you struck from ambush, which means that you don't have the slightest clue how we can *really* fight, do you?" Kitania taunted, ducking Haral's whip as it lashed at her. She'd seen what it could do and didn't want it hitting her in the head.

"Shut *up!*" Haral growled, winding up for another strike, but

Kitania caught a flicker of movement from the corner of her eye and took a step to her right.

Isalla rushed past Kitania, her shield up as she charged Haral, who yelped as she hastily drew her sword and blocked the strike, stumbling backward as she did so.

"Haral!" Sorm exclaimed, and Kitania took the chance to press the attack, stepping toward him.

What she *didn't* expect was for him to step toward her as well, and Sorm's concerned expression turned to a grin as he drew a dagger with one hand, a ring of keys jingling on his belt as he slashed at her with the dagger, his sword trying to get past her cloudpiercer. Kitania dodged as best she could, but he kept moving toward her, not letting her open the distance.

"The problem with cloudpiercers is that they're almost useless if you get inside their reach," Sorm said coldly, dodging slightly as she tried to slam him in the face with the shaft. "I'll disable you, then kill Isalla, once and for all."

"You'll *try*," Kitania corrected and dodged the dagger again. Even if she could regenerate, she couldn't afford the time it'd take to recover.

$\sim$

"YOU WORTHLESS BRAT. I should have just killed you and been done with it," Haral hissed, trying to catch Isalla's foot with her whip, but Isalla managed to get out of the way in time. "No one cared about you enough to search properly, and all you've done is cause problems."

The battle was in their favor, Isalla knew, even if the defenders had initially had better positions. They were outnumbered and had been injured in the opening blast, which gave the attackers a significant advantage. Now she just had to finish Haral, and one of her long-standing grudges would be over with.

"Maybe so, but fortunately you didn't. You're a bitch, Haral," Isalla retorted, blocking with her shield as she probed for an opening, but Haral was a little more agile than she'd expected. In fact, Isalla hadn't expected Haral to be so good in a fight, which was a little frustrating, and rage was seething in the back of Isalla's mind. "You betrayed me, and I'll bet you betrayed Rose. I'm going to kill you and rip your conspiracy to shreds."

"Oh, you might try, but you'll fail. And Rose... well, she may not remember it, but I'm the one who stabbed her and handed her over to the demons. I should've killed her as well, but it was amazing how gullible she was," Haral said, her eyes narrowing, then she smiled thinly. "On the other hand, I've already cleaned up some *other* loose ends. Your family, for one."

"You *what*?" Isalla demanded, shock and fear freezing her in place for a moment. Haral took advantage of the opening, striking like a snake as her sword shot at Isalla's face.

Ember flashed by at that moment, blocking Haral's sword as Rose stepped up next to Isalla, her face calm as she spoke softly. "Don't let her distract you, Isa. She'll say whatever she needs to in order to win."

"T-thanks," Isalla said, catching her breath, only to have her blood run cold as Haral laughed.

"Oh, but that's where you're both wrong. I was ordered to kill *both* of your families," Haral said, laughing as she took a couple of steps back, grinning at them. "I only killed Isalla's, because Rose's family was too large to easily eliminate. I killed them and burned the house to the ground, Isalla."

"You *bitch*!" Isalla roared, and she charged Haral recklessly as her vision practically turned red, her thoughts overwhelmed by rage. Haral dodged at the last moment, slipping behind Isalla, and her sword hit the ground in a clatter as a loop of the whip slipped over Isalla's head and around her neck. The angel tightened it suddenly, wrenching Isalla around to block Rose.

"Yes, that's right, that's how I feel about *you*," Haral crooned in Isalla's ear venomously, tightening the whip to where Isalla couldn't quite breathe. "Sorm will cut down your precious demon while you watch, then I'll kill you, too. Even if the others somehow survive this, the Lord of Light and other council members will hunt them down, Isalla. You're all dead, you just don't know it yet."

Isalla choked, her eyes going wider as Rose hesitated, obviously torn on what to do, and behind her Kitania was trying to open enough distance between her and Sorm to fight him properly, but he'd almost pinned her to the wall.

$\sim$

KITANIA BARELY CAUGHT sight of Haral and Isalla, and what she saw chilled her blood. How Isalla had let herself get caught up in *that* sort of situation was beyond her, and it was almost a fatal distraction.

Sorm's knife glanced off her skin as he shoved it into her armpit, and only the fact she dodged kept it from penetrating fully. He cursed, growling as he hissed, "Would you go *down* already?"

"No," Kitania retorted, a couple of ideas rushing through her mind on how to turn the fight around, with Sorm's sword pressed hard against the haft of her cloudpiercer. Then she caught a glimpse of Vinara and Eziel in the doorway and smiled.

"Hello, Sorm," Eziel said calmly, an arrow nocked and aimed at him, at the same time that Vinara was casting a spell, one which Kitania recognized.

"Eziel? What are you—" Sorm began, his eyes widening in shock.

Kitania took the chance to will her cloudpiercer to collapse into a hair stick, and Sorm lurched forward as he was suddenly pressing against nothing. Eziel loosed her arrow at the same time, causing him to flinch and dodge, and in that moment Kitania flipped the hair stick around and slid it under the edge of his breastplate before willing it to return to its normal size.

Vinara's spell caught the arrow and twisted its path, whipping it around the room in a half-circle that terminated in Haral's left knee, and the angel screamed as she collapsed and a fountain of blood erupted from under Sorm's armor. His expression turned to one of shock as his gaze dropped, blood dribbling from his mouth as he tried to speak, yet couldn't.

Isalla pulled away from Haral, barely having gotten the whip away from her neck. She'd drawn her dagger, Kitania realized belatedly, and Isalla savagely stabbed the angel, burying the blade in Haral's throat, then ripping it out again as she stepped back, panting as she looked around the room.

Kitania shrank the cloudpiercer to free it, then returned it to its normal size, wincing at the gore covering her weapon. The last of the enemy angels were going down as she watched, and she took a deep breath, then let it out as she murmured, "Well, *that* was unpleasant."

"Yes… we have a couple of injured, but nothing major," Karakel said, stepping away from the pair of angels she and another two soldiers had dealt with, looking at Kitania warily. "You were… impressive. I don't think I could have beaten him."

"It would've been harder without Eziel's help, but thank you," Kitania said, nodding to Eziel as she did so, and the angel smiled warmly in return. Kitania's attention turned to Isalla, who was being examined by Rose closely, and Kitania asked worriedly, "Is she alright, Rose?"

"I'm fine, thank you," Isalla replied, taking deep breaths as she looked around, then down at Haral in distaste.

Rose clicked her tongue in disapproval but spoke calmly. "She'll have a couple of bruises, but nothing more. Fortunate, considering the fight."

"No I won't," Isalla disagreed, but Rose ignored her.

"We have a few injured, as well as at least a few potential prisoners," Karakel informed Kitania, frowning as she looked at the squad. "I'm trying to decide what to do, considering that."

"Rose? You're the one who's more practiced at military matters," Kitania asked, looking at her. "I'm a bit out of date, I'm afraid."

"Have half the squad wait here and keep anyone from ambushing us from behind," Rose said instantly, looking at Karakel with a smile. "The rest of us can see what they were guarding."

"As you say," Karakel acknowledged, and quickly turned to snap out her orders.

Kitania turned and looked at the large doors at the back of the room. Before the fireball had detonated, they must have been pristine and breathtaking, but now they were soot-covered and charred in places, which ruined the images of angels kneeling before an immense, four-winged figure. The doors also bore a lock, and she frowned, then looked down at Sorm, since she vaguely recalled him having a ring of keys on his belt.

The key ring was where she thought it was, and Kitania grimaced, realizing that she'd inadvertently covered them in gore when she'd killed Sorm, and she carefully removed the ring, trying to wipe off the worst of the mess.

"What's that?" Vinara asked curiously, stepping close to Kitania, adding with a smile, "Also, that was an interesting way of killing him. Gruesome, but interesting."

"I was going for speed, nothing more. At least it was quick for him," Kitania said, standing and nodding at the doors. "I saw it has a lock, and I'm hoping he has the key."

"Ah, much is explained. Why don't you go take a look? I'm afraid I haven't seen that conduit since we entered the mountain... I think it entered at an angle that hasn't intersected with any of the rooms we're in," Vinara said, frowning. "That, or we passed it. I don't think so, but it's possible."

"Hopefully not," Kitania said, quickly heading for the door. They'd wasted more than enough time in the room, and she examined the door for traps for a moment, then began testing the keys to see if any fit the lock.

It took six keys before Kitania found the right one, and she let out a breath of relief, looking at the others as she smiled slightly. "Here we go. I'm taking point from here, I think."

"Are you sure? If we run into anyone..." Isalla began, then her voice trailed off and she laughed softly, shaking her head. "If we run into them *here*, they aren't going to listen to any excuses. Go ahead, we'll be right behind you."

Kitania smiled at her reaction, taking a deep breath, then opened a door and stepped through it.

The door opened to a short hall, at the end of which was a vaulted chamber where a circular table rested with five chairs arranged in a semi-circle across from the entrance. Like the rest of the building, the room was lit by glowing orbs on the ceiling, though they were brighter here, and positioned such that Kitania suspected that anyone sitting in the chairs would have their faces mostly shrouded in shadow. There were three short hallways attached as well, each with a door set into them, but Kitania focused on the one directly behind the table, up a half-dozen stairs. The door was ajar, and Kitania could hear voices from beyond them, only faintly but rather upset from the sounds of things. She paused as she heard Vinara's breath hiss out.

"The conduit enters through the ceiling, and goes into that room," Vinara murmured, glancing at Kitania, worry in her gaze. "It's... more potent than I thought."

"Then let's go," Rose said, her gaze fixed on the door ahead, Ember seething with flames.

"Keep toward the back, I don't want your sword giving us away," Kitania told her, smiling as Rose flushed a little, then headed for the doors in the back, taking care to give the table and chairs a wide berth.

She quickly ascended the steps, reaching a plainer door, and as she did so, she heard a woman snarling venomously in angelic. "How is she still alive? We've hit her a dozen times, and she just keeps getting back up!"

"We're hitting her in mid-air, so it loses a lot of its force, instead sending her back," a man replied, strain in his voice. "If we could pin her down, one or two hits and she'd be done, archangel of war or no. But these damnable other deities—"

"Reinforce the armor!" another woman interrupted, a trace of panic in her voice.

Swearing ensued, and Kitania blinked, her blood chilling as she slowly pushed the door open to look into the room. Fortunately, whoever maintained the door kept the hinges well-oiled, so it opened silently.

The room she looked into was darker than the other had been, but she could easily see the five angels around the small table in the room. Three were men, while the other two were women, and they were channeling a veritable *river* of glowing light into a crystal orb over a foot across, its surface covered in faint symbols. It was the images within the crystal that caused Kitania to freeze for a moment, though.

She could see a battlefield raging in the sky, and blood was trickling down Anna's face as the angel fought fiercely alongside Gandar, whose armor was riddled with cracks. She caught

371

glimpses of the other deities, including a grim-looking Alserah, and the battle was raging at a speed she could barely keep up with. Blasts of light ripped through the air, blasting craters into the ground below, and between movements Kitania could see a raging battle on the ground and skies as well.

"Hellfire. They're channeling their mantles into it," Vinara murmured, her eyes widening still more. "Anna and the others… they're facing the combined power of *five* archangels in one? Or more?"

"What?" Karakel demanded, her eyes going wide. "How… Milady, she's in danger!"

"Yes, she is. They're all in danger," Kitania replied in a whisper, then smiled thinly. "On the other hand… if their mantles are *there*, they're not here. What do you think would happen if we stabbed one of them?"

The others fell silent, and Vinara smiled wryly, almost sounding amused. "I suppose that *is* the direct solution. I'm all for it."

"Then I'm going for the woman nearest the door," Kitania said, nodding toward the brunette facing away from her, the one who'd been complaining.

"I'll take the man on the left," Karakel said, her eyes narrowing slightly.

"The woman on the right," Rose added.

"I think my bow has little place here, so I'll join you," Eziel said, glancing at Isalla as she added, "Shooting past everyone would be difficult. Who do you wish to target, Isalla? I'll join you, and the guards can go after the other."

"The big man in the back," Isalla whispered, and blanched as she said, "Hurry!"

Kitania flinched as she saw a blast of light and a sword in the orb, just as Anna went flying backward and hit a tower, which began to teeter, then collapse as the viewpoint rushed after her.

"Got her! Finish her off before that archer interferes again!" the brunette snarled, and Kitania couldn't wait any longer. Even if she wasn't sure how she felt about Anna at this point, she was *not* going to let them kill her.

Kitania rushed into the room, barely sparing a glance for the orb, her cloudpiercer snapping out to its full length. She was only two steps into the room when there was a startled gasp from her right, and a female voice exclaimed, "Attackers, Milord!"

Kitania caught a glimpse of an elderly female elf to her right, the woman in the midst of drawing a dagger, but she didn't pause. Even if the archangels had a warning, they only had an instant to react, and she was practically in reach.

Before the brunette could react Kitania swung her cloudpiercer, and the blade cut through half her neck effortlessly before catching on bone, but that was quite enough, and the demoness ripped her weapon free.

"What in the, where were the—" the other woman began, only to be brutally interrupted.

Ember blazed with immense flames as it shot across the room, punching a hole through the woman's chest, the chair behind her, and shattering stone as it embedded itself in the floor. Kitania almost paused in shock, her eyes going wide at the sight, but she didn't dare, not with the others in the room.

Karakel was dueling her target as he tried to get out of his chair, and Kitania was quite sure he'd drop quickly. The only question was if it'd be enough, and she rushed to help the soldiers attacking one of the two remaining archangels, ignoring the clatter from Vinara and the elf behind her.

Vinara could deal with a single elven woman, Kitania was certain.

CHAPTER 47

*A*lserah cursed as the Lord of Light shot down after Anathiel, fear rushing through her. If he hit the archangel, Alserah sincerely doubted that she'd survive, based on how hard he'd been hitting thus far, and she simply couldn't seem to *hit* the figure, which filled her with more fear than she'd felt in centuries.

It didn't help that none of her allies were uninjured, save possibly for Ratha, who was mostly out of sight, while Ire, Phillip, and Sidina were doing their best to keep the other archangels out of the fight. It helped that all three opponents had been injured early on, but even so, the Lord of Light was too destructive for *any* of them to face head-on.

So Alserah's heart clenched as she flew to the side, trying to get a good shot on the angelic deity, praying that Anathiel would survive, but there was no time, and—

At that moment the figure of the Lord of Light suddenly lurched and *slowed*. Not a little, either, but to the speed of a normal angel. Anathiel managed to drag herself out of the wreckage at that moment, and when she spun her weapon and hit the Lord of Light's blade, for the first time the glowing golden figure was blown *backward*. Alserah stared for a long moment, her mouth agape, then took the opening to shoot at him.

The glowing arrow shot through the air like a lightning bolt, and unlike every other time, where the man had deflected her arrows with blade, magic, or even his gauntlet, *this* time the arrow hit hard. It exploded violently, marring his armor as the golden glow around him dimmed.

"What just happened?" Alserah muttered under her breath, but she didn't pause, instead manifesting an even more powerful arrow as the forces of the Society of Golden Light seemed to pause, almost wavering in shock.

Anathiel seemed to agree, as the archangel launched herself at the Lord of Light fearlessly, ignoring the multiple wounds she'd taken, and for the first time they began to drive the glowing angelic deity *back*.

Alserah just hoped that Gandar would drag himself out of the pit in the side of the hill to help. Getting catapulted there by an attack was no excuse, in her mind.

ROSE EXTENDED HER HAND, willing Ember to return to her grasp, and the sword responded instantly, almost joyfully. Ever since she'd woken again, Rose felt like the connection between her and Ember had grown stronger, and what she'd just done had confirmed that, since the attack she'd just made had previously been enormously draining, but now barely impeded her.

Karakel buried her sword in the chest of her target, even as the man managed to drive his blade through her shoulder, and Kitania was on the table next to the crystal orb, attacking the man under assault by Estalia's soldiers. Rose thought she recognized the archangel but refused to think about it.

The orb had mostly gone dark, she realized belatedly, which made her wonder how the battle was going, but instead she focused on the last archangel, the one who'd been farthest from the doors initially. The man had managed to get up in time, and he was now wielding his sword expertly as Eziel and Isalla attacked him. Rose started toward him, and it was at that moment that one of the soldiers managed to get past the guard of the other archangel.

"Alright, that is *it!*" the archangel growled, his eyes blazing with an orange-brown light. "Enough of you!"

The angel suddenly radiated the same light, and he grew several feet taller in the process. Rose paled, as suddenly she realized who he was. Ordath, the archangel of strength and endurance. His sword grew with him, and he drew the blade back to swing as Isalla hesitated.

"No!" Rose screamed as the blade came down like a thunderbolt.

Blood sprayed through the air, but Rose paused for an instant as she realized it wasn't Isalla's blood, that her beloved was bouncing backward across the floor instead. No, the blood sprayed outward from where Eziel had shoved Isalla out of the way, a faint smile on the angel's lips as she staggered, then fell in two pieces, diagonally bisected by the blow from shoulder to hip.

"Eziel?" Isalla's voice was surprisingly audible in the room, as almost everything seemed to have come to a stop.

"One down, many more to go," Ordath said coldly, glowering at them as he flicked the blood from his weapon. "You've ruined *centuries* of work, and for that you'll pay with your lives."

Suddenly Rose was *incredibly* aware of the fact they were in the room with an archangel in full command of his powers... and she didn't think any of them could stop him.

ESTALIA WINCED as an arrow struck the Lord of Light above them, the shriek of rent metal echoing across the battlefield, but she smiled viciously as well. He'd done damage to her army simply by attacking near them, and the renewed fervor of their opponents had been terrible. She feared that a quarter of her army was down and hoped there hadn't been too many deaths.

The sudden weakness of the seemingly invincible attacker had caught her off guard, though the reactions of their opponents had been telling, as their improved morale suddenly turned to shock and fear, something she and the army had taken advantage of. They had little other choice if they wanted to survive against the zealots, though she *did* see what she hoped were reinforcements in the distance. Hopefully not for the society, but there was no way to know, not under the circumstances.

Gandar yelled loudly as the battered dwarf hit the Lord of Light from above, and *this* time the angelic god came crashing down in the middle of the Society of Golden Dawn's army. For a moment the world seemed to have gone still as he and Anathiel chased after the figure, and Estalia paused, hoping that they might have defeated the Lord of Light at last.

The sound of ripping metal split the air again, and Estalia heard Gandar curse, then the dwarf bellowed loudly, ascending into the air as he held something over his head. "Alright, you deluded featherbrains, have a look at what you thought was a *god*! You're not just fools, but *damned* fools!"

Estalia looked more closely at what was in his hand, and shock rushed through her, enough that she almost dropped her guard. What was in Gandar's hand was a head, but it wasn't the head of any angel, demon, or mortal. The skin was like polished brass, while the glowing eyes looked like they'd been inlaid with topaz gemstones, and gears and wires extended from the neck where Gandar had torn the head free. If she hadn't been able to see the gearing, Estalia might not have realized the head wasn't from a living creature, which meant someone had spent an immense amount of effort making the construct as realistic as possible.

"Retreat!" one of the archangels above them snapped out, and the woman immediately began trying to fall back with the others. The deities quickly moved to obstruct their paths, slowing the archangels down as the society army wavered, then broke and began to run.

"We can't let them regroup to do this again! All soldiers, *advance*!" Estalia snapped out, extending her rapier over her head, then quickly pursued the retreating soldiers.

Anna and Gandar quickly joined the attack on the three remaining enemy archangels, and as they did so Estalia looked up and blinked. The reinforcements she'd seen were approaching far more quickly than she'd expected, and why was readily apparent. The angels flying in formation wore the colors of the Order of the Eagle as well as the Order of the Phoenix, and at their head were the three deities of Uthren. She only recognized Cyclone personally, but his power would certainly make it easier to speed up the flight of a thousand angels.

As Estalia drove into the retreating angels, many of the members of the Society of Golden Dawn began throwing down their arms in surrender. The approaching deities seemed to hesitate, but then they moved to support Anna and the others above, something which Estalia was certain would seal the fates of the three archangels.

With the battle well in hand, Estalia spared a moment to worry about Kitania and her friends. Mostly about Isalla, Rose, and Vinara, if Estalia was being honest, though she also hoped her soldiers were alright as well. Kitania would be fine... probably.

THE HAFT of Kitania's cloudpiercer bent like a bow and she went flying sideways almost like she was launched from a catapult from the sheer force of Ordath's attack, and Rose cursed under her breath as she charged forward desperately. Fortunately, Kitania's magical wings snapped out and brought her to a stop an instant before she hit the wall, but it was a near thing.

"You've ruined *everything*," Ordath growled, backhanding a soldier into the wall, and the man screamed as his wings snapped like twigs, much like Karakel's arms had a few moments earlier. Unlike Eziel's armor, Karakel's had held, if only just. "Seven centuries of preparations, all down the drain because of *you*."

"Maybe that should be a clue that you were wrong to do this!" Rose snapped, channeling mana into Ember as she tensed, then swung her sword just outside of his reach. The flames around Ember raged, emitting a razor-sharp crescent of flame that shot toward the archangel.

Ordath's body glowed still more brightly as the attack struck, and Rose's eyes went wide. His armor was barely marred by the flames, and he didn't seem to even care about the heat it'd carried, either. Her shock didn't stop her from dodging when he attacked, though. The results of what had happened to Eziel and Kitania told her that trying to simply block his attacks was a losing proposition.

"No, it's merely evidence that I have to try harder," Ordath said bluntly, shrugging off a blast of lightning from Vinara, then kicked the table across the room at her and the angel mage, and Rose barely ducked in time to avoid the hurtling object. "I'll kill you all, retreat, and bide my time. Eventually I *will* destroy the hells, I promise that."

"I don't think so," Kitania's voice was soft as she stared at Ordath, her eyes narrowing. "You people are heartlessly cruel, and I won't let you do that."

"Oh? And how do *you* think you're going to stop me? None of you can so much as *injure* me," Ordath replied, laughing as his eyes narrowed. "You've killed my servant and my companions, so I see no reason not to rip you all apart."

"You think you're invincible? That we have no chance against you?" Isalla interrupted, her voice quiet, but Rose could *hear* her anger, and she blinked as she saw that her friend was next to Eziel's body and had put down her sword and shield. Instead she was holding Eziel's bow, which confused Rose, since Isalla had never been a good archer.

"Of course not! You're no archangel, and none of you are demon lords. You can't stop—" Ordath sneered, but was interrupted as Kitania suddenly launched toward him, and her movement was so quick that he couldn't react in time, at least not fully.

Kitania's cloudpiercer lashed out, and Ordath jerked back as he tried to counter, but even at his size Kitania's reach was just a bit longer than his. A line of blood appeared on his throat, and Ordath's eyes went wide, while he reached up to wipe it away and stare at it.

"That's where you're wrong," Kitania said, a trace of anger seething in her voice, while her words shocked Rose. "I am the child of Anathiel and Estalia, and *I* bear the mantle of an archangel. I'm Kitania, immortal daughter of the heavens *and* hells, and nothing you can do today will keep me from tracking you down and stopping you, even if you escape."

"Impossible. That *harlot* consorted with hellspawn? She fell even more than I believed possible!" Ordath exclaimed, his face darkening as he turned to face Kitania. "I'll just have to destroy you first."

Ordath charged toward Kitania and swore loudly as Isalla fired an arrow at him. Unlike the blade of flames, the glowing white arrow punched through his armor, making Rose wonder what Eziel had been doing with arrows like *that*. Just as Rose was about to charge into Ordath's back, she was interrupted by a male voice whispering in her mind.

"Daughter of Ember, receive a tithe of my power, that you may vanquish the corruption which lies before you," the deep, powerful voice said, and Rose felt a wave of heat strike her, and she only had an instant to choose whether to accept it or not.

The sight of Kitania dodging sword-blows, and barely avoiding attacks which could cut her in half, along with Isalla fumbling to pull arrows out of Eziel's blood-soaked quiver made the decision for her, though. Rose would *not* allow Ordath to harm them, and she let the heat rage into her, as the fires surrounding Ember grew brighter and brighter, expanding to envelop her in a corona of blue-white flames that illuminated the room.

Heat surged through Rose's veins, and she could *feel* her joints pop, her muscles strengthen, and her mana... Rose's mana core had always been like a small, gentle fire, but now it surged to life with far more power than she'd ever felt before. The heat was immense, and it seethed for release. Rose instinctively knew she had to use it before it incinerated her.

"I think you shouldn't have mocked us, Ordath," Rose spoke, her voice surprisingly calm, and rushed forward, clasping Ember in both hands as she channeled her full power into the sword.

"What—" Ordath exclaimed, two arrows buried in his left shoulder, and he took a step back and raised his sword to block Ember.

Rose's blazing sword cut straight through Ordath's, though it managed to slow her attack somewhat, and he bellowed in pain as Ember cut deep into his right shoulder, flaring with immense heat as it seared through flesh and bone. Kitania quickly spun and stabbed through Ordath's left armpit, piercing deep into his body, and Ordath froze for a moment, blood beginning to bubble up in his mouth.

"This... won't kill me..." Ordath gasped, to Rose's shock as he abruptly grabbed her wrists, clenching so tightly she almost lost her grip on Ember, while his other hand grabbed the shaft of Kitania's cloudpiercer.

"Will this?" Isalla interrupted from behind him, and Rose saw her friend standing directly behind Ordath with the bow fully drawn, a glittering arrow nocked and aimed at the base of Ordath's skull.

Before Ordath could react, Isalla loosed the arrow, and at such a close range she couldn't really *miss*. The arrow punched into the back of the archangel's head, and he froze, his eyes going wide as his mouth worked, but his hands slowly relaxed.

The archangel slowly shrank, his eyes rolling back in his head as he collapsed into a heap, and Rose felt the heat that'd been surging through her slowly sizzle and begin fading, leaving her body aching in its passage. She slumped over, groaning softly as she asked. "Was... was that it?"

"I think so," Isalla said, swallowing hard as she looked toward the door, wincing. "Is everyone alright?"

"I don't know that I'd say alright, but I think we're alive," Vinara said, leaning against the door, amidst the wreckage of the table that'd hit her, obviously dazed.

The mage who'd been next to her was slumped on the ground unconscious, and Rose realized they must have been hit by the crystal ball, based on the shape of the dent in her helmet. The elf was dead, a bloody dagger next to her body, and most of the soldiers who'd accompanied them were injured.

"All but Eziel," Kitania said, her eyes darkening as she pulled the cloudpiercer from Ordath's body, slowly approaching the woman's body.

"She saved my life," Isalla said, her voice trembling as she looked down at Eziel's body. "She... she threw me out of the way, and after I'd been so *mean* to her. Why would she do that?"

"Because she wanted Kitania to be happy. She wanted to make up for her mistakes," Rose said simply, closing her eyes as grief and relief warred within her, causing tears to well up in her eyes. Rose didn't try to fight the tears as she shook her head slowly. "I *hate* sacrifices."

"You aren't the only one," Kitania said softly, reaching down to close Eziel's eyes. "Perhaps she can be raised from the dead, but... chances are this is the end."

Rose knew Kitania was right. Even with the body of the dead, less than a third of the time a person could be brought back after their soul had departed. If they'd had someone capable of it immediately, it was more likely, but they didn't. Instead, Rose nodded slightly, murmuring. "Well, we'll find out once the others catch up. Assuming they won."

"I'm sure they did," Kitania said, letting out a sigh as she straightened. "In the meantime, let's let them know and get the injured tended to. The dead aren't going anywhere."

"I... suppose you're right," Isalla said, letting out a sigh. She set down the bow and followed Kitania toward the man who'd been backhanded into the wall.

Rose hesitated, then asked, "So, you have an *angelic* mantle, Kitania?"

"Apparently so, which is just the *tiniest* bit disconcerting," Kitania murmured, prompting a morbid chuckle from Rose as she sheathed Ember.

Turning away, Rose decided to help Karakel first, since having both arms broken couldn't be fun. She *did* wonder what the voice in her head had been from, though. It might have been Ember itself, but she wasn't certain.

Not that it mattered. What mattered was that they'd won.

CHAPTER 48

"That wasn't how I expected her to die," Estalia murmured, and Kitania looked at her mother and arched an eyebrow curiously.

"Oh? How did you expect her to die, then?" Kitania asked, not really wanting to look at the pyre that was consuming Eziel's body. It was painful to watch, and looking at Anna and Estalia helped distract her, as did Isalla holding onto her tightly. At least her mother's mantle was good for *something*.

"Honestly, I half-expected her to eventually die as your servant, not as a hero," Estalia said, prompting a slight smile from Kitania, though it simply sharpened her pain.

Kitania was surprised at how much Eziel's death hurt, in the end. It wasn't as though she'd been close to the angel, especially not since she knew that her mother had broken Eziel's mind. Yet at the same time, for weeks Eziel had been a quiet, attentive presence doing her best to help Kitania get through her life, and she'd saved their lives when they ran into Sorm. It wasn't a surprise when the attempt to resurrect Eziel failed, but Kitania had been a little startled by her need to dab tears from her eyes.

Now they were watching her pyre burn below the incredible skies of the heavens themselves. It was a private pyre, relatively speaking, and Kitania could sense the watchful gazes of members of the Order of the Phoenix watching them in the distance. She was more surprised that the angels hadn't tried to kill Estalia after they'd taken many members of the Society of Golden Light into custody, but she supposed they didn't dare, after the damage the heavens had taken over the last few days. The numerous craters and destruction surrounding the Eagle Citadel had shocked her, though at least it hadn't exploded like Rosken had.

Even so, the heavens had boiled over with a full-scale rebellion, from what Kitania had heard, though the loss of its leaders and many of their plans going awry had kept the rebellion from gaining as much ground as they might have hoped, especially as the rumors spread that the Lord of Light had been the creation of the society's leaders. Still, the fragments Kitania had heard indicated that the rebels had managed to take over several regions and minor continents, which meant that the heavenly orders had their hands full, and didn't want to risk alienating the archangel of war, not when Estalia had informed them that she'd be heading home soon.

Soon was today, in fact, and a part of Kitania was relieved to be leaving. As beautiful as the heavens were, there was also a great deal of grief here, as far as she was concerned. They'd taken a trip to where Isalla had grown up, escorted by wary angelic soldiers, and the sight of the burned-out husk of a house and overgrown fields had caused Isalla to break down in tears. Kitania thought her lover would be grieving for a long time, and she hoped that distance would help.

Even more frustrating had been how nearly twenty elders from the Emberborn family had shown up and demanded that Rose return Ember to them, as she'd betrayed the family. Kitania had been fairly certain that Anna had been about to interfere, but Rose had stopped her with a look, and had carefully placed the sword on a pedestal and invited them to take it if they could.

After virtually every visiting member of the family had burned themselves trying to reclaim the sword, they'd ended up leaving much less pompously than they'd arrived, which had been surprisingly satisfying, from Kitania's perspective.

"So, you're planning to stay in the Forest of Sighs for a time?" Anna asked, looking at Kitania, then her gaze flicked up to take in the sight of Alserah behind Kitania. "I should say that I don't object, I just *would* like some time to talk more, Kitania."

"Mm, I think it's more comfortable for Isalla and Rose, and the food is *much* better," Kitania replied, smiling wryly. "Oh, I intend to come back and have some words with you, but it's going to take some time. I also need to sort things out with Niadra. I've no idea what she's been up to, and I'm... well, confused."

"I think you may find that she's moved on," Alserah interjected politely, letting out a soft sigh as she spoke. "I'm a trifle disappointed, but... I fear that my permission to court you caused her to lose restraint more than anything."

"Really? That's... well, a bit surprising," Kitania said, blinking at the goddess, and her mood dimmed a little more. A tiny part of her was relieved, but at the same time she noticed that the goddess was staying rather close. That was particularly interesting, since the rest of the deities who'd participated in the battle had already left.

"Indeed, but such is what it is," Alserah said, smiling at Kitania warmly. "Regardless, I've already taken measures to correct *some* of her mistakes. Cecilia isn't in quite as honored of a position, but she'll be in charge of your stay when you visit. If she messes *it* up, she's never going to return to court, however, and she knows it."

"Ah, I see. Well, it sounds like you have things planned out," Rose said, a hint of amusement in her voice, as well as melancholy. She paused for a long moment, then murmured, "What do you think the consequences of all this will be?"

No one spoke for a long minute. Finally, Anna sighed and murmured, "I think that the unity of the heavens and the northern alliance has broken at last. If the hells decide to attack, things may go... poorly. That's something I fear, especially after the destruction in the hells."

"On the other hand, the devices have been destroyed, and the angels who created them destroyed their research," Estalia said, smiling thinly as she shrugged. "I wish I could say that nothing like them will be created again, but there are no guarantees in this world. I'll try to mitigate any calls for war, but there's only so much I can do."

"We'll just have to deal with it a day at a time," Isalla said softly, speaking at last.

"I'm mostly surprised you didn't decide to claim one of the mantles yourself, if I'm being honest. Either you or Rose would make *excellent* archangels, if you asked me," Estalia teased, her smile lighting up the clearing a little more.

"Thank you, but no. I don't want that power, or the responsibility which would come with it," Isalla said, shaking her head firmly, then grinned at Kitania as she added, "Kitty can keep hers, too. She obviously needs it."

Kitania let out an exaggerated sigh, and laughter echoed around the clearing in response. After a moment she replied softly. "I like them as they are, Mother. Life will move onward, no matter what choices we make. You have your choices, and I have mine."

"Very well. I just hope to see you in the *near* future, hm?" Estalia said, smiling a little more. "That said, I think it's time that we paid our final respects to Eziel."

Kitania nodded, looking back toward the pyre with a pang of guilt. She looked at what remained of the angel, taking a deep breath, then let it out uselessly as she bowed her head to pray for the woman's soul.

Beside her, Isalla murmured. "Thank you, Eziel. I'm sorry I didn't treat you as well as I should have... but you saved my life anyway. I'll remember that, I promise."

The only answer was the crackling of flames as the pyre slowly continued burning, but despite that Kitania felt the faintest sense of relief. She hoped it was from Eziel.

CHAPTER 49

"*H*ello, Niadra," Kitania said calmly and resisted the urge to grin as the elf almost jumped, pulling away from the blonde woman she'd been about to kiss.

The gardens in Alserah's palace were as beautiful as they'd been the last time Kitania had visited, though different flowers were now in bloom, and the sun was shining brightly overhead, even if there was a faint haze in the sky. She'd been told that was from the destruction of the portal, as an immense amount of dust had been thrown in the air.

More importantly, she hadn't seen Niadra when she returned to the palace, and no one had seemed to know where she was. Considering for a moment, Kitania had decided to check the corner of the gardens where Niadra had taken her during the ball, so she wasn't *too* surprised to find the princess here. With Alserah's warning, she also wasn't surprised that someone else was with her, though both elven women were blushing brightly.

"Oh, Kitania! I didn't realize you were back!" Niadra exclaimed, quickly climbing to her feet, smoothing out the deep purple dress she was wearing. Her hair was a little mussed, Kitania noticed in amusement, though Niadra probably didn't realize that. More importantly, Kitania could see the faint frustration in Niadra's gaze, and realized that Alserah was right, which reinforced her decision.

"Mm, of course you didn't. I only got back about half an hour ago and thought I should come see you," Kitania said, glancing at the blonde, who was looking between them skittishly, looking like she was about to bolt.

"I see; that would explain it. Well, I was just—" Niadra began, but Kitania forestalled her by raising a finger and shaking her head.

"There's no need for excuses, Niadra," Kitania said gently, looking back at her calmly. "In fact, I came here to thank you, and to say goodbye."

"What?" Niadra asked, blinking in shock.

"You saved me at one of the lowest points of my life, Niadra. Your company kept me from collapsing into despair, and for that I'll be forever thankful. However… it's obvious to me that it was fleeting. You and I come from different worlds, and not in a figurative sense, either," Kitania said, staring into Niadra's eyes, keeping a lid on the faint sense of loss that struck her at the sight of Niadra's confusion, then trepidation. "You've moved on, I can see that. I've also moved on, I'm afraid, so… I think it's time for us to part. Live well, Niadra. I will be in the country for a time, so feel free to call upon me, but… I think all we are at this point is friends."

"I… I…" Niadra began, but she didn't manage anything more, and after a few moments Kitania inclined her head slightly and turned away to leave the elf behind.

It hurt a little, Kitania had to admit, but now they were both free to do what they willed with their futures.

"You really like our food that much?" Cecilia asked, carefully pouring tea into the cups. "I often wondered why you seemed to enjoy meals here so much."

"Oh, you have *no* idea," Kitania said, picking up the cup and inhaling the fragrance with half-lidded eyes, a happy smile on her face. "Compared to the hells, food here is… is *ambrosia*. Mostly, anyway. There are some good wines there, and a few other things."

"I particularly liked the apples," Isalla chimed in, taking her own cup as well.

"The apples?" Alserah asked, looking over curiously. Her presence was a little odd, but the others seemed to be slowly adapting to the goddess's aura, and Kitania enjoyed her company. A tiny part of Kitania wondered how Maura and Yain were doing on their way back, since she'd been told they were being teleported to the coast.

"They're interesting, like they almost have a bit of cinnamon mixed into them. Not quite as sweet as most apples, but tasty," Isalla explained, and Kitania chuckled softly.

"You particularly liked the pie I made," Kitania murmured, smiling as she opened her eyes and took a sip of the tea. After savoring it for a moment, she looked at Cecilia and nodded at her. "Thank you, Cecilia, I think I needed this."

"You're most welcome. I'm simply glad I'm not stuck at home, dealing with my parents' disappointment," Cecilia said, setting the pot down and busying herself with rearranging her cart.

"I can't say as I blame you. I had some difficulties with my family as well," Rose said sympathetically, taking a moment to stretch, then looked at Alserah. "So, were there any plans for today?"

"Not in specific, but I thought I might invite you to go hunting with me," Alserah said, gracefully taking a sip of her tea, and the goddess smiled. "I particularly like the outdoors, and even if we don't take any game, I find hunting restful."

"Mm... that seems like it could be nice. Particularly in an environment where most of the wildlife isn't inclined to eat me," Kitania said thoughtfully, sitting up straighter. "What do you two think?"

"Sure, I wouldn't mind," Isalla agreed, rolling her shoulders as she added, "My wings need to stretch, anyway. I slept funny last night."

Rose laughed softly, and Kitania blushed a little, since she knew that it wasn't that Isalla had slept oddly, but more that she'd rolled onto Isalla's wing.

"After lunch, then?" Rose asked, looking at Kitania with a warm smile, and Kitania felt herself relaxing as she nodded.

"Sure, that sounds absolutely lovely," Kitania said, and her blush deepened as Alserah looked at her, a *faintly* predatory look in the goddess's eyes.

She had a suspicion that the goddess wasn't planning on just hunting game, as it were. Based on what she'd seen, Kitania suspected that the goddess was settling in for a long chase where Kitania was concerned, which amused the demoness. She also didn't particularly mind it, either.

At least the other two didn't seem to object.

EPILOGUE

$\mathcal{L}$ooking into the room, Anna shook her head incredulously as she glanced at Estalia. "I cannot believe you got away with that, dear."

"You'd be surprised at how easy it was to make a couple of bodies go missing," Estalia replied, grinning broadly as she did so. "Besides, would you rather those zealots had gotten their hands on them?"

"No, of course not. They're bad enough as it is," Anna said helplessly, then chuckled under her breath. "The question is, what are you planning to *do* with them?"

Sitting in the room on a series of tables were the bodies of three angels. Not just any three angels, either, but three *archangels*, including Aelon himself, which somewhat startled Anna. The man had fallen rather far from where Estalia's army had been, so she had no idea how Estalia had gotten her hands on it. More importantly, all three bodies still held their mantles, which would probably give most of the heavens heart failure if they knew about it. Any angel who got their hands on the bodies could absorb the mantles, after all.

"Mm... I plan to offer them to some of the angels in my service. The ones I can trust, of course," Estalia explained, looking at the bodies, just a hint of nervousness in her voice. "I don't trust the other demon lords to leave us alone, now that you've unveiled yourself."

"I can't say as I blame you, there," Anna admitted, tilting her head as she thought, then smiled a little. "That said, I think you have the right idea. It also helps with your plans to help bring more people into your faith, hm?"

"Indeed! I've heard that my followers in the heavens have found people to be *far* more receptive of late, too," Estalia agreed, her worry fading as she grinned up at Anna. "We're making progress, one day at a time. Now we just have to keep it up, hm?"

"Very true," Anna agreed, and she smiled as she closed the door, then pulled Estalia into an embrace as she murmured, "That, however, can wait until tomorrow. We haven't had *nearly* enough time together, so I suggest we take advantage while we can."

Estalia simply giggled and stood on her toes as she murmured. "Come down here and kiss me, then."

Anna happily obliged.

AUTHOR'S NOTE

With this, the Mantles of Power trilogy comes to an end. It's funny, since less than a year ago I started writing the opening scene of *Heaven's Fallen* on a whim, only to have it take over in a way I never expected. I had to set it aside to finish the rest of the Through the Fire trilogy, but I kept coming back to the story, and I'm glad I did. There were a lot of twists and turns to the story, and when I started I had no idea where the end point would be. If you'll review this book I'd greatly appreciate it, as it does wonders for convincing others to look at my books.

For now, it's time for me to move on to other projects. I'm working on a book in the Ancient Dreams series, *Crisis of Faith*, and it appears that this time my muse is with me! However, another book snuck up on me called *Sting & Song* which I wrote as a side project on Patreon, and it just came out. After *Crisis of Faith*, I intend to start on the next book of the Lilith's Shadow series, the first of four more books I have planned. I hope that many of you will join me in the future!

May your imaginations soar, and allow you to dream of impossible things.

Made in the USA
Monee, IL
16 September 2021